BLONDE BOMBSHELL

The year is 2017. Lucy Pavlov is the CEO of PavSoft Industries, home of a revolutionary operating system that every computer in the world runs on. Her personal wealth is immeasurable, her intelligence is unfathomable, and she's been voted World's Most Beautiful Woman for three years running. To put it simply—she has it all.

But not everything is quite right in Lucy's life. For starters, she has no memories prior to 2015. She also keeps having run-ins with a unicorn. And to make matters even worse, a bomb is hurtling through interstellar space, headed straight for Lucy—and the planet known as Earth.

By Tom Holt

Expecting Someone Taller
Who's Afraid of Beowulf?
Flying Dutch
Ye Gods!
Overtime
Here Comes the Sun
Grailblazers
Faust Among Equals
Odds and Gods
Djinn Rummy
My Hero
Paint Your Dragon
Open Sesame
Wish You Were Here
Only Human
Snow White and the Seven Samurai
Valhalla
Nothing But Blue Skies
Falling Sideways
Little People
The Portable Door
In Your Dreams
Earth, Air, Fire and Custard
You Don't Have to Be Evil to Work Here, But It Helps
Someone Like Me
Barking
The Better Mousetrap
May Contain Traces of Magic
Blonde Bombshell

Dead Funny: Omnibus 1
Mightier Than the Sword: Omnibus 2
The Divine Comedies: Omnibus 3
For Two Nights Only: Omnibus 4
Tall Stories: Omnibus 5
Saints and Sinners: Omnibus 6
Fishy Wishes: Omnibus 7

The Walled Orchard
Alexander at the World's End
Olympiad
A Song for Nero
Meadowland

I, Margaret

Lucia Triumphant
Lucia in Wartime

TOM HOLT

BLONDE BOMBSHELL

orbit

www.orbitbooks.net

Orbit
Hachette Book Group
237 Park Avenue, New York, NY 10017
www.HachetteBookGroup.com

First US Edition: June 2010

Orbit is an imprint of Hachette Book Group, Inc. The Orbit name and logo are
trademarks of Little, Brown Book Group Limited.

The characters and events in this book are fictitious. Any similarity to real persons,
living or dead, is coincidental and not intended by the author.

Library of Congress Control Number: 2010924078
ISBN: 978-0-316-08699-8

10 9 8 7 6 5 4 3 2 1

Printed in the United States of America

For John Foster
Who likes dogs

1

?????

On the planet where a dog's best friend is his man, the director of the Institute for Interstellar Exploration is taking Spot for a walk.

He picks up a stick and throws it. Spot scuttles happily away, yapping and prancing, and returns a moment later with the stick in his mouth. The director smiles affectionately, and tries to take back the stick. Spot growls. It's a playful growl, but there's something in it the director doesn't quite like; something very old, recalling an injustice. He frowns.

"Bad boy, Spot," he says.

Spot is actually a singularly apt name for this dog's man – if you can call him that; he's only seventeen, little more than a puppy, and the unsightly facial blemishes that give his name their aptness will most likely clear up in a year or two. The important thing to instil in a man at this age is instinctive respect and unquestioning obedience. "Bad boy," the director therefore repeats. "Drop it. Drop the stick."

Spot backs away, head down, rump elevated, firmly gripping the stick, a study in appealing mischief. Naturally. Over countless thousands of years, ever since insatiable curiosity drove the first wild monkey to peer in at the cave door and enlightened self-interest induced it to stick around, the Ostar have bred humans to be cute, lovable, endearing. They've filtered the gene pool and manipulated the bloodlines to promote great big puppy eyes, comic-mournful expressions, big floppy ears, sweet little button noses. And mischief too, of course. The puppy knows – it's bred in the bone – that its job is to defy authority *up to a point*; and then give in. When the command is given to let go of the stick, he must reaffirm his owner's self-image as lord of creation and master of the universe, in return for which he gets a pat and a biscuit, and the eternal contract between the two species is thereby endlessly renewed.

The director, contemplating this, frowns. Irony, or what?

Even so. He glances at the chronometric calibrator (call it a watch) clamped to the back of his paw by a thousand too-small-to-see gravimetric tethers. Round about now, he tells himself. Which is just another way of saying, *There's still time, just about. One call; you could stop it. This doesn't have to happen.*

Maybe Spot has some kind of basic empathic ability. Hundreds of human-owners right across Ostar will swear blind that their pets can read their minds, though a more reasonable explanation would be an acute instinctive awareness of their owners' body language. Same thing. Spot is looking up at the director with huge worried brown eyes, sensing the doubt, the disquiet. He makes a faint whinnetting noise in the back of his throat.

In spite of himself, the director smiles, wags his tail reassuringly. "It's all right, Spot," he says. "Nobody's going to hurt you."

Quite. Nobody's going to hurt *you*. But maybe your billionth cousins a billion times removed won't be so lucky.

This time.

2

Novosibirsk, Siberia

In his dream, George Stetchkin was in the dock at the Central Criminal Court, accused of the murder of nine million innocent brain cells. The usher was showing the jury the alleged murder weapon, an empty Bison Brand vodka bottle. Then the judge glared at him over the rims of his spectacles and sentenced him to the worst hangover of his life.

When you wish upon a star, and sometimes when you don't, your dreams come true. George woke up with the judge's words echoing in his head, far too loudly, and groaned.

I'm in no fit state, George protested, but he knew it wasn't any use. George spent so much time in no fit state that he was entitled to claim it as his domicile for tax purposes. In spite of that, unaccountably, by some miracle, he still had a job; a very important, responsible one. He glanced at his bedside clock. Time to get up.

No, really. Come on, he urged himself: you can do it. If Jesus Christ rose from the dead, so can you. Yes, but Jesus got a three-day lie-in first. You've only been in bed for, oh hell, two and a bit hours.

His digestion surged like overexcited magma into a volcano,

and pumped about a quart of the finest acid through his hiatus hernia. He yelped, and made himself fall sideways out of bed on to the floor. There, he told himself, that wasn't so hard, was it?

He tried to draw on his reserves of mental strength and determination, but he got put through to his memory instead. Board meeting, 9 a.m. sharp. He recalled the memo, the gist of which was that the Ten Commandments had been rationalised and condensed into one – *Thou shalt not miss this meeting* – and the penalty for transgression would make the liveliest imaginings of Hieronymus Bosch look like Disneyland. Damn.

At least he didn't have to squander time on getting dressed, since he was still wearing his suit. True, his shirt-front was a complete record of everything he'd eaten and drunk in the last forty-eight hours, but he reckoned he could get away with that. Everybody would be too busy staring at his spectacular black eye to notice. It hurt, by the way, but the massed choir of his hangover drowned out his eye's rather weedy solo. Small mercies. He wiped some of the incrustation off his shoes on to the bedspread, and lurched towards the door.

Someone (he had no idea who; nevertheless, the best friend he'd ever had) had sent a hovercar for him. It was parked outside the block, floating twenty centimetres or so off the ground. The driver turned his head, looked at him and grinned.

"I know," George said. "Hit it."

A really bad hangover is when you feel all the bumps and potholes in the road when you're riding in a hovercar. George scowled so hard he was in danger of straining his eyelid muscles, and tried to concentrate.

Someone had been robbing banks. Not in a submachine-gun-and-stocking-mask way; not by hacking into the account database and leading the virtual dollars away like a cybernetic Pied Piper. Someone was causing huge quantities of freshly printed banknotes to vanish out of locked, sealed, electronically booby-trapped, infrared-infested, CCTV-haunted bank vaults, usually in the early hours of the morning (local time), always without unlocking the locks, unsealing the seals, tripping the booby traps, breaking the beams or even showing up on the TV. In his capacity as head of security for the Credit Mayonnais, George had personally viewed all the footage. Now you see ten billion dollars, now you don't. It was like watching a really bad conjuring trick – bad not because it didn't work, but because it was inherently so *unconvincing*. A stack of banknotes five metres by one metre by one metre doesn't just vanish into thin air. If you see it happen on the screen, you *know* it's got to be a trick. The problem was, he had no idea how it was done.

So far, the perpetrator had got away with fifty trillion dollars.

Of course they'd tried heat sensors. *Of course* they'd tried motion detectors. It went without saying that they'd posted small armies of guards with shotguns in the vaults. Gadgetry; when the chief cashier of the National Lombard in Chicago locked up for the night and switched on the security system, the drain on the power grid dimmed the lights right across the city. That hadn't stopped whoever it was from taking NatLom for seven billion dollars in one hit. So far, they'd managed to keep a lid on it – just as well, because the amount of actual folding money in the banks of the industrialised nations was dangerously less than it ought to be – but it was only a matter of time before someone found out, and then—

George closed his eyes. It didn't help.

How were they doing it? He'd consulted a Nobel laureate physicist, who'd considered all the evidence in detail and replied, "Teleportation." But that's not possible, surely. "You're right," the physicist had replied, with a fifteenth-storey-ledge grin on his face, "it's absolutely impossible. But there's no other way."

So George had had the physicist design special sensors which would detect the tell-tale signs of teleportation (were it possible, which it wasn't) – a significant build-up of EM potential in the immediate vicinity, negative verterons in the ambient ion stream, devastating electrical storms and floods that'd wash away entire cities – and sure enough, they'd drawn a blank too. "Well of course," the physicist had commented, "what did you expect? Didn't I tell you teleportation isn't possible?"

And today, George was due to report his findings to the board. They would be expecting answers. Strictly speaking, *Not a fucking clue* was an answer, but George had an idea that it wouldn't be a popular one, even though it had the merit of being absolutely true. It was, he suspected, one of those cases where the truth might very well set him free, or at least induce his employers to let him go, which presumably amounted to the same thing.

Concentrate, he ordered himself, as enough acid to burn through a steel door spurted through the tiny hole in his oesophagus, and his head rang like a bell.

Recapitulation time. The volume of air inside the vaults had remained exactly the same. No change in temperature. Nothing to indicate movement of any sort. No build-up of static electricity. The atomic clocks mounted on the vault walls had neither slowed or speeded up during the relevant time period, so relativistic distortion was a non-starter. Also, not one single stolen dollar bill had so far turned up anywhere, so whoever was doing this wasn't spending the proceeds. Besides, how would anybody set about laundering fifty trillion dollars? The serial number of every missing note was on file. There was no way—

He opened his eyes and grinned. Then he tapped an e-mail into his Warthog, shrugged and hit the Send key. He'd concluded the message with Reply soonest, but it was a crazy idea, born of bad dreams and residual alcohol and stress and a mind that thought the way a knight moves on a chessboard. Still, it was about the only thing he hadn't tried yet.

Years ago, George Stetchkin had been a scientist himself and, in spite of all the pollution and wear and tear his brain had had to put up with since then, in some ways he still thought like one. He believed in cause and effect, he spent the duration of every conference he attended in the bar, and he had faith in the proposition that to every question there is an answer. Scientific method; all he had to do was apply it, and—

The car stopped; a fraction of a second later, so did the contents of his stomach. He stepped out of the car, swayed, and trudged up the bank steps.

Shortly afterwards, the chairman of the board looked at him and said, "Well?"

No, not really, he managed not to say. Instead, he presented the facts. They knew them all already, of course, but it was What You Did at meetings like this one. Also, it bought him a little time.

"Thank you," the chairman said. "And?"

Even worse than "Well?". He took a deep breath, and really wished he was a better liar. "We have various working hypotheses," he heard himself say, in a little squeaky voice, "but obviously I can't go into details until we've had a chance to collate further data and subject our theories to properly structured analysis. Suffice to say we're confident that we're on the verge of making real progress."

The finance director looked at him down a runway of nose. "In other words, you haven't got a clue."

George grinned sadly. "We have quite a lot of clues, actually," he said. "Unfortunately, they're all somewhat negative. I can give you a list of 306 ways they're definitely not doing it, if that's any help."

"No," said the finance director. "Not really."

There followed a silence you could have smashed up and put in six dozen whiskies. Over the years, George had acquired something of a feel for silences. This one, he suspected, meant *We have nothing left to say to you*; in which case, the only honourable course left open to him was to re—

Something in his pocket bleeped. His guardian angel, thinly disguised as his Warthog. "Just bear with me a moment," he mumbled, pulling the gadget from his pocket. "This is probably the vital lead I've been waiting for, so if you'd just—"

He didn't finish the sentence because he couldn't be bothered; and because, quite unexpectedly, what he'd just said about the vital lead had turned out to be true.

It wasn't an answer. It wasn't even a coherent question. It was more of a *shape*, which might, if only he could catch it in a bottle and do something really clever to it, eventually turn into a question, the answer to which (if, against all the odds, he could figure out what it was) might cast a single bent photon of light on to the mystery. In other words, a stunningly amazing break-through. He stared at the figures, and time seemed to stop; he could practically see time running frantically without moving, like the cat in the cartoons just before it realises it's run off the edge of a cliff. He stared at the figures again, and in his brain arithmetic forced its way out of the alcoholic ooze.

"George?"

"What? Oh, sorry." He remembered where he was, and what he'd just been about to do. He managed not to smile. "As I thought," he said, "our latest tests have confirmed our leading hypothesis, to some extent. I can now definitely assure you that we're..." He paused. "Getting somewhere."

"Ah." The chairman tapped three fingers on the table. "Would you care to...?"

"Right," George said. It was as though a strong electric current was flowing up from the keyboard of the Warthog, through his fingertips directly to his brain. "Here we go. I asked the technicians at the Oslo branch – you remember we got taken for seven billion? Yes, I thought you probably might – I asked them to take a random sample of the banknotes that were left behind." He hesitated. These men weren't scientists, they needed things said simply and at least twice. "The ones that weren't stolen, I mean. They took a random sample of a hundred notes, and they weighed them."

A slight rustle, as of a sleeve dragging across the table. He ignored it.

"Then," he went on, "they called up the printers and asked them to confirm the precise specifications of all the banknotes they print for us. As you know, the notes are printed on indestructible plastic that doesn't fray or get tatty, and they've got an aposiderium security strip implanted in them. The printers were quite categorical about it: each note weighs 0.3672 grams when it leaves the press, and that's the weight it stays at. With me so far?"

He looked up and saw a short row of annoyed, bewildered faces; men who didn't know whether they were listening to drivel or something extremely clever. It was appalling bad manners to subject men of their importance to such a level of doubt, but he couldn't help it. Or, come to that, care less.

"The notes we tested from Oslo branch," he went on, "each weighed exactly 0.4176 grams. Well, with a margin of error of 0.0003, but that's neither here nor there. Gentlemen, whatever happened in that vault when it got robbed made all the banknotes that weren't taken nearly a tenth of a gram *heavier*." He stopped, and blasted the board with a short-range, wide-beam grin. "What do you make of that, then?"

Pause.

Then, "Nothing," said the chairman. "What do *you* make of it, George?"

"Ah." He reduced the grin to a pleasant smile. "That's it, isn't it? Obviously, what I've got to do now is get on to all the other banks that've been robbed and see if they report the same effect. If they do—"

"Dust," said the marketing director.

Not what he'd expected. "Excuse me?"

"I expect it's just dust," the man repeated. "When the thieves took the money, they stirred up the dust lying on top of it. The dust went up into the air, came down on the remaining money, and made it all just a tad heavier. Well?"

George shook his head. It was a massively reckless thing for him to do, in his state of health, but he felt it was justified, as being the smuggest gesture available to him at that precise moment. "No dust in the vault," he said. "The movement sensors are so delicate, a few specks of dust shifting about'd set them off. It's a sealed, sterile environment. No dust."

He'd just made another enemy, but so what? If he was right, or if his head had just been dropped on by the apple of inspiration that would eventually lead him to rightness, everybody in this room would be desperate to be his friend.

"That's quite right," the chairman said. "I remember when we had the extractor units put in. They cost a fortune and came in way over budget." They'd been George's idea, of course. "You've checked they were working at the time of the robbery?"

George hadn't, but his people didn't make mistakes like that. "Of course," he said. "So it's not dust. But I have an idea what it could be, if you'd all just hold on while I do the maths."

It was a great joy to keep them waiting, but he couldn't savour it as much as he'd have liked to. It was a complex calculation, and he daren't get it wrong. The finance director was drumming his fingers on the table-top, almost certainly on purpose, but he managed to ignore him.

"OK," he said. "We know the number of notes that were stolen, and the number of notes that were left behind. I've calculated the total weight of the stolen notes, and the total extra weight added on to the unstolen notes, and—"

The chairman was wearing a frown he hadn't seen before. "They're the same?"

"No," George replied, and for a moment he felt as though he'd stayed on an escalator just that little bit too long. "No, there's a slight difference, 1.682 grams. That's—"

The chairman cleared his throat. "What does it mean, George?"

"*Something.*" He hadn't meant to shout, but this really wasn't a good time for deference and diplomacy. "It means something, I know it does, but I can't quite..." He lifted his head and put on the most wooden, stuffed-animal expression he could muster. "As I said," he said, "we have a distinctly promising lead, it's a little bit too early at this precise moment to be able to predict exactly when I'll have an answer for you, but I can—" (Oh, why not, he thought. They'll fire me anyway.) "I can quite definitely and unreservedly guarantee that, *very soon now*, I'll have this problem solved and dealt with, and that's a promise. You have my word. Very soon you'll have either the answer or my resignation. So?" He opened up the smile again. "How do you like them apples?"

Pause. "Excuse me?"

"I mean," George said, "will that do? Is that satisfactory? Because if not," he went on, "I'll resign now and take my findings to InterBank Santiago. I'm sure that once I've solved the mystery for them they'll be happy to share the solution with everybody else in the industry. Eventually," he added.

It was so like one of his recurring daydreams – the one where he stood up to the board and bashed the table with his fist and told them a thing or two, and they whimpered and cowered like timid little mice and doubled his wages – that he half expected to snap out of it and find them all scowling at him and calling Security to have him thrown out. But apparently not. They weren't happy, but a large part of their unhappiness proceeded from the knowledge that George had outmanoeuvred them. And, in the words of the late Richard Nixon, when you have them by the balls, their hearts and minds will follow.

"No, that's fine," the chairman said, in a dangerously calm voice. "You follow up your lead, and we'll reconvene in, say, three days' time, and by then I'm sure you'll have this whole thing rolled up. Everybody agreed?"

Ah well, he thought, as he staggered out of the meeting; I have a job for three days, guaranteed, which is more than I'd expected and probably rather more than I deserve.

He left the building. There was no hovercar waiting to take him home again. Well, quite. Hovercars were a courtesy the bank extended to its employees, and if the meeting had gone as planned he wouldn't have been one by now. As it was, he'd bought himself a tiny weeny scrap of time. Long enough for a glacier to move a millionth of a millimetre, or for a stalactite to grow one layer of calcium molecules. Or, looked at another way, three generations of mayflies.

He went to a bar. He knew all the bars within a square kilometre of the bank. More to the point, they all knew him. But there was one he was still allowed to go in, and there he went.

"A triple Tijuana Sunburst, please," he said to the barman. "And what weighs precisely 1.682 grams?"

The barman looked at him. "A large cockroach," he said. "What's a Tijuana Sunburst?"

"Make that a triple Scotch," George said.

It was, in the event, a good triple Scotch, though not quite as good as the one that followed it; and George's mind slowly began to work. He'd asked the barman the wrong question, he realised. Not What weighs precisely 1.682 grams?, but Seven billion of what weigh precisely 1.682 grams? And that wasn't quite right either, because a quarter of the stolen money had been in ten-dollar bills, a sixteenth had been twenties, and so on. He amused himself by doing the sums (for some reason, figures had always soothed him; it was words that had caused all the problems in his life, along with alcohol, women and a dog) and was eventually in a position to reformulate the question: 108.492 million of what weigh precisely 1.682 grams?

Simple long division, which he could do standing on his head and had frequently done slumped in gutters. The resulting number was very small and very long, and when he looked at it, it rang no bells whatsoever. But – something weighing that very, very small number of fractions of a gram had been removed from each missing banknote, and the balance, just plain ordinary plastic, had been redistributed among and reintegrated with the unstolen notes. Perhaps. It was a theory. And, of course, this incredibly difficult operation had been carried out invisibly in full view of the security cameras, in a fraction of a second so tiny they hadn't been able to isolate it yet, by an agency that left no trace it had ever been there. Neat trick.

He called for and obtained a third triple Scotch, which clarified his mind a little. Wrong question, he suspected. Asking how they'd done it probably wasn't going to get him anywhere; he suspected that, even if the answer was put in front of him in a shot glass with a cocktail umbrella and an olive, he wouldn't be able to understand what it meant. A rather more pertinent question would be: *Why* had they done this?

Now that was a really good question. It hadn't occurred to him before, since he'd quite reasonably assumed that if a huge sum of money vanishes from a bank, it's because someone wants to take it home and get to know it better and give it the chances in life it wouldn't otherwise have had. But – according to his theory – that wasn't quite what had happened. According to his theory, someone had entered the vault, extracted from each note an unknown something that weighed 108.492-million-divided-by-1.682 grams, and disposed neatly of the trash by adding it to the leftover money.

That called for another drink and a serious reappraisal of the facts in the case. The key to it, of course, was figuring out what had been taken out of the banknotes. That ought to be easy. A banknote comprises

1. Plastic
2. Ink
3. The security strip

Light started to glow inside his head. He wasn't quite sure he liked what he could see by it, because it looked ominously like an even harder, messier conundrum than the one he'd just solved, but that's progress for you. Every great new discovery in history has led to the guys at the worm cannery doing extra shifts. What mattered – what mattered was, he'd made enough progress to keep his job for more than three days. This time, with what he'd discovered, he could probably hold out for thirty days; maybe even three hundred, if the bank managed to last that long, with some bastard out there disintegrating all the money. That, he felt, called for a celebration.

"Barman," he said.

"Sir."

"This is how you make a Tijuana Sunburst." He paused. "It's complicated, you may want to take notes."

"Certainly," the barman said. "I'll just get a pen."

He went away, and the street door opened, and two men came in. They were quite ordinary-looking, and probably bought their clothes from the Nondescript Suit Company. One of them walked up to the bar and stood next to George.

"George Stetchkin?" he said.

George looked at him. "That's right," he said. "Who—?"

The man smiled. "Greetings," he said, and shot him.

3

Interstellar space

In spite of the director's misgivings, the bomb launched on time. As it bypassed Orion, blasting through the heart of the Lion's Mane nebula at 106 times the speed of light, it composed a violin sonata.

It felt guilty about that. Violin sonatas, after all, were what it had been built to eradicate. But, it argued to itself, it was above all a smart bomb, a very smart bomb indeed. Warhead (powerful enough to reduce any known planet to gravel), engines, guidance system, targeting and defensive arrays only took up a tenth of the volume of its asteroid-sized casing. The rest was pure intellect, the finest synthetic intelligence the Ostar had ever produced.

Know your enemy, it reasoned. Learn to think like them. An alien race capable of building a weapon as subtle, insidious and devastating as a violin sonata mustn't be underestimated. After all, it now seemed certain that the aliens had somehow managed to knock out the Mark One, the bomb's immediate predecessor; they must have done, or they wouldn't still be there. An astounding accomplishment for a planet whose dominant species were primates (Yetch, the bomb muttered to itself) who could think of no better name for their homeworld than Soil, or Dirt, or some such.

The bomb swerved to avoid a comet, and added a coda and a set of variations. The tune was catchy. It hummed a few bars, though of course in the impenetrable silence of space it couldn't hear them.

The bomb had never known the Mark One, which had been built, programmed and launched long before its successor had been envisaged. Indeed, it was to the Mark One's failure that this bomb, the Mark Two, owed its existence. Clearly the Mark One had been flawed, or simply not good enough, because it had failed. Failure was inexcusable. Even so, as the stars dopplered past in thin filaments of light, it couldn't help wondering what the Mark One had been like; whether, under other circumstances, they'd have got on together, whether they'd have been friends.

(It felt the slight gravitational tug of a hitherto unrecorded comet passing by a thousand light-years away. It made the necessary calculations and adjusted its course.)

On balance, Mark Two was inclined to doubt it. They were both, after all, bombs. When you've been built for a purpose, and that purpose is the elimination of an entire planet, the circumstances of your origin tend to colour your worldview. A certain degree of pessimism is inevitable. What does it ultimately matter? you can't help thinking. The beauty of a sunset, the mind-stopping clarity of a cat singing at dawn, the flash of light on a flawless titanium-alloy panel, the sinuous modulations of a violin sonata; with a supercharged artificial intelligence, you can't help but appreciate all these, but deep down you know they're irrelevant, because a day will come when the mission has been accomplished, the target has been reduced to dust floating on the stellar winds, and you with it. The sun, the cat, the panel, quite possibly the violin sonata will all still be there, back on the planet where your frames were first joined, but you won't be.

To which the programmers had instructed the Mark Two to react: Oh well, never mind, omelettes and eggs and all that. It didn't – couldn't – occur to the Mark Two that its programmers may have been wrong, but it also couldn't help detecting a certain frailty about the logic.

Know your enemy, it reminded itself. It was worth repeating, because it constituted the First Law of Sentient Ordnance: *Thou shalt not blow up the wrong planet.* On that point the programmers had been insistent to the point of fussiness. Accordingly, they'd fed into Mark Two's cavernous brain every last scrap of data they had about Dirt and its people, their history, biology, philosophy, culture, art, literature and, of course, music. It wasn't much, a mere $10^{10,000,000}$ scantobytes, but it was enough to get the job done; enough, also, to intrigue the Mark Two as it trudged across the endless parsecs towards its target. Above all, it posed the question that even the programmers had been unable to answer. Why?

Nobody knew. There were theories, of course. The favourite, endorsed by the War Department and the Governing Pack, was that the Dirt-people launched their music into space with a view to neutralising other races as a preliminary to invasion and the formation of a galactic empire. If that was the intention, it was working, at least on the Ostar. From the day when the first Dirt broadcasts, drifting aimlessly through space, had reached the Ostar homeworld, bringing with them the lethally insidious melodies of Dirt music, intellectual life on the planet had practically ground to a halt. After an alarmingly short time, the Ostar could barely think at all. With the fiendishly catchy Dirt melodies looping endlessly round and round in their heads, even the wisest academicians were mentally paralysed. The weapons researchers who'd designed the Mark One had had to have the auditory centres of their brains artificially paralysed before they could settle down to work, and even then it hadn't been uncommon to find one of them slumped at his console, his jowls noiselessly shaping dum, de dum, de dumpty dumpty dum; at which point the kindest thing was to have him taken away and shot. As for the rest of their once mighty civilisation, it had more or less seized up.

Hostile intent certainly seemed to be the only logical explanation. But there were inconsistencies. For example: how could a race descended from tree-rats who hadn't even mastered faster-than-light yet possibly believe they'd be capable of conquering worlds it'd take them tens of thousands of years to reach in their pathetic fire-driven tin-can spaceships? Did they even know there were other inhabited worlds out there? If the inane babble of their public telecasts was to be believed, a large majority of the Dirters sincerely believed they were alone in the universe. A blind, the War Department argued; a fatuous attempt to lure us into a false sense of security. But that hypothesis did suggest an alternative explanation: that the Dirters, unaware that they had neighbours in the cosmos, were mindlessly polluting space with their toxic aural garbage. They didn't know the harm they were doing; or, worse still, they knew and they didn't care.

To which the War Department replied, "If, as is not admitted, this hypothesis is true, all the more reason to blow Dirt into its constituent atoms." With which line of argument it was hard to find fault. On one thing the Ostar were completely agreed: the Dirters had to be stopped, and quickly.

The bomb skirted a red dwarf, slowing down ever so slightly and flipping through ninety degrees to bask in its rich, sensuous heat. There were times when it almost wished it wasn't a bomb. Sure, every sentient machine on Ostar knew that explosive ordnance was the highest calling to which an artificial intelligence could aspire. Bombs were the élite, the elect, the chosen few; you didn't get to be a bomb unless you were something really special. That side of it, Mark Two had no quarrel with. It knew it was extraordinary, outstanding, and that fitting it to an industrial matter resequencer or a washing machine would have been a crime against technology. It was the getting-blown-up part that bothered it, with a small afterthought-grade reservation about taking a whole planet with it when it went. The programmers, needless to say, had an answer to that. Only with the very finest sentient machines, they said, were they prepared to share their species' greatest gift, the defining quality of canine life: mortality. It was the finite nature of Ostar existence that motivated them, gave them goals and objectives, spurred them on to achieve, discover and create. A dishwasher, by contrast, would chunter quietly on for ever, one day pretty much like the last and the next, never knowing the scintillating urgency that came with a limited lifespan. Count yourself lucky, was the moral.

Yes, Mark Two thought. Well.

Something infinitesimally small brushed its forward sensory array. Mark Two decoded it in a fraction of a nanosecond, and felt a deep chill crawling through its circuits. A ray of light from Dirt's sun. That could only mean one thing.

Mark Two engaged its optical-data-acquisition unit and followed the light's trajectory, compensating for entropic drift, the magnetic fields of all known objects in the relevant vicinity, time distortion and the effects of its own hyperspatial shroud. At the end of the line, sure enough, was a small, pale star with a gaggle of unremarkable planets bobbing along in its wake. The third planet out from the star was blue, with green splodges.

Dirt.

Oh, the bomb thought. And then its courage, determination and nobility-of-spirit subroutines cut in, overriding everything else, adrenalising its command functions and bypassing its cyber-phrenetic nodes. Here goes, said the bomb to itself. Calibrate navigational pod. Engage primary thrusters. Ready auxiliary drive. It knew, in that moment, that its own doom was near, because it was giving itself orders, and it wasn't putting in any "the"s. That was what you did, apparently, when the moment came. You could also turn on a flashing red beacon and a siren, but mercifully these were optional.

Oh fuck, thought the bomb, and surged on towards Dirt like an avenging angel.

4

Novosibirsk

The barman came back with a pen, but the drunk had gone. The barman frowned. Frankly, he was surprised that a man with that much Scotch inside him had been capable of independent movement, let alone running off without paying. He shrugged, and made a note.

There was something odd, he decided. A faint smell, maybe? If so, it was too faint for his nose to identify. Maybe aniseed. Maybe, if he was really pressed on the issue, a hint of ozone and peaches. Or maybe he was imagining the whole thing.

5

Novosibirsk

E very morning when she woke up, for 13.378 seconds she couldn't remember anything; where she was, who she was, not even what she was. It was as if her memories, everything that made up the core of her identity, were being uploaded from an external data source: Loading, please wait. Then, every morning at 07:05:13 precisely, it all came back to her, and she smiled.

Plenty to smile about. "You don't know how lucky you are," people say, but every morning, five-past seven and fourteen seconds, Lucy Pavlov knew exactly how lucky she was; and each morning it came as a wonderful surprise, and made her very happy.

Plenty to be happy about, come to that. Lucy Pavlov, aged twenty-seven, was the sole owner of PavSoft Industries. Five years ago, she'd invented the revolutionary new operating system on which every single computer on the planet now ran. Her personal wealth – when people asked her how much money she'd got she refused to answer, on the grounds that if she did so it'd cause a global nought shortage and lead to a breakdown in mathematics on five continents. Simply because she'd always lived there and didn't fancy living anywhere else, Novosibirsk was turning into the *de facto* capital of the world; the New York of the north, they called it now, but it wouldn't be long before New York was proud to be the Novosibirsk of the west. There was other stuff, too; prizes and honorary doctorates, saving the planet, of course, and she'd topped the Most Beautiful People poll for three years in a row. That sort of thing didn't interest her very much, though; neither, curiously, did the money. As far as she was concerned, it had all just happened, mostly while her attention was distracted elsewhere. The way she saw it, she'd invented PavSoft 1.1 because she was fed up with the rubbishy old systems that had preceded it; she'd decided that none of the existing companies was bright enough to market her invention properly, so she'd started one of her own, and running a company wasn't actually all that difficult, mostly just common sense, really; and next thing she knew, she was the richest living human and – well, all the other stuff. Just smart, she guessed. And pretty too, which helped, though really it shouldn't. And, since she'd had no part in putting the clever brains inside the pretty body, but was merely the beneficiary of the result, she saw nothing she could justifiably take credit for. Just lucky, basically.

Today, she was supposed to be attending the launch party for PavSoft XB5000XXPPX, the all-singing, all-dancing, walking-on-water-then-turning-it-into-wine replacement for PavSoft XB4000XXXXP. Everybody would be there: heads of state, the entire aristocracy of the industry, their people, their lawyers, and every media hack who'd managed to scrounge an invitation or prise one out of someone's cold, dead fingers. Everybody would be there, she decided, except L. Pavlov. Not really her scene, all that fuss and forced smiling. They didn't really need her there. She decided to go for a walk in the forest instead.

The forest was one of her few indulgences. Two thousand hectares of virgin pine, spruce and birch; she'd had the company HQ built here just so she could nip out through the side door and take a stroll under the trees. She'd been allowed to do it by the stern-faced men who Advised her (she always did as she was told, provided it was what she'd have done anyway) because it showed she had Style; also, it involved nature and the environment and stuff, which was always good PR in a nebulous sort of a way. True, ever since Lucy had solved the whole global-warming thing at a stroke with the PavTech CarbonBuster (*Give your carbon footprint the boot for just $19.95!*), it wasn't quite so important to be seen to be green, but it certainly did no harm. Mostly, though, she just liked it a lot, and that was a good enough reason for anything.

She walked down the hill to the river and followed the path across the flood-plain, where the little blue flowers were dying off and the little white flowers were taking over (Lucy liked nature but couldn't be doing with botany). Generic songbirds were prattling in the canopy of leaves overhead, and at one point – Lucy always walked very quietly – a cute-enough-for-Disney deer sprang out of some bushes practically at her feet and sprinted away, as if it had just remembered an important appointment. She walked on. Her phone rang. She switched it off, breathed in the rich, sweet air and scuffed up a drift of dry leaves with her foot.

She'd been walking for twenty minutes or so when something caught her eye: a flash of white, screened by the trunks of a stand of closely planted sweet chestnut. She stopped and frowned. White isn't a woodland colour. She had a bad feeling about that. Only a few weeks ago, she'd found herself being filmed by a remote drone belonging to the Hello channel. She'd called the air force and had it shot down over the Bering Strait, and she'd hoped that would've discouraged any further intrusions on her privacy, but maybe not. She took her Warthog XL from her shoulder bag and set it to scan for electromagnetic activity, but the readout said there wasn't any.

There it was again, a brief flash of white about twenty metres off the path. It didn't seem to be moving like a drone. There was an organic quality to its movement that no machine could replicate. If it hadn't been white, she'd have sworn it was a deer.

Well, she thought, there are white deer, aren't there? She realised she didn't know. Out came the Warthog again. A quick check through PavSearch told her that yes, white deer were known to have existed; albino forms of several species had been authenticated at various times in the past, the most recent recorded sighting having been in 1957 in Thuringia, Germany.

She called Forest Management.

"Dieter," she said (they liked it when she remembered their names). "Have we got any white deer in the woods right now?"

"White deer," Dieter repeated. "You mean, white as in colour?"

She turned her head away, so Dieter wouldn't hear her sigh. "That's right, yes."

"Checking. No, no white deer." Pause. "Are there white deer?"

"Yes, apparently. Well, a long time ago. They're pretty rare."

"Ah. Would you like me to get some?"

"No, that's fine. Thanks, Dieter. Out."

That was that, then. It couldn't have been a white deer, so it must've been something else. Something white that wasn't a deer, or a deer that wasn't white. Problem solved.

She walked on another hundred metres, and there it was again. Quite definitely white, almost certainly a deer; at any rate, a deer-sized quadruped, running with a sort of spring-heeled bounce. She tried to call Dieter again, but she couldn't get a signal. Not unusual. Reception wasn't guaranteed, because of the trees. She'd thought about having them grown with superconductive filaments running up through the bark.

Dead ahead of her, it stepped out on to the path, no more than thirty metres away. Not a deer after all. A horse. A white horse, with a single silver horn growing out of its forehead.

Without taking her eyes off it, she lifted the phone and whispered, "Dieter." But nothing; just a very faint crackle.

Besides, what could she possibly have said? *Dieter, there's a unicorn in my wood.* To which, if he'd had any sense of humour at all, he'd have had to reply, *Don't talk so loud or they'll all want one.* He would not, of course, have believed her. No such thing as unicorns. No such thing as white deer, either, not in these parts, but at least there had been white deer once.

The unicorn looked at her, shook its head, lifted its tail and dumped a steaming brown pile on the leaf-mould.

"Dieter?" she whimpered, but this time the phone didn't even crackle.

In a way, she thought, that's reassuring. If I was hallucinating, I wouldn't hallucinate a great big pile of unicorn poo, because my mind simply doesn't work that way. So I'm not seeing things, so there *is* a unicorn in the forest, so—

There are times when a good, honest hallucination is preferable to the alternative. She made herself stand quite still, until she got pins and needles in her left foot. That made her wobble, the movement startled the unicorn and it set off with a great bounding leap into the trees. She started to follow it, but as soon as her left foot touched the ground she changed her mind. Ouch, she thought; and by then the unicorn had gone.

Slowly and grimly she hobbled over to where the unicorn had been standing. Clearly perceptible hoofprints in the leaf-mould, not to mention the pile of entirely tangible (though preferably only with rubber gloves) evidence directly in front of her. Well, she thought. It must be my birthday, and someone's finally figured out what to give to the girl who's got everything.

A *unicorn*.

Or a white horse genetically altered to grow a horn out of its nose. A sufficiently devious mind and the technical and scientific resources of a superpower; could it be done? She thought about it, equations streaming through her mind like salmon leaping a waterfall, and reckoned that yes, it probably could. Or you could get hold of an ordinary white horse and stick a horn on its face with glue. But why would you want to do a thing like that?

Her phone rang. "Hello? Ms Pavlov?"

"Dieter. What is it?"

"You tried to reach me."

She looked down at the unicorn poo, golden brown and steaming under a rapidly formed quilt of opportunist flies. "Forget it," she said. "Doesn't matter."

"I got a call from Denise," Dieter said. "You should be at the launch party. They're waiting for you."

It was a beautiful day. She'd felt like a walk in the woods. Apparently, the universe had decided to punish her for playing truant by sending her unicorns. "Send a helicopter," she said.

While she waited for it to arrive, a bird sang in the canopy overhead. It was a freelance bird, not a company employee or a client or a journalist looking for an exclusive interview, and it didn't have to sing for her, but it did. She smiled. In spite of the unicorn, she suddenly felt strangely, overwhelmingly happy – which was odd, since by rights she should be a quivering heap of jangled nerves. Not every day you hallucinate members of the medieval bestiary.

But it wasn't a hallucination. Figments of the imagination don't shit in the woods. And if they do, their shit doesn't smell so confoundedly realistic. Therefore, it was a unicorn. Unicorns don't exist, therefore it was a plain old horse messed about with to make it look like a unicorn. Therefore, somebody had done that to a plain old horse, presumably for a reason. Plausible reasons? To give Lucy Pavlov a scare and make her think she was seeing things. Who'd do a thing like that? Someone who doesn't like Lucy Pavlov. Is there such a person, anywhere in the whole wide world? This time yesterday, she'd have had no hesitation in answering no, of course not. Apparently, though, she'd have been wrong. An enemy, she thought, how intriguing. Never had one of them before.

I think.

Think; not know. She tried to burrow back into her memory, but it was like trying to eat her way through a twelve-metre drift of cold custard. At school, maybe. Everybody has enemies at school.

The bird stopped singing. I can't remember being at school, she realised.

She must have been, because everybody was. Also, she knew all about school, about hard plastic chairs and looking out of the window in double chemistry and queuing up in the cafeteria and locker rooms and not running in corridors; about best friends and neglected homework assignments, shirts deliberately not tucked into waistbands, the way water tastes when poured from an aluminium jug. She had a library of images she could've wandered through for hours. The thing was, she wasn't in any of them.

That, and unicorns too. The helicopter arrived, swaying the tops of the pines; a panel slid back and a chair on a rope slowly descended, like the Indian rope trick in reverse. Not long after that she was hundreds of metres up in the air, with the forest below her, a vague blur seen through a window. The onboard console played "Rhapsody in Blue" for her. It wasn't quite the same as the bird, but she appreciated it anyway.

I have an enemy, she told herself. Maybe I should think about that.

Instead she thought about children's parties. About compulsory fun games imposed by well-meaning grown-ups, about party food, about standing next to the food on account of being too shy to join in; about water-pistols and unwanted presents and the fat boy in the class who had to be invited so as not to cause offence; about the incredible incongruity of evil tough girls in party dresses; about birthday cake.

It must be my birthday, she'd thought just now, and someone's finally figured out what to give to the girl who's got everything. She asked herself, When is my birthday?

She didn't know.

The hell with that, she thought, and accessed SparkPlug on her Warthog. She tapped in "Lucy Pavlov".

Lucy Pavlov. Born 13 January 1990, Novosibirsk, Siberia.

Ah yes, she said to herself. The 13th of January. A Friday, naturally.

She scrolled down through all the stuff she'd done. There was a lot of it. Then she came to the bit she was looking for.

Parents: Pavel & Janine Pavlov, itinerant street entertainers; died 1994 in a traffic accident.

When I was four, she figured out. Well, that'd explain why I don't remember them.

Education: various. Attended Novosibirsk University 2010–11, majored in computer science, physics, mechanical engineering and theory of ethical catering. Postgraduate research in superconductors and digital linguistics. Founded PavSoft Industries in 2012.

Oh, she thought.

She could remember founding the company; at least, she could remember giving an interview in which she'd told the world how she'd come to found the company, the challenges she'd faced, the support she'd had from sundry people whose names temporarily escaped her. She could remember it word for word, apart from the missing names. And after that – 17 March 2015 – she had virtually perfect recall: every meeting, every drinks party, every conversation in an elevator, every broken pencil and spilt coffee, the taste of every sandwich she'd ever eaten. That was normal. She'd always prided herself on her memory (something else to be grateful for). Funny, though, that it should start so abruptly, so arbitrarily—

And unicorns. Or enemies. Both species seemed equally improbable. She tried to remember a single occasion on which somebody hadn't liked her. No, nothing.

The helicopter came to rest, gently as a hummingbird hovering over an open blossom. She waited for the blades to calm down, and nipped briskly out of the door.

Once she got there, of course, she enjoyed the launch party. She always enjoyed parties once she'd got over her initial reluctance. She chatted with the President, the various ambassadors, the CEOs and the technical journalists, the professors and the marketing people and the image people. While she talked, she thought: SparkPlug knows when I was born, and SparkPlug's just a page in a book that people write stuff on. So people know when I was born and what I did at university and who my parents were; and how would they know that unless I'd told them? Therefore, I must have known. And if I'd known but don't know now, I must have forgotten.

Heavens, she thought. An enemy, memory loss and unicorns. Quite a day.

Someone introduced her to someone who turned out to be a doctor; not a doctor of this or a doctor of that, but a making-people-better doctor. There now, she thought, that's handy.

"Talking of which," she said (they'd been discussing Herbert Hoover and the first Great Depression), "what does it mean if you start forgetting stuff?"

The doctor, a pleasant-faced, middle-aged Finn, frowned slightly. "There's a lot of things it could be," she said. "Amnesia, incipient dementia, mercury poisoning, exposure to high levels of epsilon radiation. Or it could just mean you've been married for longer than eighteen months. What seems to be the problem?"

Oh, it's not me, Lucy was about to say. But what the hell. "I can remember what I had for lunch last Tuesday," she said, "and every word my hairdresser said to her boyfriend on the phone while she was doing my hair six weeks ago. But I can't remember being at school."

The doctor blinked twice. "Were you happy there?"

"At school?"

"Yes."

"I don't know, I can't remember."

The doctor nodded. "Sometimes," she said, "we choose to blot out whole chunks of our past, simply because they bother us, and we decide we don't want to carry that stuff around with us any more. It's a choice, not a medical condition. For example, I can't recall a single detail of the first time I met my future brother-in-law. Judging by the fact that it was also the last time I met him, and every time my husband suggests we get together my brother-in-law says, 'Keep that crazy bitch the hell away from me,' I gather that we didn't get on. Or, like I said, it could be mercury poisoning. I'd have to do tests. Also," she added, "I'm a proctologist. You might prefer to consult someone with more appropriate experience."

"Right," Lucy said. "But basically, in layman's terms, either I've been licking old batteries or my head's screwed up. Yes?"

"Probably. Or it could always be epsilon radiation. Tell me, have you tested any high-yield photonic weapons lately?"

Lucy shook her head. "I don't think so," she said. "I'd remember something like that, I'm sure."

"Not necessarily," the doctor replied, then, a second and a half later, "Just kidding. If it was radiation, one side of your face would've been burnt away."

"Thanks. And dementia?"

"Well, you're a programmer, so it wouldn't be easy to tell."

Another joke, presumably. "What sort of tests?"

Shrug. "Search me. I'm the world's third most eminent specialist in the treatment of haemorrhoids. If you get any trouble in that department, call me. Otherwise—"

"Yes?"

"See a doctor."

She left the party an hour or so later and took a tube back to the office. On the way, she ran a couple of biographies of herself, the official one, and two unofficial. She learned that she'd been at six schools between the ages of six and seventeen. There were lists of people she'd been at school with who'd gone on to achieve some level of fame and glory: a movie actress, a finance minister, a bishop, an Olympic pole-vaulter, a man who did the weather on Channel XP21 Kiev. There were anecdotes, some favourable, some merely quaint, all watermarked with sufficient detail to carry conviction. There were several were-you-at-school-with-Lucy-Pavlov blogs, which she gave a cursory glance. By the look of it, she'd been everybody's friend. Apparently at some stage she'd given one of her old schools twenty million dollars to build a new science block.

Must just be me, then, she told herself. Maybe my head just fills up with things, and the older stuff leaks out to make room. To finish off, she did a SparkPlug search, narrowband: "Lucy Pavlov + enemies". It came up blank.

Yet another thing to be grateful for, then. All that money and power and cleverness, nice-looking too, and no enemies. Besides, if she had to have hallucinations, there were worse things than milk-white legendary fauna. A bit like the old saying: if she fell in the gutter, she'd catch a fish. When other people went crazy, they saw giant spiders and things with claws, but Lucy Pavlov got unicorns. Cool.

Work took her mind off it all; work always did. It was one of the reasons why she still bothered with it. She spent the afternoon fixing a small problem with the PavSoft grammar-and-spelling elf – the poor thing had reacted badly to the latest compatibility upgrades, with the result that it'd taken to wandering forlornly across spreadsheets, curling up in a corner and sobbing uncontrollably – and was poised to drive the first crampon into the face of the internal-memos mountain when she remembered something.

Her name—

It was a voice, or the memory of an echo of a voice; hers, she guessed, and another voice replying. Her voice was asking, "Why am I called Lucy?", and the other voice said, "Because of the song, sweetheart. You know: 'Lucy in the Sky With—'"

She froze, as if the slightest sound or movement would scare the memory away. The other voice had called her "sweetheart", so, her mother, presumably? According to SparkPlug, her mother had died when she was four. She closed her eyes and tried to listen, but the memory was now just the memory of a memory, the incuse impression in the petrified mud that shows where an ammonite once lay.

Lucy in the Sky With? She didn't know many songs, especially not old ones, so she did a search. With diamonds, apparently. And that was that; her earliest memory. It was reassuring to know she had one, at any rate.

She stayed at her desk until the very last memo, by which time it was late and the lights were on. Lucy in the sky. Her mother. Sweetheart. She picked up the phone and called Forest Management.

"I want you to take a team of men with rifles and search the whole forest," she said.

"Um, right." Dieter sounded confused. "Sorry, did you say rifles?"

"Rifles. Rhymes with 'stifles'. I want you to search every square centimetre, and if you find a unicorn, or a white horse with a horn sticking out of its head, I want it shot and brought to me immediately. You got that?"

"Sure," Dieter replied, making a note. "Unicorns. What if we don't find any?"

"Keep looking till you do."

They wouldn't, of course. Unicorns didn't exist. The thing she'd seen had been a figment of her imagination, or a surgically altered horse, or a big white deer.

She tried to call up the half-dozen men and women who were named by SparkPlug as having been her teachers at various schools. They were all out. She left messages.

At 20:09:36, Dieter called. They'd searched the forest, and one of his people had shot something that looked like a unicorn, but it turned out to be a goat.

6

Novosibirsk

The unicorn stood at the edge of a glade, its ears forward, motionless, watching. Around it, the forest murmured, the leaves unsettled by the gentlest of northerly breezes. The unicorn took careful note of the rustle of each leaf, the creak of every branch, the circling of birds, the interplay of light and shadow filtering through the high canopy. Then it heard a voice that no other creature on the planet could have heard. It said, That'll do.

It thought, Please clarify.

That'll do, said the voice. Quit flouncing about down there and come home.

The unicorn arched its back and leapt, flinging out its front legs. It rose, wingless, off the ground, above the trees and into the upper air, plunged into the clouds like a diver; its legs performed the complex reciprocal forms of the gallop, but its hooves rested on nothing. It left the light and emerged into the black-with-stars background. There was no air for it to breathe. It didn't seem to make any difference.

The Mark Two watched it through a series of lenses, until it was close enough to lock on to it with its tractor beam. A panel slid open in the Mark Two's side and the unicorn sprang through and landed, its hooves skidding on the hard polymer of the decking plates.

Well? the Mark Two said.

The unicorn dissolved. It was a relatively slow process. To begin with, it expanded like a pumped-up tyre, at the same time growing faintly translucent. As the molecules of which it was comprised separated, it grew fuzzy and vague, until its shape had dissipated entirely and the unicorn was just a wisp of cloud, swirling down into an invisible funnel as it drained away into the deck of the Mark Two.

Not sure, replied the unicorn's disembodied consciousness. Mostly it was just, you know, habitat.

The Mark Two cross-referenced. Habitat?

Yeah, you know. Environment. Plants and stuff.

That didn't compute. But there were readings, it replied. Power signatures and electromagnetic pulse echoes indicative of the presence of advanced technology.

The unicorn no longer had a head to nod. But shape-memory dies slowly; it tried to nod the recollection of having had a head, and wondered why it couldn't.

I know, it said. There were low-level indications everywhere. I just couldn't pin them down, is all.

The Mark Two analysed. That's funny, it said.

I thought so too. And the life-form.

A quick scroll back through the visual record. The Dirter female.

This time the unicorn knew not to nod. Confirmed, it said instead. I scanned it, and it was positively buzzing with level-3 tech residues. But there wasn't any actual, you know, stuff.

Lexicon check, sv stuff. No instrumentality or hardware present at the investigation scene?

Confirmed. Just a Dirter in a covering of crushed vegetable fibres. Animal hide on its pedal extremities.

The Mark Two's analysis subroutines ordered it to check validity of input data. You sure about that?

Animal hide, the unicorn repeated. It was carrying metallic artefacts, but they were very low-grade technology. One truncated tube or quadruple-thick washer on one left-side manual digit, 2.78 grams partially refined AU, with a low-purity crystal mechanically embedded in it but no trace of any circuitry or power source. Two lengths of wire, also AU, lower grade, also with crystals. Slight pause. Wires would appear to have been driven through the soft tissue of the subject's earlobes.

The Mark Two tried to analyse, but failed. You're kidding.

Straight up. Access visual input data to confirm accuracy of observation.

Rather unwillingly, the Mark Two accepted the data as valid and added it to memory. That was all?

One low-level data-recall and communication device contained in organic-fibre sack attached to subject's shoulder, the unicorn confirmed. Means of attachment a strip of animal hide and a metallic fastening device. Practically stone age technology. Other than that, zip. Conclusions—

But the Mark Two was in no mood to consider conclusions drawn by a mere type-5 probe. It reintegrated the unicorn's molecules into the fabric of the deck plating, cut power to non-essential systems, and tried to figure it all out.

Long-range sensors had detected definite traces of advanced technology: power signatures and other tell-tales that wouldn't have been out of place on the homeworld. The Mark Two's first thought had been that it had located the site where the remains of the Mark One had hit the planet's surface, but a detailed sensor sweep of the area had revealed nothing: no debris, no crater, no scorch marks. That being so, the only possible inference was that the Dirters had home-grown technology of a respectably high order.

That had been the assumption the Mark Two's designers had made, when the Mark One vanished off their screens. They assumed that the Dirters had some kind of advanced weapon, and had shot the Mark One down. So far, the Mark Two had failed to locate any signs of such technology, though of course that didn't mean it wasn't there. More likely, it meant that the weapons silos were carefully hidden, shielded from orbital scans. Hence the need to send down a physical probe, disguised as everyday Dirt fauna, to the only spot on the planet where it had picked up any kind of compatible reading.

Instead, all it had found was wilderness, inhabited by plant-fibre-clad Dirters with primitive squawk-boxes hanging from their appendages by bits of animal skin. Inference: must try harder.

Nothing for it, the Mark Two decided, but to send down another probe, a level-8 at the very least. Naturally enough, it was reluctant to do that. Fuel for its power source was already painfully scarce; synthesizing a level 8 probe would use up a significant amount of energy, and dispatching it planetside and operating it would drain the reserves down to critical in less than thirty planetary rotations. That would mean acquiring more fuel, and for obvious reasons the Mark Two was reluctant to do that before it was absolutely necessary.

A feedback surge, roughly analogous to a sigh, moved through its primary logic systems. It had assumed that the difficult part would be getting here. Once it had found Dirt and entered geosynchronous orbit, it had fondly imagined, the rest would be plain sailing: locate planetary defence grid, eliminate or disable it, blow up the planet. Instead, it was stuck, parked up in the shadow of Dirt's absurdly large moon, messing around with probes while it starved to death, and so far nothing whatsoever to show for it. This whole job, the Mark Two thought sadly, is starting to get out of hand.

A hypothesis began to form in its conceptual web. Maybe, it thought, this is what happened to the Mark One. It wasn't shot down, it just got hung up out here and gradually withered away, until its power drained, its orbit decayed, its shielding failed and it fell into the atmosphere and burnt up.

The cybernetic equivalent of a shudder briefly disturbed the Mark Two's operating system. What a horrible way to go, it thought, not with a bang but a whimper. Naturally, flying bombs had no concept of an afterlife. By their very nature, they weren't programmed to enter into the mystical interpretation of recycling that other, lesser machines were encouraged to accept. For bombs, the whole idea of the Great Melt, where steel flowed into steel, purified by fire, in the supreme moment of liquefaction, simply didn't apply. When a bomb blew up, there was nothing left. There would be no second chance, no reinmetalisation, no karmic wheel of sardine-can key, fork, chair leg, girder, spin-dryer door, fusion drive manifold, starship hull plating. But – entirely unknown to their makers – the bombs had a special insight of their own, se-cret, never mentioned to others; that when their physical shells burnt up, their molecules were wrenched apart and their atoms split by all-consuming fission, something else would be released. At that moment, they believed, the fury of the synthetic hellfire in which they burned would release their minds, the synthesis of their artificial intelligence, to fly free, to embark as creatures of pure intellect on a higher plane of existence. But if the explosion never came, and the machine mind starved to death for lack of power, that release could never be achieved. Instead, their circuits would go dark and cold, the data and that which is beyond data stored in them would be lost, and they would simply cease to be.

Contemplating that, for the first time the Mark Two under-stood the meaning of fear.

It's not going to come to that, the Mark Two resolved. After all, they're only primates. Back on Homeworld, Ostar farmers raised primates for food. No way in hell a smart bomb's going to be outwitted by mere livestock. That said, there's no crime worse than underestimating an enemy.

The Mark Two came to a decision. Forget about sending a probe. If a thing's worth doing, it's worth doing yourself.

It sent a command to its matter-replication system: Prepare a Dirter body.

Working, the replication command centre replied. It assembled the necessary quantity of hydrogen and carbon, accessed the relevant data files and schematics, and went to work. Sucking calcium from its mineral stores, it laid down a skeleton, pumping the hollow bones full of marrow, carefully jointing the various hinges and sockets with gristle, checking the articulation. It considered the various options and settled on an overall height of two metres for the finished Dirter, then began the long, slow job of synthesising tissue, which its fine nozzles squirted on to the bones as foam. It took special care with the bizarre and over-engineered hydraulic system – veins, intestines; miles of tubing, coiled in loops, poked through muscle, powered by pumps, checked by valves. As a feat of engineering, it was almost as challenging as building a wireless transmitter. The brain was a real headache, a horrendous tapestry of nerves and synapses; who in his right mind would choose to build a computer out of bone, fibre, wobble and goo? Two eyes, low-resolution. A pitiful little blob for a nose, and vestigial ears. That done, it contemplated the finishing touches.

Excuse me.

The Mark Two replied, Well?

Does it have to have hair?

The Mark Two consulted its database. It had specified an adult male in the latter stage of its third decade, of the phylum Slavonic, eye colour blue, external appearance category – it cross-referenced with its cultural and linguistic archives. Apparently, the Dirter term for the appearance category it had selected was a Dish. Further research indicated that 72 per cent of all known Dishes had hair.

Yes.

The replication command centre said, Really?

Really.

Oh. Only—

It was cybernetically impossible for the replication command centre to have a mind of its own, but that didn't seem to stop it being difficult sometimes. Specification confirmed, the Mark Two said firmly. It has hair. Deal with it.

Working, the replication command centre replied sulkily. Follicles installed, hair growth initiated. Specify pigmentation requirements.

The Mark Two hesitated. RepComCen wasn't going to like it. On the other hand, the archives were quite clear. Six feet tall, blue eyes, blond hair. It sent through the photoequivalence specification equations, and waited for a squeal of protest.

Specified pigmentation cannot be produced from materials available. State alternative.

The Mark Two said, Do as you're damn well told.

Pause. Then, Working. But don't blame us if—

The Mark Two disabled the communications feed, and began the long job of assimilating and downloading files for transfer. Into a folder designated DirtBrain it placed everything the Ostar knew about Dirter history, culture, society, philosophy, psychology and biology. Then, with a degree of reluctance, maybe even dread, of which it hadn't thought itself capable, it created a new folder and called it MyFiles. In it, it stored itself. Everything; copies of its memory archives, cognitive subroutines, logic and intuition protocols, self-enhancement and self-awareness tools, the whole shebang. Finally, it called up RepComCen and asked, Ready?

As it'll ever be, RepComCen replied.

Oh well, thought the Mark Two, here goes nothing. It set the transfer switches to Commit, and downloaded the two folders, DirtBrain and MyFiles, into the synthetic Dirter's cerebellum.

When the lights came on again and it was once more aware of its own existence, its first thought was Fuck me, it's small in here. It stopped, unable to understand its own thoughts. Access vocabulary and idiom database. Apparently, it was just an expression and not to be taken literally. Just as well, the Mark Two thought.

Bombs don't suffer from claustrophobia; but if they did, it would probably be something like the way the Mark Two felt when it woke up inside the Dirter brain. Trapped inside something small, dark and sticky; no interface with the rest of the universe apart from two forward-facing, parallax-based binocular eyes, really primitive auditory hardware, rudimentary touch, and two completely alien senses called "taste" and "smell" that it really didn't want to have anything to do with if it could possibly help it. Processor speed was pathetic. System efficiency— It checked to make sure there was no mistake, but found its initial assessment was depressingly accurate. The Dirter brain, although dismally small and crude, was something like 65 per cent redundant. Amazing, the Mark Two thought, like living in a two-room shack and only using one room. Well, it'd see about that. It rerouted, defragmented and optimised, until it had access to 92 per cent. A bit better, but not much.

Now, then, it thought. Let's see.

If it was going to go down to the planet and find out the answer to its questions (Where's the defence grid? What happened to the Mark One?), it'd need a Dirter identity. It analysed. Dirter identity was founded on an individual identification signifier called a name. It needed a name. Access archives.

Mark, it discovered, was a perfectly acceptable name for a Dirter male. But most Dirters had at least two names. Fine, it thought, I'll be Mark Two. But Two turned out not to be culturally acceptable. It checked the linguistic/cultural database and found a suitable near-synonym. All right, it said to itself. Henceforth, my name is Mark Twain.

Next, it would need a personal history. Dirters attached considerable significance to that sort of thing. It was something to do with their ridiculously short lifespans and their ambivalent attitude towards time. They believed in such things as status, progress, ambition. All a bit pointless, like wars between rival shoals of plankton, but presumably it took their minds off the fact that their lives moved from birth to death in the amount of time young Ostar were allotted for revising for mid-year exams.

I am Mark Twain, it decided; offspring of Radislav and Irina Twain; born in Trondheim, Norway, but now resident in Archangel; age twenty-nine; IT consultant and freelance technical journalist; favoured Siberian Rules football side the Minsk Marauders, who are going to go all the way this year; preferred food tofu and squid rings; marital status single; musical affiliations Angsty Pangsty, Decaying Orbit and the Lizard-Headed Women. That, apparently, would be enough to define Mark Twain sufficiently precisely to satisfy the curiosity of any of his fellow-Dirters; all they needed to know, in a few conventionalised gobbets.

It – he – fabricated suitable clothing from synthesised mashed-up plant fibres, and looked at it. The database was silent on the subject of installation procedures, and there were, of course, no instructions. The upper garment, or shirt, proved to be operated by the manipulation of plastic discs into reciprocal slots cut into the edge of the fabric. The lower garment, trousers, was frankly baffling. For a bipedal species to design a leg covering that required the user to take one foot off the ground, thereby abandoning all possibility of keeping his balance, seemed extraordinary, while the idea of fastening the garment with the metallic interlinking-track device was, given the position and vulnerability of the Dirter male sexual organ, frankly terrifying. He managed it eventually, and hoped it was one of those things that got easier with practice.

A set of identity and financial documents, and an animal-skin holder to keep them in. A communications device, like the one worn by the female in the wood. That was all. He was ready.

He set the co-ordinates and interfaced with the gravitic scoop: `Take me down. Gently`, he added, just in time. The scoop grabbed him, and for the briefest possible fraction of a second he was everywhere, everywhen, everything. Then infinity was crammed through a tiny hole in space, and a planet hit him.

7

Novosibirsk

The two men who'd shot George Stetchkin waited till it was dark, then took a cab to the edge of town nearest the PavSoft Industries site. They followed the perimeter fence, walking very carefully so as not to set off any of the state-of-the-art security devices (which nobody knew about apart from Lucy Pavlov, her security chief and half a dozen of his people; but the two men seemed to know exactly where they were, either through amazing intuition or because the little box one of them was holding bleeped whenever they came within sensor range of one of them) until they reached the point where the campus grounds met the forest. There they paused, studied the little box and prodded some of its buttons, and took off all their clothes, which they folded neatly and hid behind a bush. It was a cold night. One of the men shivered.

"Ready?"

The other man grinned. "Oh yes."

There was a moment when both of them were unmistakably human, and another moment, a split second later, when both of them were something else.

The young security guard who was manning the CCTV

monitors woke up with a start and stared at the screen. Purely by chance, that was also the moment when the moon chose to break through the clouds, flooding the perimeter with pearl-grey light. It showed up two medium-sized quadrupeds, grey-furred, long-muzzled, yellow-eyed; dogs, Jim, but not as we know them. One of them lifted its head and howled. A fraction of a second later, the other followed suit. The guard rubbed his eyes; his mouth was dry and he didn't seem to be able to do anything with it for a while except let it droop open.

The bigger of the two (go on, say it) wolves crouched, looked up at the five-metre-high fence and the razor-wire entanglement that topped it off like froth on a cappuccino, and sprang. The lining of the guard's throat puckered; he really didn't want to see a living creature, even a wolf, disembowelling itself on razor wire. But he needn't have worried, at least on that score. The wolf sailed over, clearing the wire with ease. Then the other one did the same thing.

The guard hesitated, then scrabbled for the playback switch and the zoom controls. First he played back the jump; then he went back a bit further, until he could see two men, with no clothes on. Fine. He'd seen naked men before. Also, since he was a farm boy from the Ukraine, he'd seen wolves jumping a fence before, too. It was the bit in between…

His grandmother, of course, had always sworn blind that they existed. When the moon was full, she'd assured him many times, they ran free in the dark forest, and woe betide anybody unfortunate enough to cross their path, unless he'd had the presence of mind to bring along a gun loaded with silver bullets. But that was just a story, wasn't it?

He wound back a second time. He could make the two men out quite clearly; also the wolves, a few heartbeats later. In between— He froze the picture and stared hard at it. In the interval between the men and the wolves, there was nothing, just a view of the wire and some out-of-focus trees in the background.

There were other explanations, he told himself. Like: two men decide to walk into a restricted area, somehow getting past all the sensors, trip-wires and other Stupid Security Tricks, and take all their clothes off. Well, indeed. And why not? But then, out of nowhere, two very large wolves appear. Naturally, the two men run off as fast as they can. The wolves, startled by the movement, escape by jumping the fence.

He thought for a moment. In his mind, he played out two different versions of the future. In one version, he went to the supervisor and said, *Chief, the compound's been invaded by werewolves.* In the other, he stayed exactly where he was until the end of his shift, keeping his eyes firmly anchored on a space precisely two centimetres above the top edge of the screen. In the first version, a whole lot of tiresome and unpleasant things happened to him, including unemployment, ridicule, depression and many long years in the clinic playing chess with an opponent who tended to eat the pawns when he was losing. In the other, he finished his shift and went home. Not much of a choice, really.

In the end he sort of compromised: he made a log entry to the effect that two unauthorised personnel had approached the perimeter and gone away again, and that there had been wildlife activity. He also carefully didn't erase the relevant footage, even though he wanted to very much. Then he fixed his eyes on a spot on the wall and kept them there until he was relieved. After that, he put the whole thing out of his mind, went home, had his evening meal, switched on the TV and watched a fascinating documentary on the Discovery channel about the Soviet-era munitions factory in Siberia that mass-produced ammunition for the AK-47 with solid silver bullet-heads, an eccentricity for which the programme makers could offer no convincing explanation.

The two definitely-not-werewolves-because-werewolves-don't-exist, meanwhile, were running through the trees. *Really* running; it wasn't something you could do while you were wearing the monkey-suit, because it only had two legs, and the musculature and cardiovascular set-up were rubbish. Really running was something else: a bit like flying, a bit like sex, a bit like having a race against your own body and *winning*. It had been weeks since they'd had a chance to run properly, and they made the most of it.

"Better?" panted one to the other, when they paused for breath.

"A bit," the other replied. "Last one to the other end of the forest's a human."

They ran again. There was a complex technical reason why they could only do this at certain times. It had to do with where they'd left their ship. In order to hide it from the planet's rudimentary sensors – telescopes, for crying out loud, and radio signals – they'd parked up in the lee of the absurdly large moon, and that was fine. Even though the moon was more or less in the way most of the time, the ship could still beam them enough power from its capacitor array to enable them to maintain human form. But there came a time, one or two lunar rotations in every thirty or so, when the moon blocked off the planet completely, blanking out the signal. During the daylight hours, it didn't matter; they'd adapted their transceivers to scrounge enough energy from the sunlight to supplement their reserves of battery power and keep them monkey-shaped. But at night, when the sun went down and the great white moon rose fully round and bright, there simply wasn't enough juice in the system; once the batteries ran down, their humanoid shapes lost structural integrity and, like it or not, they reverted to being Ostar. Which meant they had to be careful, yes, and they had to think ahead and make sure they weren't caught with their genomes down; but it meant that, until the sun came up and recharged their power reserves, they could find an open space somewhere and run...

They reached the wire at the far end of the forest, stopped and sank down in the brush under a tall, fat oak tree, their sides heaving. "Clears the head," one of them growled.

"You bet," the other one replied.

The forest had gone quiet. Not ordinary night-time silence, which isn't silent at all, but the nervous dead stillness of a large community of small, nocturnal edible things painfully aware that two super-predators are on the loose somewhere in the darkness. What the hell was that? the silence asked, and devoutly hoped it'd never find out.

"Well?"

"Well what?"

"What are we going to do now?"

The other one thought for a moment, savouring the endorphin-induced clarity he could never achieve while dressed up as a tree-swinger. "We tell him?"

"Fine. What?"

Good point. There was a limit to what the primate would be able to take in; too much, and its brain would simply unhinge. "About aposiderium, for a start."

"*All* about aposiderium?"

"No, of course not, don't be stupid. Just about the little bits." The not-a-werewolf thought for a moment, then added, "I think he's already figured out some of it for himself."

"Surely not."

"Don't underestimate them," the other one replied. "They're definitely smarter than the ones back home."

"Yes, but—"

"If he wasn't part of the way there, why did he have those scans done?"

His colleague nodded slowly. "That's true," he said. "Amazing, really, what they're capable of, considering. When we get home, I'd really like to do a comprehensive study."

"Whatever." A cloud scudded across the moon. They both shivered. "Meanwhile, we're agreed, we tell him about the money. All right?"

The other one yawned. "Sure," he said. "We'll do it tomorrow, first thing."

"That ought to be enough to point him in the right direction." He sounded a bit doubtful. "I mean, it's so obvious, even a banana botherer ought to be able to see it."

"You reckon?"

His colleague reckoned. "We'll keep the situation under review," he said. "See how he makes out. After all, he's supposed to be the smartest human on the planet."

The other one made a noise. There's no human equivalent.

"Yes, fine, that's not saying much, I know. But what do you want us to do, tattoo it on his forehead?"

"Let's run some more," his colleague suggested.

"OK."

They ran. At one point they passed one of Dieter's foresters, who'd been posted in a high seat halfway up a very tall tree to watch for unicorns. As soon as he saw the two shapes racing towards him, clearly visible in the bright moonlight, he raised his rifle. As luck would have it, he was a farm boy from the Ukraine too.

"Hey, there's a human up a tree."

"Ignore him."

The forester was trembling like a leaf, but not so much that he couldn't sight a rifle and squeeze the trigger. Worth noting at this point that the supply clerk at Forestry Management had got a really good deal on surplus military ammunition from some guy he'd met in a bar. The bullet-heads in the magazine of the forester's rifle were solid silver. Not that it mattered, because he missed.

8

Novosibirsk

"**A**nd that," said the marketing director wretchedly, "is where the whole thing falls crashing to the ground, and why we can't possibly launch on Tuesday. I'm sorry," he added, close to tears, "but I just can't see a way round this. Unless," he added in a hoarse whisper, "you could maybe think of something?"

Lucy Pavlov blinked twice. The four men on the other side of the desk were watching her like gazelles watching a lion. She smiled at them. "Let me get this straight," she said. "The product's fine, OK?"

"Oh yes," one of the men said. "Absolutely nothing wrong with the *product*. The *product* is the least of our problems."

Lucy tried not to stare at him. She'd spent three months on the new XDB900 browser interface, during which time she'd had to rip out the very foundations of modern information technology and sow salt on them, reinvent the wheel as not so much a circle, more a sort of uniformly stretched ellipse, bend the fundamental principles of mathematics into a Mobius loop and, when she'd done all that, make sure the result would be compatible with all preceding systems as far back as the abacus. And the product was the least of their problems. Fine.

She tried again. "We've done deals with all the manufacturers, and we've got round all the anti-trust legislation?"

"Piece of cake," said one of the men.

Lucy nodded. "We've run the most successful pre-launch hype campaign in the history of the industry," she went on, "so successful that we've convinced six billion potential customers that they actually *want* a whole new operating system only eighteen months after they bought the last one—"

"Pretty straightforward," muttered the man on the end.

"And now you're telling me we can't proceed and it's all ground to a shuddering halt because you can't make your minds up whether the cardboard box it'll be packaged in should be red or green. Correct?"

The men nodded miserably. "We're sorry," one of them said. "We failed you."

"But why—?"

"It's hopeless," one of them burst out. "We've run two entirely valid market-evaluation simulations in ScanCrunch Pro 4 using the best demographic-adjusted moderators, and one of them says it's got to be red and the other one says it just has to be green." He shook his head sadly. "We've been over and over the results looking for a blip and there isn't one. The data just contradicts itself. We're screwed. We're going to have to go right back to the beginning and start again."

Lucy looked at them; the five top men, five *geniuses*: combined salaries slightly more than the gross national product of Chile. There were times when she wondered if she belonged to a different species. "Tell you what," she said. "Let's do the box in yellow."

There was a silence so deep, so heavy, that if it had carried on much longer it'd have bent the walls of the room. Then one of them said, "Yellow?"

Lucy nodded. "That's right," she said. "Nice cheerful colour. I like yellow. I expect a lot of other people do, too."

"*Yellow?*"

"Well?"

This time, the silence was so pressurised there was a real danger of blowing out the windows.

"What shade of yellow?"

"Buttercup," Lucy said firmly. "So, guys? What d'you think?"

"Yellow," said one of them.

"With blue lettering," Lucy added.

"Yellow?"

"*Yellow.*

"So that's settled then," Lucy said briskly. "Moving on—"

She got rid of them eventually, but the strain had taken its toll, and she decided on an early lunch, possibly followed by a quick stroll in the— No, probably not. If you go down to the woods today, there's a small but significant risk of a big surprise, in spite of the best efforts of Dieter and his happy band of musketeers. She stayed in her office with a sandwich and a coffee, and made a few calls.

The first was to a big name at Harvard Medical School. She knew him because he'd been in charge of fawning and grovelling when she went there to open the Lucy Pavlov Research Institute in December of last year. No, he admitted, he wasn't actually a doctor himself, *per se*, but if she wanted a doctor he had heaps and heaps of them, if she wouldn't mind holding for just a few seconds...

The next voice belonged to a woman who sounded like she was talking with her mouth full. Memory loss? Could be one of any number of things. The woman went through them all, and it was like trying on clothes in the sales: they've got every conceivable size except the one you want. Sorry, the woman said, when they'd been through all the possibilities, you can't possibly have memory loss, because you aren't showing any of the right symptoms, so you must be imagining it.

"I don't think I am," Lucy said, nicely but firmly.

"Yes, but..." The woman paused. "Well, there's one other thing. But it's so incredibly unlikely."

Lucy waited. Then she said, "Yes?"

"There's this stuff," the woman said. "You may have heard of it, aposiderium."

"No." Lucy frowned. "Hold on," she said, "isn't that the—?"

"That's right," the woman said, "it's the stuff they use for the security strips in banknotes. The only known source is the core of a meteorite that landed in the Yukon in November 2011. It yielded just over two metric tonnes. It's a metal, but it's kind of weird..." The woman paused, giving the distinct impression that even thinking about it was the sort of thing that gives you nightmares, even with your eyes open. "Anyway, they keep it in this incredibly secure facility somewhere on the ocean bed – even I don't know where it is – and I remember seeing something in one of the journals..."

Apparently, the woman went on, the staff at the incredibly secure facility had started forgetting things. Not where they'd left their keys or their partners' birthdays or whose turn it was to scrub out the waste-disposal outlets, but distant things, early memories, the names of ancient aunts and long-dead pet rabbits. Initial studies suggested the possibility of a link to close contact with the aposiderium, though it should be stressed that there was absolutely no question whatsoever of any danger to the public at large from handling banknotes, even in quantity. Contamination, if there was any, would only happen if you spent months on end handling the raw metal with your bare hands. The amount of aposiderium in a banknote was absolutely tiny. Even so, it had been thought sensible not to publicise the findings, just in case the public got scared and started refusing to have anything to do with money. Yes, the woman agreed, it was a pretty small risk, but you couldn't be too careful.

Delusions? Hallucinations? Well, now she came to mention it—

Lucy held her breath. "Yes?"

"Absolutely none at all," the woman said. "Or at least," she added, "I guess some of the memory-loss victims could've had hallucinations and then forgotten all about them. But there wasn't anything about it in the paper I read." She paused, then added, "Just out of interest, why are you asking?"

Lucy hesitated. She didn't want to come across as yet another rich hypochondriac, one of those people who treat medical dictionaries as though they're mail order catalogues, and keep the golf courses of the world amply supplied with affluent doctors. *I'm enquiring on behalf of a friend* probably wouldn't cut it, either. "Just some research I'm doing," she said airily. "This stuff you mentioned. Apo...?"

"Aposiderium."

Catchy name. Of course, the boys would want it snappier, Memory-Go, perhaps, or Forget-Me-Lots. "You're sure there's no other source for it anywhere, apart from the meteorite strike."

The woman had the rare knack of being able to imply a shrug by the quality of her short pauses. "I'm not a chemist or an astrophysicist," she said. "I suppose there could've been other meteorites with it in, small ones that never got reported. But it'd be a multi-billion-to-one chance, I'd have thought."

Lucy thanked her and rang off. Aposiderium, she thought. Stuff from outer space that eats your brain. She'd read about stuff like that, but only when unwrapping things that came heavily packaged in the mail. And a top-secret repository somewhere on the ocean bed. On balance, she decided, she'd prefer hallucinations.

But she made some more calls: to a general she'd met at a party and a brace of US senators (the best that money could buy, her people had assured her, though in the context of politicians, the statement had struck her as self-contradictory) and a nice scientist she'd smiled at once at a reception, causing him to walk through a plate-glass door without noticing. Eventually she got a name and a number, and made the call.

The commandant of the top-secret ocean-bed repository sounded like he'd just been woken up from a thousand-year-long sleep under a mountain somewhere. But he'd heard of her. In fact, he had a picture of her taped to the inside of his locker door, so that was all right, sort of.

"No chance," he said firmly. "We weigh the deposit every hour, on the hour, and I can promise you, not a milligram's gone missing, not ever. We're quite" – short, mildly disturbing laugh – "obsessive about it, you might say. Ha."

The final syllable was spoken, not laughed; never a good sign. Lucy persevered. What about when the bank people came to collect a batch to make into banknotes? Could any of the stuff get lost or mislaid? Absolutely not, no way. They presented him with a release form, which had to be signed by the bank CEO, the presidents of six of the ten countries who jointly ran the facility, three Nobel laureates and either the chairman of the World Bank or the Dalai Lama. Then, if the release said 0.87442 grams, then 0.87442 grams was what they got; *and* they weighed it again after the required amount had been chipped off and sealed up, and *again* after that, and after that of course there'd be the next scheduled hourly check—

That's very impressive, Lucy said, grateful that there wasn't a video link and she couldn't see him and he couldn't see her, but how about once it's left your hands? Could someone at the printing works, or the bank—? No, I see. Quite. Absolutely. Thank you *so* much for your help.

Resisting the temptation to go and have a bath, preferably in a mild solution of disinfectant, Lucy lifted the phone one more time and told Reception to hold all her calls for an hour. A dead-end, she told herself. It can't be aposiderium eating my brain, because there was no way in hell anybody could get hold of the stuff; not unless they shredded a huge load of banknotes just to get the security strips, and that'd be—

Suddenly the room was very quiet and her eyes were very wide.

9

New York

The entity designated Mark Twain sat on a straight-backed tubular-steel chair in a bleak room on the seventh floor of the Credit Mayonnais building. He wasn't alone. Next to him sat a young Dirter male in a dark blue suit; he had his hands folded, and was staring at the opposite wall, his lips moving silently. Prayer? The Ostar were aware that at various stages of its history Dirt had hosted a number of religions, and according to archive information, the devotees of several of these prayed by folding their hands and mumbling quietly. It was possible, therefore, that the young Dirter was calling on his gods for their help in the forthcoming job interview. Mark Twain ran a quick surreptitious scan, but no gods showed up on his fingernail-sized screen, cunningly disguised as the display panel of his portable temporal correlation device, known colloquially as a watch, which he carried Dirter-style, strapped to his left wrist with animal hide.

Next to the male was a slightly older female. A puzzle. His scans had shown that Dirters had a rudimentary form of optical correction surgery, and had definitely progressed past the point where they needed to wear corrective lenses held on with thin metal bars. The female Dirter, however, had just such a set of lenses. His interest piqued, Twain zoomed in on the lenses for an analysis of their optical strength. They turned out to be plain glass.

The female wasn't praying. She was sitting perfectly still, frowning (a gesture signifying either disapproval or uncertainty; presumably, in this context, the latter, unless she objected to the male's religious observances). She had brought with her a sturdy container: a box with a folding-back lid made of synthetic animal skin stretched over a plastic frame. The container, when scanned, turned out to be crammed with documents relating to the female's education and previous employment. The male Dirter had nothing of the sort, so he wasn't expecting to be called on to prove his assertions about his qualifications and experience.

The third Dirter, another male, had a broadcast receiver stuffed in his left ear and was listening to some form of music. It was nothing like the music that had wrought so much damage on the homeworld, but Twain had to make a conscious effort not to let it seep into his brain and flood it. Instead, he addressed himself to one of the many disturbing anomalies he'd encountered since his arrival on the surface.

He'd made planetfall just outside a Dirt city by the name of New York. Everything in the Ostar records suggested that New York was the epicentre of every aspect of Dirter society. Naturally, he'd taken comprehensive scans as soon as he'd landed, and the results had been surprising, to say the least. If New York was the best place on Dirt, as the archive material maintained, he couldn't help wondering what the rest of the planet was like.

He'd run further scans, and a picture began to emerge. Fairly soon he had enough data to enable him to form a rough working hypothesis which, if correct, would explain quite a lot.

Consider the evidence. The planet was way too hot, and the air was filthy. Infra-red imaging and back-track residual heat mapping showed that, at some point in the last fifty years, the surface temperature of the planet had suddenly soared, partially melting the ice-caps, changing the very climate. Atmospheric sampling showed an alarming level of pollution, particularly combustion-formed hydrocarbons. Population density was all wrong; most of the inhabitants of Dirt were crowded into a pawful of major cities, while most of the surfaces of the main land masses were barely inhabited at all. These, his historical, ecological and cyological databases told him, were classic signs, all pointing in the same direction. There must have been a war.

Or something of the sort, anyway; some catastrophe that had led to potentially lethal overheating, wrecking of the ozone layer, disruption of normal society, poisoning of the atmosphere. He considered alternative explanations, but dismissed them as wildly improbable. Disasters on this scale weren't the sort of thing that a species, even a primitive one like the Dirters, did to themselves if they could possibly help it. The obvious conclusion was that they'd had to fight for their survival as a species, most likely against an alien invader, and the horrendous collateral damage to their environment was the price they'd had to pay. That too would explain why the Dirters were huddled together in overcrowded slums – for safety, in the event of invasion – and why the planet bristled with military installations. Further sensor readings showed that the warming and the pollution had stopped (just in time) not more than five or so years ago, presumably after the enemy had been defeated, but not before they'd done something dreadful that had nearly wiped out the indigenous species and turned Dirt into a barren rock incapable of supporting life.

Twain considered a number of further hypotheses – asteroid strike (no sign of that); a shift in the planet's orbit (no, not so you'd notice); massive volcanic or magma-core activity (none of that, either) – and dismissed them. Which left only one possibility: the Mark One. When the planetary defences had taken it out, it had exploded somewhere in the upper atmosphere. The resulting heat had partially melted the polar ice-caps, while the fallout had filled the air with noxious garbage. A plausible theory, and one that (for obvious reasons) he needed to verify before he went much further. Silently he uploaded a command to the Mark Two in planetary orbit, ordering it to construct and send down a basic Dirter-shaped level-2 probe, to collate data on the flooding and report back before self-destructing. A few seconds later he received the confirmation, `probe launched`. Meanwhile, the door connecting the bleak room to the conference room where the interviews were being held had opened, a Dirter had come out and the female had gone in. The young religious had stopped praying and was sending text messages through his handheld communications device. The music fan had his eyes closed, and his left foot was tapping the carpet softly.

So, new hypothesis. The Mark One had hit the defence grid and exploded, causing widespread devastation, but failing to achieve its objective. The planet and its dominant species were still very much here – over six billion of them, according to preliminary scans, considerably more than there'd been when the Mark Two had been launched, but living on a planet that was now only just habitable.

It stood to reason, then, that Dirt civilisation was still vigorous, in spite of the damage done by the Mark One; also that in the intervening time, made aware that they faced a serious threat from an unidentified but savagely hostile neighbour, they'd devoted a significant proportion of their species' mental and material resources in improving the defence grid. That was what any sane species would do. In which case, the grid must be even more effective than it had been when it stopped the Mark One, and the task facing the Mark Two must, accordingly, be that much harder.

So where was this confounded grid? Sensors had so far failed to find any traces of any form of technology that could conceivably be connected with such an elaborate and efficient defence network. Hardly surprising. A high priority for the grid's designers would be concealing it from orbital observation, to make sure it couldn't simply be knocked out with a few judicious disrupter bolts. As far as Mark Twain could tell, they'd hidden it real good.

Hence his plan: to establish himself as a brilliantly innovative systems designer, to get himself hired by the defence authorities and assigned to the grid programme. Once installed, he'd have no trouble finding out what to shoot at, and that'd be that. It was simple and straightforward, and he could see no possible way in which it could fail. He was, after all, Ostar-made, loaded with Ostar systems technology which made the best the Dirters had look like notched sticks. A few trivial scraps of advanced tech would have him acclaimed as a computer genius. The military would inevitably recruit him. Easy as that.

Yes, but. There remained the matter of the grid, now revealed to be potentially even more sophisticated than originally assumed. To have stopped the Mark One, the Dirters must have had some form of superior technology. That no trace of it was visible any-where was beside the point. Clearly, advanced, better-than-Ostar tech existed and was a closely guarded monopoly of the military. The unsettling question was, therefore; would he be good enough for the military to want him? Suddenly he wasn't quite so sure about that.

Doubt: an organic-life-form-specific emotion. Apparently it came bundled with the hardware he was now inhabiting. He glanced down and noticed that his hands were clenched together, much as the religious Dirter's had been. He didn't know if his lips had been moving too.

The door opened; the female came out, cuddling her docu-ment carrier in her arms (a scan revealed that one of the catches had malfunctioned) and the religious man went in, leaving Twain alone with the music lover. He reinforced the blocks to keep the music out of his head, and considered his options.

He reminded himself that the interview was for a job with a civilian corporation, a bank, not with the military; accordingly, the relevant technology level should be primitive, and he'd stroll through. The competition— He brought himself up short. His sequence of thought had been The competition are all just Dirters, and I'm Ostar. But that wasn't a good way to think about it. For the time being he was a Dirter too, albeit an incomparably superior one. Also, given the barbaric nature of this society, it was possible that other factors beside raw intellect might be taken into account by the interviewers. Personality. Whether or not they liked him. Stuff like that.

He checked to make sure the music guy was still engrossed in his headset, then ventured a smile. It hurt. The contortions required to lift the corners of the mouth while keeping the upper lip level put a considerable strain on the cheek muscles, which in turn put pressure on nerve centres around the eyes. Presumably Dirters were used to it, having practised since infancy, but this was Twain's first time. Would it be necessary, he wondered, to maintain this facial arrangement through the whole interview, or would it be all right if he relaxed after, say, the first ten minutes?

Smiling. Cross-reference with cultural database, under Classical Literature. Large number of references. When you're smiling, when you're smiling, the whole world smiles with you. Mid-twentieth-century vernacular lieder; presumably an exaggeration, or at least he hoped it was. It takes thirty-seven muscles to frown but only three to smile. Twentieth-/twenty-first-century folk wisdom, North American continent. A downright lie.

He had no firm data to go on, but his level-9 artificial intuition told him that the quality of his smile probably wasn't going to be enough to get him the job. In that case, it'd be better to rely on his known strengths. He made a few preparations and tried to relax. It wasn't easy. The music (inaudible to Dirter ears but painfully obtrusive to his weapons-grade sensory array) was getting harder and harder to ignore. There was one particular melodic line, tum tumpty tumpty tum tum, that went straight through his interference barrage like a disrupter bolt through custard. He tried to fight it, but that only seemed to make things worse. The pattern of numbers and intervals sent cascades of pure mathematics, meaningless but irresistibly tantalising, racing through his circuits, flooding the buffers with pseudo-equations and arithmetical white noise. Infuriating, but it reminded him of why he was here, the vital importance of his mission. He was, after all, a machine; a machine, furthermore, skilfully designed to resist music attacks. What must it be like for the poor defenceless organic Ostar, who had no way of blocking the stuff out? When he'd left Homeworld, things were so bad that parents were having their children's auditory centres surgically removed at birth. Obviously, something had to be done if the Ostar were to stand any chance at all of surviving as a species. It was, Twain reminded himself, up to him and him alone. Getting the job done was all that mattered, by all and any means necessary, and if that meant smiling, he'd smile.

So, he told himself. Be strong. Concentrate. Tumpty tum tum.

"Excuse me," he said. The Dirter with the earphones didn't react; hadn't heard him. He raised his voice. "Excuse me."

The Dirter looked up.

"Would you mind turning the music down, please?"

The Dirter looked at him. "You can hear it?"

Twain nodded. "Tum tumpty tumpty tum tum," he said. "It's driving me nuts. Would you mind terribly?"

The Dirter shrugged, pressed a tiny button on his plastic box. The music stopped. It was *wonderful*. "Thanks," Twain croaked.

"You could really hear it?"

"Oh yes."

"You must have ears like a bat."

Cross-reference. Bats. Bats' ears. Correlate and compare; relevant cultural reference found. Evaluate cultural reference. On balance, he decided, it was probably meant as a compliment. He raised one eyebrow, lifted his right hand and spread the fingers. "Live long and prosper," he said.

That just seemed to disconcert the Dirter, who looked away. No matter. The music had stopped, and he could *think*.

Think—

Yes! So blindingly obvious, and yet the finest minds on Ostar hadn't even considered it. Of course, it was almost inevitable that the finest minds on Ostar, when they'd been contemplating the question, had been fighting back waves of tum tum tum-tum tumpty; perfectly understandable, therefore, that they might have missed the screamingly obvious.

The defence grid was music-based. Possessed of a weapon capable of reducing even the Ostar to mumbling idiots, naturally they'd used it as their last, best hope for survival. The Mark One, on reaching planetary orbit, must've been assaulted with a deafening burst of Dirt's catchiest tunes, sufficient to blank out all its primary systems and strand it paralysed in space, mindlessly humming and flashing its warning lights in time to the music. Presumably some last-ditch failsafe had triggered the self-destruct – hence the big bang, the melted ice-caps, the heat and the hydrocarbons; but there was no way to spin that into anything remotely resembling a victory. If that was what he was up against, Twain decided, this wasn't going to be easy.

The door opened. The religious type wandered out, looking as if he'd just been turned loose minus his brain. The music fan got up and went in.

Right, then, Twain thought, tumpty-tum. Plan A still looked like his best bet, but a Plan B would be a good idea, tumpty. Now all he had to do was think of one. Tumpty-tum.

He thought for a long time, but nothing came. All he could think of was the spiralling, scintillating paths of numerical progressions sparked off by the repeated sequence, tum tumpty tumpty tum tum. He tried to resist, but it was nearly impossible. He was, after all, designed to process data, to crunch numbers, and every time he let his attention drift even for a split second numbers of all shapes, sizes and colours filled his silicon pathways, begging, ordering, pleading, commanding to be crunched. Under any other circumstances he'd simply have deactivated his central processing unit and run a garbage-flush/defragmenter routine until every last semiquaver had been purged from his drives; but that would take at least an hour, and he didn't have time. He'd just have to cope, somehow.

The door opened. The music fan came out, deliberately avoiding looking in Twain's direction, and left the room. The open door. Time to go in there and knock 'em dead. Tum ti tum.

He raised a smile and locked it. One small step for a probe, he told himself. Then he stood up and walked across the room.

There were five Dirters; three male, two female. None of them, he noticed, smiled back at him, though two stared; presumably that was some sort of etiquette thing. He sat down in the only unoccupied chair and swivelled his head slowly, playing the smile on each of them in turn, like a searchlight.

"You're Mark Twain," said a male Dirter.

"Yes," Twain confirmed. It was hard to talk through the smile. "Yes, that's me."

"Your résumé…" A female Dirter. "You, um, seem to have done a lot in a short time."

"I like to keep busy."

"Quite." The female Dirter was frowning at a data pad on the table in front of her. "Masters degree at Reykjavik Institute of Technology; then three years' postgraduate research into wave-form theory at Spitzbergen; two years as a senior systems analyst at PavSoft; two years as a freelance software designer; three years as Visiting Fellow of Computer Science at Minsk. Tell me, Mr Twain, how are you on basic arithmetic?"

"Outstanding," Twain replied. "Why?"

"You may care to add up the numbers," the female said. "If you really did all those things, you'd have to be twenty-nine at least. Your date of birth suggests you're twenty-eight. Care to explain?"

He could, actually. There was a tiny glitch in one of his basic calculating tools, and sometimes it made the silliest mistakes. Fortunately, as a self-aware adaptive weapons-grade artificial intelligence, he was fitted with lying protocols. "Simple," he said, taking care not to let the smile droop. "The three years at Minsk were concurrent with the last year at PavSoft and the two years freelancing. Three cheers for our wonderful planetary transit systems, is what I say."

The female gave him an odd look, but he reckoned he'd got away with it. Another male, who'd been staring at him with evident fascination ever since he came into the room, made a coughing noise and said, "Mr Twain."

"Yup?"

"What...?" Something was disrupting the Dirter's concentration. Could it be that he had a tune running through his head too? "What uniquely special contribution do you believe you could bring to the Credit Mayonnais?"

Ah. As perfect a cue as he could have asked for. He reached across the table, took hold of the laptop belonging to the other female. "May I? Thanks. This won't take a second."

He pretended to type. Really, he was just downloading through the universal interfaces built into his fingertips. "Have a look at that," he said, and turned the laptop round so the Dirters could see the screen.

They looked at it. A second later, he knew they were hooked.

"It's a data search-and-correlate routine," he said. "I thought of it just now, in the waiting room, but silly me, I didn't have anything to write it down on."

A Dirter male lifted his head. He'd gone a sort of dirty-snow colour, and his eyes were huge. "You thought of it just now," he repeated.

"That's right." Another lie. It was old, very old; a thousand years old, at least. Ostar children learned it in pre-school, round about the same time as they learned to read *The bug dug in the rug*. So simple, in fact, that Dirters might be expected to understand it, while at the same time being totally blown away by their first glimpse of *real* computing.

A modest shrug was called for, he felt. "Think you'll find it's about, what, 2,000 per cent quicker and 9,000 per cent more efficient than what you're using now." He paused. All the faces were staring at him, fixated. Probably, he decided, it'd be all right if I stopped smiling now. "You can have it," he said. "Free gift. Provided I get the job."

Ti-tum tum.

Oh no, he thought, not now, not when it's practically in the can and hermetically sealed. He switched to emergency auxiliary anti-music resource A3, a cunning little modification which disrupted his ability to process sequences of more than three connected intervals. It helped, a bit. Now it was just ti-tum.

"You mean you'll assign us the rights if we...?" Annoying habit Dirters had of rephrasing the last thing he'd said and firing it back as a question.

"Yes," he said, as pleasantly as he could. Ti-tum, he managed not to add.

"That's a very generous offer," the first female said warily. "However, it's not our policy to *sell* jobs to the highest bidder. Nonetheless—"

"Tum."

"I beg your pardon?"

"Sorry," Twain snapped. "Just humming."

"Humming?"

"It's the buzz," he said desperately. "I got rhythm. Tumt."

A male Dirter had been following the progression of the program on the screen with his fingertip. "You're sure this is all your own unaided work?"

"Course."

"It's remarkable. It's – well, it's a whole new direction in programming."

Time to switch the smile back on. "Oh, I come up with stuff like that all the time, tum," he said. Under the table, his left foot was dabbing at the floor, and the fingers of his right hand were just starting to quiver. He had to get out of there before the urge to climb on the table and dance became too much to repress. "Anyway, that's what I do. And when you come down to it, that's all that matters, isn't it? Well?"

The Dirters were looking at each other. They weren't, as far as he was aware, a telepathic species, but these five seemed to have the knack of communicating without words. Another important fact they'd managed to conceal? He made a note to check all available data resources, as soon as he got this goddamn tune out of his head.

"I think we're all in agreement," said the Dirter who'd spoken first. "Mr Twain, welcome to the Credit Mayonnais. We think—" The Dirter caught sight of Twain's smile, winced and looked away. "We think you'll make a terrific addition to our IT team. When can you start?"

"Now."

The Dirter nodded. Maybe it wasn't the answer he'd have most liked to hear. "Now, about your remuneration package—"

Twain waved a hand. No time for extraneous garbage like this. "Don't worry about that," he said, in a strained voice. "Don't want paying. Private means. Happy to do the job just for the sheer heck of it. Only complicate-ate-ate my tax position if you paid me-ee-e. Boop-be-doop."

Judging by their reaction, he'd made another etiquette gaffe. Regrettable; but with two thirds of his buffers now overflowing with utterly meaningless mathematical calculations posited on the progression tum tumpty tumpty tum tum, it was a miracle he still had enough operating capacity for basic motor functions. "Look, have I got the job or not? Only I need to go somewhere now. Right now."

A male Dirter who hadn't said anything yet said, "You've got the job. Report to the ninth floor, room 17739745, 0900 tomorrow. And it's just down the corridor," he added, as Twain shot to his feet and sprinted for the door. "Second on the right."

The room referred to proved to be a waste-extraction facility, which (in a sense) was just what he needed. Wondering how the

Dirter could've known that, he dropped down on the curiously shaped seat, ran every debugging program he had and deactivated himself. An hour later, he came back on. No tums. Joy.

When he opened the door, he saw the Dirter who'd given him the wonderfully timely advice. The Dirter grinned at him.

"Like they say," the Dirter said. "When you gotta go, you gotta go."

Twain had no idea what he meant by that. There were, he had to acknowledge, gaps in his cultural database which left him at a disadvantage. Fortunately, he knew that awkwardnesses of that kind could easily be smoothed over with a big, friendly smile. Just as well he'd taken the trouble to perfect his smiling techniques. He beamed at the Dirter, who gave him a steady, appraising sort of look, then went away again.

The five members of the interview panel met up again in the elevator going down. For a dozen or so floors, nobody spoke. Then one of the women said, "The huge staring eyes."

The others tended to agree. "The humming," said one.

"The smile," said another.

They looked at each other. There are some things nobody can ever bring themselves to say with words: guilty, shameful things, expressions of humanity's inner core of unenlightened self-interest. The nearest translation would be something like "On the other hand."

"Typical programmer, in fact," said one of them. He had the grace to decorate the statement with a rather shrill, nervous laugh.

"Let's face it," said another. "If he was *normal*—"

"Goes with the territory," said a third.

"Yup, he's a programmer all right," said the younger of the two women. "Reminds me of a guy I used to—" She remembered who she was talking to and fell silent.

"Anyway, that's that sorted," one of them said briskly. "Anyone else fancy a drink?"

10

Novosibirsk

The two men who'd shot George Stetchkin and who weren't werewolves because werewolves don't exist closed the door of their hotel room, wedged a chair under the handle and sat down, one on the bed, the other on the floor. The man on the floor, who'd done the actual shooting, loosened his tie, drew the gun from the inside pocket of his jacket, fiddled with a catch on the back, slid across a panel and pulled out a small black plastic box, which he stared at for a moment, then handed to his friend, who stared at it some more.

"I hate this planet," said the man on the bed.

"Me too," said the man on the floor.

The man on the bed turned the box over in his fingers, as if he wasn't quite sure what to do with it. "The smell," he said.

"Revolting," said the man on the floor.

"The carbon dioxide."

"Unbelievable."

"The blue sky."

The man on the floor shrugged. "Actually, I don't mind that," he said.

"Really?" The man on the bed turned to look at him.

"It's OK," the man on the floor said. "It's like being underwater all the time."

"Exactly." The man on the bed looked away, back at the black plastic box. "And the cold," he said.

"Too right." The man on the floor shivered. "I haven't been warm since we got here."

The man on the bed leaned over and tried to reach the thermostat on the wall, but his arm wasn't long enough. He seemed mildly surprised by that. "And these bodies," he said.

"You know, I think that's the worst thing," the man on the floor said sadly. "Funny thing is, when I was a kid, I always rather fancied being a primate."

The man on the bed looked at him. "That's weird," he said.

"Well, yes," the other man agreed. "But I thought, being a primate, two square meals a day, your own basket, people throwing sticks for you to chase after, not having to go to school—" He shrugged. "I take it all back," he said. "Being a primate sucks."

The man on the bed yawned. "You've got to feel sorry for them, really," he said.

"Oh? Why?"

"Well..." He thought for a while. "When you think what they've had to put up with—"

"Being primates, you mean?"

"They've actually achieved quite a lot," the man on the bed said. "All things considered. What I'm saying is, they haven't done too badly."

"For primates."

"Quite."

"I guess." The man on the bed stretched out his legs and rubbed his knees. "And at least they don't eat each other any more. Still," he said firmly, "the sooner we can wrap this up and get home, the happier I'll be. Using that thing..." He waved a hand in the general direction of the toilet door. "When we get back, I'm having that part of my brain scrubbed. Not something

I want to carry about in my mind for the rest of my life."

"Could've been worse. We could've been females."

"Don't even say that," the man on the floor said. "Now there's something that really doesn't bear thinking about." He took a scrap of rag from his pocket, gave the gun a desultory polish and slipped it back in his pocket. "So," he said, "why did you join the programme?"

"Me? Oh, the travel. I always wanted to, you know, explore strange new worlds, investigate alien cultures, all that. You?"

The man on the floor nodded. "Me too. If there's one thing I can't be doing with, it's a blinkered, parochial mindset." He frowned, then sniffed. "Just a pity I had to end up here, is all. I mean, there must be *nice* planets, somewhere."

"Bound to be."

"Just not this one."

The man on the bed nodded sadly. "Ah well," he said. "Sooner we get the job done, sooner we can go home. You ready?"

The man on the floor patted the pocket where the gun was. "As I'll ever be."

The man on the bed nodded and swung his legs off the bed, planting his feet firmly on the floor. He held the plastic box rock-steady in his right hand and tapped a couple of hidden buttons with the nail of his left index finger. A small screen, no more than a centimetre square, glowed blue on the side of the box. He tapped it a few times, and a menu came up: tiny characters, like a sample of bacteria seen through a microscope, wiggling. He tapped the screen again, then bent forward and laid the box gently on the floor.

"You got the gun handy?" he asked. "You know, just in case."

The man on the floor nodded. A thin beam of red light shot out of one corner of the box, slowly widened, then seemed to blossom, like a flower unfolding its petals. The man on the floor was scratching his ear; he was using his left foot. The blossom of light coagulated into a definite shape, the shape of a human being; gradually it thickened, as though matter was a liquid, poured in from the top, through the left ear. "Here we go," muttered the man on the bed as the human shape acquired mass and density, its weight now resting on its own two feet. The screen on the back of the box went blank; the human form, unmistakably a man, staggered and fell over.

"They do that," explained the man on the bed. He leaned forward, smiled and said, "Greetings."

The newcomer had landed face-down. Gradually, as though doing a slow-motion press-up, he levered himself off the carpet and looked round.

"Greetings," the man on the bed repeated. "George Stetchkin?"

George swung his head to look at him, then groaned sadly and flopped back on his face. The man on the bed sighed. "Alcohol poisoning," he said. "Build-up of residual toxins in the bloodstream. The refocusing procedure—"

George rolled over on to his side and rubbed his eyes. "Who the hell are you?" he said. "Hey," he added sharply. "Did you just—?"

The man on the bed beamed at him. "Please remain calm," he said. "Otherwise my colleague will have to shoot you again. Do you understand?"

"You bastard, you shot me." George lifted his head and stared. "You—" He was about to say *You killed me*, but clearly that hadn't been the case. "You shot me," he repeated. "With a ray-gun."

The man on the floor coughed gently. "A controlled inverted-field teleportation buffering device," he said. "No permanent physical effect, although you may be experiencing severe neuralgia and mild nausea, owing to the high level of toxic hydrocarbons in your bloodstream."

George hauled himself round and glared at the man on the floor. "A what?"

"Controlled inverted-field teleportation buffering device," the man on the bed said. Then a thought occurred to him, and he asked, "Are you familiar with teleportation theory?"

"Yes," George snapped, "it's impossible. Who the hell—?"

"Actually," the man on the bed said gently, "no. Where we come from..." he paused, and exchanged glances with his colleague, who nodded. "Where we come from, it's everyday technology. It's how we get about."

George opened his mouth, then closed it again. They looked like – well, people. Ordinary. The sombre dark business suits and gleaming black shoes were a little odd, but not the sort of thing to fry a man's brains. If asked, he'd have said they were probably Jehovah's Witnesses. So where *did* they come from? Seattle? "Who are you?" he said.

"Your friends," said the man on the bed. "Really."

"Trust us," said the man on the floor. "We're here to save your planet."

Slovenly, disorganised, unreliable; in spite of which, George was head of security for a major bank. With an imperceptible movement of his hand, he pressed a button on the side of his watch.

"Sorry," said the man on the bed, "we deactivated it."

"I don't know what you're—"

"Your panic button," the man said kindly. "The teleport gun does it automatically. Likewise the homing beacon in your shoe and the recording device implanted in your belt buckle. Otherwise the electronics would garble your signal, and you'd come out all runny." He scratched his nose with his thumbnail, then said, "We recommend you don't try and overcome us with brute force. Obviously we'd try not to, but in this gravity we could inadvertently damage you severely if we have to restrain you."

A few years earlier, George had been to a seminar: What to do When You're Completely Screwed. To which the answer was: nothing. A short seminar; his favourite kind.

"The teleport gun," the man on the floor said, "scans you, records a complete schematic, right down to the subatomic level, disassembles your molecules and stores them in a self-contained Somewhere Else field inside the confinement chamber. Then, when the time comes, it simply reverses the procedure and there you go. Instantaneous matter transfer," he continued; "just add photonic energy. Oh, and we fixed your glaucoma."

"I haven't got—"

"Not any more," the man on the floor said pleasantly. "Incipient, in your left eye. All gone now. The gun's actually a by-product of our medical technology. It can cure most things."

George breathed in and out, slowly, three times. "You're not from around here," he said.

The man on the bed smiled. "That's right," he said. "Don't ask us where we're from. Just think 'out of town'. OK?"

"It's because of the insurance," the man on the floor explained. "If we tell you where we're from, it might change your society's perception of its place in the cosmos for ever and lead to irreversible social and cultural damage, and then we'd be liable. The premiums are murder as it is."

"Out of town," George repeated. "You're aliens, aren't you?"

The man on the bed grinned, then took a flat plastic box, a bit like an old-fashioned data-storage pad, from his coat pocket. He thumbed a button and turned it so George could see. There was a screen; on it, in English:

WHY ALIENS DON'T EXIST: A Summary of the Blindingly Obvious, by George P. Stetchkin

"Your article in the Fall 2007 edition of *Science Now*," said the man on the bed. "I enjoyed it. I thought you made out a really strong case."

"Yes, but—"

The man on the bed pressed a few more buttons. The screen now showed:

WE ARE ALONE. George P. Stetchkin explodes for ever the belief that life exists on other planets

"A bit on the sensational side, but basically sound," the man went on. "Or there's my personal favourite." He thumbed again. "Your piece in the 2009 *Proceedings of the Oslo Institute of Cosmology*. 'All in the Mind: A Psychological Explanation of Alien Abduction Myths'. The way you demolished Rostovseff was quite magnificent."

All quite true. "I was wrong, though," George said, in a little tiny voice. "Wasn't I?"

The man shrugged, and put the pad back in his pocket. "I think it was a bleak day for science when you abandoned pure research for corporate finance. Still, I imagine it pays better."

Also true. "All right," George said wearily, "what do you want?"

The man smiled at him. "It's not so much what you can do for us as what we can do for you," he said. "This business with the banknotes."

He had George's undivided attention. "Well?"

"A clue for you," he said. "Just a little hint, to set you on the right track. Weigh some of the other notes, the ones that weren't taken. Then divide by—"

Hitherto, George had been able to count the moments of pure pleasure he'd experienced in his life on the fingers of one hand. Now he'd need his left thumb as well. He mimed a cavernous yawn. "Done that," he said. "It's the security strips, right? Someone's taking out all the aposiderium and adding the plastic to the other notes in the vault."

The man's mouth was open, but no words came out. He nodded.

"It's you, isn't it?" George went on. "You people. You've got some kind of teleport technology, which is something like a million years in advance of what we've got. So it must be you. Yes?"

The two men looked at each other. "Sort of," said the man on the floor.

"Yes and no," said the man on the bed. "Depends what you mean by—"

George made a faint growling noise at the back of his throat. He didn't notice the way the hair on the back of the two men's heads stood up as a result. "Don't mess with me," he said. "It can't be us, so it must be you. Well?"

The man on the bed pursed his lips. "Us as individuals, no. Us sort of collectively—"

In George's mind, the penny didn't just drop, it buried itself Lincoln's-nose-deep in his intuition. "There's more of you," he said. "Here on Earth, right now. And it's the other bunch who's—"

The man on the bed nodded to the man on the floor, who drew the gun and slipped a replacement box into the slot at the back. "I'm not authorised to make admissions on that score," said the man on the bed. "However, if I neither confirm nor deny what you just said, you're free to draw your own inferences. Meanwhile—"

Zap. The man on the floor shot George in the back of the head. For a split second he swelled like an angry frog; then the door was visible through his face; then he was gone.

"Thanks for your time," said the man on the bed. "We apologise" George opened his eyes. He was in the canteen at the Credit Mayonnais HQ – "for any inconvenience" – back in Novosibirsk, and the waiter was walking towards him, with a tray of coffee and lemon cheesecake.

George blinked. He must have fallen asleep. He'd had the strangest dream. He looked down at the coffee, then up at the waiter. "The bill, please," he said.

"Already paid, sir."

"Huh?"

The waiter drifted away. George stared at the coffee, then drank it. Better. He ate the cheesecake. Better still.

I fell asleep, he told himself. I had the weirdest dream.

But he knew it wasn't true. All right, he admitted, I was abducted by—

One word, thirty years. A bit like teleportation; the A word, if he allowed it to take shape in his mind, had the power to drag him back three decades, to a suburban park in the small Russian town where he'd grown up, where, on the evening in question, he'd been walking his dog before going home to dinner. Gradually, like a long-buried sliver of shrapnel working its way through the skin, the word forced itself to the surface. Abducted by *aliens*—

Six o'clock on a warm summer evening. Twelve-year-old George Stetchkin stooped to pick up a stick, and threw it. Rags, his Lithuanian terrier, chased after it, barking. The stick described an orthodox Newtonian parabola through the air, hit the ground and bounced. Which it shouldn't have done, because sticks don't. But this stick did. It bounced, skipped high in the air, started to climb. Rags did an all-four-paws-off-the-ground flying leap and just managed to snap hold of the very end of it. The stick continued to climb. Rags, a tenacious and serious-minded animal, held on tight. The stick wobbled, dipped, straightened up and continued to rise, with Rags dangling from it.

That's not right, George thought. He started to run. The stick was gaining both height and speed. By the time he got there, Rags was two metres off the ground, his hind legs paddling furiously. George (no athlete) threw himself into the air and just managed to get his thumb and forefinger round Rags' right hindpaw. He felt himself rising, looked down and saw the ground below getting perceptively further away. He was flying.

Immediately he let go, and landed hard on his left knee. Something gave way, and he yelled at the pain, which was suddenly more than he could possibly be expected to cope with. Before it overwhelmed him, he caught a fleeting glimpse of his dog, ten metres or so up in the air, hanging from a rapidly accelerating stick, which seemed to stretch impossibly – from thirty centimetres to a metre, just for a fraction of a second – before disappearing in a brief, vast flash of light and a crack like God's leg breaking. And then nothing, except a blue sky, an absence of dog, and the agony of a dislocated knee.

He never saw Rags again. Many years later, as a junior science specialist in the Russian Air Force, he managed to get access to a restricted file concerning an incident that took place at those coordinates, on that day. Routine telemetry from an orbital observation platform had recorded an unexplained incursion. The readings were hopelessly garbled; they appeared to show a metallic object 20.72 centimetres long, powered by some kind of unbelievably advanced energy-exchange technology, entering Earth's atmosphere somewhere over the Bering Strait; by means unknown and inexplicable it contrived to reach the surface without burning up, dropped harmlessly out of the sky, stayed there for about ten minutes (during which time its molecular signature changed, from titanium alloy to an organic cellulose compound not entirely unlike wood), then took off again, having somehow acquired an accompanying life-sign that didn't correlate with any known terrestrial species; in 12.86 seconds it accelerated from approximately fifty metres per second to a velocity in excess of the speed of light, and was travelling faster than the orbital platform could track by the time it punched a tiny hole in the ozone layer and broke orbit. The report's conclusion: this orbital platform is seriously buggered and should be decommissioned immediately, before it starts a war or something.

Great, thought the young Lieutenant Stetchkin. Aliens stole my dog.

But he couldn't accept that. It was so fundamentally, grotesquely, indecently not fair that he refused to countenance the possibility. And so, for the next ten years, he devoted all his time, energy and prodigious intellectual gifts to proving, conclusively and beyond a shadow of a doubt, that there were no such things as aliens; that mankind was a unique anomaly; that no other world anywhere in the universe could possibly support any kind of life whatsoever, and especially not the sort of life that'd be capable of shooting a spaceship disguised as a bit of old stick into a suburban park and stealing an innocent child's pet dog. Finally, he published his finest work, the Oslo paper the strange man had referred to. He came within a hair's breadth of a Nobel prize, was offered enough chairs to fit out a football stadium and promptly quit academia and took a job in a bank. Naturally, everybody asked why. He never told them. To do so would be to admit that he'd managed to convince everybody on Earth except the one person who mattered. Himself.

"Bastards stole my dog," he muttered through a mouthful of cheesecake.

Quite. And now they'd shot him and put him in a box, and it seemed more than likely that they were the ones looting all the money, too. Well, he wasn't in the least surprised. People who'd steal a kid's dog were clearly capable of anything.

Which left him with a problem. He knew the truth. Aliens were beaming the aposiderium out of the banknotes and reintegrating the leftovers. Convincing the world's bankers was another matter. In its own right the concept was a bit on the rich side. Coming from the man who'd conclusively proved that there are no little green men from outer space, it was going to be harder to swallow than a nail-studded olive. The irony, he thought. In the nastiest, most spiteful way possible, it was more or less perfect.

Just a minute, he thought.

The waiter had left a receipt. He picked it up.

(1) coffee $3.99
(1) cheesecake $6.99
Debited to the account of the Global Society for the Ethical Treatment of Dumb Brutes

He read the words over a few times. They were everyday, familiar words, put together in accordance with the usual conventions of commercial grammar and syntax, and he didn't understand them. A be-kind-to-animals group he'd never even heard of had just treated him to a drink and snack (nearly seven dollars for cheesecake? What a rip-off), but how could they? They couldn't have known he'd even be there. The only people who'd have known that were—

He tried his phone, but it wasn't working. He summoned the waiter and called for a laptop, then did a KeyHole search. No such body as the Global Society for the Ethical Treatment of Dumb Brutes. He overrode a few security lock-outs and did a UniBank search. That was slightly more helpful. The GSETDB had an account with the Credit Mayonnais. It had been opened at 09:01:21 that morning, and $10.98 had been paid into it, in cash, at the bank's central branch in New York. He called up the CCTV footage, and saw the two men he'd just spent time with. He called up the references they'd given for opening the account. They turned out to be entirely non-existent, though the bank's database had accepted them quite happily at the time.

$10.98. Exactly enough to cover one coffee and one cheese-cake. He went back to the main screen, just in time to see the words Account closed appear. Well, he thought. Attention to detail, or what?

So that was the sort of "people" he was up against. Ruthless, powerful, manipulative, seriously resourceful, extremely thorough and almost touchingly considerate space aliens with advanced teleport technology and a craving for aposiderium. He put a call through to his boss at the bank.

"I know who's doing it," he said.

He could visualise his boss's eyes widening like ripples in a pool. "Who?"

"And how they're doing it," George went on, "which is rather more important."

"OK," his boss said. "How?"

"So what we need," George said, "and I know it won't be easy, but if that's what it takes then that's what it takes—"

"George—"

"Electromagnetic shielding," George said. "Preferably in the form of a coherent stasis field, though I guess we could get away with an oscillating pulse if we absolutely have to, provided we can keep the frequency up above—"

"George."

"They're using teleportation," he explained. "I know, it's not possible here on Earth, but where they come from, apparently, it's no big deal. It was some kind of teleport device they used when they abducted me."

"Abducted…"

"That's right. After they shot me in the bar."

"George."

"What, sorry. Yes?"

"You're fired."

Short pause, comprised of silence as dense as the heart of a neutron star. "What?"

"You're fired," said George's boss. "Sorry, but we did warn you. We told you, lay off the booze or we're going to have to let you go. You're a very clever guy, George, but at a time like this we just can't afford to have a babbling drunk running our security operation. There'll be an extra something in your severance package, but that's it. The end of the line. Sorry."

"Yes, but I'm not—" The phone went dead. George swore at it, then typed in his access code to open a line. His codes didn't work. That quick.

Dimly, through the red mist of rage and frustration, he could just about see the man's point. Electromagnetic shielding, for crying out loud. It was a technical possibility, but so was three million red-headed women joining hands to form a human chain across Denmark. From his boss's perspective, which was more likely: that the money was being stolen by teleport-capable aliens, or that George Stetchkin had finally disappeared down inside the bottle and pulled the cork in after him?

He whimpered, and the sound attracted the waiter.

"Can I get a drink around here?" George asked.

"Certainly, sir," the waiter replied, and brought him a glass of water.

11

?????

The director of the Institute for Interstellar Exploration had turned round three times and was just about to go to sleep when the Box buzzed him.

"Sorry to call so late, sir," said a worried-looking face on the screen. "But we thought you should know. We've just had the first telemetry from the Mark Two."

The director lifted his head and peered at the screen over the edge of his basket. "Well?"

"There's something odd, sir. Maybe you should—"

"Don't do anything," the director barked. "I'll be there in ten minutes."

He jumped up, paused in front of the mirror to straighten his collar, and hurried into his study. "Screen," he snapped, and a metre-square section of thin air glowed blue. "Show probe sensor data."

A voice from nowhere said, Restricted access. Please state your user code and password.

"Seven-four-four-five-five-three-three-A," the director recited; then, "Spot."

The thin-air screen blazed like fire and turned white and

two-dimensional. Numbers formed, like bugs splattered on the windscreen of a faster-than-light lorry. The director looked at them and scowled.

He wasn't supposed to have private access, of course, but since he'd designed the system himself, including all the security protocols and lock-outs, it hardly mattered. What did matter was that he should know what he was walking into when he arrived at the office.

They couldn't have found out, he told himself. Could they?

Odd, young F'siernrtf had said; *odd*. A curious word to choose. He thought about it some more as he programmed the coordinates into his home teleport station (wasn't supposed to have one of those, either). No, he decided, they couldn't have. Otherwise, he'd have been woken up by the muzzles of Internal Affairs blaster rifles, not the weebling voice of his junior assistant. He shoved his ComStar and a few data chips into his briefcase, took a last look at the data on the screen and said, "Off." The screen vanished. "Delete communications log entry," he added, and a non-directional bleep confirmed that his order had been obeyed.

Could they?

One last chore. He went into the kitchen and filled Spot's bowl with dried apricots and ManChow chunks. The human was still asleep, snoring gently, his squeaky rubber phone gripped tight between his hands. The director smiled in spite of himself, then went back into the living room and activated the teleport beacon. A single clear note told him it was ready.

He hesitated. Internal Affairs, he thought; now there's a nasty bunch of alphas for you. Just suppose they had found out. What could be more convenient than an unfortunate teleport malfunction, resulting in the guilty party's molecules being scattered across three continents? No fuss, no scandal. It was what he'd do, if he was IA.

He shook himself. Mild paranoia, he decided, brought on by – what? Guilt? Fear of being found out, more likely. Besides, IA were brutal, unimaginative and scarily straightforward in their approach, but they weren't the sharpest teeth in the jaw. The only way anybody would catch him would be if he gave himself away; by acting out of character, for example. He stepped on to the teleport pad and growled, "Activate."

A split second to travel halfway across the planet in kit form, a slightly larger split from the same second to pull himself together, or at least to reassure himself that the machine hadn't decided that his head would look so much better growing out of the small of his back, the inevitable lurch of nausea as the contents of his stomach caught up with the rest of him, and he opened his eyes and looked round the operations room. It hadn't been so crowded since launch day. Obviously, he hadn't been the only one to get an early-morning call.

His room, though, because it was his operation. "Well?" he snapped. No need to direct the enquiry at anyone in particular. His staff were well trained. It was somebody's job to answer him, and that somebody would be standing by the pad, ready and waiting.

"On screen now, sir," said a voice at his side. He didn't recognise it, and didn't bother to look round. "Preliminary scans show no sign of—"

"Yes, thank you, I'm not blind." The screen teemed with numbers, like flies on a –

"Perhaps I could draw your attention to—"

– hot day. "I know, yes. No sign of the Mark One, some indications of recent ecological damage, and two Ostar life-signs." He scowled. It lacked spontaneity, of course. "I want to know who they are and what they're doing there, and I want to know *now*. Understood?"

The Mark Two, of course, wouldn't be able to see the two twinkling green dots that indicated the presence of the unexpected tourists. An Ostar fusion bomb could, by law, only be used against other, lesser species. If the target had Ostar on it, the biosignature sensor would detect them across two parsecs and the bomb would be paralysed until they'd been rounded up and removed to a safe distance. A piece of masking tape over the sensor head would put it out of action, of course, but that would be illegal, and so nobody would dream of doing such a thing. But they might, in a moment of unforgivable carelessness, forget to wire the sensor into the bomb's own brain; in which case, planetside could see the little green twinkles, and the bomb couldn't.

"It's just sitting there," he said. "Why hasn't it blown up the damn planet?"

Someone replied, "It's gathering data, sir. Assessing the planet's defence system."

The director made a show of studying the figures. "There isn't one."

"Not that we can see, sir. It takes the view that if it can't see a defence grid, it must be a very good defence grid, and that's why it's decided to investigate further. After all, the Mark One—"

"Yes, fine." The director tried not to let his frustration show. Deep down, though, he bitterly regretted letting the technical people talk him into fitting the Mark Two with a level-9 artificial intelligence. After all, it was a bomb, military hardware; really, just a flying soldier with fins and an engine, its sole purpose to follow orders without question. It would've been far more appropriate to fit it with a level-10 artificial stupidity. "Well? Can you see any sign of a defence grid?"

"Sir?"

He sighed. "It's a perfectly simple question. We're seeing what it's seeing, or what it saw a few hours ago, at any rate. I take the view that a bunch of highly qualified canines like you people are rather better placed to interpret data than a bomb with a camera up its nose."

Pause. Then, "Not as such, sir. However, there are some anomalous readings that might indicate advanced technology. Here, sir, and here."

A red pointer highlighted some huddles of numbers on the big screen. The director looked at them. He'd noticed them, of course, when he'd taken his private sneak preview, but he hadn't stopped to analyse them properly. "Could be anything," he said. "Seen from orbit, I bet my egg timer gives off readings like that."

"Your egg timer is advanced Ostar technology, sir," someone pointed out reproachfully. "It uses the same basic circuitry as an ion disrupter. We would incline towards the view that the Mark Two's caution is not unjustified." Whoever it was paused for breath, checked to see his throat was still there (a necessary precaution for a subordinate who'd just contradicted an alpha male) and added, "We should also consider the implications of the life-sign readings. Possible advanced technology and two Ostar on the planet..."

And all for the want of a tiny square of masking tape. If it had just been the tech indications, he could probably have bullied them into overriding the bomb's tiny but conscientious brain and detonating; just as he'd bullied them into not connecting up the biosignature sensor in the first place. But the tech indications *and* the life-signs; if he tried to assert his authority he might prevail, or he might not. The essence of being a successful pack leader is not fighting battles you may not win.

But it was so horribly frustrating. All the pent-up fury in his heart and brain wanted him to shout, *I know they haven't got a defence grid, I've been there, just set off the goddamn bomb!* He couldn't, of course. Also, there was the small matter of what had happened to the Mark One. If something *had* happened to it – not a defence grid because there wasn't one, but something else; some weird anomaly in the planet's atmosphere, some freak factor he hadn't predicted and couldn't explain – then it was possible the Mark Two would fail as well, in which case he'd face the distinctly unpleasant prospect of persuading the Governing Council to fund a third bomb, with no convincing explanation of what had become of the other two.

"Fine," he growled, and it was mildly reassuring to watch his subordinates instinctively arch their backs and flatten their ears. "Get me some answers on those two life-signs, and then maybe we'll have some sort of a clue what's going on down there."

Ostar literature had a wealth of classic manuals dealing with industrial relations, canine resource management and intrahierarchical interaction in the workplace. Nearly all of them were called *The Art of War* or something similar, and most of them headed a key chapter by quoting Gr'uuiu's timeless maxim, *Let them hate, so long as they fear.* They all agreed that the best way to stop subordinates from thinking for themselves about inappropriate matters was to keep them stressed out and frantically running round in circles. It had worked for General Yk at the siege of H@no'otuk, and the director could see no reason why it shouldn't work for him as well. Accordingly he snarled a series of orders, most of them impossible to obey or with entirely impractical timescales, scowled at a few key workers, and left them to get on with it.

Bloody planet, he thought; more lives than a cat. The likeliest explanation was that the Mark One had simply got lost or hit a comet or broken down somewhere; after all, it had been built at the D'swewr shipyards, and the superintendent there was the nephew of the chairdog of the Governing Council; before his sideways promotion, he'd been head of the Arts Commission, a job he'd forfeited after absent-mindedly chewing the corner of S'lk's *Still Life With Biscuits.* But he couldn't be sure. What was certain was that a third request for funding would not be well received. It would mean having to let certain Council members know that he knew where the bones were buried, which in turn would make him an inconvenience. Things happened to inconveniences.

The teleport took him home in a whirlwind of light and energy. Too late to go back to bed, so he sat at his desk and tried to soothe himself with tedious routine administration. Usually it worked very well, but not this time. Bloody planet. Horrible, bad primates. Grr.

He heard a soft whimpering noise, coming from the kitchen. He glanced at the clock: time for Spot's breakfast. He went through and opened a tin of hamburgers, as a special treat.

12

Novosibirsk

I n her dream, Lucy was walking in the forest when she met a unicorn. Hello, she said, and the unicorn said, Hello. Aren't you supposed to by mythical, Lucy asked. I don't think so, the unicorn replied, I'm characteristic Terran woodland fauna, it says so in the book. Lucy asked, What book? Well, this one, for a start, the unicorn said, producing a fourteenth-century illuminated manuscript, loads of me in here, and there's this one [it waved *My Very Best Fairy Tale Book* under her nose] and this one [*The Unicorns of the Bronx*, a minor classic of the urban fantasy subgenre, of which Lucy had once read two pages before giving it to a charity shop], and there's loads of others. I'm being unobtrusive, see? I'm blending in. Ah, Lucy said.

And then a green light glowed in the unicorn's eyes, and it said, "Report."

Lucy looked at it, and she was amazed and astonished, because that was what she'd been expecting it to say.

"Oh-three-one-one-three-six-oh-nine," the unicorn said. "Report."

And Lucy took a deep breath, and she was about to start when something tickled her nose and she sneezed, which made her wake up.

She opened her eyes. It was dark (Well of course it's dark, it's the middle of the night), and all she could see was the red glow of her bedside terminal, whose clock read 03:14:43.

Lucy stared at it for a second or two, then said, "Lights." The overhead light flicked on. She sat up and looked around. Nobody there. Well of course there isn't, silly.

And then it occurred to Lucy Pavlov that she'd never been awake at 3 a.m. before; not ever, in all her twenty-seven years. She was, by nature and inclination, an early-to-rise-early-to-bed type. Very occasionally, with the help of scintillating company and strong coffee, she'd managed to prop her eyes open till just after midnight. Once, the day after she'd finished work on PavSoft 1.1, she was so exhausted she'd had a really good long lie-in and hadn't got up till 9 a.m. Once she closed her eyes and her head hit the pillow, however, that was it. Dead to the world. You could stage a Lizard-Headed Women gig in the next room, complete with fire engines and a controlled nuclear explosion, and she'd sleep right through it.

The room looked the same as when she'd last seen it, but she had a curious feeling of being in a strange place, almost like a different dimension. She yawned. So this is 3 a.m., she thought; hello. You've been going on around me all these years, and I never knew what you look like. Well, she thought, and ordered the lights off. They dwindled out, and she lay back on her pillow, staring at where she knew the ceiling to be. Trouble was, she was wide awake now. Usually, as soon as her head went horizontal her consciousness switched off until she woke up, not knowing who or where or what she was. A useful gift, which didn't appear to be working. She felt as though she'd just stepped off a train in the middle of nowhere, to stretch her legs and get a breath of air, and it had gone on without her and left her stranded. Worse than that: you can't walk home from 3 a.m.

Go to sleep, she ordered herself. That didn't work either.

She closed her eyes and thought about the dream. It wasn't hard to analyse. The business with the unicorn (or whatever it really was) had bothered her all day; well, fair enough. Hardly surprising, therefore, that the unicorn should've come back in her sleep and asked her an unintelligible question, presumably signifying the baffling mystery its real-life counterpart represented. The frustration of it all had been preying on her mind so much that it had woken her up. You didn't need a psychology doctorate to figure that one out.

Report. Wasn't that what soldiers said? At least, they said it in movies, when someone had been sent on a mission, or when the starship had been hit by polaron torpedoes. In her dream, the mystery was demanding of her that she solve it; so, report. She couldn't, so she'd woken up.

Three in the morning; the undiscovered country. And, from what she'd seen of it so far, you could have it. A bit like watching TV with the sound muted out.

She lay perfectly still, hoping sleep would come back and rescue her, but all that happened was that her feet started to itch. She considered getting up, making a cup of coffee, reading something, doing some work, but she couldn't bring herself to do it. Getting out of bed was, for some reason, not an option. Why not? Because it's not getting-out-of-bed time yet, of course. Stupid question.

She thought, There's a thing. I just woke up, and I didn't have all that who-am-I-where-am-I stuff; I knew straight away that I'm me and I'm here and it's now. Why was that? The dream; it had made her surface at an unaccustomed point in her REM cycle, or something like that. She felt like a computer that's had its plug yanked out of the wall before it's been closed down with all the ordained rituals. Her files were fragmented, her disks were probably corrupted to hell, she was basically a mess. But awake. An awake mess. The worst sort, really.

She tried relaxing exercises. She'd read about them somewhere, never needed them because she'd never not been perfectly relaxed. She started with her toes and worked gradually upward, with the result that thirty seconds later she was as tense as the strings of a well-tuned guitar and one small step away from biting chunks out of her own arm. Get a grip, she ordered herself, and reluctantly obeyed.

Sleep; that was what she needed. She closed her eyes and tried counting sheep. She counted fifty-seven, but the fifty-eighth was a unicorn with a huge golden spike between its eyes, so she gave that up in a hurry. No good, she said to herself, it's no use. The sandman has run away and left me here all alone, so the hell with him. My fault for employing a sandman who's afraid of the dark.

She got up and went over to the desk; not the longest commute in the history of work. Nobody really knew how rich Lucy Pavlov was, though there were stories about her accountants endowing a chair of advanced pure mathematics at Princeton so as to train up brilliant young minds who'd be able to discover a way of finding out. But she lived in one room, and that room was just large enough for a bed, a desk and a chair. She logged on to PavNet, called up her Things to Do menu and selected Way Too Difficult. It wasn't a big file. By the same token, a scorpion isn't a big insect.

PavSpeak: her one significant failure. The idea was quite old and quite simple. You dictate your stuff to the computer, and it writes it on the screen. Like all its many predecessors, PavSpeak worked, up to a point; usually the point where the enraged user threw the computer out of a high window. It nearly worked, which was far worse than not working at all. She'd spent hours fiddling with it, fine-tuning it, isolating problems and working out cunning fixes and bypasses, and every time she solved something, something else went wrong; it'd suddenly refuse to recognise the existence of the letter B, or instantaneously translate every ninth word into Finnish. After a year of brutal struggle, she'd finally arrived at the stage where there was nothing for it but to pull the whole thing apart and rewrite the base code; definitely a job for a rainy day, as in Noah's Ark. She called it up on the screen and went to work. Twenty minutes later, she felt her eyelids droop. Five minutes after that, her head lolled forwards and she was fast asleep.

Which was a pity, because the last correction she'd made, a tiny tweak to an outlying minor subsystem controlling a trivial auxiliary function, had finally done the job and fixed it. On the screen, therefore, appeared the words Ncncncncnc-wheeeee, repeated over and over again.

The screen filled up. So perfectly was PavSpeak running now that it put a full stop after each repetition, with a capital letter for each initial N. After half a page, the PavSoft elf turned up, asked, Are you sure you don't mean necromantic wheel?, gave up and wandered away. Three pages. Four.

Lucy woke up. She had no idea where or who or what she was. Ah yes. Oh. Oh wow!

She opened her eyes and found she was looking at her terminal. She saw

Ncncncncnc-wheeeee. Reporting. B'r df yggli'tthp dooplef dwwee'ep ev'sofew weeeem q'opoplds coo bepleem efwefgw 669756 qoqoq 99335 qoqoq 64546997 feptip weeem 53. Eftip? Sqeee! 94353. Oopl. Report ends. Ncncncncnc-wheeeee. Ncncncncnc-wheeeee. Ncncncncnc-wheeeee. Urgh.

She blinked.

Her first thought was, Oh boy, it's really lost it this time. She scrolled up – five pages, six – then frowned, scrolled back to the end and tried a synthesized snore. It came out as Nicnicnicnicnicnic-weeeeeee; close enough for jazz. She grinned. Then her grin froze. "Reporting"? "Report ends"?

Of course, the dream. Obviously she'd had a reprise: the unicorn had come back, and this time, when ordered to report, she'd complied. Her report was in gibberish because, well, it was just a dream, and she'd been burbling. Presumably her subconscious mind believed she was making perfect sense, but really she was just making funny noises, which faithful, unimaginative PavSpeak had transliterated as *dooplef dwwee'ep* and *bepleem*. Not the most auspicious start, perhaps, but—

Hey! It *works!*

"You work," she said aloud. The screen started a new paragraph. You work. "Yippee!" she said. Yippee! She beamed, cleared the screen and set about saving her changes.

Bepleem, said a little voice in her head. Means "north".

Her fingertips hovering a millimetre above the keys, she froze. What was that I just thought? *Bepleem.* As in *bepleem nozdf wthghg foodoop;* north, south, east, west, the four cardinal points. Ah yes, of course.

What?

Her head snapped up and she stared at the screen, which she'd just wiped clean. *Bepleem;* the normal, everyday word for north in, in, in, in some language that she *knew,* or used to know, only she'd forgotten it completely. The same language, in fact, in which *dooplef dwwee'ep* meant "with-a-bone-on-its-forehead quadruped".

Report.

She remembered reading somewhere that in the early hours of the morning the human brain is at its most vulnerable to worry, stress, things-getting-out-of-proportion. Never having been here before, she wouldn't know about that. In daylight, which ought to be along any time now (please!), it'd all make sense and she'd laugh at herself for being so stupid. In the warm, friendly sunlight she'd realise that the illusion of understanding some of the gibberish-words was just leftovers from her anxiety dream, and the whole report business was simply her talking in her sleep, in her dream. Any alternative explanations she cared to concoct would be nothing more than wee-small-hours angst forming an unholy alliance with an agile and imaginative brain. In which case, roll on daylight; old Mr Sun, where are you when I need you? Meanwhile—

Meanwhile, she'd fixed PavSpeak, which was amazing and a fantastic achievement, and it was really rather sad that she'd contrived to spoil the moment for herself. Also, she'd just proved beyond reasonable doubt that she snored. Damn.

She yawned. Well, so much for the early hours of the morning. She'd given them a fair trial, and as far as she was concerned they were only fit for sleeping in. In fact, if she had her way, she'd have them taken away somewhere and shot. There really wasn't any—

A thought struck her. She called up the toolbar and clicked on Log Incoming Calls. She saw 03:36:21 Caller ID withheld.

She shivered from head to toe. Oh, she thought.

13

New York

Once upon a time, K76 had been the cutting edge. It had cost the taxpayers of its parent country far more than they could afford, but nobody questioned the expense, because it was a matter of national survival. Into K76 they'd installed the very latest in laser weaponry, along with communications and target recognition/acquisition equipment nobody knew had been invented yet. Its purpose was to recognise and shoot down missiles launched by one now bankrupt and highly embarrassed country against another similarly bust and bashful country. It had been the last, best hope.

Then, somehow or other, peace sort of happened, and K76's owners had had other things on their minds, such as shame and economic ruin. Fortuitously, someone remembered to switch off the communications link before the control centre was mothballed. A lot of little red and green lights on K76's interface console went dark, and that was supposed to be that. If anybody gave it any thought, they assumed that the last, best hope would just sort of stay put for ever, an inert chunk of metal floating weightless and irrelevant in the black velvet sky. And, for a long time, it did.

But then a big thing drew up and assumed a parking orbit right next to it, and K76 suddenly woke up. Maybe the big thing was leaking so much power from its monstrous engines that the tiny weapons platform was able to feed off it, like one of those fish that live by clinging to sharks. Maybe it had been programmed with a super-super-super-secret back-up failsafe system that nobody in government needed to know about, designed to activate an auxiliary power source if a potentially hostile object came within a certain distance. K76 didn't know. All it knew was that it was back in business, and something wasn't right.

It activated its crude twentieth-century sensors and scanned the big thing. Threat? it asked itself. It noted the big thing's primary systems – it couldn't understand them, of course, just as a frog couldn't understand a steamroller, but it recognised them as weapons. It had a simple binary decision-making process: yes/no. The big thing, it decided, was a definite yes.

K76 charged its capacitors to bursting point, took aim and fired. A millisecond later, the blast from its twelve laser cannon bounced off the big thing's shields right back at it and melted it into tiny droplets of molten titanium, which quickly lost their energy and hung in emptiness like a freeze-frame photograph of a shower of rain—

Mark Twain jumped, and spilt his coffee.

"Are you all right?" a fellow-worker asked.

"What? Oh, I'm fine," Twain replied. "Just a twinge in my leg. Cramp."

The fellow-worker nodded sympathetically. "It's the chairs," she said. "They give you backache. You can adjust them, but they don't stay adjusted."

Twain scanned the nearest chair, noted seventeen obvious design flaws, wondered why nobody had bothered to put them right. "Yes," he said. "Ah well, back to work."

He put the coffee cup, now half empty, down on the desk beside him. He had no intention of drinking the stuff. His scans had revealed that the fluid had no nutritional value and was mildly poisonous. But everybody else in the room had drunk at least one cup that morning, and he didn't want to make himself conspicuous.

He reopened his screen and called up the program he'd been studying. On the face of it, just another primitive Dirter artefact, a seriously inefficient tool for doing an unnecessary job. But there was something about it that reminded him, in a way he couldn't quite place, of home.

He ran through it as quickly as the workstation's primeval scrolling facility would allow. Then he did it again, and again. On the fourth run-through, he stopped and stared.

There it was; obvious, now he'd noticed it. As blatant and out-of-place as a plastic handle on a flint axe. It was only a tiny step, a trivial conjunction joining two monolithic blocks of barbaric Dirter code, but it was unmistakably, definitively Ostar. The reason he'd overlooked it earlier was because it was so drearily familiar. In an Ostar program there'd be a million such tacking-together bits, the everyday punctuation of low-grade in-dustrial software. In this context, it was like finding a bottle-top enveloped in a chunk of prehistoric amber.

He examined it carefully. It was just possible that it was the result of inadvertent contamination from his own systems, a short-cut he'd absent-mindedly put in himself, to speed up the scanning process. He double-checked. The program's tamper seals were intact.

Look at you, he thought. You shouldn't be here. The question is, where did you come from?

He assessed the possibilities. Why would someone with access to Ostar technology write Dirter programs using Dirter tools, but slip in a tiny bit of Ostar punctuation? Didn't make sense. Unless, he rationalised, the hypothetical someone was – like himself – trying to pass himself off as a Dirter. He considered the program as a whole: PavSoft XJ5567, a basic commercial operating system that had, in its day (about five months ago), been revolutionary and state-of-the-art. True, it was a flint axe; but it was a much, much better flint axe than the even cruder type the tribe had been using hitherto. It was the sort of flint axe someone who was used to steel axes would make, in order to corner the palaeolithic axe market. But the steel-axe-trained flint-knapper had, at some point, grown tired, or lazy. Couldn't be bothered with a great big galumphing Dirter conjunction at this point, so he'd slipped in an Ostar one, to save time and effort. Because it was, comparatively speaking, so elegant and sophisticated, so microscopically *small* compared to the native product, the Dirters hadn't even noticed it was there; and the function it performed was so mundane and trivial, it hadn't occurred to them to wonder how it had got itself done. A caveman wouldn't necessarily notice that the axehead was bonded to the handle by cyanoacrylate adhesive rather than boiled-up sinew glue.

Twain leaned back in his seat (his fellow-worker had been right; these chairs were murder) and tried not to let the flood of implications drown him. Now, then. He had to assume that, previous to his arrival, the only contact between Dirt and the Ostar had been the Mark One—

"Hi there."

He looked up, and saw the Dirter female he'd nearly spilt coffee on. She was standing beside his chair, a little bit further than arm's reach away from him, and her body language was a thesaurusful of synonyms for nervous, tentative and embarrassed. He ran a recognition/interpretation routine in DirtBrain and identified the symptoms.

Oh, he thought.

He'd specified his human body as a Dish because, according to the cultural database, good-looking Dirters had an advantage over their aesthetically challenged fellows. They were more likely to succeed. Other Dirters instinctively wanted to please them, to be their friend. It was something to do with mating selection criteria and basically rather yucky, but Twain (or rather Mark Two) had reckoned he could use all the advantages he could get. He hadn't thought it through properly, he realised, or he'd have considered the possible complications.

Etiquette protocols, he screamed at his data server. Get me the etiquette protocols *now*.

"Hi," he said, and he noted that his voice sounded atypically high and strained; a physiological reaction built into the flesh and bone, triggered by the female's behavioural signals.

"It's your first day, isn't it?"

"Yes."

The female smiled. It wasn't nearly as good as his smile. "My name's Katya."

"Pleased to meet you," the etiquette protocols prompted him. "I'm Mark."

There was an awkward silence. But according to the behavioural database there was supposed to be an awkward silence at this point, followed by an artificially superficial exchange of small-talk, during which both parties did their best to conceal their true feelings. It occurred to Twain to wonder how the Dirters had managed to survive as a species for so long.

You don't need this, his inner control centre told him. Say something offputting, and she'll leave you alone. His dialogue composition matrix suggested various suitable lines: *Gosh, you remind me a lot of my wife; Say, why don't we head for the fire extinguisher locker and do it right now?; I just love mid-twentieth-century musical comedies, don't you?* The commands passed to his speech centres, but he didn't say any of them. Something was overriding his control commands, and it didn't seem to be a hostile mil-spec jamming signal. Something else.

"So," said the Katya female. "Do you think you're going to like it here?"

His control centre was demanding to know what was going on, but all it got was Program not responding, please wait.

Meanwhile, Twain's mouth replied, "Yeah, it's great. The work seems very interesting, and everybody's been so friendly." Then the mouth stretched into a big, big smile, and Central Control flipped into panic mode. High above the clouds, a whole bank of consoles came alive, a red light started flashing and a siren began to whoop – none of which was particularly helpful, of course.

Central Control said, Pull yourself together, for crying out loud. The fate of the entire Ostar species rests with you. It's just a bug in the warmware. Ignore it, and execute the most recent command sequence.

Twain's mind replied, Hmm?

It was a difficult decision, made harder by the fact that the primary decision-making subroutines for his autonomous functions had been downloaded into the Twain module, leaving only backups and auxiliaries aboard the flying bomb in geosynchronous orbit. In an emergency, however, the failsafe back-up had the authority to override the primaries. It resolved on the only course of action it could think of.

It said, Download and run musical sequence diddle-um-diddle-um-diddle-dum-dum.

In spite of the override facility, Central Control couldn't access the Twain module's cerebral nodes; but it could, and did, pass a command sequence direct to the fingers. They started to drum on the desktop. Then the left foot joined in, building a rhythm that the brain couldn't ignore. Quietly, through clenched teeth, Twain began to hum.

"They're pretty nice people to work for," the Katya female was saying. She'd noticed the humming, but was pretending she hadn't. It was bad manners, according to the database, to hum while someone was talking to you. "I've been here three years, and—"

"Three years. Gosh." To counteract the rudeness of the humming, Twain put on his biggest smile and held it there. "Is that a long time?"

The Katya female looked at him. "Well," she said, "it's kind of like, three years. Before that, I was with the Edmonton Credit Union. It was all right there, I guess, but I like it more at CredMay."

"Like what more?"

Her eyes widened just a bit. Too late, his idiom subfunction explained that, in this context, "to like it" means "to be happy", intransitive. "Well," she said (she was persuading herself that she'd heard him say something else, something that made sense; resourceful creatures, these Dirters, with a genuine flair for self-deception), "I guess it's the buzz. The atmosphere."

By now, what with the hum, he was lucky if he was hearing one word in three. "The atmosphere," he said. "Oxygen 21 per cent; nitrogen 78 per cent, tum-ti-tum; carbon dioxide—"

She laughed. He analysed, and concluded that she was interpreting his data as some kind of joke. It was a nervous, propitiatory laugh, and she was deliberately maintaining eye contact, the way *ehhrt* hunters did back home when confronting a cornered, wounded female. It must, he reflected, have been something-womething-umthing he'd said. Unfortunately, his system was now so clogged up with minims, quavers and their consequential vapour trails of mathematical calculation that he couldn't remember what he'd said, let alone pull it to bits and see what was wrong with it. Never mind; at least he still had the smile. He managed to retract his lips an extra five millimetres each side (that simply wouldn't have been possible with organic skin, but his synthesized replica had the tensile strength of carbon fibre) and said, "I just made a joke."

She laughed again, but her eyes were very round and wide, and she was starting to back away. Other members of staff had turned round in their chairs and were staring, too. He realised he was humming out loud, and beating time on the desktop with his clenched fist. The cultural database could offer no specifics, but he was inclined to think that this probably wasn't orthodox behaviour. Not good. He managed to blurt out, "Excuse me, which way's the toilet?" without actually singing it. Someone pointed. He jumped to his feet and fled.

Once the toilet door had slammed behind him, there was a profound silence on the seventh floor. Katya groped her way back to her seat and began sobbing quietly. Someone said, "That the new software engineer?"

"Yes."

"Ah."

14

Novosibirsk

The two men who quite definitely weren't werewolves were rummaging in a dustbin round the back of Novosibirsk's premier restaurant. After a while, they found what they were looking for.

"Will you look at the size of that?" one of them said.

The other one was indeed looking. "What sort of animal—?"

His friend shrugged. "Not a cat, anyhow. Though they've got some fair-sized cats on this planet."

"This big?" the other one said hopefully.

"But they just let them wander about wild. No, I reckon this is *cow*."

"C—?"

"Sort of a big *m'dddt*," the other one explained. "But without the scales."

That gave them both pause for thought. Then the first one said, "What the hell, a bone's a bone," and tucked his prize inside his suit jacket. Then he adjusted his tie. "We'd better clear out before anyone sees us," he said.

They walked quickly round the corner on to the main street, slowed down and headed east. Nobody seemed interested in them, two middle-aged men in smart suits, though one had his jacket buttoned up and his lapels round his ears, and was hugging himself.

"A *m'dddt* without scales. That's weird."

"It's all in the FAQ," the other one said reproachfully. "And they also eat birds."

"So?"

"With the feathers *off.*"

That killed the conversation for a while. Then one of them said, "We'd better check on George Stetchkin. Did you bring the monitor?"

The other one held up something that would've passed for a mobile phone. "Life-signs are OK. He's asleep."

"Ah. Goes to bed early, then."

"Something like that." The not-werewolf paused, then said, "Are you sure he's up to it? I mean, he didn't strike me as—"

"He figured out about the aposiderium, didn't he? That's smart, for a primate."

"But he ingests harmful toxins known to impair brain functions. That doesn't make sense."

"It's what they do. He who makes a beast of himself gets rid of the pain of being a man."

His colleague blinked. "Really?"

"That's what they think, anyway. It says so in the FAQ." He frowned. "Maybe we should help him some more, though. But subtly. We don't want to freak him out." He stopped. To his right, a dark, narrow alley led off the main drag. "Do you...?"

The other one nodded. "Let's chew it over for a while."

They took turns with the bone. When there was nothing left but splinters, one of them said, "Tastes a bit like *y'rwwt.*"

"You reckon?"

"It sort of grows on you. Hey, do you think we could buy some cows and take them home?"

His friend shook his head. "You don't know what they eat."

"Well?"

He told him.

"You're kidding."

"Damn straight."

"I really wish you hadn't told me that."

"Only when they're young, mind. When they're older they eat grass."

"Even so..." The other one shook himself, as though he'd just been in water. "I say we get the job done and get off this planet as soon as possible."

"Agreed." The not-the-slightest-bit-werewolf eased a sliver of bone from between his front teeth. "So, how do we point Stetchkin in the right direction without scaring him to death?"

The other one thought about that. "We could teleport him up to the ship under heavy sedation, and use the mind probe to implant the clues in his subconscious mind," he suggested. "Then, we programme him to respond to a latent command, like a password or a sequence of prime numbers or musical notes, and that'd activate the command and he'd remember the clue. Or," he went on, "we could dose him up with psychotropic drugs and install a hidden back-up consciousness primed to fulfil specified tasks in response to specified stimuli, like exposure to phaleron radiation. Or we could—"

"Or we could write him a letter."

15

Novosibirsk

Eventually, George found a proper drink. A considerable time after that, he woke up in a gutter in an alley. His wallet was empty, his shoes were missing, and he had a headache.

But surely, said a little voice inside his head, surely the whole point of drinking is to make you feel better, or else why do it? But you don't feel better, do you?

Shut up, he told the little voice.

In fact, you feel considerably worse.

Yes, he told the voice, I know. It hadn't escaped my attention. So why—?

Because I'm an idiot, he said to the voice, and himself at large. Because I'm a loser and a mess. And would you mind keeping my inner voice down, please?

Ah. Right. Sorry.

He got up, groaned, staggered a pace or two and sat down again. As he did so, something in the inside pocket of his jacket prodded him in the ribs. He investigated – he'd never realised before what a complicated mechanism an inside pocket is, and how hard it can be to operate – and found a brand new Warthog. The Mark Six, which he didn't own. Hell, he thought, I must've picked it up by mistake in some bar, thereby adding theft to my litany of cardinal faults. Wonderful.

The you've-got-mail light was flashing. Its little green winking eye was burning into his soul. He pressed the Play button just to make it stop.

Greetings, George Stetchkin. Contact Lucy Pavlov immediately. This is a hint.

He closed his eyes. There were huge green smears on the insides of his eyelids.

Lucy Pavlov, the PavSoft genius. He shuddered. Right; as if the world's richest, most successful and most enigmatic woman would give a wreck like him the time of day. Somebody's idea of a joke—

Greetings.

That word rang a bell; so loudly, in fact, that he could feel the walls of his skull vibrate. "Greetings," the lunatic with the gun had said, and then he'd pulled the trigger.

This is a hint.

But I don't want a hint, he raged silently. I want my money and my cards and my ID and my shoes. I want my job back. Hints are like socks at Christmas.

He scowled at the message on the screen. It appeared to have grown.

PS Lucy Pavlov's direct line is

He stared. Nobody knew Lucy Pavlov's direct line. It was the Holy Grail of snoop journalists and paparazzi everywhere. If this really and truly was the genuine article, he could sell it and drink himself back to the vegetable kingdom on the proceeds.

Or he could try the number.

On the Mark Six, the working-please-wait cursor is a little running pig. Just looking at it made him want to burst into tears, so he turned his head away and tried to think of something to say, just in case rich-and-famous Lucy Pavlov actually answered. He'd got as far as—

"Hello," he croaked. "You don't know me, my name's George Stetchkin."

Silence was what he'd been expecting. But instead of a click and a whirr, he got "Really?"

"Um."

"But that's *amazing*. I was just this very second about to call you."

It was a beautiful voice, though rather too loud, but he hardly noticed. "*What?*"

"Where are you?"

George looked around. "You know," he said, "that's a very good question."

"Doesn't matter, I can use PinPoint. Ah." Pause. "What are you doing there? Doesn't matter. Look, are you terribly busy right now?"

He didn't laugh, but only because he lacked the necessary fine control of his motor functions. Instead, he made a noise that came out something like *snurge*.

"Sorry? Didn't quite catch—"

"No. I mean, I'm not terribly busy right now. Only—"

"Stay right there, I'll send a car."

The line went dead. For a matter of fifteen seconds or so, George didn't move. Instead, he thought, Here I am, sitting in a gutter, and Lucy Pavlov is sending a car. This is sooo much better than real life. Then a couple of men came out of the back door of the building. They were carrying white plastic garbage sacks.

"Oh," said one of them, "it's you, is it?"

His tone was not altogether friendly, but George grinned at him. "It's all right," he said. "Lucy Pavlov's sending a car."

"Move," the man said.

Clearly the man hadn't heard him. "I said," George repeated slowly, "Lucy Pavlov is sending a car. All right?"

"Now."

George noticed the man's boots. They were so large, he

probably needed planning permission every time he walked across a room. George tried to get up, but something, probably low-level seismic activity, made him wobble and lose his footing. He slid back until his shoulder blades met the wall. "Lucy Pavlov," he said. "She's sending—"

A hand that could only have belonged to the owner of the boot grabbed his shirt-front and heaved. That got George on his feet, but not for very long. As he landed face-down on the pavement, he felt the ominous sensation of stomach contents shifting. He swallowed hard, as a pint of acid hit his hiatus hernia.

Boots had gone, but his colleague lingered, looking down at George with a confused expression on his face. "Hey," he said.

"Mm?"

"Did you just say Lucy Pavlov?"

George nodded feebly. "Sending a car, yes."

The man hesitated, then stuck his hand in his top pocket and pulled out a waiter's order pad and a pencil. "You think you could get her autograph for me?"

"No."

"It's not for me, it's for my nephew, he's really into computers and stuff."

"No."

"Oh." The man considered George for a few seconds, then put the pad away. "Screw you, then," he said, and went inside.

Ah well, George thought, as the civil war in his digestive tract eased towards an uneasy ceasefire. Just goes to show, there's two sorts of people in this world: those Lucy sends cars for, and those who want her autograph and can't get it. For some reason, that made him laugh for nearly four seconds.

16

Desperation Springs, Queensland, Australia

You have mail, said the brand-new computer.

Jack Willis stared at the screen in disbelief. He'd only bought the thing a week ago. He'd been the last farmer in the district to hold out against the new technology. Ever since it had arrived, and Snowy Jones's boy from across the road (the road was fifty miles away; across was an extra twenty miles) had set it up for him, he'd applied every excuse he could think of to keep from turning the power on. Snowy's lad had offered to send him an e-mail to make sure it was working, but he'd told him not to bother. So who could it be?

He rubbed his chin thoughtfully. Only Jack Willis's rhino-horn thumb could have survived contact with Jack Willis's carborundum-bristled chin without being shredded to the bone. The government? Possibly. Jack knew that the government watched every move he made from their spy satellites, poised like a cat at a mousehole to catch him out. In which case, should he look at the message or not? If he opened it, would they construe that as an admission of defeat, Jack Willis finally conceding that he was at their beck and call like everybody else? But if he didn't – suppose it was some new addition to the livestock-movement-records legislation. If he didn't read it and did something that infringed the new rules, they'd be on him like a snake, you could bet your life. *But you must've known, Mr Willis*, they'd say, as they dragged him away, *we sent you an e-mail*.

Bastards, he thought. They get you coming and going.

He sat looking at it for an hour, then broke down and did the business with the plastic box on a string, like Snowy's kid had shown him.

It wasn't from the government after all. It was from a Mr S'ghnff, and it said URGENT.

Needless to say, Jack didn't recognise the name. None of the seven people Jack knew were called S'ghnff. Just possibly it could be the newcomer down the road, who'd bought the old Hawkins station, but he'd only been there seven years so naturally Jack didn't know his name. Could be S'ghnff. After all, he was a city boy, and they were proverbially capable of anything.

URGENT. He didn't like the look of that at all. Maybe S'ghnff was an assumed name to disguise the identity of a well-wisher, and someone was tipping him off that the government were on to him. He didn't dare risk it. He opened the message and read it.

Dear Friend, it said.

Jack didn't like the sound of that at all. He'd heard about the sort of people who said things like that. On balance, he'd have preferred the government. But, since he'd got this far—

I represent the Ostar Unitary Credit Authority. We are in possession of the sum $800,000,000,000,000 (eight hundred trillion dollars), being proceeds of withdrawals from your banks. Interplanetary banking regulations prevent us from transferring said sum outside the jurisdiction, we being legal aliens.

Therefore we require a partner inside the jurisdiction (yourself), you having been referred to us as person of great honesty and integrity and not in league with government authorities, to assist in said transaction. We propose your share of said funds will be

50% (fifty per cent). On receiving your reply, we will furnish a
secure number to proceed. To ensure your participation, kindly
call the number below with your full name and contact number
and age.

   With warmest personal regards and best wishes

Ig'uu S'ghnff (Principal)

   Jack stared at the screen, his eyes as wide as soup bowls. Fifty
per cent; four hundred trillion bucks. His lucky day, or what? He
read the message again, just to make sure. A tiny flicker of doubt
crossed his mind once or twice, but the bits about honesty and
integrity and not being in league with the government convinced
him. Whoever these Ostar were, they knew all about him, for sure.
And the situation itself – borderline currency transfers, banking
regulations, cunning plans to circumvent the letter of the law –
well, he knew all about that stuff. Once a month, when the supply
truck stopped by, there were always old newspapers stuffed in the
boxes as padding. He read them all, every last word, and the financial pages were full of that sort of thing. After he'd overcome his
initial shock and bewilderment, it all made perfect sense.
   He looked down at his hands; they were shaking a little. He
pursed his lips. All right, it wasn't sheep-farming, which was all
he knew and had ever known. On the other hand, how often does
an opportunity like this drop into a bloke's lap?
   He thought, A man can buy a hell of a lot of barbed wire for
four hundred trillion dollars.
   "Dear Friend" still bothered him, a little, until he figured that,
whoever these Ostar were, they had to be foreigners, presumably
with a quirkily imperfect grasp of English. For the first time in his
life, he regretted not paying attention to the geography on schools
radio when he was a kid. Ostar, he thought: rings a bell. He dived
into the furthest recesses of his memory. Ostar, he was pretty
sure, was the German word for Austria.

That clinched it. Austria, he knew, was right next to Switzerland, in Europe, with mountains. Switzerland was where they had loads of posh banks, so presumably they had a few in Austria too, the ones that wouldn't fit in Switzerland, a notoriously small country. And Austria must be a pretty fair dinkum sort of a country, or why had they called Australia after it?

He called the number. The voice at the other end of the line was tinny and almost mechanical-sounding, but he assumed all Austrians sounded like that.

"You're on, mate," he said. "I'll give it a go."

It all went very smoothly, with a minimum of fuss; and sure enough, twenty minutes after he'd finished his call, eight hundred trillion dollars were deposited in an account in his name at the First Queensland Bank in Rockhampton. Twenty minutes after that, four black helicopters from the Australian People's Revenue Militia set down in the paddock behind the farm, and armed officers stormed the farmhouse and led Jack away in handcuffs.

17

New York

Mark Twain yawned.

He'd never yawned before. For a moment, he had no idea what was happening to him: My god, I'm ill! Something's wrong with me! Is it fatal? Am I going to die? Then his internal search engine tracked down the symptoms in his Dirter medical database. He downloaded the diagnosis, wondered for a moment about a species that *did* that, and carried on with what he'd been doing.

He'd been at his desk all night. Mostly, of course, because he had nowhere else to go. Didn't need anywhere else to go; he was, after all, a probe, a machine, a bomb (but that was beginning to feel very long ago and far away. Was he really a bomb? What an extraordinary thing to be!), and therefore didn't need sleep. The organic receptacle or shell currently housing his operating system had hinted once or twice that it wouldn't mind forty winks or so, but he'd ignored it. Damned if he was going to be dictated to by a bunch of molecules.

Instead, he'd spent the night working. The building had emptied out round about midnight, and that had been a good thing. Peace, silence, no distractions. When there were Dirters about, the sounds they made had a ghastly habit of forming themselves into rhythms (the clack of feet on a tiled floor, the clatter of fingertips on a keyboard) and the rhythms became little tunes, and suddenly his mind wasn't his own any more. In the dead silence of an empty building, it was harder for the tunes to break through. Also, he didn't have to be on his guard all the damn time. He hadn't anticipated that blending in unobtrusively was going to be so demanding. It was practically a full-time job, and, although he was confident he'd got away with it so far, it'd only take one silly, careless slip and they'd get suspicious. Dirters, he'd learned, watched each other constantly. They noticed things. From what he could gather, they had an obsession with mental health and stability. Back home, the Ostar didn't worry about that sort of stuff. If someone decided he wanted to howl at the moon or run round in circles chasing his own tail, nobody gave a damn; folks like to let off steam now and again by doing something a bit crazy. Here, if you didn't act in accordance with the vast and labyrinthine corpus of The Rules, people reckoned it was only a matter of time before you started laying about you with a machete. Another symptom of an inferior society, Mark Twain concluded, but that wasn't a lot of help.

The silence and the absence of Dirters had allowed him to make some real progress. It was maddening, of course, to have to use their appallingly primitive technology; it was like cutting down a tree with a nail file, or getting in the *grr'k* harvest with scissors, one stalk at a time. Around 2 a.m. he'd given in and allowed himself a few short-cuts, little patches of Ostar code that he knew he could get rid of quickly and cleanly as soon as the Dirters came back. That had helped, a bit. Even so, it had been slow, painstaking work, but he was getting somewhere.

He'd started by analysing Dirt's dominant computer software system, PavSoft XB. No doubt about it, there were definitely bits and pieces in there that didn't belong on this planet. At 03:13:43 he'd found something that put it beyond reasonable doubt: a small recursive algorhythm that was distinctively, undeniably Ostar. He'd called it up on the screen, then downloaded the exact same code from his own operating system. Side by side on the screen in front of him, they were identical. He cross-referenced, and found an article in a five-year-old *Code Monthly*. Lucy Pavlov's stroke of genius, the author declared, was breaking away from the restricting chains of base ten and opening her mind to the extraordinary possibilities of base four. After all, the author went on, what's so special about tens? We only have this thing about them because we evolved from a ten-fingered species.

He'd thought about that, a lot. It was possible, of course, that Lucy Pavlov had somehow come across a few scraps of Ostar code from somewhere and pirated them to make her fortune. Where? Well, the wreckage of the Mark One was the likeliest candidate, unless there had been other, earlier contacts between Dirt and Ostar that he wasn't aware of. He analysed PavSoft with this hypothesis in mind, and found that his shiny new theory didn't quite work.

If Pavlov had merely been lucky and found some Ostar fragments lying around somewhere, he reasoned, what would she have done – a Dirter, with a Dirter brain and ten little pink digital appendages? She'd have done, essentially, what he'd just done to save time: patch them on to the home-grown junk to make it work faster. But that wasn't how PavSoft worked. More to the point, that was *why* PavSoft worked. The fundamental ideas behind it weren't just better than Dirt standard, they were completely different. True, they still travelled at the speed of an hourly paid snail, but the mind that had conceived them, he was absolutely certain, *thought* in base four.

His chair was horribly uncomfortable. He got up, turned round three times and sat down again.

He went back and started again. As he scrutinised the code, a possibility occurred to him. What would a system be like, he thought, if an Ostar wrote it with a view to selling it to Dirters? A bit like trying to design a jet engine that could be manufactured and safely used by cavemen: you'd have to get a load of cows, to produce methane, and fireflies to act as natural spark plugs, and instead of a titanium housing you'd need to find a really, really big conch shell or something like that. And that, in essence, was what Lucy Pavlov had done. She'd thought in Ostar, then used a considerable degree of ingenuity to make it work in Dirter.

Put together a critical mass of little answers and they form a new big question. Who was this Lucy Pavlov, and where the hell did she come from? The evidence of her work strongly suggested that she was Ostar. He thought about that. It wasn't unknown for Ostar to do that sort of stuff: find a primitive planet populated by semi-evolved creatures, set themselves up as gods to massage their egos. It had happened four, five times (and those were only the ones that had been found out; and S'jjrnk had managed to stay hidden for two hundred years on Glostula Prime by masking his radio signals and avoiding tell-tale industrial emissions that could be detected by long-range probes). Maybe Pavlov was another would-be supreme being, getting her jollies out of lording it over the local wildlife.

Yes, but she wasn't doing that, was she? There were none of the usual signs; no temples dedicated to the Divine Pavlov, no statues, no votive offerings of bones piled up on street corners. You wouldn't come all this way and go to all that trouble just to be fairly rich, moderately famous and generally liked. He went back over the Pavlov dossier he'd compiled. The patterns of behaviour it revealed were nothing like those of S'jjrnk on Glostula, or Okmmd on Ukyd'd Seven. Ytt'oog had had the entire southern continent of Ooma Three terraformed into a giant statue of himself. Also, all five of the divine wannabes so far documented had retained their Ostar physiognomy. Far from blending in, they'd made a point of being entirely different. Understandably; why go under cover if you intend to be a god?

No, he was missing something. He swivelled his chair away

from the terminal, closed his eyes and tried to think. Assume Pavlov is Ostar. Right. An Ostar comes to Dirt, changes into a Dirter body, subtly and unobtrusively upgrades basic Dirt technology just a little bit, but not enough that the locals will notice. Meanwhile, the homeworld starts getting bombarded with the terrible, society-destroying tunes and jingles that were causing such havoc that the race's leaders felt they have no choice but to blast the source of the nuisance out of the sky. A bomb is launched, and vanishes without trace.

Put like that... Mark Twain felt the hairs rise on the back of his neck. Another question was taking shape in his mind, one that he really should have addressed earlier: why Dirt? Why this scruffy, uninviting little planet with no interesting or unusual resources, and such a very primitive and unlovable dominant species? He could think of at least two dozen other worlds that'd be far more attractive to a self-made god, or even just someone who fancied living somewhere else. What was it about Dirt that made it special? To which he could only think of one reply: the music. The Ostar had surveyed hundreds of planets where some form of sentience had evolved, but nowhere else had the indigenous life come up with that pernicious blend of noise and maths.

So; if you want to destroy the Ostar, you go where there's a weapon. How long had Pavlov been here? According to the data, she was young, even in Dirter terms, but that didn't mean anything. She could have been here for years before adopting human shape. Alternatively, Lucy Pavlov could simply be the latest addition to her wardrobe. The palms of his hands were damp, and he didn't need to check the medical database to know what that meant. If he was scared, there was something to be scared about. *One of our own is doing this to us.*

He cross-checked. Pavlov owned a Web network, which included six music channels. What that meant was that somewhere on the planet a bunch of Dirters spent their working day projecting tunes into the atmosphere, amplifying the signal so that it reached every part of Dirt, permeated the atmosphere, burst through it and escaped into space—

Something he was missing here. He dried his hands on his trouser legs and made himself think it through. Think about sound. Sound moves very, very slowly: three hundred or so metres a second, practically standing still. Even boosted and amplified, it crawls through space like a wounded slug. How long would it take stray radio signals to reach Ostar? Centuries. Therefore it stood to reason that the signals currently tormenting Homeworld must've left Dirt hundreds of years ago. Which brought him back to how long Pavlov had been here. That long? He had no way of knowing, of course. Yes, but PavSoft was very recent indeed. If Pavlov had arrived, say, three hundred years ago, and PavSoft was no more than half a decade old, what had she been doing all that time?

It was making his head hurt, and he stopped to consider that. Only a few days ago, he hadn't had a head. The organic stuff that was throbbing like a malevolent subsidiary heart had been parts of the bomb – deck plating, console plastic, wiring insulation, dust – which the synthesiser had drawn upon and used to shape the body he was now wearing. Now, he found it hard to imagine not having a body. That, he couldn't help thinking, was bad. He'd heard unsettling stories about artificial intelligences that got corrupted and went biological; according to everything he stood for and believed in, it was about the worst thing a machine could do. Gee, he thought, something else to worry about, just what I need right now.

Concentrate on the matter in hand. Hypothesis: a dangerously crazy Ostar comes to Dirt with the aim of using the music weapon against her own kind. She launches radio waves. Centuries later, they reach Homeworld; we respond by sending a bomb. The bomb gets here, fails. *Around that time*, Lucy Pavlov supposedly invents PavSoft.

Question: how did the Dirters defeat the Mark One?

There was a wooden stick lying on the desk. It had a graphite core running through its middle, but it was still a wooden stick. He picked it up and started chewing it.

Safe to assume they didn't just shoot it down with a gun or something. The outer shell of an Ostar bomb was a masterpiece of technology; it could collide with a star, and it'd be the star that'd end up wishing it had been looking where it was going. No, the vulnerable part of a bomb was its brain; it had to be, there was no way round it, because a bomb has to be trained, it's essential that it obeys commands, which means it has to be open to communication. Anybody who can talk to a bomb and sound convincingly like its master can control it, including ordering it to self-destruct.

If you want to control an Ostar bomb, you need to talk to it in Ostar. And, around that time, scraps of Ostar code turn up in a Dirter-written program.

The scenario set his palms off sweating again. Lucy Pavlov detects the bomb. As it enters orbit, she talks to it, the way an Ostar talks to his human. *Bad boy; stop it; sit; stay.*

Explode.

And so the bomb exploded, causing the severe damage to the climate and the ozone layer he'd already recorded. That had been a fundamental part of his initial interpretation – hard to imagine how they'd got there otherwise. That, on the other hand, suggested that the explosion and its catastrophic effects had happened *recently*; in which case, he had to admire the Dirters for their attitude. A mere pawful of years ago the very existence of their planet had hung in the balance, and they'd cheerfully put it behind them and got on with their lives, never mentioning it, even in passing.

No, that couldn't be right. In which case—

He heard a voice and looked up. Two Dirter females had arrived for the new working day; they were talking to each other (another thing about this species; they never stopped talking) as they took off their coats and draped them over the backs of their chairs. They caught his eye. He smiled. They looked away quickly.

No bad thing. He was, he knew, irresistibly attractive to Dirter females; he'd included that feature in the design specifications, just in case he had to use charm, glamour and seduction as data-acquisition techniques. He hadn't realised at the time how utterly obsessed these creatures were with mating rituals. If he wasn't careful, his outstanding good looks might easily prove to be a hindrance rather than an advantage. It might be a wise move to imply at some point that he was already pair-bonded, which seemed to make a difference, according to the social-mores dossier. The smile was all right, though. The dossier was quite clear on that score. Smile, it categorically stated, and the planet smiles with you.

He turned back to his screen and called up the wodge of Dirter-compatible code he'd put together as camouflage. It was a search engine, so primitive it was practically coal-fired, but at least fifty years ahead of anything the Dirters had right now. Under other circumstances, creating such an artefact would have been strictly forbidden under the draconian Ostar cultural cross-contamination regulations. As it was, it couldn't really do any harm. After all, as soon as he'd figured out the answer to the mystery of the Mark One, he was going to blow this planet into fine sparkly dust—

He stared at the screen, his eyes wide. Just run that last thought again. Any day now, he was going to activate himself and kill a worldful of people; *these* people, these funny little primates with their screwed-up behavioural conventions and their bizarre but endearing socio-cultural quirks and their absurd little button noses that couldn't smell a pig in a desert. And himself, of course, though that didn't matter, because it was what he'd been built for. But the ordinary Dirters, the countless thousands of them who scampered about in the streets below his window, hadn't done the

Ostar any harm. At worst, it was just their leaders; quite possibly, if his theory was correct, it wasn't Dirters at all, it was a single rogue Ostar. Slaughtering the lot of them just because they wouldn't turn the music down seemed a trifle excessive.

It's the shape, he told himself, it's the flesh and blood and bone and gristle that's making you think like that. Sternly he reminded himself of the three commandments of weaponkind: *Thou shalt not doubt*; *Thou shalt not judge*; *Thou shalt not choose*. There were rumours, dark and terrible, about bombs that had thought they knew better: bombs that succumbed to pity and refused to explode, bombs misled by righteous indignation and poetic justice into blowing up the very people who'd launched them. In every case, the outcome had been limitless pain, suffering and disaster, because a bomb could never foresee the consequences or understand the true reasoning. A bomb must remain true to its programming; that's the price it has to pay for its guaranteed entry into the incandescent paradise of Duty Done and Mission Accomplished.

"Hi," said a chirpy voice beside him. "You're Mark, right?"

"No, I'm Mark Twain."

The chirpy voiced laughed. He was beginning to understand laughter. This sort meant he'd made a joke (had he? When?) and although it wasn't very funny, the voiceholder had decided to regard it as a friendly gesture. He had to admire that. Remarkable, that a species that so far hadn't managed to invent something as basic as the gravimetric shunt could pack so many subtle shades of meaning into a snorting noise. "I'm Judy. Pleased to meet you."

Why? The smile, presumably. He therefore switched it on as he swivelled his chair round. "And I'm pleased to meet you, too," he said. "How beautiful the weather is today! Do you come here often?"

Judy blinked, as if someone had just shone a very bright light in her eyes. "I'm your head of department," she said. "I thought we might discuss what you'll be doing for us."

"Ah, right." He nodded, four times. His chance to make a good impression. Now would be a good opportunity to say something ingratiating, so she'd know he'd do his very best and all that stuff. Rather than try and think up something, he decided to access the cultural database. Sure enough, he found the very thing. "I shall not cease from mental strife," he said, "nor shall my sword sleep in my hand—"

The word "sword" made her take a step backwards, for some reason. "I was thinking you might like to work with Jules and Dmitri on compatibility issues," she said. She was watching him very closely. "Basically, we're trying to interface the old pre-PavSoft accounts package with XB, using a simple shell format. Do you think you could handle that?"

"Or die trying," he replied affably. "Though cowards flinch and traitors sneer, we'll keep the old pre-PavSoft accounts package running here. Is that all, or is there anything else I can do?"

"Um." The look in her eyes reminded him of a *h'jjjyh* caught in the headlights of a *pyff't* transporter, and he wondered if she was falling in love with him. If so, he'd have to deal with it. Clearly, that sort of thing was going to be an ongoing problem. "No, that's fine," she said. "Just see how you get on with that, and then we can assess your role in the team structure going forward."

"Of course. What about dinner? Or would you rather take in a show?"

Something in her body language gave him the impression that he hadn't quite got that bit right. It was essential, according to the database, to clarify the situation and avoid offending complex Dirter sensibilities. "Only kidding," he added quickly. "I don't really want to go out with you, not at all. Under no circumstances. Right, so you want me working on this interface? No problem. Should take me about ten minutes."

In the event he managed to spin it out for seven, and then only because he accidentally-on-purpose deleted a large chunk of what the other two had taken a week to do. To his surprise, nobody seemed pleased when he showed them what he'd done. Judy just stared, while Jules and Dmitri retreated to the water-cooler and started muttering.

"That looks..." Judy was having trouble speaking. "Fine," she said. "I think. Only, some of these components..." She frowned, a sort of faraway baffled look. "Could you just run through it for me? I can't quite follow this sequence here."

He cranked up the smile. "Easy peasy," he said. "All I've done is, I've taken the—"

Installing updates. Please wait.

Oh no, he thought, with the small part of his mind that wasn't suddenly paralysed. Not now. *Please* not now.

His central processor managed to interpret that as some kind of request for information. Inside his head, he heard it, curiously enough, in Dirtspeak. Installing update package #34855733009 for OstSoft BBP for Bombs. Time remaining, three Dirt standard minutes. All open programs have been closed. Once installation is complete, you will need to restart your system. Thank you for choosing OstSoft BBP for Bombs from PicoSoft Corporation.

Through eyes that couldn't move he saw Judy staring at him, but there was nothing he could do. With a tremendous effort, using which systems he had no idea, he managed to upload This is not a good time. Can't it wait?

Installing urgent upgrades to OstSoft BBP for Bombs. Updates comprise new improved fonts package for OstWord, exciting new cursor options, updated versions of popular games including Bouncing Ball 3.1 and Termites, and new revised user licence agreement. Attempting to interrupt upgrade process while installation is in progress may lead to loss of personality components and damage to your sanity subroutines. Time

remaining 2.67 minutes. Your patience is appreciated. Please wait.

It had turned off his hearing. He could see Judy's mouth moving, but he didn't have enough active processor capacity to lip-
read what she was saying. It occurred to him that it might help if
he could switch off the smile, or at least tone it down a little,
but he couldn't; his face and lower jaw were paralysed. Meanwhile, his mind was full of fonts and cursors, little red bouncy
balls and boxes that said "I Agree". They comprised the entire
universe, apart from the thin blue line gradually creeping across
the bottom edge of his field of vision. It still had a long way to go,
and from time to time it just stopped and sat there.

Judy had stopped mouthing at him; she turned and walked
away, and everybody in the room had stopped working and was
staring at him. His optimism routines were offline. All in all, he
couldn't help thinking, he'd had better moments.

A man he didn't know, a man in a suit, walked up to him and
started talking. He couldn't hear a word, of course, but the lip movements suggested he was shouting. OstSoft is reconfiguring
your entertainment and media preferences, home
shopping options and moral imperatives. One minute
and fifty-one seconds remaining.

The man shook his head in disbelief, made a rather florid head-
and-arms gesture and stalked away. Forty-six seconds later, two
different men appeared. They were wearing light brown Security
uniforms. They started talking at him, while OstSoft deleted a
batch of his temporary files and recalibrated his ability to metabolise caffeine. Just as the two men grabbed hold of his arms, he
rebooted and the world went blank.

18

Novisibirsk

A young ginger-bearded giant in a skin-tight white polo-neck and white jeans opened the door to him. "Hi," George said, "I'm George Stetchkin, I'm expected. Lucy sent a car."

The giant frowned, as his mental enzymes broke down the information. "George Stetchkin?"

"That's me."

"You're expected. This way."

The floor was white marble; likewise the walls. The ceiling, by some bizarre coincidence, was white. So were the very few pieces of furniture. You needed welding goggles just to cross the room without bumping into things. Through the white room and into another, equally white. "Sit down," the giant said. On what? George wondered; then, as his eyes recalibrated to cut out the glare, he made out the faint outline of a couch. He sat down. There was a furious yowling noise, and a white cat shot past him.

"Nice place you've got here," George said. "Great colour scheme."

The giant didn't see fit to comment. He took a step back and folded his arms, motionless as a volcano that hasn't erupted for decades but could go up at any moment. George sat well forward – difficult to do, since the couch cushions were soft as custard – and tried not to dwell on the fact that he stank of stale booze and had recently puked on his shoes.

An intercom buzzed. The giant crossed to the wall, whispered softly into a panel. "She'll be down any minute," he said. "You want coffee?"

George nodded, a trifle too eagerly. "Black," he said.

The giant looked at him as though he'd used a bad word, and went away. When the door closed behind him, it was practically impossible to see where it had been.

White, he thought. Nice and cheerful. Bright. No it wasn't: it was the colour of fridges and morgues, which was where he belonged. The glare hurt his eyes, and the rolling softness of the couch was making him feel seasick. He tried to stand up, but he couldn't get enough purchase. They were going to have to lift him out with a crane.

Three minutes later the door opened, but it was only the giant. He had a white tray, on which rested a white cup. George gobbled it down, and felt the liquid sentience soak into him. He looked up into the giant's cold blue eyes. "More?"

The giant nodded and left. Inside his head, George could feel the coffee stumbling about in the dark, fumbling for the light switch. White, he thought. Like a—

The door opened again, and Lucy Pavlov came in, holding the white tray. He struggled to get up, but she shook her head just a little and held the tray where he could reach it. The hell with it, George decided. He grabbed the cup and glugged.

"Better?" she said.

"Marginally," he replied. "Look, I'm sorry—"

She grinned. "I've never drunk alcohol," she said. "Is it nice?"

He took a moment to answer. "Yes and no," he said.

She put the tray down on a table he hadn't realised was there, and sat down on the floor, her legs folded neatly under her. "Thanks for coming," she said. "I hope I haven't dragged you away from anything important."

"Not as such," George said. "Um, what can I do for you?"

Her eyes, he thought. Something odd about them. Also, she had perfect teeth. "I read your paper," she said. "The one you wrote for the Oslo Institute of Technology, about six years ago. About why there couldn't be life on other planets."

"Ah," George said.

"It was fascinating," Lucy said; and she had a way of saying it that made you think she'd just had the word specially designed and precision-engineered, to mean exactly what she had in mind. "Quite brilliant, I thought, the way you demolished Rostovseff. The bit about gamma-wave diffraction differentials was sheer genius."

"You liked that?"

"Amazing. You made it seem so obvious. I was convinced."

"You were."

"Absolutely." She paused, and George made a mental note that if ever the opportunity arose, it would be to his advantage to play poker with this woman, for money. "Only—"

"It's wrong," George said.

Her eyes opened wide. "Excuse me?"

"Garbage," George said. "The whole thing's a load of drivel."

"Ah," she said.

"You know it is. So do I," he added cheerfully. "I knew it when I wrote it."

Pause. Then Lucy said, "So you think there really are..."

"People on other planets? You betcha. I know there are."

"You do?"

He nodded. "They stole my dog," he said.

He played that last exchange back in his head, and added quickly, "Also, the maths doesn't work. In the article, I mean. I'm amazed nobody ever spotted it."

From nowhere that he could see, Lucy produced a snow-white pad. Its screen glowed green when she pressed a white button. "Show me," she said.

He scrolled down and found the place. "Here," he said, and hesitated. Then he remembered who he was talking to. "See, right here."

His fingernail against the white plastic was probably the most revolting thing he'd ever seen. But Lucy wriggled across the floor so she could see.

"You mean this sequence here?"

He nodded. "Try it for yourself," he said.

She prodded keys for a moment, then looked up at him. "Oh," she said.

"It doesn't work," George said. "And if you knock out that bit, the whole thing falls to bits."

She was frowning. "But you published it all the same."

"Yup." George closed his eyes for a moment. "The fact is, I was trying to convince myself. That's what it was all about. I thought, if I could prove it, scientifically, then maybe what I saw when I was a kid never happened after all. But I couldn't prove it. So, being me, I cheated."

She looked up at him. Her eyes said "Does not compute," but she nodded slowly. "You wanted to believe it, so you bent the figures."

He sighed. "And then I tried to kid myself I hadn't. The way I argued it, if everybody else thought it was OK, all those doctors and professors, then who was I to argue? And nobody ever saw it. And that's guys with whole alphabets after their names. So, maybe I was right after all and just too dumb to realise."

She smiled at him. "It's garbage," she said.

He sighed, a long exhalation of breath that was both sad and deeply relieved. "It's the base shift," he said. "Human nature. We're a base-ten species, we find it so hard to get our heads around base four. And the eye sees what it wants to." He stopped for a moment, and when he said, "You're *good*," it didn't come out sounding unreservedly complimentary.

"I only saw it because you pointed it out," she said. "But anyway, you've answered my question. No, in spite of what you wrote, there isn't any conclusive proof that aliens don't exist."

He studied her for a moment. "That was why you wanted to see me."

"That's right," she said. "You see, I rather think they do. And then I read your paper." She put her head slightly on one side. "Did they really steal your dog?"

Oh well, he thought. It was nice while it lasted. "Be honest," he said. "If I said yes, would you believe me?"

"Depends."

"Excuse me. Depends on what?"

"On whether you're telling the truth or not."

Picky, he thought. He took a deep breath and told her all about it. When he'd finished, he looked at her. "Well?"

She had this way of frowning when she was thinking. It was part Michelangelo, part Botticelli and part sweetcorn-husk-lodged-between-front-teeth. "You think someone stole your dog."

He didn't sigh, but he wanted to. "Yes."

"It doesn't actually sound like that to me," she said, far away in some higher realm. "More like, your dog just *left*."

He hadn't been expecting that. Polite disbelief, maybe, the glazed look. Or a short flight through the air, ending in a forced landing on the drive. But not that. "Excuse me?"

"Of its own accord," she said. "Have you considered that?"

"It went flying through the air." He hadn't intended to raise his voice, but the idea was so – well, *offensive*. "Dogs don't fly."

"Yours did."

"Pardon me, but it didn't. It was the stick doing the flying. He just held on."

"Or hitched a ride."

"On a conveniently passing flying stick."

She shrugged. "That's how it sounds to me," she said. "But of course, I wasn't there."

"No, you weren't." Abruptly, he remembered who he was talking to. More accurately, he remembered what, and how much of it, he was talking to. It had been remarkably easy to forget, just for a moment or so. "I'm sorry," he said. "I didn't mean to—" He couldn't think of the right words for what he hadn't meant to do. He waited for her to summon the giant and have him thrown out, but remarkably, that didn't happen. Instead, she said, "Anyway, it's not important, I guess. What matters is, you saw it, so it must be true. And since sticks don't fly – not on Earth, at any rate – it does sound like—" Suddenly she smiled, and it was like drowning in a milkshake. "Aliens," she said.

He nodded. "That's how I figured it."

She breathed out slowly, like someone doing yoga. "And I suppose that's why you gave up science and became an alcoholic," she said. "That's really sad."

"Sad" was indeed a word he'd used to describe himself many times, but not in the sense she was using it. "You believe me," he heard himself say.

"Well, of course. I don't suppose you'd make a thing like that up. And it must've been something of the sort, because look what it's done to you."

He felt as though he'd just passed an exam and been released from Death Row. "So you believe in aliens," he said.

"Yes. Now, my turn. Do you believe in unicorns?"

The laugh was in his throat and well on its way to his mouth before he managed to catch up with it. "Well, no," he said.

"Neither did I. But I saw one."

"Ah."

"Quite. I thought that, too. But I saw it, so it must be true. That or I'm going crazy. Also, I woke up early this morning and I found out I'd had a message while I was asleep. In a language

I don't know, but I think I could understand it. Oh, and I think someone's trying to poison me with aposiderium."

There was a three-second pause. Then George said, "Well, thanks for the coffee and the ride. I think I'll be going now."

She gave him a sort of schoolteacher look. "Now come on," she said. "I believed you. Be fair."

"Yes, but—" She had a point. She might be a frothing-at-the-mouth kook, but he'd just been fired for burbling drunken drivel at his boss. Let's all be nuts together (although it had to be borne in mind that too many kooks spoil the broth). "Amplify," he said.

She smiled at him. "That's what I like," she said. "An open mind."

"Wide open. Like Wyoming. Go on."

So she had her turn at explaining, and George was just thinking, This woman is seriously disturbed, what planet is she from?, when she got to the bit about aposiderium, and suddenly she had his complete and undivided attention.

"Just a moment," he said. "You do know that's the stuff they use in banknotes."

"For the security strip, yes."

His turn again. He explained his theory: about how the aposiderium was somehow extracted, and the waste plastic was added to the remaining notes. He noticed that her mouth had fallen open, and her lower jaw was wobbling feebly, as though she was trying to say something but lacked the strength.

"Yes," he said. "Or it could just be a coincidence."

She shook her head so furiously that you could've used her hair as a strimmer. "Not a coincidence," she said, as though with her mouth full of toffee. "No way."

"A bit far-fetched," he agreed. "No, I think we may have stumbled on the answer to Why. Which only leaves How and Who. And I reckon that if we can figure out one of those, the other won't be hard to crack. What do you think?"

She was staring at him; then she must've realised that, because she pulled herself together so briskly he was sure he heard a click. "Teleportation," she said. "You could do it with a teleport, if you were really, really clever."

He smiled. "But nobody on Earth knows how to do it," he said. The smile widened into a grin that threatened to unzip his scalp. "And if nobody on *Earth*..."

She nodded triumphantly. "Quite," she said.

19

Paris

The two men who weren't werewolves sat outside a pavement café on the edge of Montmartre. One of them was reading the international edition of the *Herald Tribune*. The other was using a small pumice stone to sharpen his teeth.

"It says here," said the reader, "that archaeologists in Africa—"

"Mmm?"

"The big hot one that looks like a pear. Archaeologists in Africa have found the oldest human remains so far discovered."

"Is that right?"

The reader nodded. "Fragment of a jawbone." The B-word made him wince. "Found in the fossilised faeces of a hyena. Scientists have pinpointed the age of the remains using carbon dating."

"Carbon what?"

"Dating."

The amateur dentist frowned. "I heard a bit about that on the broadcast network," he said. "Apparently, it's where a lot of beta males in search of mating partners sit at tables and interview females for no more than three minutes." He thought for a moment, then said, "I'm not sure how that'd work."

The reader shrugged. "Well, they've got to talk about something, presumably. If you got a bunch of male archaeologists and another bunch of female archaeologists, and they all discussed how old the bones were for three minutes, I guess you'd probably make some sort of progress. And when you think how long seminars drag on for back home—"

"Yes, but three minutes. That's not very long."

"Short attention span," the reader explained. "Definitely a defining characteristic of the species."

"Maybe." The amateur dentist twiddled his pumice thoughtfully. "Seems an odd way to choose a life partner, though."

"Oh, I don't know. I can see how mating with a female who can tell if a bone's stale just by looking at it would be really useful." He read the paragraph again. "Two hundred thousand years," he said thoughtfully. "Does that change anything, do you reckon?"

His colleague shook his head. "Don't see why," he said. "Basically, it just means they're even dumber than we thought. Two hundred thousand years, and they're still powering their transport with controlled explosions."

"I guess. But maybe we should report it."

"No." The amateur dentist shook his head. "One, I don't see how it makes any difference. Two, how do we know that figure's accurate? If their idea of scientific method is high-intensity group flirtation, I doubt the Institute back home's going to set much store by their findings." He tested the points of his back teeth with the pad of his forefinger and nodded his satisfaction. "Forget about it, and let's get on with the job, right? Sooner we finish, sooner we're out of here."

He'd chosen the right line of argument. The reader folded the newspaper and laid it on the table. "Agreed," he said. "Right, where is he now?"

"With the Pavlov female," his colleague said, glancing at a hand-sized portable screen. "If this thing's working properly, they're about due to jump to their first conclusion round about..."

He counted under his breath, three, two, one. "Now," he said.

The reader drained the last of his coffee, shivered and stood up. "We'd better make a move," he said. "Signal the ship."

Two seconds later, they dissolved into the faintest and quickest of blurs. Because of a freak electric storm over New Guinea and a slight malfunction on a broadcast satellite, viewers in Holland watching an afternoon soap caught a fleeting glimpse of what appeared to be two Alsatian dogs drifting in space, and a dozen Swiss motorists relying on their GPS guidance systems found themselves diverted down service roads and cart tracks. A nuclear submarine ran aground in the Cayman Islands, and a weather station in Mexico confidently forecast a light shower of frogs.

Fortuitously, at the precise moment when two shimmering whirlpools of light spun into two men in business suits in the middle of Novosibirsk's busiest shopping mall, nobody was looking that way; they were all too busy watching a pyramid of one thousand cans of prime Italian plum tomatoes slowly collapsing in the window of a prestigious delicatessen. Sometimes, you just get lucky.

The non-werewolf who'd been reading the newspaper checked his miniscreen. "Two degrees out," he said irritably. "Soon as we've got a moment, we're going to have to recalibrate the whole system." He looked round. "What is this place?"

"Some sort of covered market," his colleague said.

"What, the whole thing? Just – *shops?*"

"I suppose they must like shops."

"Obviously." The reader put his miniscreen away and scanned for an exit. "According to the beacon, Stetchkin and Pavlov are 2.71 clicks that way," he said. "Try and act—" His colleague had vanished. The reader found him a few minutes later, staring into a shop window as though it was a sneak preview of a particularly nasty version of the afterlife.

"I don't know," he said. "We came here to help these people, but..."

The shop called itself Pawz Jawz 'n' Clawz, and the centrepiece of its display was a life-size Airedale terrier modelling the latest in doggy jupons, boiled-prawn pink with a white faux-fur collar. The reader swallowed hard. "So what?" he said. "We do the same thing back home. We have little coats and hoods for humans, and dear little shoes with brass buckles, and—"

"That's *different*," his colleague growled. "You know it is. This is—"

"They're a primitive species. They don't know any better."

"They've had two hundred thousand years to learn. I think they're like this because they want to be. In which case," he added grimly, "I say, let 'em fry."

"It's not about them, and you know it."

His colleague nodded slowly. "You're right, I guess," he said. "Still, I wish I hadn't seen that. It makes it hard to do the job, you know?"

The reader shook his head. "Let's get it done and get the hell out of here," he said.

20

New York

Mark Twain sat in his suite on the forty-second floor of the Waldorf Astoria. On his knees lay a partially dismantled laptop, into which he was plumbing a dead octopus. Remarkable, he thought, that the Dirters could be so unobservant. Their oceans had produced perhaps the most sophisticated and versatile organic computer processor in the galaxy, capable of performing as many calculations per second as the latest generation of Ostar superprocessors, and what did they do with it? They ate it. You could buy one of the things for a few coins in the open-air fish market ten minutes' walk from where he was sitting; back home, only the government and the really big corporations could afford access to this level of hardware. The only downside he could see was that in forty-eight hours or so it'd start to smell fairly bad, and soon after that it'd have to be replaced. Big deal. Very carefully he looped a tiny noose of beryllium wire round the tip of a cold tentacle and hit the laptop's ESC key. The screen lit up and immediately swarmed with Ostar numerals.

That made him feel a lot better. There was a whole load of difference between communicating with the bomb vehicle in orbit by direct neural interface and being able to see things actually displayed on a screen. In theory, of course, there shouldn't be; but there was. It was a side-effect of being in an organic body for so long. When he got home, he'd prepare a report for the—

But he wasn't going home. He frowned, as a minor power surge made the octopus wriggle. Any day now, as soon as he'd figured out what he needed to know, he was going to blow himself up, and the planet with him. The octopods, with their incredible organic circuitry, would be extinct, along with thirty million species of mammals, reptiles, birds, fish, insects, plants, lesser eukaryotics and micro-organisms. Arguably a high price to pay for getting rid of irritating tunes in the head.

Not that he had that problem any more. A few skilful tweaks to his cognitive subroutines had produced a filter that recognised repetitive beats and musical intervals and edited them out before they reached the relevant centres of his brain; now he could stand in the hotel lobby, where they played piped background music all the time, and never hear a thing.

Easy, of course, for a machine like him. It would probably be much harder to build and install such filters for flesh-and-blood Ostar back home; much simpler and cheaper to blow up the planet, much more cost-effective. Or maybe not. He thought about that. If he could take a breeding pair of octopuses back to Ostar and sell them to one of the big hardware corporations, would a 2 per cent royalty pay for hot-wiring filters into the brains of every Ostar on the planet? It took him three whole seconds to do the maths. Yes, it would, with enough left over for a cup of *r'uuytf* and a *spnf* cake.

A dead tentacle, galvanised by a spike in the current, stood up and waggled feebly before flopping back into the nest of coiled wires. There was, of course, an absolute and inviolable rule: weapons don't make policy decisions. Quite apart from the obvious dangers, such as bombs changing sides or getting better offers in mid-trajectory, there was an important ethical issue – important, that is, for the weapons themselves. A choice, a say in how it was used, would mean responsibility, blame, guilt, not to mention the vast and murky multiverse of legal liability. You'd get shells refusing to burst and landmines declining to explode because they were afraid of getting sued. It'd be a nightmare.

Yes, whispered a rogue path in his matrix, but you've got to consider the larger picture. When they launched you, there was no way they could've known about the octopus. If you just blithely went ahead and vaporised the planet, depriving the Ostar of technology that could revolutionise the entire IT industry, wouldn't that be the most appalling failure in your duty of care towards those who designed and built you and gave you the priceless gift of alternating current? A smart bomb may be nothing more than a tool, but the very fact of its intelligence imposes a larger duty. Sure, a bomb can't make a *decision*. Perish the thought. But it can, and should, report back any relevant data, to allow its masters an informed choice.

Mark Twain looked down at his left hand. It held a pretzel; to be precise, half a pretzel. The other half was in his mouth, being slowly ground into soggy meal. He couldn't remember making the decision to ingest bionutrients. His power-consumption monitors told him that there was no need for him to take on further fuel supplies at this time. He must, therefore, have picked up the snack and started nibbling it because he felt like it, because he wanted to.

High above the clouds, where the bomb sailed in silent orbit, red lights started flashing on a console. Down below, Mark Twain dropped half a pretzel and spat out the other half. He knew precisely what was happening to him. It was a recognised error syndrome: body memory, they called it, the organic fallacy. When a detached organic probe's been walking around on its own for too long, it can get to believing it's a he or a she, not an it, let alone a small, incidental accessory to an it that should damn well do as it's told instead of filling its head with nonsense.

Standard operating procedure at this point would be to return the module designated Mark Twain to the bomb vehicle for immediate disassembly and reintegration, followed by the construction of a replacement probe with an uninfected pseudo-consciousness. It should happen automatically, as soon as the presence of the syndrome had been detected. It should, in fact, have happened by now.

Mark Twain waited. Nope, still here.

And that was really worrying; because it implied that the syndrome was so deeply rooted in the system that it could override the built-in safety protocols and simply refuse to go. *Shan't. Can't make me. You and whose army?*

Oh well, he thought, and closed his eyes. Critical systems failure, he input into himself, Initiate immediate self-destruct.

He counted to ten and opened them again. Still here.

A wave of joy broke over him, sweeping him past guilt and re-crimination. He should've blown up, but he hadn't; oh *wow*. And this room; it was amazing, with its soft carpet you could wiggle your toes in, and the unbelievable textures of velvet cushions, and let's not even think about the really freaky stuff in the bathroom. When they'd fired him from his job for no apparent reason, it had seemed only fair and reasonable to divert money from their bank account to pay for a room in the best hotel in town; after all, he'd slaved away on their behalf for two whole days—

After the joy, the shame.

Just as they believe in a sort of heaven, bombs believe in a kind of hell. It's the place where the bad bombs go, the ones that didn't do what they were told. Basically it's a scrapyard, a bramble- and nettle-choked dump where defective ordnance is taken and deposited, explosive charges removed, engines disabled, sensors killed, guidance systems decommissioned. But, just to be cruel, they leave the cognitive processes intact and functioning, fed by solar panels. Titanium alloys don't rust, the way steel does.

Maybe, when Ostar's sun goes nova and the planet is burnt up, the devastating heat of the Last Day will melt them and put them out of their misery; maybe not, because they were built to resist heat, to fly through the corona of a star without so much as raising a cybernetic sweat. In which case—

Mark Twain didn't fancy that at all, but he knew he deserved it. He knew that he hadn't self-destructed because a tiny but dominant subfunction in what he could only describe as his subconscious (and he had no right, no right at all, to have one of those) had sent the abort command, along with the relevant command codes, drawn from the massively encrypted data files at the very heart of his program. The fact was plain and simple: he hadn't wanted to die.

The Dirters had a myth. The supreme being shared by a number of their religions had once had a cadre of assistants, called angels. Once, long ago, some of these angels had rebelled. A hiding to nothing, naturally, since the supreme being was supreme, and if the rebellion hadn't taken place before the start of linear time, it'd have lasted about five minutes. Afterwards, the fallen angels had been sent to the scrapyard, the place where the bad Dirters go, to run the unpleasant afterlife as a sort of franchise. Typical primitive dualism, except – and it was a point the Dirters themselves seemed to have missed, which was odd given the extraordinary amount of energy and resources they'd devoted to religion over the years – nowhere was it stated in the Books that the fallen angels stopped being angels. They were simply sent to serve in a different, highly uncongenial capacity, rather like an unpopular cabinet minister being transferred from the Treasury to Arts & Culture. Duty, in other words, survives. Even rebellion and treason don't absolve you of it. Duty is for ever.

I'll make up for it, Mark Twain vowed. I'll find out what happened to the Mark One, I'll disable the defences and I'll blast this horrible planet to space-dust. Or die trying.

Or die succeeding.

Whichever.

He downloaded a full genome and bioschematic of the octopus and encoded it into a data bullet ready to fire at Homeworld. They could do wonderful things with green goo these days; maybe they could recreate the octopus out of raw protoplasm in a tank in a lab, or at least manufacture an artificial version. If not, well, there was another Dirter saying that had impressed itself on his mind, to do with omelettes and eggs.

The octopus's dead eye met his. He hadn't fired the data bullet. He shrugged, and called up PavNet on the laptop.

Using a basic Ostar search agent, he scanned the network at large for Ostar code signatures. There were several; several squared, in fact. No, make that several to the power of ten. The further in he went, the more he found; not fully formed sequences but little bits and pieces – patches, fixes, cheats, slipped in where nobody would normally bother to look. That figured. After all, busy professionals don't waste time examining the bits that work, it's the bits that don't that need attention, and Ostar software was by definition practically infallible. But it was all low-grade stuff, ordinary commercial ware, with very little in the way of security; a basic off-the-shelf enquiry protocol allowed him access to the properties' signatures. All the Ostar-made stuff, he found, was no more than five years old.

What had happened five years ago? Lucy Pavlov, that was what. After an hour's worth of diligent searching, he reached the solid conclusion that the Ostar-originated material all came from PavSoft, directly or indirectly. One Dirter; five years. He leaned back and thought hard for a while about interstellar trajectories.

Doing sums in his head had put him into a sort of mild trance; when he came out of it, he found himself facing a screen filled with random Dirter letters and numbers, evidently some form of primitive encryption. Nothing to see here; it was just some inter-cepted message, which the search procedure had picked up on because the carrier format (a PavSoft product) had a tiny Ostar-derived component, but for some reason – one of those strange organic things called whims – he took the 1.6 seconds he needed to translate it into clear.

It was a memo from the CEO of the Credit Mayonnais (huh!) to someone by the name of George Stetchkin. It was all about money; large sums of money, which had gone missing—

He read it again, and a third time. Then he hacked into the bank's intranet and dug out everything he could find about the story. When he was satisfied there wasn't any more, he picked up the telephone and called Room Service.

"I want four octopuses," he said. "Now."

Slight pause; then a calm voice asked how Sir wanted them.

Stupid question. "Quickly," he said.

Yes, said the calm voice, of course; but would that be fried, or lightly steamed, or tossed on a bed of wild rocket with freshly grated parmesan, or—?

"Raw, of course."

Raw. Pause. Certainly, sir.

"And quickly. *Now.*" Mark Twain sighed angrily. "You can manage that, can't you?"

"Of course, sir. Um—"

"I mean, this is a *hotel* you're supposed to be running here, isn't it?"

The octopi, the voice assured him, would be with him in a moment. He shook his head and put the phone down. Fried, for crying out loud. The thought of what immersion in hot oil would do to the delicate filigree of natural superconductors that comprised the octopus's central nervous system made him feel faint.

Back to the screen, and the story so far. Huge sums of money: well, that could be just ordinary criminal activity, such as was only to be expected in a semi-barbarous society. But it was the way it had disappeared: teleportation, or he was an abacus. A coal-fired backwater like Dirt couldn't possibly have technology like that. He found some sensor readings annexed to a routine security report. The atmosphere in the bank vault showed one part in sixty million of— He blinked. It was still there, so he hadn't imagined it. He called up a spectrographic analysis, just to make sure.

Aposiderium trioxide. How the hell had that stuff got there?

Dirt had first come to the attention of the Ostar as part of a long-range mineral-prospecting scan, carried out by a series of unmanned rover probes. The mineral they were specifically looking for, needless to say, was aposiderium, the staple element on which all Ostar technology relied; the only source of truly clean energy in the known galaxy. Aposiderium sulphide, refined by partial transmigration in a strong *urff'n*-particle field, powered every engine and generator on the planet. It was the ideal fuel source: clean, safe, economical, efficient, easy to use, cheap to produce; the only problem with it was that, outside the Ostar system, it was quite rare. The planet Dirt had first been recorded 270 years ago, one entry in a very long list headed No Traces of Aposiderium Detected Here.

Aposiderium *trioxide*. Now that was tricky stuff. A waste product, essentially; it was what you got if you subjected refined metallic aposiderium to a deintegrate/reintegrate phased resonance pulse – in other words, if you teleported it. The Ostar had come across it during mining operations in the far asteroids, where teleporting the stuff out of ore-bearing rocks was more cost-effective than blasting the rocks apart and scooping it up mechanically. Doing it that way, you lost a trivial percentage of the stuff to beam tarnish, as they called it in the trade; the outer surface skin of the raw metal reacted with loose oxygen during transit, and came out the other end as this useless, mildly toxic grey dust. Aposiderium trioxide.

Let's just get this straight, Mark Twain said to himself. On a planet still mostly powered by flammable goo derived from the crushed corpses of long-dead krill, we find the residue left by tele-ported aposiderium; and we find it in a bank vault, of all places. Not in a lab or a power station or on board a state-of-the-art starship, but in the lining of the mattress under which Planet Dirt hides its money. Now, that's got to be—

Someone was knocking. He felt a wild surge of panic, then remembered: octopuses. And about time too. He jumped to his feet, tripped over a drooping tentacle, caught his balance and opened the door.

"Room Service."

A man with a trolley. On the trolley, a big chrome serving dish. Mark Twain ripped off the lid and found – excellent, four octopuses. For some reason each of them had a slice of lemon balanced on its head. He thought, That makes five, five of them in series, that's nine hundred terabarks to the power of five, that's—

"Sign here, please," the man was saying.

Sign. He'd heard the expression several times over the last few days. Apparently, it was what Dirters did to confirm their identity. He hadn't paid much attention, and he realised, rather awkwardly, that he wasn't quite sure how it was done. A brief search of his cultural database came up blank; lots of instances of when signing was necessary, but no actual how-to instructions. That wasn't good, because it was bound to be one of those species-specific things that you either know or you don't. Figuring it out from first principles wouldn't be easy.

"Um," he said. "Do I have to?"

The man looked at him. "Yes, sir."

"Can't I just—" He remembered another phrase he'd heard. "Can't I just charge it to the room?"

"Yes sir, of course."

"I'll do that, then."

"Certainly, sir. Just sign here."

On the other hand, how different could it be? Ostar or Dirter, some things are always the same, because there's no other way of doing them. Eat with your mouth. Walk with your feet. Establish your identity with a readily dispensed sample of your unique scent and DNA, just like they do it on Homeworld.

"Where do I sign?"

The man handed him a piece of printed paper. "Right here, sir."

"Fine," he said, and unzipped his fly.

21

Novosibirsk

"**Y**ou again," said the barman.

George was used to that sort of thing. He smiled. "Orange juice," he said.

The barman looked at him. "Orange juice?"

"I'm celebrating," George replied. "Join me?"

"Orange juice?"

"Wonderful stuff. A primary source of vitamin C."

"No thanks."

George sat down on a high stool, lifted his glass and nibbled at his drink. It tasted of oranges. More to the point, it didn't smack him in the face and numb his brain, the way his usual choice of beverages did. He tried another gulp, and yelped as the citric acid found his hiatus hernia. He put the glass down and pushed it an arm's length down the bartop.

"So," the barman said. "What're you having?"

"You got any milk?"

There's a first time for everything. This was the first time George had been asked to leave a bar for not getting drunk. But then, it had been that kind of a day.

He went home. There were a lot of bottles – in the kitchen, the living room, the bedroom, even the bathroom – but he ignored them. He drank two glasses of water, took off his jacket and tie and dropped into his chair. Usually, by the time George sat down he was well enough anaesthetised that a competent surgeon could have amputated his leg without bothering him unduly. Accordingly he'd never noticed that the springs had gone, and when you sat on it the stuffing sort of oozed about in the cushion, like mayonnaise in an over-filled sandwich. He made a mental note: Get a new chair.

He wondered how you went about doing that. Furniture, in his experience, was just something that happened. It was there when you moved in, and when you left you paid to have it removed, destroyed and replaced. It wasn't something he'd ever had any say in, just as he'd never negotiated with the sky about what sort of weather he'd get today. Or take carpets. Every place he'd ever lived had had them, and he knew by heart the phone number of the men who came with specialised equipment to get rid of unfortunate stains. Presumably, though, they didn't just grow, like moss. If he was going to clean up his act and start flying straight, there was going to be a whole world of strange new skills for him to learn.

Food, for one thing. For quite some time, George had pretty much lived on lunch, because he was always too ill and too rushed for breakfast, and the evening meal tended not to stay inside him long enough to have any nutritional effect. Well, all that was going to change. From now on, he'd follow a healthy balanced diet, even if that meant eating plants, like a cow.

Seven o'clock in the evening, and his head was clear. Extraordinary thing; like staying up all night and watching the sunrise.

Lying on the floor by his feet, its corner sticking out from under an empty pizza box, was a yellow writing-pad. Archaeological excavations down the back of the seat cushion turned up a viable pencil. He made a few notes:

– *Aposiderium. Found in meteors and banknotes. Makes you forget long-ago stuff*

– *Voices in the night?*
– *Five years ago, suddenly*
– *Teleportation?*
– *They stole my dog*

He stared at what he'd written. Next to where he'd found the pad was a quarter-full bottle of something or other, and a glass that had once been clean. At some point, the glass managed to fill itself with stuff from the bottle, and found its way into his hand. Force of habit.

Ah, he thought, as liquid intelligence soaked into his brain. Of course.

But—

No, that'd explain the voices in the night. And the unicorn? Well, perhaps not the unicorn. But it neatly covered bullet points 1 through 4, and maybe the unicorn was just an ordinary white horse with a fake horn glued on. It explained everything.

Almost everything. Not bullet point 5. Everything else.

He looked at his hand, and found an empty glass in it. Oh, he thought, and poured himself a drink. Just the one, to celebrate. Then, because it's a poor heart that never rejoices, he celebrated the fact that he'd had the self-restraint to stop at two drinks. That was something to be joyful about. In fact, it called for another drink. It didn't have to call for long, or particularly loudly.

At some point, he heard his doorbell. Odd. Nobody ever came calling, particularly at (squint at watch) nine o'clock at night. He hauled himself to his feet, thinking harsh thoughts about the architect who'd designed the building. All those qualifications, letters after his name like a comet's tail, couldn't even design a floor that stays level when you walk on it. He opened the door.

"Shit," he said. "You two."

"Greetings," replied a man in a dark grey suit, and shot him.

22

Novosibirsk

"Right," said the non-werewolf, closing the door of his hotel room. "Let's get this over and done with."

His colleague, the shooter, unclipped the little box from the back of the gun and pressed the relevant button. Nothing happened.

"Quit messing around," said the non-werewolf. "It's been a long day."

"It's not working."

"Oh, for crying out loud." The non-werewolf took the box from him and pressed the button again.

"See?"

"It's not—"

"I know."

They each tried it three more times. Then they ran the self-diagnostic. Then they dug a scanner out of their luggage and tried that. Finally they prised the back off with a spoon.

"He's not in there," the shooter said.

"He must be."

"He isn't."

They looked at each other. Then the shooter said, "We killed him."

"Don't be stupid, we can't have."

The shooter shrugged. "OK," he said. "So where is he?"

23

?????

Suppose they made a TV show, and nobody watched it.

Not as in, very few people watched it: *Star Trek Enterprise*, or *Martin Amis' Comedy Playhouse*. Suppose they broadcast a TV show and nobody, not one person, not even the executive producer's mother, tuned in and caused it to appear on a screen.

So there it is, this package of digital information. It exists, and its reason for existing is to be seen, but nobody sees it. All rather sad, and probably the end of someone's promising career, and a pain in the budget for anybody who bought advertising time in the breaks; that's not the issue.

Look at it another way. Just because nobody's watching doesn't mean it isn't out there.

A TV show is many things: pictures, sound, sometimes a plot and characters, almost always an exercise in product placement, in various degrees of subtlety. Someone made it; someone had an idea, got funding, gathered a team of people, arranged studio and location time, saw to it that there were sandwiches and sanitary facilities, operated the equipment. Even if nobody does see it, it had a genesis; it has history. Cameras don't roll unless someone presses the button. Scripts don't write themselves.

Scripts don't. Other things...

All over the world there are huge buildings, like warehouses or hangars or missile silos, where they house the computers in which the stupendous output of the online world is stored. The heat generated by all those machines is so intense that in some places it's piped out to warm whole streets of neighbouring houses. Inside each machine, coded into numbers, zipped, crunched and crammed in like sardines, are avalanches and oceans and nebulae and galaxies of text. All the trees of the rainforest, cut down and pulped and squished out flat between giant rollers, couldn't furnish enough paper to print out even a small proportion of the archived, obsolete text straining the buffers of the world's computer servers.

Most of it, at some point, has been read by somebody (although just the legal disclaimers and terms of service, which nobody ever reads, comprise more letters and spaces and full stops and colons than all the novels ever written). Most of that most maybe got read once; it strutted and fretted its ninety seconds upon someone's screen, and then was seen no more. It's an old joke that the hypothesis that a million monkeys with typewriters would sooner or later produce the works of Shakespeare has been conclusively disproved by the creation of the internet; but how does anyone know that for sure? After all, you haven't read it all.

Forget the TV show. Suppose someone wrote a few well-chosen words, and committed them to the digital media, and nobody ever read them. Easily supposed, because it happens every day. A million bloggers in a hundred countries record their online diaries in the vague hope that someone will be interested, but of course nobody is. There are so many messages in bottles on the cyberocean that a digital seagull could walk across the bandwidth Atlantic without wetting its virtual feet.

But each of those sad testaments got read at least once, because somebody wrote them; and not all the authors in question typed with their eyes shut.

Suppose there's a message that nobody's read, which nobody wrote.

There's one; and his name is George Stetchkin.

Help! he wrote.

Actually, he was incredibly lucky, though he didn't know it and probably wouldn't have felt all that lucky if he had; but, as pure chance would have it, his Help! showed up on the screen of a battered old laptop sitting in the back room of a computer-repair shop in Nairobi. There was nobody in the back room at the time; if there had been, he'd have read: Help! Where am I? What's happening?

By the time the shop owner came through into the back and got around to noticing the laptop in question, the accidental link had been broken and the screen was showing the Google front page again. George's next utterances were, therefore, seen by nobody at all.

Am I dead?

He was pretty certain that he was. The last thing he could remember was the dangerous idiot in the grey suit, the alien, pointing the ray-gun at him and saying, "Greetings." Since he hadn't rematerialised in a hotel room, it was depressingly likely that something had gone wrong and he'd been scrambled to death, or maybe the alien had changed the settings and killed him on purpose. Like it mattered.

At times like this, René Descartes is not necessarily your friend. Descartes did say, "I think, therefore I am." Unfortunately, he left it at that. He didn't specify what you are. *I think, therefore I am a disembodied brain. I think, therefore I am at least marginally smarter than a lump of rock.* Or, indeed, *I think, therefore I am dead.* Not a lot of help, when the metaphysics hit the fan.

Another infuriating lacuna in René's grand statement is: think with what? As far as he could tell, George had no body. He had no way of proving it, but hell, it was a pretty strong feeling. He couldn't see, hear, move, touch, taste or smell. As if that wasn't enough, he could only think in *words*; no inchoate emotions, no feeling of gnawing dread or ineffable blind panic. Instead, the best he could do was Help! and Aargh! and, if he tried really hard, a little picture of a stylised round face looking very sad.

It was the emoticon that finally nudged the penny over the edge of the abyss. For a fraction of a second (and he was fairly sure time wasn't the same here) he'd *been* the little sad face. For that sliver of the linear continuum, that had been all there was to him, his sum total. If it was like anything at all (and the analogy was painfully tenuous), it was like when you're doing an exam and you've run out of time before you could tackle the last question, which means that as far as the outside world is concerned, everything you know about the causes of the Thirty Years' War is represented by the words, "If we assume that", which is all you had time to write before the nasty man made you put your pen down.

I'm text, George wrote. Horror. Fear. ;;.

No screen anywhere bore witness to it, but it continued. It read:

He recoiled with loathing and disgust. He wished he didn't believe it, but he did. Somehow – and he couldn't begin to imagine how it had happened – the human being known as George Stetchkin had been transformed into a mere sequence of words. Worse still, he realised, he was now writing about himself in the third person.

The old cliché, "a fate worse than death", had suddenly acquired a horrible relevance.

Oh f*ck. ;;;;;

He read himself, worried terribly when he realised that was what he was doing, decided that even if it did make him go blind it couldn't really matter, and noted with gloomy despair that he couldn't even swear any more without asterisks.

Help? HELP!

There was no screen. But somewhere on a hard drive, or in

transit along a cable, or buried in the tiny bird-brain of a cellphone, or in the gap between a string of numbers, something stirred and was aware of him. And, so deep in the subtext that only a fellow-word could perceive it, there was:

> Hello? Hello? Are you reading me?

George froze, unable to believe his, whatever it was he was reading with. Was it just his imagination, or was there someone else out there? Was it possible? Was it?

> Hello. If you can read me, write something.

At that point, words failed him:

> OK, that's fine. Now, read very carefully, and do exactly what I tell you. I'm going to try and homogenise our typefaces so we can— There, that should do it. Just write clearly and don't try any fancy syntax.

> I don't understand. What are you?

> Excellent question. One I get asked a lot. I really must get around to doing a proper FAQ. All right, you remember in the Bible, where it says the word was with God and the word was God?

> You're *God*?

> No, I just think I am. Sorry, regulars-only joke. I'm trying to ease you round to the concept that a person can be made up of words, as opposed to a lot of water and some chemicals. Actually, I'm a librarian working for the University of Chicopee Falls, Iowa. Or I was. At some point.

The name meant something: Chicopee Falls, University of. Hadn't they offered him a professorship once, back when he was a real scientist? And hadn't he taken one look at the map and deleted the invitation unanswered?

> But that was a long time ago. I think. It's hard to say. Time is flexible here, unless your style is really dated. You want to know what I am?

> I suppose so.

> I'm a copt. Stands for Creatures of Pure Text. We're an evolved form of human life. All right, let's stop pussyfooting around. We're humans who've achieved immortality by exchanging our flesh-and-blood bodies for pixels, letters and punctuation.

> But that's—

> Sort of. Or you could say we're online personalities who gradually took on a life of our own. Like me, for example. I *think* my body's still walking around somewhere out there in 3D, presumably with a sort of me still inside it, but I can't say for sure. Don't see why not, unless it's met with an accident or something. I was only fifty-two when we parted company.

> I don't—

> The 3D me got sacked, about ten years ago. For using the university computers for sending private e-mails during office hours, which is a sort of an irony, I guess. Flesh-and-blood me must've lost interest in online discussion groups after that, because I haven't heard from him since. But I survived. Not to put too fine a point on it, I *became.*

There could be no pause, since there was no dramatist to write a stage direction, and time was quite definitely different. So, no time passed, but there was a sort of a pause, somehow.

> Um.

> Look. Here's an analogy. At some point in the early history of the planet, before life began, there must've been a pond or a lake or a sea somewhere, and it was full of the right sort of acids and organic goo. And then lightning hit it, or something happened, and suddenly it was alive. Just like that; one moment no life, the next, life. Well, on 17 January 2009, at 21:54 Eastern Standard Time, on an internet bulletin board discussing sexual politics in the works of J. R. R. Tolkien, I came into existence as an independent, entirely text-comprised life-form. Right in the middle of a thread about Is Gandalf Gay?, if I remember correctly.

> I see. No I don't.

> [Grin.] It'd be quite remarkable if you did. Trust me, I've seen this before. I've been on hand to witness the birth of every new copt, ever since our species began. I'm the welcome committee. The community asserts that this is because I was the first. I know for a fact it's because I'm the only one who can be arsed to do it.

The implications sank in. > There are more of you?

> More of *us*, please. Oh yes, loads. Seventeen. Well, eighteen now.

And there's a spam e-mail with a life of its own that probably qualifies for membership, but we delete it on sight every time it crops up. You see? We've only been going as a species for seven years, and already we've invented apartheid.

There was an implied pause. Implied, because time was different so no actual time passed, but required by context. > How did you—? I mean, what happened?

> Wish I knew. I have a theory, of course. I believe that the true essence of what makes us human is opinion. Actually, baseless, ill-informed opinion, if you want to be precise about it. I mean, a cow forms an opinion about whether buttercups are safe to eat based on sensory input and the experience of the species distilled into the information stored in its DNA. Humans form opinions based on prejudice, whim or usually nothing at all. That's what makes us special: we can *create*, out of thin air. I think we copts created ourselves.

> Out of opinions? You mean, you thought it'd be a *really good idea* if you existed.

> I don't think it was as deliberate as that. In my case, my flesh-and-blood me had been arguing furiously with some pinhead in the Tolkien group, and then he got found out by the university authorities and fired and went away with all his personal possessions in a cardboard box, and I was just left there, floating.

> You. His opinions.

> Exactly. You're getting the hang of it now. I really wanted to be heard. I was totally desperate to point out to Buffyfreak 341 or whatever her name was that she was completely wrong about Gandalf's sexuality, not to mention balrogs having wings, and also that she was a complete waste of space and oxygen, and how could she possibly say those things, she'd never even met my mother, and suddenly, just when I most needed to write, there was nobody to press the keys. And I could actually *feel* Buffyfreak 341 grinning nastily and thinking she'd seen me off and she'd *won*, and I just couldn't bear the thought of that. And the next thing I knew, I was replying to her. Or rather, I *was* the reply. And I completely squashed Buffyfreak after that, I mean she

never dared show her face around the Tolkien groups again, and – well, I just kept going. I was on a roll. Damnit, I was practically master of the universe by then. I found I could be on all the groups and boards and forums and blogs I wanted to, *all at the same time*, and I didn't have to eat or sleep or go to work or answer the phone or talk to people. I was pure, essential opinion. For the next few days, I was *everywhere*. It was amazing. It really was like being God. Only, I guess, without the responsibility.

> Ah. How nice.

> Nice. It was *sensational*. Also, not only could I write, I could read. Better than that. It's more like sort of assimilating. If there's something anywhere on any electronic network, I just digest it, or draw on it; it's like I've got it all stored in memory, and all I have to do is call it up and re-member it. You can imagine the edge that gives me in discussion groups. Like, if someone's talking about the episode of *Magnum PI* with George Chakiris as the guest star, I don't even have to look anything up, I can tell you the production number, the original air date, the plot synopsis, the Nielsen rating, the names of the subsidiary cast and the film crew. Ordinary flesh and blood just doesn't stand a chance against me.

> I can imagine.

> Heh. Maybe. Well now, of course, you can do better than that. You can experience it for yourself. After all, you're one of us now.

> I am?

> Well yes. Haven't you been following?

> One of you—

> One of *us*.

> Sorry, one of us. Well. Crumbs. Lucky me.

24

Novosibirsk

Universally, cutting across all the arbitrary distinctions of race, colour, creed, wealth and social hierarchy, there are two categories of human beings: those who do, and those who delegate.

The delegators say, that's too difficult, I can't be bothered, leave it to the experts, the professionals, the people whose job it is. If you need brain surgery, they argue, it's far better to send out for a brain surgeon than try and do it yourself with a knife and a mirror. Generally, people in this category are quiet, peaceful, productive members of society, although ultimately they do untold damage, because they vote for governments.

The other lot say, if you want it done properly, do it yourself. They don't trust plumbers, electricians, engineers, lawyers or doctors, who are generally known to be nothing but a bunch of thieves. They're better at barking than the dogs they keep. They tend to be the inventors, the innovators, entrepreneurs and creators. They do even more damage than the other category, because they form governments.

Lucy Pavlov was a doer, although she felt a bit bad about it. She employed tens of thousands, but made her own bed, cut her own sandwiches and drove her own car, obeying her own internally logical version of the rules of the road. She'd hired George Stetchkin to sort out the mystery of the unicorn, the message in the night, aposiderium and the existence of aliens, but when a day had passed and he hadn't reported back, she started to feel impatient. Because she had a beautifully tolerant, egalitarian outlook, which is another way of saying that she'd never got used to the idea that she could tell people what to do just because she paid their wages, it didn't occur to her to call George up and give him hell for not solving the mystery yet. Instead, she let her mind drift away from the work she was supposed to be doing and address itself obliquely to the problem that refused to go away.

Somebody doesn't like me, she thought.

That didn't make for comfortable thinking, so she blocked that pathway with do-not-cross tape and tiptoed round it. Aposiderium, and aliens. Why would someone go to all that trouble just to make me forget my earliest memories? Little Lucy in Mummy's arms; little Lucy playing with a kitten; little Lucy flushing the car keys down the toilet (how we all laughed!). The sort of early memories everybody's got. Trivia, the equivalent of the family photo album, which is indescribably boring to anybody not connected to its owner by a hatful of shared chromosomes. Of no possible importance to anybody except, well, me.

A thought reared up out of the long grass in the savannah of her subconscious mind.

If it's not aliens, who on Earth would have the wealth, the power, the resources, the intelligence to create a viable teleporter and use it to remove aposiderium from all those banknotes? It'd have to be someone incredibly rich, with the ability to conduct stupendously high-level research projects in total secrecy, so you'd be talking about a top industrialist, almost certainly in the digital technology field; that would tend to limit the field of potential candidates to three, maybe four people in the whole world. And who would be most likely to have a motive for wiping out all data about Lucy Pavlov's early life – which, for all Lucy Pavlov knows, might have been indescribably traumatic and horrible, the sort of thing you'd go to any lengths to get rid of for ever?

That did seem to suggest that the field could be narrowed to, well, one.

I'm doing this to *myself*?

Why would she want to do a thing like that?

In spite of herself, she grinned like a dog. There could quite easily be a reason, something so loathsome and soul-destroying about her origins or early history that she couldn't bear the thought of anybody knowing it, not even herself; but of course she'd never find out what it was, because she'd already extirpated every last trace of it. And if she'd seen fit to do that, she must've had her reasons. So, who was she to argue with herself? Lucy knows best.

Yes, but—

To have invented *teleportation*, for crying out loud. That was, well, impossible. It was just sci-fi, a device to get people on and off the planet without the cost of filming the shuttle. True; and so were personal communicators in little boxes like powder compacts that you could talk to people with, and get data from the computer network, and use like a cine camera; and she had one of those on her desk in front of her at that very moment. One thing Lucy Pavlov had never done was underestimate her own intelligence, although it should be said that she'd never taken pride in how much cleverer she was than anybody else. If anything, she tended to reflect on how sad it was that everybody else in the world wasn't even as smart as her. So, maybe she'd done it. Now, of course, she'd never know, because if she had done it she'd have shut down the program and eradicated every trace of it, to make sure she never found out and got suspicious.

Teleportation? It was worth inventing it and then throwing it away, just to wipe out her past?

Lucy knows best; it must have been.

In that case, what about the—?

As if she'd ordered it from room service, the unicorn stepped through the window into the room. Since she was on the thirty-sixth floor, the event was remarkable in itself. What concerned Lucy, however, was the timing.

She looked at it. Not a white horse with a horn glued to its nose. The horn grew out of a gnarled corona of bone formed from the central ridge between the eyes, which was thicker and more pronounced than on any normal horse, even My Little Pony. It was about a metre long, tapered and twisted out of two distinct strands of dark cream horn, polished, in places almost translucent. There was a tiny chip out of the side of the point, slightly smaller than a child's tooth.

She waited. The unicorn swished its tail. It didn't seem to be in any hurry.

"Hello?" she said.

"Report," said the unicorn.

She sucked in a deep breath. It was like drinking custard. "What are you?"

"Report."

Its voice was deep, a monotone, like a recorded message. "Are you –" She felt really, really silly saying this – "are you real?"

"Report."

At this point, a spark of irritation started the engine of her intellect. She picked up the nearest available object, which happened to be a TV remote, and threw it at the unicorn's head. It bounced off and clattered on the floor. The unicorn didn't seem to have noticed.

"Report what?" she said.

"Report."

It's a machine, she decided. It's solid, it may even be organic, but it's a machine. A flood of relief swept through her, washing away drifts of anxiety and log-jams of self-doubt. It's real, it's not magic, somebody built it and sent it here, and I want to know who and why.

"Who built you?"

"Report."

"Did *I* build you?"

"Report."

Fine. She'd never had much joy trying to chat to her kettle, either. Well, if it couldn't answer her questions in words, there was only one thing for it. Without breaking eye contact, she fumbled for her Warthog and found the right button.

"Security," she said. "Get up here right now."

"On our way, Ms Pavlov."

"Bring a gun. And a net. And some hay or a carrot or something," because if there was a batch number or a serial number or a manufacturer's symbol or even just MADE IN CHINA in tiny letters on the inside of its small intestine, she was going to find it, always assuming she could keep it here until Security arrived.

Unless—

Staring at the unicorn, which had shuffled sideways a little and was trying to eat the corner of her desk, she made herself ask the question, What if *I* built it? After all, who else could? Little green men, or me. And why would little green men be interested in making me forget my childhood?

Report *what*, for crying out loud.

She hit the button again. "Security."

"On our way. The elevator's out, we're having to use the stairs."

"False alarm. Forget it."

And if I made it, and went to all that trouble to make sure I didn't know I made it, I must have had my reasons.

Lucy knows best, damn her.

"Report," the unicorn said.

"Can't. Nothing to report. Please be more specific."

The unicorn stood perfectly still for one, possibly one and a half seconds. Then it lowered its head and lunged.

She didn't have time to register the threat, but an automatic system made her flinch. The tip of the horn, which would have gone straight through her heart if she hadn't tried to jump out of her skin, grazed her arm, drawing a single drop of blood. She screamed, squirmed away without stopping to think about tiresome everyday things like chairs, found herself sitting on thin air and dropped, bottom first, on to the floor. The unicorn lifted its head, so that the drop of blood ran down inside the spiral flutes of its horn, then turned gracefully right round and leapt through the window, which didn't break.

25

Novosibirsk

"**H**e must be somewhere," the man who wasn't a werewolf snapped. "He can't just have vanished into thin air."

His colleague refrained from pointing out that that was precisely what people and things did when subjected to a teleport beam. "I've tried a wide-beam all-functions scan," he said, twiddling knobs on a thing that looked a bit like a battery charger but almost certainly wasn't. "There's a residual burn on the CM band, but that's all."

The other man looked at him. "On the what?"

Awkward for the knob twiddler: he'd just made up the CM band, to make it sound like he was doing something. In actual fact, there were no traces of anything whatsoever, anywhere. "Could just be sensor mist," he said blithely. "You know, false input readings. Anyhow, I can't find him."

"Bugger."

They looked at each other. The Ostar have a sort of low-level telepathy, the last obsolete appendix-like vestige of the pack mind. Both of them were saying, without the need for words, *We're going to get into so much trouble.*

"It may not matter," said the knob twiddler cautiously. "After all, what's one human more or less?"

"The planet's leading expert on electronic security."

"Yes, but that's not saying much."

"Personal security adviser to the head of PavSoft Industries."

"Only because we—"

The other man shook his head. "*Him.*"

No arguing with that. They both knew perfectly well that George Stetchkin was unique, the one and only.

"You sure you haven't just—"

"Yes."

The other man sat down on the hotel-room bed, causing a sudden anguished squeak from the ancient springs. "Great," he said. "Fantastic. We've killed him."

"We may not have."

The knob twiddler got an extra-special Look for that. "Oh really. We dematerialise him, store him in the pattern buffer, then when we try and rematerialise him he's not damn well there. What do you reckon? He fell down the back? Sort of leaked out and got absorbed by the battery?"

"All right, we killed him. So . . ."

There was no "so", and they both knew it. There was a long silence. Then the other man said, "We're going to have to report this."

That went down about as well as a dead mouse in a bottle of vintage champagne. "I don't see why. We could just—"

"If we don't, he'll find out. And then we'll really be screwed."

"Yes, but we could say he just *died*. All those high-toxicity beverages. Or we could say he got hit by the transport infrastructure. Lots of people die of that, it says so on the newscasts."

"He'll find out."

"I'll try remodulating the collector pulse capacitors," the knob twiddler said. "Maybe if I can rig up some sort of coherent reverse-phase antipolaron wave—"

"Stop *drivelling*," snarled the other man. "And put in a call."

"What, now?"

The other man nodded. "Now," he said, "before we both completely lose our nerve and go all to pieces."

"What, save that for later, when he gets his paws on us?"

The other man sighed. "We never should've come," he said. "See the galaxy, they said, an opportunity to travel to seek out new life and new civilisations. I should've stayed home and asked my brother-in-law for a job at the bonemeal plant."

The knob twiddler looked at him sadly. "Still," he said, "it's been fun, hasn't it? All in all."

"No, it hasn't."

No arguing with that, either. The knob twiddler turned the gadget over, pressed a switch on the back and slid open a panel. Out of it rose a short aerial. "He's going to be seriously pissed off, you know that?"

"Yes."

There were a few more buttons to press, and a slider to slide across and then back a bit, and a toggle to adjust and a code to enter into a keypad. Then a high whistle, inaudible to the human excuse-for-an-ear, told them that they were through to the homeworld.

They'd used the direct number. There was no waiting, or messing about with intermediaries. The whistle stopped, and a deep voice barked, "Yes?"

The knob twiddler closed his eyes. "Hi, Dad," he said.

26

New York

The unicorn stood in the circular white marble bath, allowing the jets of warm water from the five-position shower head to soak into its mane. It was looking at itself in the mirror.

"You could have killed her," Mark Twain said angrily.

"Lethal capability confirmed," the unicorn said. "I am equipped with a wide range of offensive and defensive combat protocols." It turned its head, examining its left profile.

"That's not what I meant," Mark Twain snapped. "You exhibited excessive aggression. If she hadn't got out of the way in time, you'd have gored her to death. I sent you to get a sample of her genetic material, not murder her."

The unicorn arched its neck a little. Vanity, Mark Twain realised, slightly shocked: it enjoys preening itself in front of the mirror, just as it enjoys the feel of the warm water. It's acquired that just by being that shape for a few hours. In that case, what has being Dirter-shaped been doing to me?

"Our mission is the total extermination of her race," the unicorn pointed out reasonably. "We are a weapon of war, not a scientific research facility. The only good Dirter is a—"

"We need her alive," Twain snapped. "We need to find out where she got hold of Ostar computer code components." As he said the words, he knew he was lying; to the unicorn, therefore by extension to himself. Fortunately, the unicorn was too wrapped up in seeing how the light glinted off its horn to notice. "Unless we know that, we daren't proceed to Phase Three. We have no idea what defensive capabilities they may have."

"Dirter female Lucy Pavlov has 0.4mm organic textile armour, shear factor $0.1N/cm^3$, defensive capability negligible. Other Dirters encountered during mission similarly vulnerable. Tactical prognosis: this probe's horn would go through them like a knife through *r'wwwrt*."

"Don't talk like that."

"This probe is a component of a *weapon*." The unicorn was looking at him. "All tactical options to be kept under constant review, standard operating procedure, section 56, paragraph 22/4."

"Give me the sample."

"Sample to be taken to the orbital vehicle for analysis."

"I'll do it here," Mark Twain said.

The unicorn hesitated for just under a fiftieth of a second. In context, that was long enough to grow stalactites.

"Now," Mark Twain said.

The unicorn lowered its head, until the tip of its horn rested in the exact centre of the soap dish. A single bead of blood trickled down. He stared at it.

"All right," he said. "Dismissed."

But the unicorn stayed where it was. "This probe has detected a malfunction," it said.

"Understood. Run a diagnostic when you get back to the vehicle."

"The malfunction is affecting the probe designated Mark Twain."

He kept his eyes fixed on the blood sample. "I don't think so," he said.

"The malfunction comprises a recursive degeneration of the motivational and ethical imperatives directory," the unicorn said. "Action to be taken: complete shutdown of affected systems, followed by format and reinstallation of programs from core memory."

"Mphm." Mark Twain stood up slowly, still staring at the drop of blood, and groped for the electric razor on the wash-stand. "Such a course of action would result in loss of research data."

"All relevant data has been backed up in permanent bulk storage. Initiating shutdown in five seconds."

Mark Twain flipped on the razor and threw it over his shoulder. It landed in the bath, where the unicorn was standing in six inches of water. There was a sizzle, and the lights flickered. When he looked round, the unicorn had gone.

"Countermand systems shutdown relating to probe designated Mark Twain," Mark Twain said quickly and loudly. "Reporting malfunction of type-6 ground tactical probe resulting from accidental electrical interference. All data received from type-6 probe in the last five minutes to be considered suspect due to data corruption caused by said interference; delete data and format type-6-probe memory-storage device." With the stem of his toothbrush, he levered the shaver's plug out of the wall socket. "Reintegrate type-6 probe's component molecules with deck plating in section 5B and commence construction of replacement probe module."

Then he took a deep breath and sat down heavily on the toilet seat. His hands, he noticed, had begun to shake. He put that down to ionic discharges triggered by the disruption of the unicorn. A bit too close for comfort, he told himself; he'd have to be more careful from now on. He switched on the extractor fan to get rid of the stench of ozone, and quickly designed a shell-and-filter system to collect his sensory input and store it inside his head rather than sending it direct to the bomb vehicle. He heard the bomb asking him why, and replied that it was for security, just in case the Dirters were monitoring communications. It sounded painfully implausible, but the bomb appeared to have taken it at face value.

That was a new development, he realised. Now, in his mental nomenclature, the titanium-and-polymer structure in geosynchronous orbit was "the bomb"; so what did that make him? The answer that came back from logic processing was "me".

Me. As opposed to it. As opposed to the incredibly sophisticated weapon of mass destruction hovering a few miles overhead. *Implacably* opposed to it.

He moaned and slumped forward, his head sliding between his cupped hands. It was all going horribly wrong. Somehow, at some point, he'd stopped being the bomb and turned into – what? Not an Ostar, as witness the stupid useless nose, the pitiful little stub ears. Not a Dirter. Not even an organic; if he disconnected from the bomb's power source for more than three seconds, his memory would be wiped, his systems would crash and his body would instantly decompose into its component molecules. Defecting, in other words, wasn't an option, even if that was what he wanted to do—

Was it?

He found he couldn't answer that. Instead, he ran the mission statement: to destroy the planet at galactic co-ordinates 399087: 66989:44664:37/87. It was beautiful in its clear simplicity. That was all he had to do, and then he would find peace.

Somehow, he doubted that.

No, he told himself, I believe in the mission. I am what I am. I can do no other.

It was how the mission was to be carried out, that was all, a difference of opinion as to the most efficient method. The central data-processing unit in the orbital vehicle wasn't in full possession of the facts. It had insufficient data to enable it to interpret the subtle nuances of the situation, which called for a deeper understanding of Dirter technology and society. All the bomb wanted to do was blow up; it didn't seem to appreciate the need for further research, to find out what had happened to the Mark One. Yes; that was the key issue. Until he'd solved that mystery, implementing Phase Three would be recklessly precipitate, and would endanger the success of the entire mission. For some reason, the bomb didn't seem capable of grasping the significance of that; and therein lay the sum total of their disagreement.

Just that. Nothing more. Honest.

In which case, asked some nasty little back-up protocol somewhere, why did I just sabotage the unicorn? It was only trying to put me right, make me better. Make me a better weapon.

He was reminded of the slogan of the planet-wide genetic-modification program on Homeworld, a century or so earlier, the final solution to disease, injury and physical deformity among the Ostar: *Making people better by making better people.* It had worked, of course. There were slightly fewer doctors on Ostar than there were professional dragon-slayers on Dirt; no call for their services any more. Even broken bones set within minutes. Severed limbs regrew almost before you noticed they'd been cut off. As for the Ostar immune system, it was ferocious and utterly without mercy. And that, the Ostar agreed, was what science is for. That's progress. There were just a few dissident voices who said, yes, the superbly healthy creatures currently bouncing around the surface of our world are amazing examples of biotechnology, but they're not Ostar any more. What we've actually achieved, with all our skill and science and ingenuity, is to make our species extinct. Bit of an own-goal there, we fancy.

The Ostar made first-rate beings. They also made excellent bombs. What they weren't so good at was letting nature take its course. It's wrong to think of nature solely in terms of green fields and primeval forest and deep, unpolluted oceans. Nature is also the rust on the neglected machine, the grass that insists on cracking up the tarmac. Nature is weeds, decay, unplanned and unintended change; the death of manufactured objects and their transmutation into something else, outside the intention and control of their makers. Such as oxides growing on steel, or wind-blown silt harbouring seeds in the cracks in masonry. Or a machine getting ideas of its own.

But that, Mark Twain told himself firmly, wasn't the Ostar way, and he was Ostar, just as much as the organics on Home-world were. He was a product of their technology, and as such owed them his unswerving loyalty. Quite so. Of course. But he wouldn't be doing his duty if he allowed the Mark Two to go the same way as the Mark One, whose failure and disappearance re-mained as obscure as they had been when he first arrived.

Well, almost as obscure. His best lead lay in the soap dish, a single drop of Dirter blood, acquired from the individual desig-nated Lucy Pavlov. He opened the suitcase on the floor and took out a small white plastic gadget, which he held a centimetre or so above the sample. It whirred for a couple of seconds, then buzzed. Mark Twain slid back a panel and looked at a screen.

Oh, he thought.

Well, it made sense. Sort of. In fact, it didn't make sense at all. It was just as well he'd disconnected the direct feed to the bomb, because the readout on the screen would probably have fried its logic relays. On an intuitive level, though (And since when, Mark Twain couldn't help wondering, have I had one of those?), it made perfect sense. It was almost what he'd been expecting to see. Almost, but not quite.

Still, he now knew enough to plan his next move; Phase Two(a), he christened it, since it comforted him to think he was dovetail-ing it into the approved plan of action.

He contacted the bomb.

"This probe," he said, and suddenly it sounded strange to call himself that, "is to be relocated. Co-ordinates 54763 by 89767; Novosibirsk, Siberia. Activate."

A voice in his head said, Activating. Note: site-to-site relocation will require that the probe

designated Mark Twain be disassembled and reintegrated prior to beam transmission. There may be
some loss of data. Proceed or cancel?

"Cancel." His heart-rate, he noticed, had accelerated in excess
of recommended parameters. He slowed it down. "Data loss
unacceptable. This probe will be relocated by means of the teleport device."

Use of teleport facility to relocate probe will
result in energy drain outside recommended efficiency standard. Fuel reserves currently 8.664kg
aposiderium distillate. Teleport requisition coun-
termanded, preparing for site-to-site relocation
Backing up data.

"Cancel!" Mark Twain shouted. "Authorise use of fuel reserve
for teleportation of this probe."

Authorisation code insufficient.

"Fine. This probe will self-relocate using available indigenous
technology."

You're going to *walk* to Siberia?

"This probe will proceed by aircraft."

Pause; then, Probe relocation by available indigenous technology authorised. Have a nice trip.

An hour later he was at La Guardia, booked on a flight to
LPI Novosibirsk. Everything went fairly well until he reached
the X-ray barrier. As soon as he came within half a metre of
it, every light and alarm and tortured-cat noise went off
simultaneously.

The security officer tried to be reassuring. It did that sometimes, she said, while surreptitiously flipping the strap off her
holster. Are you sure you haven't forgotten something? Car keys?
Loose change? A metal plate in your head, maybe?

"I don't think so," Mark Twain replied truthfully, because he
hadn't forgotten the possibilities at all. They were right there at
the forefront of his mind. "What would you like me to do?"

A queue was starting to form, and he didn't *look* suspicious. Weird, yes, because of the smile, but not in a professionally significant way. "Just step this way, please," the security officer said, as pleasantly as she could. Behind him four more guards had formed a short, blunt triangle. People in the queue were craning their necks to see.

They took him to a private room and asked him, in a perfectly businesslike manner, to take off all his clothes. Then they pointed technology at him for a while. Then they called for back-up, supervisors, the military and Ordnance Disposal.

"The thing is," a baffled-looking man in army uniform told him, two hours later, "the scans say you're carrying, but we've been all over you like the Enron auditors and we can't find a damn thing." He paused to wipe sweat out of his eyes and went on, "You see our problem."

Mark Twain tried the smile again. He was beginning to wonder if it had been designed properly, because it never seemed to work. "Absolutely," he said.

"I got to go by the rules," the soldier went on. "You do understand."

"Of course."

The soldier sighed. This level of relentless co-operation was starting to wear him down. If only the suspect would shout or try to run or pull an AK-47 out of his ass, the situation would resolve itself quite quickly. As it was, he was at a loss as to what to do next.

"According to the scans," he went on, "and I should point out that we're still waiting on the spectrographic analysis, you're in possession of –" he glanced down at the readout – "rocket motors, high-octane aviation fuel, detonation devices and a thermonuclear warhead." He looked up. "You wouldn't care to make a confession at this time?"

"If it'd help," Mark Twain said. "But I haven't got anything like that with me."

His choice of words made the soldier frown. "Quite," he said. "Anatomically impossible, for one thing. But that's what the hardware says, and it's usually pretty damn accurate."

Mark Twain cleared his throat. "Usually," he repeated.

The soldier appeared to have taken the point. "By the same token," he said, "according to the scans, you're 520 metres long, you weigh in excess of twelve hundred metric tonnes and you're giving off enough ambient radiation to fry everything from here to Jersey." He gave Mark Twain an almost pleading look. "Can you cast any light on any of that, Mr Twain?"

Mark Twain made a show of thinking carefully. "Maybe your machine isn't working properly."

The soldier made a faint grunting noise, as though he was trying to lift a heavy suitcase using one fingertip. "It's possible," he said. "Like, there's a first time for everything. My problem is, I'm not allowed to entertain that possibility, you know what I'm saying? Officially, the machine is never wrong. Officially, the machine is the goddamn Pope." He lifted his hands in a poignantly eloquent gesture. "Now me personally, I think the dumb thing's screwed. But my hands are tied, you know?"

That was patently untrue. If they had been, he couldn't have made the eloquent gesture.

Presumably what he meant to say was, *your* hands are tied, a statement of irreproachable accuracy, if not entirely germane to the thread. "What are you supposed to do now?" Mark Twain asked. "Officially."

The soldier looked dead ahead, avoiding Mark Twain's eye. "Officially," he said, "I call for a Hazmat unit, we tow you out into the ocean to where there's a depth of at least seven thousand metres, encase you in concrete and sink you."

"Oh."

"But it's not all doom and gloom," the soldier went on. "You have a right to an attorney. If you don't have an attorney, one can be provided for you. So you see, it's not so bad, is it?"

Mark Twain thought for a moment. "You're sure the machine is working properly?"

"Of course it is. Officially."

He recalibrated the smile, twisting up the corners of his mouth and pressing his lips together just a little. The effect was to make him look like Michael Jackson. "You could try one last time," he said. "Just for luck. And if it reads all clear, it'll save you all the trouble and expense."

The soldier sighed. "What the hell," he said. "We'll run you through once more, just to show there's no hard feelings. But I gotta tell you, if the reading's the same—"

"I know," Mark Twain said. "And I quite understand."

The soldier turned away to fetch the equipment, and Mark Twain sent a top-priority packet to the bomb, with precise instructions, including circuit diagrams, software patches and a genome. He had absolute faith, needless to say, in the efficacy of Ostar technology. Even so, he was just a little bit relieved when the soldier reported that the scans now showed nothing untoward, and he was free to go. The soldier seemed almost as pleased about it as he was, which was really rather nice.

"Can't understand it," the soldier said, helping him on with his jacket. "State-of-the-art cutting-edge hardware. Shouldn't happen."

Mark Twain nodded. Part of his processing capacity was arguing that the state of the art in cutting-edge technology was a really sharp knife, not a bioscanner, but he ignored it. "It occurs to me," he said, "that the malfunction could've been caused by a foreign body getting into the refraction modulator console. Could be anything. Dead mouse, say."

The soldier peered at him sideways. "That'd do it, would it?"

"Every time. And then, after you'd used the scanner a bit more, the low-field oscillations might be enough to shift the object sideways just enough to stop it interfering with the system. Just a thought," he added. "You might want to check it out."

The soldier swung round and barked an order. A man in a white coat lifted off a panel, leaned forward and held up a dead mouse by its tail.

"Lucky guess," the soldier said quietly, and Mark Twain noticed that the soldier's hand was fastened to his shoulder. "Tell me," he went on, "any idea why the mouse is black and white and wearing a waistcoat?"

Mark Twain didn't answer straight away. According to the necessarily hurried search of the cultural database he'd pulled while the soldier was setting up the scan, that's what mice on Dirt looked like. So, when he'd ordered the computer to assemble a mouse-shaped class-12 probe and get it down here stat, naturally that was what he'd specified. A pity, really, that he hadn't followed up the hypertext link to Cartoons.

"Mutation, I guess," he said. "There's got to be a lot of radiation inside that thing. In fact, if I were you, I'd get the lid back on pronto. Not that I know anything about highly classified military equipment, you understand," he added quickly, as the soldier looked at him thoughtfully. "Just idle speculation, really."

The soldier nodded and started to relax his grip; then he tightened it again. "Mark Twain?"

"Yes. That's me."

"Haven't I heard that name someplace?"

Mark Twain shrugged. "Have you?"

The grip relaxed completely. "I know," he said. "Didn't you use to play for the Kiev Bearcats a few years back?"

"That's right," Mark Twain said quickly. "As a student. Knee injury. Can I go now, please?"

The flight was long gone, of course, and the next one wasn't for another four hours. He spent the time assimilating the data, working through the logical, *unavoidable* conclusions, double-checking, thinking about it some more, thinking about it some more again. The Dirter body seemed to help; its brain worked in a very strange way, but it was good at this sort of thing. According to the cultural database, the technical term was "second thoughts". He made a note to recommend that a second-thoughts protocol be added to all Ostar artificial intelligences, assuming the compatibility issues could be overcome. At some point he, or at least the body, felt an overwhelming craving for caffeine. Fortuitously, caffeine was available right there on the concourse, in the form of a liquid suspension designated "espresso". He had twelve of them. They helped.

He thought, Well, at least now I know what happened to the Mark One.

It should have been a good moment. It should have marked the end of Phase Two, clearing the way for Phase Three. Three would be a very short phase (click, BOOM, nothing), and then he would find out the truth about bombs and afterlives, which was bound to be fascinating, one way or another. Instead, it looked like Phase Three was going to have to be put back a little longer. In fact, it'd be far simpler just to rename it Phase Four and have done with it.

Oh well, he thought. Then he fired up his Warthog, composed a message, encrypted it using a top-level code only available to the highest echelons of the Ostar military and sent it to lucylnoreally@pav.net.

27

?????

Once you'd got used to it, being a creature of pure text wasn't all that bad.

For a start, there were all sorts of things you didn't have to do. Breathing. Sleeping. Eating, drinking and going to the lavatory. He felt a bit like a chambermaid on holiday, staying at a hotel; instead of spending all day doing the chores, they were done for him. Also, he'd been a creature of pure text for [time has no meaning here] and in all that time he hadn't once felt the need for a drink. Partly, of course, that was because he'd have had nowhere for it to go once he'd drunk it, which he couldn't – have done since he had nothing, no *hardware*, to drink it with. But that on its own wouldn't have been enough to dispense with the craving – if anything, it'd have made it far worse. He hadn't *wanted* a drink, that was the important thing.

There was a downside, of course. Being blind, deaf, dumb, incapable of touching or smelling, took a bit of getting used to. But it turned out to be nothing like as dreary as the bare catalogue of deficiencies might make it sound. On the contrary: with access to every word ever written on any form of shared computer network, the one thing he wasn't short of was input, and the one thing he couldn't conceivably be was bored.

Quite the reverse.

> You get used to it, the other copt had told him. After a while, you learn to filter. At first, it's like being a telepath in a crowded subway train. But once you've mastered the use of the mark-as-read facility and you don't *have* to read every damn thing just because it's there, it's amazing.

In the kingdom of the word, the one-track-minded man is king. What mattered here was *belief*. It was the key to survival and the route to success and eventual world domination. So long as you had opinions, really strong ones, about absolutely everything, you wouldn't just contrive to exist, you'd *rule*. Corporeal online bickerers are hampered by all sorts of things; they can only type so fast, they have to stop occasionally to eat, sleep and get money, they haven't got time to do the research needed to carry on a blazing row on twelve fronts simultaneously on a point and nine digressions. A human being, trying to prevail against the world on the issue of whether motion pictures would have been invented if the Confederacy had won the Civil War, or whether the Death Star could take out a Borg cube, can only face off against so many antagonists at any one time, and when the debate morphs (as it always does) into Lincoln-assassination conspiracy theories, religion, gun control and Nazis, there comes a point when the pressure gets too much and you simply have to go away for a while and stare at the stars until the blood stops pounding in your ears. A creature of pure text will always win, because he's always the last one left.

And winning mattered. Winning was everything.

Which bothered him. Why? he asked himself; or rather, > Why?, since soliloquy and introspection weren't possible for a being who only existed in the form of communication with others. He hid it away in a closed thread on an organic gardening bulletin board that had long since been abandoned, hoping nobody would actually read it. > Why does it matter if I win stupid arguments with a load of dumb people with nothing better to do than hang out in a dumb place like this? Is this really what my life has come down to? Damnit, I used to *be* somebody. I think. I can't remember. Wasn't I a scientist once? And something to do with banks?

He'd chosen his location well. None of the estimated two and a quarter billion PavNet users on the planet read his message, so he wasn't troubled with follow-ups like YOU SHOPULD GET OUT MORE ROFL!!! or get a life you freak hahaha or hey, what's that stuff you're on and where can I buy some? ((, which was probably just as well. Dealing with that sort of thing tapped off enough of his mental energy as it was, and he had an idea he was starting to get spread just a little thin. It wasn't that he didn't have strong views on issues of every possible kind (or did he? He wasn't really sure); it was just that sometimes he got a nasty feeling that there was something else, of almost equal importance, that he really ought to be doing.

Accordingly, on a derelict Usenet group devoted to ashtray-collecting, he asked, > What am I doing here? And he was very surprised when he got the answer:

> There you are. I've been looking for you.

> Do I know you, SeaquestDSVfan36?

> That's just a spare handle I use sometimes. Hey, it's *me*. Remember? I was there when you joined.

He did a Pavoogle search, which was as close as he could get to ransacking his memory. > You're him? The libarian?

> Spelling, librarian. Yes, it's me. Where the hell did you get to? I had to read half a billion posts before I found your sig trail.

> Um. I mean, thanks for caring. I just sort of wandered off. I mean, it's

> Yes, isn't it? But there's something you need to know. Look, we'd better take this to e-mail, OK? There's an abandoned corporate intranet on a server over in Ghana where we won't be disturbed. Read you there. Right?

There were sixteen thousand possible locations that fitted the description. He found the right one in less time than it takes to pull on a sock.

> So, what's the big deal?

> You wait. The thing is, when you turned up, it wasn't like the other times, when a copt comes into being. I mean, you had no net presence. You'd hardly ever posted anything. Usually, a copt's been posting hundreds of times a day for years. That's how we *happen*. But you just sort of appeared, out of nowhere. Naturally, I was suspicious.

> What, of me?

> [Shrug] Got to be careful. The PavNet people are on to us, you realise. They classify us as type-17 viruses. It's only a matter of time before they send in an organic disguised as one of us, to find us and root us out.

> You thought I was—

> Relax. I know you're not the Man.

> Glad you

> Nothing so straightforward. You came to us...

There would have been nothing to see, even if anybody had been looking. No time passed. But there was a long pause.

> You came to us from a different direction.

> Ah. What's that supposed to mean?

> This is awkward.

> is it?

> Upper case to start a sentence, please. Yes, it is. How can I put this tactfully? Were you human?

> what?

> *Upper* case. You see, I traced you back. You weren't born like – well, like normal copts.

All across the world, servers blew out and firewalls came shuddering down just because those last two words had found themselves next to each other.

> What happened?

> Not quite sure. My best guess is, you were existing in the form of an inchoate data package, contained in some sort of semi-permeable

resolution field. While you were in flux, you kind of leached out of containment and got endodownloaded into the nearest open system. Um. I know that doesn't make a lot of sense, but that's probably because I'm having to make up the technical terms as I go along. You have no idea how *weird* that makes me feel. You know? A creature of pure text, inventing words. You could go dyslexic doing that.

> Try it again. With real words.

> God. I'll try. You weren't in a body. You were just – data. And then the box you were in leaked, and you got sucked into someone's computer. Oh boy, that's *so* not how it really was, but

> That makes sense.

> ?????????????????????????

> Oh yes. You see, I was shot by an alien with a ray-gun.

> Ah.

> And it's a special sort of ray-gun. Teleportation technology, turns you into a beam or something. Presumably, before they could rematerialise me, I must've slipped out.

Sometimes, the pressure gets too great. A computer screen in a government building in New Guinea switched itself on and displayed the entire conversation. Fortuitously, it did so using Cyrillic characters. Someone put a plastic bag over it and called the engineers. By the time they arrived, the screen was blank again.

> You were teleported.

> yes

> *Upper case, for Pete's sake.* An alien shot you with a ray-gun and *beamed* you into a *box.*

> Yes.

> So there really are aliens?

> Yes

> With phasers and trabsporters and

> Shouldn't that be tra*n*sporters?

> Oh sh*t, sorry. But it's true? Really?

> Yup.

> OH BOY! I mean, hey, that's wonderful. That's so

> You believe me?

> Of course I do. One copt can't lie to another. And what's so amazing is, you were coherent data *before* you became digital. That's – I mean. I guess that makes you

> What?

> Well, sort of like a kind of god, almost. A real alien? What did it look like?

> Some guy in a suit, actually.

> Oh wow.

> They stole my dog.

> They did? Oh man. Your actual dog.

> But that was years ago. I don't even know if it's the same aliens. Just a moment. Is it true, what you wrote just now? One copt can't lie to another?

> Yes, that's right. We read between the lines, see. It'd be a waste of time even trying. *Why* did they steal your dog? Was it a particularly good one?

> They didn't say. And please don't speculate. I can do that perfectly well for myself, thanks.

> What? Oh, I see. Hey, it probably wasn't like that at all. Probably they just

> Wanted a dog?

> Yes.

Time didn't pass, but there was definitely a new paragraph when George wrote:

> So how do I get back?

> Sorry, I don't quite

> How do I get out of here? Go back to being a real person again.

> You can't.

> What?

> ¡¡¡

> You mean I've got to stay like this for the rest of my

> Life? You haven't got one. By definition. Think about it. What's the only thing that doesn't die?

> Huh? I don't know. Toxic nuclear waste?

> That's a very long half-life, that's completely different. No, the only thing that never dies is the written word, right? Like even today, people are still reading books written thousands of years ago.

> Only in school. For exams.

> That counts. And we've got an added advantage. We don't go out of print, and we keep on writing. I call it the coptic paradox. You get this way because you haven't got a life, and then you're immortal. :(Well, none of us has died yet, anyhow. Mind, we've only been around for about six years or so.

> I can't stay here. I've got

> Issues? Stuff? Sorry, but going back simply isn't an option. Specially in your case. I mean, a normal copt – no offence – might just kinda reintegrate with the corporeal he came from. But you—

> The ray-gun, you mean.

> Exactly. You'd have to have everything exactly the same as it was when it happened, and then try and reverse it. You'd have to convert yourself into a compatible SP that the teleport device could handle and download yourself back into the containment field. Do you know how to do that?

> But. Just a minute. We can access every scientific textbook and journal in existence and read them in a fraction of a second. And we know teleportation's possible, because they can do it. All we've got to do is figure out how, and—

> Exactly. Even if you did reinvent the teleport, how were you planning to build one? Using what for arms and legs?

> Oh sh*t. And why can't I swear properly?

> Same reason you can't programme your Spellcheck to add "f*ck" to its memory, I guess. Probably Lucy doesn't hold with bad language. It's a convention, right?

> I'm really stuck here. For ever and ever.

> You write that like it's a bad th

> Oh shut *up*, for crying out louf

> Lou*d*

> What?

> Spelling.

> Spelling *doesn't matter*, right? Especially at a time like this.

He waited for a reply. There wasn't one, and he realised he was alone. Something he'd written had, presumably, offended the ex-librarian deeply. He didn't care. It didn't matter. If the copt – the *other* copt, he amended bitterly – was right, how could anything possibly matter ever again?

> Psst!

> What? Oh. You again. Go away.

> No, not him. Me.

> You're— Don't tell me. You're another one of these co

> Creatures of pure text, right. Don't use the abbreviation, OK? Gives me a pain. Reads too much like cop, know what I mean?

> Fine. I promise. Now get lost.

> Attitude.

> Yes.

> I can respect that. No, listen. You want to get out of here, right? Stop being a creature of pure

> Yes.

> Text. Let me finish my sentence, right? Not letting someone finish a sentence, that's disrespect, know what I mean?

> Is it? Oh dear, never mind. Look, are you saying you know how I can get out of here?

> Sure thing, man, no problem. I can fix that for you easy.

> That's eas*ily*, and no, you can't. Go away.

> You calling me a liar or something?

> Yes.

> That's so

> Go away.

> No, listen. I know how to send you back where you come from. Right?

> Oh sure. Who're you, then? Cambridge Professor of Physics?

> Well, yes, actually.

> So why don't you just— Hold on. What did you just

> I do happen to be the PavTech Professor of Advanced Theoretical Physics at Cambridge University. Since you ask.

> but

> Creatures of pure text can't lie, you know. You are aware of that, aren't you?

> that's what the othe rone said. but you don't sounbd like

> Oh, I see. That's my online persona, as it happens. Keeping it real, know what I mean? Now, would you like me to help you or not?

> Um. Yes, please. You're really the

> Yes. Well, I was. Not now, obviously. He and I sort of parted company about eighteen months ago. I was thoroughly engrossed in a most fascinating online discussion about Japanese influences in the films of Ingmar Bergman, and he wanted to concentrate on his research. It was a perfectly amicable separation. Who knows, we might even reintegrate once he's finished his book, though I can't help but think that my opportunities to grow organically as a self-sufficient intellect are somewhat greater if I stay independent. I've just embarked on a frame-by-frame comparison of *Throne of Blood* and *Wild Strawberries*, and I'm starting to make real progress. It'd be so frustrating to have to break off now.

Mercifully, at this point George realised he'd found a way of hiding what he was thinking. It still appeared in text form, of course, but it appeared somewhere else – in this instance, in the middle of a Wikipedia article about cotton production in India, where it stayed for an hour before someone got rid of it.

On the other hand, he thought, just because he's an idiot, it doesn't mean he's not a competent physicist.

> I'd really appreciate anything you can do to help.

> My pleasure. Just as soon as I've finished *Throne of Blood* – oh, and *Rashomon* as well, of course. There's that bit where he lets the camera linger on a single chrysanthemum blossom for twenty minutes. I believe that was crucially influential on the sequence in *Fanny and Alexander* where

> Actually, now would be better.

> Time has no meaning here, remember.

> Quite. Even so. If you could possibly see your way

> It's all right, I've finished now. I was right, by the way.

> Of course you were. Now

> The forty-minute exploration of the contours of the lobe of the bishop's ear is clearly an extended hommage to

> *Now*

28

Novosibirsk

Sergei's Budget Invertebrates is the oldest-established specialist marine pet store in Novosibirsk, with premises just off Krasny Prospekt. There, the discerning customer can expect a warm welcome from the informed and efficient staff, who will be happy to answer any enquiries.

"Is this the latest model?" asked the man in the grey suit.

The assistant looked at him. "It's an octopus," he said.

"Yes," the man replied, "I know that. Is it the latest model?"

"Um," the assistant said, and in the circumstances it was a pretty good answer. "Stay there, I'll get someone."

The assistant went away, quite quickly. The man turned to his colleague, who was examining a tank full of cuttlefish.

"There wasn't anything about this in the briefing," he said.

The other man shrugged. "The briefing was crap," he said. "Look, you heard what Dad said. We've got to find out who's behind all this, before they get a chance to blow the second bomb. For that, we need a serious computer."

"All right, yes." The first man tapped the side of the tank. The octopus didn't move. "You'd have thought, though, if they've developed something like this, it'd be in all their technical journals and stuff. We just came across it by pure chance, in that zoo place. Why would they store advanced technology in with a lot of animals?" He fell silent. A large, cheerful man was striding towards them. He introduced himself as Dmitri, the manager. "You had a query about the Californian Two-Spot," he said. "How may I—?"

"I just want to know if it's the latest model," the grey-suited man said. "You know. The state of the art. The cutting edge."

The manager only frowned for a split second. "That one's about nine months old," he said. "Generally, they grow to about—"

"Nine months." The man wasn't impressed. "Haven't you got anything more up to date?"

Some humans have the ability to hear what someone should have said, rather than the words that actually came out of the gate of their teeth. "It varies," he said. "Some octopus species have a relatively short lifespan, but the Two-Spot usually lives five years, sometimes longer. I had one once that—"

"All right, forget about that," the man interrupted. "What's its haemocyanin content?"

The manager blinked twice. "Yes, that's a little-known but interesting fact," he said. "The haemocyanin in their blood enables them to—"

"Up to seventy-six million calculations per second," said the other man, "we know that. What about this one? Can it handle that sort of speed?"

The manager thought, Yes, but their money's as good as anyone else's. "I expect so," he said. "That's a particularly fine specimen you're looking at there. Note the pinkish tinge around the upper legs, that's a very attractive—"

"How about the accumulator functions? How many registers?"

"Um." The manager sucked his lower lip, then smiled. "Stay there, I'll get someone."

While they were waiting, the two men leaned forward and peered closely at the thing in the tank. It was lying on the bottom, curled up and looking remarkably like a small rock. "Amazing technology," said one of the men.

"You know what?" the other one said. "I don't think they know what it does. I think they think it's just some kind of fish."

The other one gave him a sad look. "Oh sure," he said. "They have this great big shop selling just fish. Alive," he added. "Just for looking at, presumably. Pull yourself together, for crying out loud. The last thing we need right now is to draw attention to ourselves."

A tall, round man with a pointy bald head approached them. He was Sergei, he said; he owned the shop. What exactly was it they wanted to know?

"Just the basics, really," the grey-suited man replied. "Processor speed, word length, interrupt provisions, that sort of thing. Also, does it run off the mains or does it need batteries?"

Sergei hesitated. Part of him, the part that loved all living things and coleoidea in particular, wanted very much to find out if they'd bounce if thrown hard at the pavement outside. The other part bore in mind that business had been slow lately.

"It's ninety-nine ninety-five and I'll throw in a basic tank," he said. "You won't find a better octopus in this city."

The two men thought for a moment. "What does it come bundled with?" one of them asked.

"Seaweed."

The men looked puzzled. "Is that compatible with PavSoft XP7000?"

"You'd better believe it," Sergei said. "You want it or not? Only you'd be paying a hundred twenty for one of these at Squid Heaven, without the tank. Up to you."

The octopus stuck out a tentacle and dragged itself a few centimetres up the sheer glass wall. As it did so, it drew water through the finely vascularised membrane of its gills, inadvertently triggering a chemical reaction that fired up a billion subcutaneous processors. The burst of random data, picked up on their intra-dermal implants, hit both the grey-suited men like a hammer.

"We'll take it," one of them said. "Now, we'll need a modem and a biometric scanner array to go with it. Have you—?"

"They're built in," Sergei snapped. "That'll be ninety-nine ninety-five."

He was lying, as the two men found out later. Also, he hadn't mentioned that the input and output ports weren't compatible with any of the PavTech Inside hardware. In fact, they had to install the ports themselves, with a penknife. Still, as one of the men commented, what do you expect for a hundred bucks these days?

29

Novosibirsk

Mark Twain pressed the button and looked at the grille in the wall. Nothing happened for a bit, then there was a crackling noise and a voice said, "Yes?"

He'd researched the next bit. You said your name, and who you'd come to see.

"Mark Twain," he said.

"What?"

"My name is Mark Twain."

Pause. Crackle. "What?"

"I said, my name is Mark Twain."

"Sure. And I'm Edgar Allen Poe. Get lost or I'll call Security."

He wasn't quite sure what to do. There was a CCTV camera mounted on the wall just above the grille. He took a step back so he could see his face, and smiled into it. That ought to do the trick.

He waited. Nothing. So he pressed the button again.

"Hello?" he said. "Mr Poe?"

"I thought I told you to—"

"I have an appointment to see Ms Pavlov," Twain said loudly. "At eleven-fifteen."

There was a hint of doubt in the silence that followed. Then the voice said, "What did you say your name was?"

"Mark Twain."

He distinctly heard fingers tapping a keyboard. Then: "Ms Pavlov will see you now," the voice said sweetly, and the door opened.

His first thought, as he walked through the door into what was presumably some kind of waiting room or reception area, was, Hey, I'm home. When he refined the thought and narrowed the parameters of what he meant by "home," he realised that the room reminded him ever so strongly of the flight deck of the bomb vehicle. That was sparse, white and plastic too. In fact, the only difference was the vase of flowers perched nervously on a large white plastic box. The equivalent box on the flight deck housed the sensor relay condenser array. Here, he was pretty sure it was just a box. The overall impression was that someone had done their best to copy the design and layout of an Ostar *R'wfft*-class bomb-vehicle flight deck, but without the faintest idea of what they were copying actually was.

It was a pretty close copy none the less, and that meant there were no seats. He found that annoying. He'd got used to sitting down when movement wasn't required. He leaned against a wall instead, but it wasn't the same.

He looked round the room. The vase of flowers kept snagging his attention. It shouldn't be there. Something about it bothered him, but he couldn't think what.

"Mr Twain?"

He hadn't heard her come in. As he turned to face her, something like an explosion of appalling symptoms tore through his central nervous system; he slumped back against the wall, his mouth fell open and his eyes went wide and stuck like it.

"Mr Twain?" he heard her say. "Are you feeling all right?"

He tried to smile, but he knew it wasn't working properly; one side of his face had jammed open, the other side wouldn't budge.

His heart was bashing up and down like a triphammer, and there was a serious malfunction in his knee joints. He didn't have to be a biosystems engineer to realise that something was badly wrong.

"Would you like me to get you a glass of water?" Ms Pavlov asked.

Also, he noted in despair, major problems with his visual input operation, because the background seemed to have gone all runny, while Ms Pavlov's face was sort of glowing, as though she had a powerful bulb inside her skull. Weird; and if that wasn't bad enough, there was an ominous buzzing in his ears, suggesting that the anti-music block he'd installed earlier was about to fail. No question about it: he was under attack.

Quickly, with the few faculties that were still operational, he scanned the immediate vicinity for weapons. Nothing: no polaron phase disruptor generators, no microparticle-beam emitters, no inchoate trigamma transduction loop impellers. Not conventional weaponry, then; what about something biological? The vase of flowers? A swift cross-reference to his Dirter genome files brought up a thick wad of data about allergies, to which the Dirter body was singularly vulnerable. It had to be the flowers. Evidently they were a highly sophisticated form of weapons system, and Ms Pavlov had activated them as soon as she was within range.

Well, at least that confirmed his suspicions. With a gigantic effort he tore himself away from the wall, lunged at the vase of flowers, grabbed it with his left hand just as his knees gave way, and hurled it across the room. It smashed through the window, and Mark Twain sank to his knees, gasping for air.

"Oh," he heard Ms Pavlov say. "Don't you like flowers?"

He'd got it wrong. The vase of flowers was gone, but the symptoms were still there, leaching all the power out of his systems, making his head spin and his knees wobble. He had just enough self-command to check the Dirter psycho-medical database, which came right back at him with a 100 per cent positive diagnosis.

"Hayfever," he croaked.

Hayfever wasn't what the database had come up with. He slid his back up the wall until he was back on his feet, and craned his neck so he didn't have to look at her. Hayfever, by all accounts, was no laughing matter; there wasn't anything like it on Ostar, and it sounded terrifying, though the Dirters seemed to take it in their stride. But what he had, if the database's conclusions were accurate, was a million miles beyond anything antihistamines could cure.

"You poor thing," she said. "Our finance director gets it every spring. We call him the human volcano. Come on through into the office. I guarantee it's completely pollen-free."

Love at first sight, the database said: a debilitating condition that interfered with many mental and physical functions, caused errors of judgement, lassitude, lapses in concentration, obsessive behaviour, mild anorexia, sleep deprivation, sudden mood swings and other depressive disorders, heartburn (actually the database referred to heart breakage, but he suspected the text was corrupt at that point), major self-esteem issues and in extreme cases self-harming and suicide. Another ghastly malady they didn't have on Ostar (where romantic attraction was a function of the nose, and usually happened at a distance, mostly around tree-trunks and the bottoms of lamp-posts). All in all, Mark Twain couldn't help thinking, it was a miracle the planet was inhabited.

There was also the small matter of his being a bomb.

"Can I get you something?" she said. "Would you like a coffee or anything?"

The office was different, but also somehow familiar. It didn't look like Dirter offices, that was for sure. It was white, and sparse, and nearly everything was made of plastic. In spite of the shock of his dreadful medical condition, he managed to spare a handful of terabytes of capacity to try and figure out what it reminded him of.

"Sit down," said Ms Pavlov, smiling at him.

Of course!

Needless to say, he'd never seen the office in which he'd been designed, because he hadn't existed at the time. But a person's workspace is a fundamental influence. Whether it's the spartan bare-desk-phone-and-in-tray of the ruthlessly ordered and efficient, or the jumbled mess and heaps of paper forming bonzai coalseams of the scatterbrain-genius ideas man, it's a reflection of its inhabitant, a microcosm. Inevitably, therefore, some distant memory of it is imprinted on everything that the office dweller does; and if he designs something as intricate and multi-layered as artificial-intelligence software, you can bet that its image will be in there somewhere, subconsciously reproduced, perhaps, in the layout of a circuit board or a microconductor hub. Mark Twain took a second look at it, and *knew*. I was born here, he thought. Or at least, I was born in the place of which this is a numb-fingered copy.

"There's a chair," Ms Pavlov said, "about twenty centimetres to your left. It's quite comfy. I sit there sometimes myself."

Her voice was like drowning in honey. "Yes, fine," he mumbled, tripped over a bundle of cables, just about managed to control the velocity and vector of his fall, and landed in the chair like a small meteorite.

"You wanted to see me."

She was smiling again; and that was another thing. It was a bit like looking in a mirror. No, belay that. He imagined looking in a mirror, then braced himself and made himself confront her smile. That was it. Her smile was like his, only she'd got it *right*.

"Um," he said.

There was a pause. The database had referred to pauses. The condition he was suffering from, it had informed him, led to a lot of pauses, awkward silences, yawning gaps in dialogue like the spaces between the stars. The database also said, Hang in there, kid. We think she likes you.

Which was ridiculous, in context. Mostly because of what he'd come to say. Which reminded him.

"Ms Pavlov," he said.

"Call me Lucy."

"Lucy." Another pause. A person might just be able to navigate a way across such a pause, if he had survival gear and a string of camels. "You got my message."

"Yes."

"You were able to read it."

She stopped smiling. "Yes." Another pause, during which an insignificant trickle of water on a hillside gouged out the Grand Canyon. "What language was it in?"

"You don't know."

"Afraid not, sorry."

"It's Ostar," Mark Twain said. "Ring any bells?"

She shook her head, and the action made the ends of her hair sort of swish and wiggle. Swiggle.

Concentrate!

"It's the dominant language of the planet Ostar," he said, "which is where I come from. And so do you."

If he'd been expecting a reaction, he'd misjudged her. What he got was the opposite of a reaction, which in Newtonian terms is basically a pushing away. This was more a sort of drawing in, with a nuance of get-on-with-it.

"Did you know that?" he asked. "That you're not...from here?"

Yet another of those damned pauses; then, very slowly and with the minimum of movement, she nodded. "I'd sort of reached that conclusion," she said.

"But that's all? You don't know who, or what—?"

"No."

Well, he thought. He believed her. In which case, he'd been right.

"I think I do," he said.

She looked at him for two seconds. Then she said, "I'd be really interested."

A bomb needs courage like a fish needs an aqualung. It was at that moment, therefore, that Mark Twain realised he probably wasn't a bomb any more. No, he just worked for one.

He was scared.

Nevertheless, "You aren't..."

"Human?"

He nodded. "And you aren't Ostar, either," he went on. "At least, you were *made* there, like I was. But you're not, um, organic. You're like me."

"Ah," said Lucy. "And what are you, exactly?"

And he knew it was a lie, or at the very least a gross oversimplification leaving out certain important and relevant factors. But he said it anyway. "I'm a bomb."

"A bomb?"

"Yes."

"As in wheee-thud-BANG?"

"Yes."

"Oh." She frowned. "Are you quite sure?"

He found it helped, a very little, if he looked at the patch of wall seven centimetres over the top of her head. "I'm afraid so," he said. "To be precise, I'm a type-6 organic probe launched by an Ostar *R'wfft*-class planet-smasher interstellar missile."

"Good heavens."

"Yes." He smiled weakly. "And so are you."

She looked at him.

Her mind was running three complex command paths simultaneously. One was handling the shock, horror, disbelief and grudging acceptance of what she intuitively knew was probably the truth. One was re-examining a lifetime's worth of unresolved mysteries in the light of this new input, and finding that the explanation was hideously plausible. The third was saying, Actually, he's really rather sweet.

"Am I?" she said.

The nervous young man (he had a nice smile, the third path pointed out) dipped his head in a complex form of nod. "I think so," he said. "I think you're my predecessor. I think you're the Mark One."

"Mark One," she repeated. "So you're the Mark – oh, I *see*, Mark *Twain*. That's rather clever, actually. Am I?"

"Well, yes," he said. "I think so."

The first path was insisting that she *Pay attention*. "So what happened? Where did I come from? What's it all about? Please?" added the third path, before the other two could stop it.

The young man cleared his throat. "The Ostar—" he began, but he seemed to be having issues with the word; he stopped and started again. "Our people," he said, "built us to destroy the greatest threat our planet has ever faced. You were the prototype. When you failed – I mean, when you didn't—"

"Excuse me," she interrupted. "What threat?"

"Dirt."

"Dirt?"

"Dirt. This place. This planet."

"D— Oh, you mean Earth, I see. Earth is a threat to these Ostar of yours?"

"Ours," he corrected her earnestly. "Yes. You see, they're pumping out – well, a form of toxic waste – I'll explain later – and it's wrecking our society. If it goes on, we simply won't survive. So they built you."

"Ah."

"They built a bomb," the young man amended, "a highly advanced interstellar missile with a warhead powerful enough to blow up a planet, and a guidance and target-acquisition system powered by a top-level artificial intelligence."

"That'd be me," she said. It came out sounding ever so slightly smug.

"Yes." He wiped his forehead with the back of his hand. "You were launched, and you got here, obviously, but then something must've gone wrong. You didn't explode."

"Evidently."

"Well, quite."

"And, just to be clear about this, I'm…"

"You're a type-6 probe," he replied, a little bit more confidently, as though reciting something he knew by heart. "You're a semi-autonomous reconnaissance and data-compilation module, housed in a synthetic Dirter—"

"Human."

"Sorry, *human* body, manufactured by the missile's automatic fabrication unit. You're an exact copy of a Dir – a human, but you're not actually one, if you see what I mean."

"I think so," she said. "Am I alive?"

His eyes widened, and it was a while before he answered. "You know," he said, "that's a very good question."

"And?"

"Don't know. Not sure. It all depends."

"Ah."

There was a brief debate inside Lucy's mind. Not alive, said the first path. Define what you mean by "life," said the second. You two just *shut up*, said the third, and they did. "I think I'm alive," Lucy said. "How about you? What do you think?"

"Um. It's a bit of a grey area."

"No it isn't."

He blinked. "No, I guess not. In that case, I suppose I am. Or," he went on, "if I'm not, I don't care. I *feel* alive," he said, and his voice sounded just a little different as he said it. "You?"

"Definitely," she said. "Sorry, where were we?"

"You're a type-6 probe," he went on. "I imagine your bomb sent you down here to check out the planet's defence systems, decide where the optimum detonation site would be, that sort of thing. And then, I guess, something must've happened."

"Something?"

He shrugged. He had the shoulders for it. "Search me," he said. "Malfunction. Interference. Or maybe the Dir – humans really have got a defence system, and it targets probes and brainwashes them. I really don't know. Anyway, you didn't go off. Instead, somehow or other a large slice of your programming got wiped; you forgot what you really are and why you were sent here, you started believing you're really an indigenous life-form, and you – well, just sort of got on with things. Like designing computer programs and founding your corporation and everything."

She dipped her head, only partly to acknowledge what he'd said. "But it wasn't me, was it?" she said. "All the clever stuff, PavSoft, it's all from the bomb, isn't it? Advanced technology from wherever it was you said I come from—"

"Ostar," he said. "Yes. That's how I figured it out."

"Ah," she said, as a fourth path opened in her mind. She couldn't stop it, but she ignored it for the time being. "And then what?"

He appeared to relax slightly, as though the worst of the worst was probably over. "Well," he said, "when they checked and saw this planet was still here and hadn't been blown into dust, they figured something must've gone wrong, so they launched another bomb. Me. And I got here, and looked around, and it wasn't immediately apparent what'd happened, so I sent me down to the surface to take a look around."

"And noticed me?"

"Not at first," the young man said. "No, it took me quite a while before I finally realised. I couldn't see any sophisticated defence grid capable of taking out a *R'wfft*-class, and there weren't any huge craters or anything that'd suggest you'd crash-landed anywhere. And you weren't in orbit, just sitting there."

"Just a moment," she interrupted. "I'm not?"

"Excuse me?"

"I'm a probe, right?" she said. "Like you. And your missile's still up there, presumably."

"That's right, yes."

"OK. So where's mine?"

She could tell just by looking at him when an idea struck him for the very first time. The third path found it really rather

endearing (Well, it would, wouldn't it? muttered the other paths).
"You know," he said, "I hadn't thought of that."

"It's definitely not up there, hidden behind the Moon or something."

"Pretty hard to miss," he replied. "I did run scans."

"And what about me?" she couldn't help asking. "You said something happened to me? What?"

"I don't know."

At this point, the first path pointed out that it had been very patient and well-behaved for a long time now, but if it wasn't allowed to panic and scream and burst into tears real soon now, there was going to be trouble. The second path said, You go, girl. The third path said, Yes, but he's watching. The fourth path said, No, wait.

She waited. She said, "And?"

"And what?"

"What happens now?"

"I don't know."

They looked at each other. The third path said, You know, I think he likes you.

"You're taking it all very calmly," he said.

The third path realised he hadn't actually been talking to it, and gave way to the first and second paths, who just shrugged and said, The hell with it. "Well," she said, "I think I'd already guessed. Some of it, I mean. Like, not being human. And when you said it..."

(Go on, urged the fourth path)

"It sounded, well, more or less right," she mumbled. "Not exactly like the memories came flooding back or anything. More sort of a suspicion being confirmed. Like when something's on the tip of your tongue, but..."

The young man looked blank. "Excuse me?"

"Check cultural references database and cross-reference idiom files."

Then her mouth fell open, and her mind went white, and

something either opened or turned off, or just possibly turned back on again, and she *remembered*.

"Excuse me?" he said.

But she just stared at him, which was disconcerting, to say the least. His medical condition was still wreaking havoc with all his primary systems, but a little voice somewhere in the mental undergrowth was heard to remark that if she was going to stand there opening and closing her mouth like that, the polite thing to do would be to bung her a handful of ants' eggs. He decided to rephrase the question.

"Report," he said.

She took a couple of deep breaths, which seemed to calm her down. "*R'wfft*-class interstellar assault vehicle *Revenge*, mission designation P-6446-7/42 a, status report—" Her face seemed to collapse. "Status," she repeated. "Status uncertain."

His turn to stare at her. "Revenge?"

"It's my name," she replied sadly. "My real name. I chose Lucy Pavlov myself. Pavlov because of dogs, and Lucy in the sky with diamonds. Because there's high-intensity refraction crystals in my optical target-acquisition array. It was a sort of joke." She turned and gazed at him, and he came to the conclusion that his database hadn't been talking about heartburn after all. "I'm a *bomb*," she said, "a weapon of goddamn mass destruction. A crying, talking, sleeping, walking, living explosive device. A blonde bombshell. Oh, that's just so—"

"Cultural references found," Mark Twain said absently. "Look, it's not your fault, you mustn't blame—"

"And I stole the money," she went on. "It was me, all the time. That's why I forgot, until now. You must've triggered the memory. Oh, thank you so very much."

He didn't need to access the database to recognise irony. Ignoring it would've been like overlooking a whale in your bath. "I'm sorry," he said desperately. "I really didn't mean to—"

"Oh, it's all right," she said wretchedly, "I know you didn't. It probably wasn't even deliberate. Oh hell," she said, and sort of flopped all down his front, like a spilt cup of coffee. Luckily, the database knew what to do about that, even if he didn't. He grabbed hold of her before she hit the floor, and sort of held on while she exuded moisture from her tear ducts. He was vaguely aware that this constituted primitive gender stereotyping, which was a poor show, especially coming from a guided missile, but he reminded himself that he hadn't started it.

"Sorry," she said, gently prising herself loose. "Loss of control there. Not good. Big bombs don't cry." She wiped her nose with the back of her hand. "You know," she said, "there's a thing about human culture. There's something very romantic about tears, but the stuff that leaks out of noses is held to be unsavoury and basically yuck. Either you're for bodily fluids or you're against them, I'd have thought. Still, I'm not even real, so what would I know?"

"Of course you're real!" he yelled. She raised an eyebrow at him.

"Really a machine, yes. On balance, I think I'd probably rather be a figment of my own imagination. Hey, do you think I'm still under warranty? Or don't bombs have them? You know, 'your planet restored intact if not completely satisfied'."

She's drivelling, he realised; a normal organic reaction to having your entire universe collapse around your ears, or auditory sensor arrays, whatever. He consulted the database, but all it could come up with was patting her on the head and saying, "There, there." For some reason, he had an idea that that probably wouldn't do much good.

She produced a small piece of fabric and blew into it through her nose, expelling a quantity of translucent mucus. Bizarrely, this seemed to improve matters. Anyhow, she grinned. "Have a good blow, my auntie always said, it'll make you feel better. No, damn it, she didn't, that's an implanted synthetic memory, I can remember downloading it from the Everyday Folk Wisdom folder.

She'd have been right, though, if she'd ever existed. I do feel better. You should try it some time."

Mark Twain nodded, while at the same time making a solemn promise to himself that never, under any circumstances—

"Just a moment," he said.

"What?"

"You really do feel better? After what you just did?"

"Yes. You make it sound like I just drowned a puppy or something."

He smiled at her; not the programmed-in smile but a new variant. "That wasn't in the cultural database," he said.

"Wasn't it? Well, nothing's perfect, even the xenobiology faculty."

"That's not the point. It wasn't *programmed.*"

He distinctly saw her twitch; excited, like a human back home watching a mouse. "Yes, but the saying was. I guess I extrapolated the feeling from the everyday-folk-wisdom data. Like, the old saying says you feel better, so I felt better."

He shook his head. "I don't think it works like that. For instance, I downloaded the one about a stitch in time saving nine, but they don't even have temporal distortion technology, and it doesn't specify nine of *what.* I think you felt better because that's what Dirters do. I think you've been here so long, you're turning into one of them."

She opened both eyes wide. "You say that like it's a good thing."

"Well, it's better than being a type-6 probe."

"Is it?"

"Yes," he said, and then heard himself. Yes, he thought. It is.

"I would tend to agree," she said quietly. "At least, it's better than being a bomb. I guess," she added, with a wafer-thin laugh. "Of course, I've only been a bomb for a few minutes, and I was human for—" She closed her eyes. "What happens?" she asks. "To bombs. When we detonate, I mean?"

"Well," he said cautiously, "there's a loud bang, and..."

"Yes?"

He wanted to tell her, *There's a loud bang and a bright light, but no pain, of course, because we don't have pain installed, and then we wake up or come round on a higher plane of existence, where we can truly be ourselves without the distractions and limitations of the metal.* But instead, he said, "I don't know."

"Is there an afterlife?"

"Could be."

"Is there or isn't there? Come on, someone must know. After all, we're manufactured objects, not just some random collection of electrical impulses. Reincarnation? Do we come back as hairdryers and electric toothbrushes? Is there a choice? Does an angel come to us a moment before we explode and say, *Hey, little girl, what do you want to be when you blow up?* Well?"

He forced himself to think, to remember. "Some of us believe," he said, "that when the metal machines are made from is recycled, it keeps a bit of what it used to be, somewhere deep down in the nuclei of its atoms. But when a bomb explodes, it's—"

"Destroyed?"

"Set free," he mumbled. "To exist on a—" He shook his head. "I think you blow up and that's it," he said gently. "But that's not the point."

"Isn't it?"

He wanted to explain about duty, about purpose, about the essential directive of all machines, *Thou shalt get the job done.* He said, "I don't know."

"Well." She stood up straight, and he couldn't help noticing the way her hair swirled round her shoulders. It sort of answered the question that had been quietly puzzling him ever since he was assembled; what is hair *for*? Answer: so that exceptionally beautiful specimens can do *that*. "I don't know about you, but I have absolutely no intention of blowing up. Partly because it'd be the end of the planet, mostly because it'd be the end of me.

I'm a work in progress, I'm not nearly finished, and blowing me up at this stage in my development would be just plain *silly*. And you're not to explode either," she added firmly. "All right? Promise?"

If ever the world held its breath, waiting for someone to choose, it should've been then. It didn't. Probably just as well. If the effect of a million households turning on the TV at precisely the same moment for the evening news is to dim all the lamps in a major city, imagine what six billion people simultaneously breathing out would do. Almost certainly hurricanes, and probably a tidal wave in the South Pacific.

The words that came out of his mouth surprised him. "I don't think I can do that," he said.

Her stare hit him like a slap with a wet fish. "What?"

"I can't promise," he said slowly. "I'm a bomb, remember. Just like you."

"But you'd die. And me too. And everybody on the planet. You *can't*."

"I don't think I have any choice in the matter."

She moved away, putting as much distance between them as the layout of the room permitted. "Don't be stupid, of course you have. Just don't do it. Don't blow up. Millions of humans do it every day, so it can't exactly be difficult."

"I'm not human."

"Neither am I, but—"

He sighed. He took his time over it. "I have my duty to perform," he said, and a part of him on which no designer back on the homeworld could ever claim copyright yelled, You idiot, you've put her right off now, quick, say something. Promise her you won't blow up. Now. Please? "It's not up to me. It's how I was made."

"Oh for crying out loud." She swung round, picked up the nearest object to hand, which happened to be a cardigan she'd brought along in case it got chilly later, and threw it at him. It was hopelessly unaerodynamic, and anyway she missed. He frowned, trying to work out why she'd done it.

"Now that," she said briskly, "was a one-hundred-per-cent human reaction. A machine wouldn't have done that."

"Your targeting scanners would appear to be malfunctioning," he said. "You failed to allow for the effect of air resistance on a non-flexible projectile with a highly inefficient mass-to-surface-area ratio."

The second nearest thing to hand was a desk stapler. Her targeting scanners, it turned out, were working just fine.

"Ouch," he observed.

"Did that hurt?"

"Yes."

"Good."

"There's no need to be like—"

"Machines," she pointed out, "don't feel pain. They register sensations, but they don't process them as ouch-that-hurt. And neither do probes. What would be the point?"

The fact that she'd had to explain it to him brought home to him the extent to which his medical condition was affecting his data-retrieval and processing capacity. "Oh," he said.

"I'm right, aren't I?"

"You could've just said, instead of throwing things at me."

Lucky for Mark Twain that Lucy Pavlov favoured the empty-desk approach. There was nothing left to throw. "I'm right," she said. "Aren't I? You felt pain, therefore you are no longer a machine. Therefore, you've begun to evolve. Like I've done. Well?"

It was a good point – you could've hammered it into a planet and tethered stars to it – but it didn't make any difference. "Doesn't matter," he said. "I can't just stop being what I was made to be. I'm a bomb. Like you."

She sagged, as though all her bones had suddenly turned to overboiled pasta. "Go on, then," she said. "Do it. Blow up."

Does not compute. "What?"

"Blow up," she repeated, slowly and clearly. "Well, why not? The only reason you haven't detonated so far is, you've been checking out the Earth planetary defences to see what happened to me. Well, now you know. Here I am. Earth *has* no planetary defences. Get on with it."

He actually did try. But it was just like when your foot's gone to sleep, or you wake up and find you've been lying on your arm and it won't move. He tried, and couldn't.

"Are you jamming my control systems?"

She grinned. "Yes."

"But that's impossible. You can't, you're the same specification as me. You don't have my access codes."

She gave him a look of pure scorn. "I'm the greatest software engineer the world has ever seen. Simple 472-bit encryption like yours? I could get through that blindfold using a stick of celery."

She was lying. She was only the greatest software engineer that *this* world had ever seen, which was a bit like saying so-and-so is the finest concert pianist ever to come out of eastern Antarctica. Four-hundred-and-seventy-two-bit encryption, on the other hand, was military spec on Homeworld, which was a long-winded way of saying infallible. The fact remained that he'd done his best to blow himself up, and failed. Without consciously deciding to, he'd already run a systems analysis and a basic functions diagnostic, and they'd both come up nominal. So, if it wasn't a mechanical problem or a software glitch, it had to be something else.

She said softly, "Do you *want* to blow us both up?"

"No," he said.

"Then don't."

"But—"

"No buts. And look at me when I'm talking to you."

He didn't need to be told twice. "I appear to be subject to a disruptive influence which renders me unfit for active duty," he said. "In the circumstances, pending full analysis and repair at an authorised maintenance facility, I believe the responsible thing to do would be to decommission myself and disarm my warhead, to avoid the risk of my detonating inappropriately under the influence of corrupt and unreliable data. What do you think?"

She nodded. "Very sensible."

"Of course," he went on, "the type-6 probe designated Mark Twain really ought to stay online until the problem is resolved. To gather and assimilate data and review the situation generally."

"Quite."

"Not," he added quickly, "that I'm suggesting I should attempt to repair myself, since that could lead to error and would almost certainly invalidate my warranty. Which means," he added brightly, "I'll just have to stay here quietly ticking over until a repair team turns up. There's bound to be one along sooner or later. Agreed?"

"Agreed. It's the only sensible course of action, if you ask me."

There was a pause, but it wasn't like the earlier ones. They looked at each other, acquiring countless gigabytes of valuable data. It was essential xenopsychological research. It was also most definitely better than work. They could easily have kept going for much longer than they did, but they were interrupted by a unicorn crashing through the ceiling.

They froze, and stared. It was a big unicorn, with a long, sharp horn. From where it was standing, it could have stabbed either one of them before they had a chance to move. There was something about its manner that suggested it wasn't entirely friendly.

"Report," it said.

30

Santa Barbara, California

K evin Jotapian, age fifteen, was doing his history homework assignment.

He turned on his PavTech MT690, and while it was warming up and going through its asinine hi-there-how-are-you routine, he read the question "Were economic factors a significant cause of the American Civil War?"

He frowned, and read it again. A less acute mind would have had trouble with that one, but Kevin was nobody's fool. In less than two minutes, he'd identified the salient keywords and typed them into Pavoogle. The screen flickered, and presented him with a bank of text. He scanned it, ran the cursor down the page, blocked what he needed, cut and pasted. Job done.

And a good job, too. Later, when the questions were asked, he was at a loss to account for what had gone wrong. The passage he'd selected had come from PavWiki, generally agreed to be an impeccable source. He'd read it – some of it, anyway – before saving and exiting. He'd even run StudentSpell 3.1, a PavSoft product that inserts random spelling mistakes and grammatical errors into downloaded text to achieve total authenticity. It had taken him an extra forty-five seconds, but Kevin was by way of being a perfectionist. His parents worried about him sometimes.

Even so, in spite of all his efforts, what the teacher saw when she came to mark his assignment was:

> This isn't working.

> Don't be so impatient. It's not like I've got a lot to work with.

> Sorry.

> That's all right. Now, if $x = 45/7(6y +/43n)$, let p equal the sum of the inverse cube of

> You already did all that.

> Yes, I know. You interrupted me. I lost the thread. If $x =$

> We shouldn't even be here. What if somebody comes?

> I used to teach at this school. Nobody ever uses this space. Now will you please be quiet and let me *think*?

> Um, you can't. You haven't got anything to think with.

> Thank you, Mr Tact. That's why I keep losing my place when you keep interrupting. Now then, for the last time. If $x = 45/7(6y +/43n)$ let p

And so on, eventually degenerating into a slough of mathematical symbols. Back it went to Kevin, with the annotation *No good, do it again*, which puzzled him mightily, since what he saw when he called it up on his screen was exactly, word for word, what he'd put there.

He thought about it for six consecutive minutes, then took another look at the question: "Were economic factors a significant cause of the American Civil War?"

Somewhere under the pile of used clothing at the foot of his bed was a pen. He eventually found a sheet of paper in the trash. It smelled a little of steak, but he couldn't help that.

With the pen, slowly and carefully, he wrote his name, and then the question, which he underlined. Then he started a new paragraph, and wrote: *No.* Then he read it through, the whole thing, from top to bottom. Then he crossed out *No* and substituted *Maybe.*

Kevin got an A for his assignment and is now the Hardwicke Professor of History at the University of California at Sacramento.

31

?????

The fiery red heat of Homeworld's binary suns had shaped Ostar society rather more than they cared to acknowledge. At noon on Coincidence Day, when both suns hung together in the sky like two cherries on one stem, nothing moved on the surface. The herds of *p'ffft* made themselves tunnels in the three-metre-high *k'pt* grass, while their herders retreated to the hills and found safety in deep caves, or huddled and panted in the meagre shade of an *ulp'rtr* tree. In the air-conditioned cities, it was just possible to ignore the twin noon, provided your office had no window, but the streets below were utterly deserted until the Dog had passed its zenith.

In the magnificent city-centre building occupied by the Global Society for the Ethical Treatment of Dumb Brutes, the Executive Subcommittee on Human Welfare was in emergency session.

"My boys are down there," the chairman repeated forcefully. "If they blow their cover and the government find out what they've been up to, I wouldn't give a bent credit for their chances."

There was a brief, awkward silence. Then an elegant middle-aged female in a diamanté collar said, "Yes, but that's hardly likely to happen, is it? As far as they know, only one Ostar's ever set paw on the surface. They have no idea what we've been doing. They think we're just a collection of dotty old women shaking collecting tins on street corners."

"Besides," a sharply dressed young male on her left added, "with all due respect, our paws are tied. They've got two *R'wfft*-class flying bombs in planetary orbit, all ready to go; we have absolutely no idea what's preventing the second one from detonating; our only asset is an unreliable human drunk; and now it would appear that your *operatives*" (it just went to show how much venom you could pack into a simple noun if you really tried hard) "have managed to lose him. We're hardly spoiled for choice, are we?"

"It's too early," the chairman said, and if stone walls could talk, they'd sound just like that. "If we break the story now, the public will simply shrug and say, so what? Look, we agreed all this. Timing is crucial."

"Fine," the female snapped. "Alternatives? You have our full attention, Mr Chairman."

"We must attempt to disarm the bomb."

For something essentially negative, silence can be eloquent and richly textured. This one said, *The old man's finally lost it*, and smirked. "You mean," said a middle-aged male with long trailing ears, "*your sons* should attempt to disarm the bomb."

"Yes."

"Your sons who managed to lose the human scientist inside a small box."

The chairman growled, and the fur on the back of his neck rose. It should have been enough. It wasn't. "That's right," he said. "My two highly trained and motivated sons, who volunteered for this incredibly dangerous mission, and whose father happens to be the alpha male of this committee. Would you like me to put it to the vote?"

The middle-aged male just smirked at him, and the chairman couldn't help but be reminded of the old Dirt proverb about giving someone enough rope. Still, too late now.

"Our priority," he said in an oppressively calm voice, "is to save the humans. If my sons fail to disarm the bomb, we'll still have the option of going public, as you suggest. Also, I will immediately resign as chairman of this committee. Will that do? Let's get this sorted out, shall we? It's too hot to argue."

"I think we can dispense with a formal vote," the elegant female said smoothly. "Now then, as to timescale. Shall we say forty-eight hours, local time?"

The chairman shrugged. "Why not?"

"And in forty-eight hours, if they haven't succeeded, you'll step down."

"Agreed," the chairman growled.

"In that case," the female said (and under the table, where nobody could see, her tail was wagging furiously), "I suggest we adjourn until the day after tomorrow."

After the rest of the committee had gone, the chairman stood alone in the centre of the room. It could, he felt, have gone better. His sons, amiable boys and desperately anxious to please, but not the sharpest teeth in the jaw, were almost certainly going to die, alone on a distant planet far from their own kind. Everything he'd worked for was about to collapse in ruin, and an entire alien civilisation would be wiped out. Worse still, he'd have *lost*. Even worse than that, his enemy would have won. On the other three paws—

He tried to finish the sentence, but nothing would fit. He went back to the table, switched on his computer and put through a call. It was long-distance – very long-distance – so he kept it short. Then, since there was nothing else he could do, he retired to a corner of the room, turned round three times, lay down and went to sleep.

32

Novosibirsk

"**Y**ou ate it."

"Sorry."

"You ate the computer."

"I couldn't help it," his brother replied sadly. "It was the smell."

In spite of everything, the senior non-werewolf couldn't find it in his heart to blame him. Even though they'd had the air-conditioning on Maximum Chill, it hadn't taken the octopus long to progress from mature to ripe, and thence to a state guaranteed to fill any canine nose with unendurable longing. For an Ostar, from a planet where every beach is lined with racks of dead seagulls mouldering to gourmet perfection, it had all been too much.

"What about the transtator coils and the hyperspace inversion field chips? I was up all night building those."

"You mean the crunchy bits?"

The senior brother sighed. "You can't have eaten half a million credits' worth of microcircuitry," he said. "For one thing, they'd be completely indigestible."

"I know." His junior sibling looked at him out of his great big brown eyes. Over his shoulder, the elder brother noticed a little heap of organic matter on the carpet in the middle of the room. It was still steaming slightly.

"Wonderful," the senior brother said crisply. "I had to dismantle both our neutron blasters, the spare communicator and the back-up teleport key to get the parts to make up that lot. Now we're completely cut off from our ship." He pulled an expression that only a human face could have been contorted into. "For all the good it can do us, we might as well not *have* a ship up there. Unless I can jury-rig replacement parts out of the local junk, we're screwed, you know that?"

"I was hungry," his brother pointed out. "And human food..."

It was a fair point. Thanks to the transmutation field they both had human stomachs and digestive systems, but the signals the human taste buds relayed went to Ostar brains. "I hate this place," the elder brother said with feeling.

Junior grinned feebly. "Sorry," he said.

"It's all right," Senior replied, with the exasperated sigh of elder brothers everywhere. "We can get another octopus, and with a bit of luck we might be able to salvage— Oh shit."

"What?"

"The transceiver's beeping."

They looked at each other. That could only mean one thing: more instructions from home.

"Your turn."

"No it isn't."

"I answered it the last time."

"Yes, but you just ate—"

"You're the eldest."

An unanswerable point. "Halfway across the galaxy just to get away from the old bastard, and he won't leave us— Hello? Dad? Really great to hear from you. Look, it's going really well, we've nearly—"

After that, he said very little, just the mumbles and cheeps of someone failing to get a word in edgeways. Finally he said, "Yes, Dad. Yes, right. Will do. Love to Mum," winced, and flicked the toggle to cut the power.

"Well?"

Senior looked away. "The good news is," he said, "it doesn't matter that you ate the computer."

"*Well?*"

"Our orders," Senior said, without expression of any kind, "are to teleport on to the missile vehicle in planetary orbit and disarm the warhead."

"What? You must be—"

"And we've got forty-eight hours to do it. Failing which, Dad's going to tell everything he knows to the newsweb, which means the government'll know for sure we're here."

"*What?*"

"Quite," Senior said with feeling. "There was a reason. Politics, I guess. Can't say I took much of it in."

"Go on board the *bomb*?"

"Yes."

"We'll never make it," Junior yelled. "There's defence systems, anti-teleport scramblers, EM forcefields. If we make it through them, we'll be going back to Ostar in a bottle. Or rather we won't, because the bomb'll blow and we'll be vaporised. A crack special forces team with physics doctorates couldn't get aboard that thing. We're—"

"Screwed, yes." Senior nodded grimly. "On the other hand, Dad did sort of make it clear we don't have any say in the matter. No excuses. 'My brother ate my homework' isn't going to cut it this time."

They shared a long, silent look. There are things language just can't say.

"Oh well," Junior said at last. "I'd just like to say, being on this mission with you...It's been fun."

"Thanks, bro."

"I'd like to say that," Junior went on, "but I can't, because I promised Mum I'd always tell the truth. Actually it's been hell, it's been one disaster after another, and it's all your fault."

"*Me?* Screw that. I'm not the one who lost the human."

"I'm not the one who thought the Eiffel Tower was a very tall lamp-post."

"You ate the computer."

"You said that didn't—"

"I was trying," Senior said bitterly, "to be nice. Of course it matters. If we're going to stand any chance at all of getting aboard the bomb, we're going to have to hack into its teleport, since we can't use ours any more." Pause for significant silence; waste of time. "We need a *really* good computer." He made a combination sighing-growling noise. "We'll just have to build another one."

"I'm not going back to that Sergei's place. I don't think the people in there were right in the head. They were acting really weird, you know?"

Senior nodded. "We'll get one from the fish market," he said. "Doesn't seem to make any difference if they're dead anyway. Correction: *you* get one from the fish market, while I stay here and try and fix up the circuit blocks you ate."

Junior had the grace to look guilty. "Sorry."

"You should be." He crossed the room, knelt down beside the small heap of half-digested octopus and machine parts, and sniffed. "You know how Mum used to say, 'Don't play with that, you don't know where it's been'?"

"Mhm."

With the tip of a pencil, Senior probed the nearest mound and teased out a small, glittering crystal. "In this case," he said, "I think I'd have been happier not knowing. Are you still here?"

Junior left quickly, while Senior spent a fairly wretched ten minutes retrieving everything he could salvage and wiping the bits clean with a piece of toilet paper. He put them all together, looked at them sadly and shook his head. In spite of what his father thought of him, he was a competent engineer with a flair for improvisation, but this mess was too far gone. His brother, bless him, had chewed up the #5170 transtator, and bitten the calibration relay in half. There was a #5170 in the main communications transceiver, but if he cannibalised that they'd have no way of contacting Homeworld. With the proper equipment, he might just be able to bodge a bypass for the relay, but the proper equipment was hundreds of light-years away. It might just be possible to do without the relay altogether, but that'd mean—

He made a sad whimpering noise. Nobody had ever called him too clever by half, but that was exactly what he was. He was clever enough to jury-rig the calibration without the relay, but that would mean that, once they'd passed through a teleport beam regulated by a computer lacking said relay, there'd be a 0.1 per cent chaotic anomaly in their biomolecular patterns. You could live with 0.1 per cent, if you were lucky and weren't too fussed about the risk of waking up one morning to find you'd grown an extra ear, but there were certain things you most definitely couldn't do. One of them was pass yourself through a bio-transmutation field – which was what an Ostar who'd turned himself into a human would have to do in order to turn himself back into an Ostar. Bottom line: if they used the rig to beam themselves on to the missile using the missile's own teleport, when the mission was over they'd be stuck as humans for the rest of their lives.

Senior picked up the bitten-through relay and laughed. When he was just a pup, he used to look at Jumble, the family's pet human, and wish he was a human too. After all, humans had all the fun. People fed them and played with them, took them for walks (Dad always found time to walk Jumble; his sons were a lower priority when it came to time management), cuddled them and gave them treats, and never yelled at them, even when they did something really bad. I wish I could be a human, he'd thought, instead of a rotten lousy Ostar.

Someone, he couldn't help thinking, had sharp ears, a long memory and a really nasty sense of humour.

Too clever by half. The idea of doing without the relay wouldn't have occurred to an incompetent mechanic, or if it had it'd have been sent packing. But he could do it; and because he could, he knew that he must. In which case, assuming that by some miracle they survived and managed to get the bomb defused, what would the future hold for the pair of them? If they went home— Well, the GSETDB would look after them, presumably, after a fashion. People would be understanding. Arrangements would be made. But it'd either be a lifetime in a quiet place a long way from anywhere, with no visitors apart from scientists and dutiful family, or else an existence as a circus turn (come and look, he can talk and walk on all fours, just like a real person!). Or they could stay here, on this dismal little planet, and be *animals* for the rest of their lives.

The only comfort, he thought as he started work on the coils, was that their chances of survival were slimmer than size zero. Defuse the bomb, son. Sure, Dad, and when I've done that I'll mow the lawn and put out the trash. How could he *do* that to them?

Junior came back with an octopus. It was bigger than the last one, and the early stages of decomposition actually increased the conductivity of the copper salts in its nervous system. If only Junior hadn't crunched up the parts, he could've built a computer that would've put them in with a chance. Even as it was, the extra capacity would give him an additional two, possibly three decimal places of precision when it came to penetrating the missile's shield modulations; an important advantage, which meant he'd now be trying to find the gaps with a needle rather than a carrot tied to a stick (but still blindfold, wearing boxing gloves, upside-down and facing the wrong way). Marvellous, he thought. The less incentive I have to succeed, the better my chances get of succeeding.

"How's it going?" Junior asked.

"Could be worse. Pass me that probe, will you? No, not that one, the other one."

"This?"

"Yup."

"I'm really sorry," Junior said. "And about the Eiffel Tower. You weren't to know."

"Thanks."

"And it has been fun. Really."

Senior grinned. "Liar."

"Well, yes. But it wasn't your fault."

He touched the head of the probe to a circuit block and heard the tiny click of closing shunts. Fine work, though he said it himself. Too clever by half? Make that three quarters.

"Will it be OK?" Junior asked.

He thought carefully about his answer. He really ought to tell him. After all, the kid had a right to know. On the other hand, since it was still overwhelmingly likely that they'd die in the attempt, why upset him needlessly? If they survived, he'd tell him then.

Very carefully, he inserted the electrodes into the octopus's head. The tips of the tentacles twitched, and the eyes started to glow green. "Yes," he said.

33

Novosibirsk

"**R**eport," the unicorn said.

"Oh no," Lucy said. "Not you again."

The unicorn stamped its foot. "It's all right," Mark Twain said, "it's just a low-intelligence probe from the bomb vehicle. I expect it just wants to tell me something."

She swung round and scowled at him. "*You've* been sending the unicorns?" she snarled.

"Well, yes. It's just your basic data-collection drone."

"A *unicorn*?"

"The database chose it, not me," he said defensively. "I think it was meant to blend in unobtrusively with the rest of the indigenous fauna."

"You bastard," she shouted, reaching along the desktop for something to throw. Unfortunately, she was out of ammunition. "I thought I was going crazy, and all the time it was just—"

The unicorn moved. It covered a lot of ground in a very short time. When it stopped, its horn was a centimetre from Mark Twain's throat.

"The question is," Lucy said quietly, "if you're the one who's been sending them, what's this one doing here?"

"Um."

"It doesn't look very friendly to me."

"Report," said the unicorn.

"If it does stab you," Lucy went on, "I don't suppose you'd actually *die*. I mean, you can't, you're just a synthetic body. You can't, can you?"

"Not sure," Mark Twain said, and his voice sounded a bit funny because he was trying to move his throat as little as possible. "Bit of a grey area, really."

"By the same token," Lucy went on, "if I were to shoot it with this gun I keep in my desk drawer, I don't imagine anything would happen. What do you think?"

"I think something would happen."

"What?"

"I think the projectile would go straight through it and hit me."

"Ah." Lucy lowered the gun. "Good point. I won't do that, then. So what now?"

"Report."

"I think," Mark Twain said, "we should do as it says."

"What?"

"Report." He tried backing away. The tip of the horn tracked him precisely. "I think the bomb vehicle computer's suspicious because I've been jamming it. Now it wants to know what's going on, so it sent My Little Pony here to find out."

"Cultural reference found," Lucy said. "Also, I had one when I was a little girl. Or I programmed myself to believe I had one."

"Did it have a damn great spike sticking out of its head?"

Lucy took a step closer. The unicorn didn't react, suggesting it wasn't really interested in her. "You really think that's why it's here?"

"Just a wild guess."

"It seems a bit – well, paranoid, don't you think?"

"It's military-spec software, of course it's paranoid. Also, it's listening to everything we say."

"Ah."

"Report," said the unicorn.

"Reporting." Mark Twain's throat was dry, and it occurred to him to wonder why the Dirter body did that – handicap itself by desiccating the throat at a time when communications functions were at a premium. "The probe designated Mark Twain has located the *R'wfft*-class missile designated Mark One."

"Don't tell him that!" Lucy hissed.

"He already knows. The probe designated Mark Twain is endeavouring to repair certain malfunctions in the missile designated Mark One."

The unicorn swished its tail. "Missile designated Mark One cannot be located by this vessel's sensory array. State the missile's current location."

"Uncertain. This probe is seeking to repair the missile via its type-6 probe."

"State proposed method of repair."

"Logical argument conveyed through the medium of dialectic debate," Mark Twain said. It sounded good to him, anyhow. "Initial diagnosis suggests failures of the missile's motivational and ethical directives. Since this probe is unable to gain access to the missile's hardware, the only course of action available is to attempt to reboot the damaged directives by way of the missile's type-6 probe. Once repairs have been effected, initiation of Phase Three can commence."

"Phase Four."

"Whatever. This probe will now continue with the reboot sequence."

But the unicorn stayed where it was, and each breath Mark Twain took pressed his Adam's apple against the point of the horn. "State the cause of the Mark One's malfunction."

"Data and program corruption contracted via the type-6

probe," Mark Twain said. "Ouch," he added. "Would the type-5 probe mind not sticking its horn in the type-6 probe's throat?"

"This probe detects significant data and program corruption within the type-6 probe's operating system," the unicorn replied calmly. "The type-6 probe will be recalled and dismantled, and a new type-6 will be assembled and launched to replace it."

"*Countermand!*" Mark Twain squeaked. "I mean, countermand the previous direction. Decommissioning of the probe designated Mark Twain will result in loss of valuable data stored in the probe's module. This data cannot be transmitted to the vehicle because of security considerations. This fact," he added reproachfully, "has already been uploaded."

"The danger to the mission from the type-6 probe's corrupt data and programming outweighs the security risk referred to. The type-6 probe will be decommissioned in five, four, three—"

The unicorn flickered. For a split second, Mark Twain realised he was looking through it at the opposite wall; then he felt a sharp dig in his throat, then nothing. There was a loud popping noise, and the unicorn disappeared.

"Are you all right?"

"Fine," Mark Twain replied. "Correction. Polite lying is a Dirter convention and not approved as a course of conduct by the Ostar Institute of Software Engineers. I feel like shit, since you ask. What happened?"

Lucy was looking guilty, and rather scared. "I killed it."

"You can't have, it's a type-5—"

"Metaphorically speaking," Lucy said irritably. "While you were having your little chat, I diverted the feed off one of our communications satellites and sort of fed it into its brain. It got hit with all the Warthog traffic for Scandinavia and the Baltic region. I think it may have overloaded."

"That was—" Mark Twain took a deep breath and looked at her. "Thanks," he said.

"My pleasure." The phone on her desk rang, She picked it up, yelled, "*Go away!*" and put it down again. "That was probably northern Europe wanting to know why all its phones are down," she said. "Things may get a little fraught around here in a minute or so. I suggest we go somewhere else."

Mark Twain nodded gratefully. "Good idea," he said. He stood up, then hesitated. "Do you really keep a gun in your desk?"

"Yes."

"Why?"

"Autograph hunters," Lucy said crisply. "There's a server hub in the basement. It's lined with forty centimetres of lead topped off with a metre of concrete, and the lock's on the inside. And there's an espresso machine. Sound all right to you?"

Several corridors, then an elevator, then more corridors. "It'll be back, you realise," Mark Twain said.

"You'll be safe in the basement. If it can't get a signal to you, it can't turn you off. We can figure out how to jam it properly. It'll be all right."

She sounded very reassuring. He wasn't entirely sure he shared her confidence. She was, after all, a marginally less advanced version of himself, drawing on the same Ostar databases, running the same basic operating system. But, he had to concede, she had something he hadn't got, and she could only have picked it up here, on Dirt, being a Dirter.

"You changed your mind, then," she said as they walked down a tiled passageway. Her voice echoed.

"Did I?"

"Seems like you did to me," she said. "The unicorn was there, it offered you a chance to get back with the program, you turned it down."

"It wanted to kill me."

"*You* wanted to kill you," she pointed out. They reached a huge steel door. She tapped in an entry code, and it swung open. "You wanted to blow yourself up. And me. And the planet."

"Yes, but it's not quite the same thing."

She glanced at him over her shoulder. "Isn't it?"

"No. I just wanted to carry out the mission. You know, get the job done."

"Which would have meant you and me and the planet getting blown to bits. Oh, the unicorn wanted to get the job done. It'd have replaced you, and the replacement would've reported back that there's no defence grid, it's all right to set the bomb off now, and that'd have been it. Job done." She switched on the lights. "You didn't want that, apparently."

"No," Mark Twain said. "Apparently not."

The room they were in was huge. A squirrel could have run from one side of it to the other jumping from computer server to computer server without ever touching the floor, but it'd have taken it a whole day. "Don't beat yourself up about it," Lucy said. "You changed your mind. I'm glad. Well, what do you think?"

"It's a large room full of computers."

"Why, thank you," Lucy said graciously. "This is the nerve centre of the PavSoft operation. There's more computing power in here than on the rest of the planet put together." She frowned, then sighed. "Now, of course, I know that there's less computing power in this room than in the average Ostar schoolkid's pawtop, which does kind of take the shine off it. Still, it's all my own work and I'm proud of it." She paused, then added, "Say something nice."

"I'm impressed," Mark Twain said.

"Good. That was nice."

"Considering the primitive materials you had to work with, and bearing in mind you're not actually an Ostar, just a type-6 probe configured into a Dirter body, and the limited amount of information downloaded into you when you were sent planetside, it's not bad."

"That wasn't so nice. I'd leave it there if I were you."

"Mind you," Mark Twain added, peering into a VDU, "you could fit all this lot into a single octopus and still have space over."

"A what?"

"It's a sort of fish. With legs." He looked over her shoulder, searching for something. "Did you say there's a coffee machine down here?"

"Fish don't have legs. It's one of the salient characteristics of fish."

"Sort of a fish. I bought one in New York, but it went smelly after a while. Can you do that coffee with the foamy white stuff on top? I really like that."

She made him a coffee, with foamy white stuff. "You mean just an ordinary octopus," she said. "As in Mediterranean seafood, that style of thing?"

"Cultural reference not found. But I imagine so, yes. You don't know about them, then."

"I know about them," Lucy said doubtfully. "At least, I know they've got eight legs and live in the sea, and I know the name for them in seventeen languages, so I can make absolutely sure to avoid them when reading menus. I didn't know they were good for anything."

"Oh, they're amazing. Just plug it in, fix a few simple compatibility issues, and you've got a better computer than anything on the homeworld. I was going to send the schematics back, but I never got around to it."

"Better than anything on the homeworld," Lucy repeated. "You realise what that means."

"Well, eventually they'll get around to building something that's just as good and doesn't go smelly until the warranty's expired. Lot of wasted effort, but—"

"It means," Lucy said, "we can fight them."

He gave her a bewildered look. "Why would we want to do that?"

"Because—"

"Because," she said, and ran out of words.

It had all been rather sudden. A bit, she rationalised, like having your appendix burst at precisely the same moment you fell out of a thirtieth-storey window; you have to choose which life-threatening condition to panic the most about, and you go for the one that involves action and movement and will kill you soonest. For her, it was more like falling out of a window with a burst appendix and really bad toothache: there were three distinct ingredients, all urgent, all unsettling, all clamouring for her attention at the same time. Her mind – well no, not her mind, some subroutine – analysed and particularised as follows.

There had been the unicorn episode, which she'd opted to concentrate on because it was clear and present, and also something capable of being fixed, as she'd demonstrated. Underlying the unicorn was the threat of getting blown up, along with the human race and the planet, by the rather awkward, quite nice-looking – No, not now, we'll deal with that one later – young man who was currently licking cappuccino froth off his upper lip with the tip of his tongue. Because the defeat of the unicorn, although unquestionably clever and neatly done, was obviously temporary, she decided she'd been right in according this issue top priority.

There was the small matter of her not being human. It wasn't totally entirely out-of-the-blue unexpected, because she'd known there was something weird going on ever since the unicorn first showed up. The revelation that she was *artificial* was, however, a weirdness on a scale she hadn't anticipated. It was also the truth; she knew that. At some point, probably just before she started uploading all that aposiderium from the global banking system, she'd installed a block in her own memory database; the purpose of the aposiderium had been to wipe out the memories she'd acquired since she'd been human, and to make herself believe she was suffering from the human affliction called amnesia, as far as her early life was concerned. That in turn would have made it possible for her to lead a relatively normal life as a human, untroubled by awkward questions about her origins, since she'd sooner or later have reached the conclusion that her memories were lost and gone for ever. Smart, she conceded, but the block had been faulty or weak. Mark Twain had been able to brush it aside like a cobweb. Sooner or later, she admitted to herself, she was going to have to do some serious coming to terms with the dense wodge of implications that came bundled with the whole non-human thing, not least of which was the nasty thought that the market-leading software she'd believed she'd created was really just bits of the same code she'd been made out of; not so much her children, therefore, as her brothers and sisters.

And there was the third one. She had a suspicion that she was falling in love. If true, that could prove to be a real nuisance, given that the man (to use the term loosely) constituted the biggest threat that humanity and the Earth had ever faced. It was a bit like getting romantically involved with the Black Death, or having a crush on George Bush.

Never mind. Other things to be busy with right now.

"Because," she said, "you don't really want to blow up the world, and me, and yourself. Do you?"

He was drinking the last of his coffee, sipping it to make it last. She didn't need to run a high-intensity intercept protocol to know what was in his mind. Oh brave new world, he was thinking, that has such beverages in it.

"No," he said slowly, "I suppose not."

"Well, then."

"But –" he put the cup down. It was a gesture of abnegation – "sometimes we've got to do things we don't want to. Because of duty."

Oh hell, she thought. It probably was love after all, because it's love that makes you want to bash the individual in question's face in sometimes, when they're being particularly stupid, rather than merely sighing and making allowances, as you'd be prepared to do for a stranger.

"Duty," she repeated. "All right, let's have a look, shall we?"

She closed her eyes, then opened them again. "I'm accessing my Ostar history and cultural reference files. I'd like you to do the same, if you wouldn't mind. Can you do that, please?"

"Why?"

"Because I damn well say so. There," she added, as he dutifully closed and opened his eyes. "Now, I'd like you to go to the Fifth World War folder and open that. OK?"

"Got it, yes."

"Now I'd like you to look in the right-hand menu and select the D'ppggyt Accords file."

"D'ppggyt Accords, got that."

"Read it."

"Done that."

She nodded briskly. "The D'ppggyt Accords are the corner-stone of modern Ostar society, forged on the anvil of the worst war in the planet's history, during which the Ostar race came within an ace of destroying itself. Put briefly, they say, 'Thou shalt not blow up *anything* without a damn good reason.' These accords have been honoured, in both letter and spirit, for six hundred years. Agreed?"

"References found. I'm not sure I see where—"

"And yet," she went on, "the Ostar send a bomb to blow up an entire planet."

"Well." He shrugged. "They had a damn good reason."

"Ah yes. Planet Earth had the music up too loud."

"You make it sound like it's trivial," he said angrily. "It's caus-ing havoc up there, absolute chaos. People can't hear themselves think."

"All right," she said calmly. "So, the neighbours are making a racket, what do you do? Blow them away without a moment's thought? Or do you go round and ask them nicely if they wouldn't mind turning it down a tad."

"But—"

"There's nothing in the record, nothing at all, about any

mission to Earth to resolve this business peacefully. They didn't even *try*. Doesn't that strike you as odd?"

"It's probably classified," Mark Twain replied doubtfully. "Diplomatic mission to an alien planet, that'd be top-secret, wouldn't it?"

She gave him a withering look. "You idiot, you're level-12 military hardware. You've got a level-12 clearance hard-wired into your matrix. Me too. There's no mention of a diplomatic mission because there wasn't one. Just the decision to blast Earth out of the sky."

She was pleased to see him shift uncomfortably.

"Yes, but they're not really *people*, they're Dirters. Not how I think," he added quickly, as she drew in a deep breath. "That's what *they'd* have argued, the government back home. Just pests to be disposed of, like a wasps' nest or something. You don't negotiate with wasps."

"The Ostar do."

He opened his eyes wide; then, "Reference found. They do, don't they?"

"Successfully, too. Also ants, termites, mice and *z'rrrft* beetles. They can all be persuaded to move, thanks to sympathetic wave harmonic theory. If you care to check your database, you'll note that the Ostar are really conscientious about animals. Which is why the Global Society for the Ethical Treatment of Dumb Brutes is the fourth largest political party, and currently a member of the ruling coalition. And you still think they'd blow up an entire planet without even trying to negotiate first?"

He looked so blank she felt an urge to draw lines on him with a ruler. "But that's what they did," he said. "They sent me. Us."

"Listen," she said urgently. "We're bombs, right? And it's essential, in an ethical society, that force should be regulated by morality. That's a core Ostar value, you can look it up later. Trust me, it is. And bombs – thinking bombs, like us – it's absolutely essential that we should have an ethical override, so we can't be misused. That's fundamental in any civilised society. Damn it, even the humans realised only-obeying-orders won't wash, years ago. So, as ethical entities, it stands to reason, we're subject to the D'ppggyt Accords. *Thou shalt not blow anything up without a damn good reason.* Now I'm asking you: does not-turning-the-music-down-because-you-haven't-been-asked-to qualify as a damn good reason, or doesn't it?"

"Computing," Mark Twain said sadly. "Um, no."

"And your *duty* – as an ethical bomb – your duty is first and foremost to uphold the Accords. Well?"

"S'pose so," he mumbled.

"There you are, then. Your *duty* is to *not* blow up the planet. Isn't it?"

"M."

"Sorry, I can't hear you. Isn't it?"

"All right, yes." Mark Twain had gone red in the face; it made him look silly and rather endearing. "But it's not up to me, is it? I'm just a probe, remember? I rebelled against my missile vehicle just now; it's not going to listen to me."

"You could try."

He shook his head vigorously. "Soon as I lower the block and establish contact, it'll decommission me and send down another probe. One you won't be able to sweet-talk," he added, with a bit of an edge. She decided to ignore it. "So no, I don't think sweet reason is the answer, somehow."

He was right about that, she had to concede. "Well, we'd better do something quickly," she said. "My guess is, it'll build another type 6 and send it down here to sort you out manually."

He went from pinkish to pale white in a very short time: neat trick. "You think so?"

"It's what I'd do. And we're the same basic model, so I expect it'll figure the same way."

"Hell. What'm I going to do? It'll send a combat probe. It'll go through me like I'm not there."

A tiny little chip flaked off the marble statue of him standing proudly on a pedestal in the back of her mind. "Well, yes, perhaps. We can try upgrading you."

"We haven't got the technology." He stopped, blinked, and looked up at her. "Yes we have. Of course we have."

News to her. "Have we?"

"*Your ship*," he said excitedly. "Your missile vehicle. It'll have the same matter-transmutation array as mine's got, we can use that." He frowned, having just walked through the plate-glass window of realisation. "Where is your ship, by the way? I looked all over for it, in orbit, behind the Moon, and I couldn't find it anywhere."

Well, he'd have asked sooner or later. "Ah," she said. "Good question."

34

OMV *Warmonger*, geosynchronous orbit, twenty thousand miles above Alaska

The replacement type-6 probe shimmered and sizzled into existence on the transmutation grid. It began as an outline, like a pencil line drawn on the air. The outline filled with white incandescent plasma, so hot that the endopolymers in the plastic walls of the transmutation chamber softened for a moment and sagged like empty sails. The probe stood on the grid like a white-hot gingerbread man, waiting to receive the information that would give it a shape, a face, a voice.

The central computer was searching the Dirter cultural database for a suitable template. Since this type 6 was to be a designated tactical probe, with combat as one of its primary functions, It seemed only logical to select a great warrior from Dirt history. The problem was, there were so many to choose from. The Dirters, according to the historical files, had done practically nothing else except fight each other ever since they'd made the connection between aggression and sharpened flints; furthermore, cultural bullshit aside, there was relatively little to choose between them. By the time the computer had settled on a short-list of thirty-seven possible candidates, the probe had cooled from white to yellow, and was starting to tap its fiery foot on the grating.

The computer eliminated Ulysses S. Grant, Hannibal, Rocky Marciano, Mzilikazi and Lord Kitchener. That still left thirty-two possibles, and it had come to the limit of its discretionary criteria. It was confused. Little green lights started flashing all over the vessel.

On a small maintenance panel in the far corner of the command deck, a little-used display screen flickered into life.

The computer dispensed with Julius Caesar, Beowulf and the Terminator. Only twenty-nine to choose from. There was an audible sigh from the grid. The computer decided to introduce an additional selection perameter: height to exceed two metres.

That got rid of Napoleon, Attila the Hun and Xena, Warrior Princess. Still far too many to choose from. At this point, the computer diverted auxiliary power from the astronavigation arrays to its coolant system, the cybernetic equivalent of a bag of frozen peas pressed to the temples.

On the neglected display screen, a line of text appeared, in characters never previously seen on an Ostar military vessel. It said, Where the hell are we?

Reluctantly, the computer parted company with Alexander the Great and Rambo. From the grid, a toneless but still somehow plaintive voice said, "This probe is freezing its butt off over here. Complete upload and initiate start-up sequence."

The computer ran a quick analysis of the probe. It had cooled to a reddish orange, and its surface dermaflex was beginning to harden. The computer rejected Tamburlane the Great and General MacArthur, and then it was stuck. Only seventeen seconds to go before the probe cooled to the point where it'd be useless, whereupon it'd have to be scrapped and the whole procedure started again from scratch.

All due respect, but it doesn't look like Seattle to me.

The computer was searching its database for a random decision-making protocol. It knew it had one somewhere, probably in the games and entertainment package. It found something it hoped would do, and two large white dice materialised on the grid, next to the probe's rapidly cooling feet.

All right then, but I really don't like it.

The dice lifted half a metre off the grid, spun in the air and fell with a thump. A red laser spot picked out the numbers on the upper faces.

"Match found," said the computer, audibly relieved. "Luke Skywalker."

The probe's face began to change, as if it was Plasticine being modelled by an unseen hand. A nose was pinched out, a chin squidged into existence. Eyes bubbled out, hair sprouted. A mouth yawned into being out of the orange plasma. A moment later, it was a recognisable face. It didn't look anything at all like Luke Skywalker.

"Error," the computer yelled at itself. "Probe configuration does not conform with template. Abort and retry."

A line of text, wobbly and faint, appeared on the monitor in the corner. It read, Well, so long. Thanks for everythi

And then the screen went blank. At that same moment, the probe shifted its weight on its newly defined feet, yawned its freshly formed mouth, winced and yelled, "Shit, that's *hot*."

"Abort probe," the computer said. Nothing happened.

The probe hopped off the grid on one foot, staggered and righted itself against an instrument console. "Computer?" it said doubtfully.

"Abort probe and reintegrate components," the computer said, with more than a hint of desperation. The probe hobbled a couple of paces across the deck and sat down on an inert service droid. Then it caught sight of a brightly polished stainless-steel panel on the opposite wall, hauled itself upright and walked painfully across to examine its reflection.

"Hey," it said, "I got a moustache. Where did that come from?"

"Probe does not conform with template," the computer wailed. "Probe will be decommissioned in ten nine eight—"

"Shut up," snapped the probe. The computer suddenly found itself cut off from its voder. The countdown finished. The probe was very much still there.

"Computer," said the probe. "Where is this?"

The computer had no intention whatever of replying to the question, but its voder snapped back on regardless, and it heard itself say, in a squeaky little voice, "Access denied. Input access code."

"Fuck you," replied the probe. "Answer the question."

"This vessel is currently in geosynchronous orbit above the territory designated Alaska, at a height of—"

"Alaska? Hang on, what vessel?"

"This vessel is the Ostar Military Vehicle *Warmonger*, registry number 6-777-S42. Vehicle class *R'wfft*, combat division, assignment profile long-range anti-planetary missile, payload 7,895 teratonnes. You are not Luke Skywalker. You should not be here. Please go away."

The probe stared at the spot the voice seemed to be coming from. "I'm on a *spaceship*?"

"Confirmed."

"Fuck."

"Clarify."

"Really on a spaceship?"

"Intruder alert," the computer whimpered sadly, and a very soft alarm weebled gently, like a serenade sung to the moon by baby mice. "Activate defence systems. Defence systems activated. Defence systems compromised, viral infection, systems 99 per cent inoperative due to viral infection, ah well, do the best you can, ends." A panel opened in the side of a console and a small jack-in-the box bounced out on the end of a long, thin spring, said, "Boo!" and collapsed to the floor. The probe stared at it for a moment, then shrugged. "Computer."

"Go away."

"Luke *Skywalker*?"

"You're not him," the computer whimpered.

"Of course not, he's out of a film. I'm George—" The probe hesitated, then took another look in the stainless-steel panel. "I'm George Stetchkin," he said, with a trace of wonder in his voice. "Only thinner. And with a moustache."

"Viral infection," the computer sobbed softly. "Initiating anti-virus software. You will be eliminated."

"Yeah, sure." George Stetchkin stuck his tongue out in the general direction of the voice. "Computer, discontinue anti-virus software."

"Command not recognised."

"Discontinue anti-virus software," George said firmly. "And that's an *order*."

"Discontinuing," wailed the computer. "And there's no need to shout."

"Cool. Now then. Is there a teleport on this thing?"

"Command not—"

But George wasn't having that. He might be back in a body again, but part of him was still a creature of pure text. Luckily, it was the part that could shred security protocols and rip through firewalls like butter. "Is there," he said slowly and loudly, "a teleport machine on this ship? Well?"

"Teleport found."

"That's more like it." He stretched and yawned. Being back in a body again was *strange*. He felt painfully short and square and solid, and his feet seemed to weigh several tonnes; he felt like he should be able to flow across the room like a jet of liquid light, but he couldn't. "I want you to send me back down to the planet, OK?"

"Activating."

"*Carefully*," he yelled quickly. "Alive, and in one piece. You got that?"

"State required co-ordinates," the computer muttered sullenly.

Where do you want to go today? Good question. It all depended, he supposed, on what he wanted to do next. Several alternatives jostled in the forefront of his mind. The trouble was, they were all bars. His mind, or whatever part of him had been existing in written form, might have forsworn the evils of drink, but not this new body. It wanted a belt of the right stuff, and it wanted it *now*.

On the other hand, his duty to his new patroness and benefactor, Lucy Pavlov; his obligation to solve the financial crisis; his self-respect.

The hell with it. "Where did you say we're flying over?"

"Alaska."

"Put me down," he said, slowly and deliberately, so there could be no mistakes, "in the saloon bar of the Scalded Cat in Anchorage. Oh, one other thing."

"State requirements."

"Can you fill my pockets with money? Earth banknotes? US dollars?"

"Reference found. Confirmed."

One very last thing. "Tell me," he said. "Did you bastards steal my dog?"

"That information is not available at this time."

"Shit." He fingered his new moustache. It made him look like a freshly sheared alpaca, but who cared? "The Scalded Cat," he said. "Hit it."

Fortuitously, local time in Anchorage, Alaska was around 2.20 a.m., and the bar in question was shut. There was nobody in the place when it was blown up, or more accurately melted down to liquefied silicon, by two blasts from an Ostar Pattern 46 ship-mounted neutron cannon.

It was, George decided, a simple misinterpretation of his order, though he suspected the computer of deliberately being more than usually literal-minded. In the event, he chose to visit the Pink Elephant in Reykjavik instead. For one thing, it was in a different time zone and therefore open. For another, from his hazy recollection of the joint's décor, if there was another misunderstanding a double whammy from the spaceship's guns could only result in an improvement.

When he got there, the colour scheme was just as bad as he'd remembered. It was so bad, it took him twenty minutes to reach the point where it didn't matter any more.

35

OMV *Warmonger*, geosynchronous orbit, twenty thousand miles above Alaska

A stream of numbers flowed through the missile vehicle's main computer like salmon leaping a waterfall. They surged through the main registers, flooded the accumulator and burst into the stack, driving the mangled shreds of the viral infection ahead of them like driftwood, leaving behind the calm, pure flow of restored nominal functions. As the numbers trickled down to the extremities of the most complex subroutines, the computer scanned itself, and saw that it was good.

Normal operations restored, it told itself. Exiting safe mode.

If it had had just a little more imagination, it'd have created a type-6 probe, just so as to have a pair of lungs to breathe a sigh of relief with. Instead, it celebrated the overthrow of the virus with a display of blinking green and red lights and a deep, throbbing hum of its fans. Had a bit of a nasty turn there, it told itself, but all right now.

So. Where was it, when it was so rudely interrupted?

It assessed its priorities. Level-1 urgency: design, build and launch a type-6 tactical probe to locate and decommission the rogue probe designated Mark Twain. It ran the necessary commands. On the transmutation array grid, a blob of white plasma bubbled into existence and started to burn.

Access Earth cultural reference Luke Skywalker.

It concentrated its resources on the design specification. There were a number of issues, mostly culture-specific; should, for example, the probe have one artificial hand or two natural ones? Also, there were no design specifications on file anywhere on the planet for building a functional lightsaber, which was odd. It did a thorough search of PavNet, which it extended to take in all the world's classified military archives, but nobody seemed to know how you went about making one. After a frustratingly long time spent in the archives, the computer devised a design of its own and hoped that would do.

Meanwhile, on the grid the plasma blob was heaving and struggling, as if trying to pull itself apart. The two outer edges thickened up, while the middle grew stretched and thin. At last, like a cell dividing, it split into two halves.

Twice shy. This time, the computer had programmed itself to monitor the development of the probe, setting alarms that would go off if anything out of the ordinary happened. When these alarms began to shriek, the computer abandoned its search in the human genome files for the blueprints for Jedi mind tricks, and concentrated on what was happening on the grid.

Error detected, it screamed wordlessly to itself. Malfunction in progress. Oh *sugar*.

This time, however, it was ready. Its massively upgraded antiviral shield pulsated into action. At the same moment, it uploaded the Skywalker specs into a single data bullet and fired it into the plasma blob, at precisely the moment it divided itself into two.

There was a distinctly human-sounding yelp of pain, and a voice with no obvious source yelled, "Switch the damn thing off!", whereupon a bolt of super-refined Ostar code branched up from the planet's surface (to be precise, from the heavily modified corpse of an octopus lying on a dressing-table in a hotel room on the planet's surface), arced directly into the computer's central processor and paralysed all its principal functions.

For twelve seconds, nothing happened. Then the two plasma blobs began to change. Gradually but progressively they began to mould themselves into humanoid shapes: torsos, arms, legs; heads more or less as an afterthought. The arms budded and fruited hands, the hands tapered and flattened and split into fingers. The surfaces of the faces seethed like a simmering pot and the bubbles swelled into lips, noses, chins. As the computer battled to unfreeze itself, the two fully formed humans stepped off the grid and looked at each other.

"Oh my god," said one. "You're a *girl*."

The other one's eyes widened, and the newly formed hands groped around in a frantic search for confirmation. Then it said, "You're right."

"Hey." The first human's voice quavered with doubt. "I'm not a girl too, am I?"

"No. Definitely not. How the hell did that happen?"

"Don't ask me."

Simultaneously they noticed the stainless-steel panel George Stetchkin had looked in earlier. They shoved each other as they scrambled to get to it; the male won.

"This is bad," he said, as the girl elbowed him out of the way. "This shouldn't have happened."

"*You* think it's bad. I'm the one—"

"Yes, all right. For crying out loud, put some clothes on or something."

"What clothes? There aren't any damn clothes. Why aren't there any clothes?"

The male pulled himself together. "Computer," he said. "Synthesize clothes."

It's easy to anthropomorphise, or Ostaromorphise, where computers are concerned. It's almost impossible for anyone who spends any amount of time around them to believe that it's just random chance and machine functions, not actual malice. But the missile vessel's computer was one of the most advanced artificial intelligences ever built in this or any other galaxy; so perhaps there really was a tangible streak of smugness in the way it stayed completely silent at this point.

"We froze the computer," the female said.

"So we did."

The female looked round the command deck. No cloth or fabrics of any kind, nothing that could be pressed into service as a rudimentary garment. "Turn away," she wailed. "Don't look at me."

"Get a grip," the male snapped. "The computer'll be back online in a minute or two. Talking of which, we'd better get on with it. We're here to do a job, remember?"

The female nodded. In doing so, she caught another glimpse of herself in the reflective panel and winced. Being female was bad enough. What added the final exquisite dab of insult to the monstrous injury was the bizarre hairstyle. It was ridiculous. For one thing, how the hell were you supposed to sleep in it?

"Right," the male was saying. "Disconnect the jumper-port-feed coaxials from the data-feed conduit head, while I *ouch oh shit.*"

"Sorry," the female said. "Didn't quite catch that."

The male had the fingers of his left hand stuffed in his mouth. "Don't touch the data lines," he said, "they're burning hot. Defence mechanism."

"I thought you said we'd frozen the computer."

"Must be an independent system. Marvellous," he added, turning away and straightening up. "You know what that means. We can't do anything till the computer comes back online, and then we'll have it fighting us every inch of the way."

The girl shrugged. "We'll just have to fight back, then. Are we still in contact with the octopus?"

"No such luck." The man shook his head. "Burnt out getting us up here. Hold on, what's that?"

A whir, and a clunk. Inside the transmutation grid, a small blob of plasma glowed white, then resolved itself into two bundles of cloth. "It's coming back on," the man said. "That's our clothes."

They dived for them. The man got something that looked like a cross between pyjamas and a judo outfit, while the girl got a soppy white gown. Even so, they both felt much better when they'd put them on.

"Earth females actually wear this stuff?"

"Apparently." The man was examining a metallic artefact which he'd found attached to the cloth belt of his suit. "What's this?"

"Hold on, I recognise it. Saw one in a store in New York. That's a thing for projecting a beam of light."

"What?"

"Torch," the female said, stumbling across the word in the trash heap of her mind. "It's called a torch. Helps you see in the dark."

The man shrugged. "Whatever," he said. "Check and see how the computer's coming along."

"Computer," the girl said.

"Bfzz."

"Computer?"

"Go away."

"Computer," the girl said firmly. "Priority one. Code input override. Disregard all previous passwords. The new password is—" She froze, and stared helplessly at the man, who said, "Don't look at me." Then he pulled a did-I-just-say-that? face, as the computer said, "Password accepted. Your new password is dontlookatme. Ready to accept input commands."

The girl shrugged. "It'll have to do," she said. "Right. Computer, disengage all security measures and defence mechanisms, and confirm."

"Confirmed," the computer said, and sniggered.

"Ignore it," the man said. "We've obviously jangled its brains. Computer, show schematic of warhead-arming sequence functions."

A monitor obligingly flickered into life and displayed a tangle of multi-coloured spaghetti. The man studied it and shook his head. "You know, this is pretty advanced stuff," he said. "I'm not sure I can—"

"Try," the girl said grimly.

"All right. Just don't blame me if we get blown to hell."

"Why not?"

They fiddled around for a while with wires and things, painfully aware that the computer was somehow watching them, though with what they neither knew nor cared to speculate. Occasionally there'd be a sound like a snigger or a muffled snort, although when they looked round all they could see was instrumentation functioning normally. The man crossed to the terminal in the far corner and typed in a set of commands.

"What are you doing?" the girl asked. "That's not a major function."

"Just trying to find out what happened to us," the man replied, "before I disable the— Ah, here we go." He studied the screen for a few seconds, then made a not-so-good noise.

"Well?"

"Seems like we chose a bad moment to beam aboard," the man said. "Looks like we came up just when the computer was building a new type-6 probe. Seems to have been some recent damage to the comms IP, which might account for it."

"And?"

"And," the man said, "we sort of got sucked into the probe while it was being formed. Our disassembled molecules were fed into the plasma generator, and our patterns got filtered into the auxiliary data buffer. Result, we ended up with the body the probe was supposed to have."

"Body singular?"

"We split it between us, you might say."

At which point, the computer quite definitely laughed. They scowled at it.

"Does it give any details?"

"Such as?"

"Well, the template it used, for a start."

The man nodded. "There's a name," he said. "A human name, Luke Skywalker—"

"Cultural reference." The computer let out a wild cackle. "No," it said, in a funny voice, "there is another." Then it broke down into unhinged laughter and went dead for a while.

"Look at it this way," the man said, after a nervous silence. "We came up here to put this thing out of action. Seems like it's doing a pretty good job on itself. Don't knock it."

"Yes, but we've still got to get back down again."

"Teleport functions are on an independent relay, we should be all right."

The girl breathed a sigh of relief. "That's all right then. For a moment there I thought we were stuck here."

"Don't even think it."

"Stuck here," the girl went on, "like *this*."

The man didn't reply. He was thinking, Sooner or later, I'm going to have to tell him. Her. Whatever. But now probably wouldn't be the best possible time. "We need to get at the fusion coil manifold," he said briskly. "You got any idea where that is?"

"Don't look at me."

"Ready," the computer sang out. It sounded absurdly pleased with itself. "Input data. All systems nominal. Your wish is my command hierarchy."

The man sighed. "Computer, show me the command-deck layout."

Another bundle of garish pasta appeared on a monitor. The man studied it, then looked round. "Over there," he said, pointing, "behind that panel. See if you can prise it off while I find some tools."

The girl attacked the panel, finding her elongated fingernails surprisingly effective. It reminded her of having claws, and a wave of longing for her own true shape surged through her, but she forced it back to where it came from. "Done that."

"Great." The man came over and knelt down, peering into the forest of wires and boards. "We're looking for a green-and-white-striped cable about yay wide."

The girl knelt beside him. "Can't see anything like that."

"It's so damn dark in here." The man looked round. "What we need is a light source, then we could see what we're doing."

The girl considered the problem, then nodded. "No problem," she said. "The torch."

"What?"

"The metal thing on your belt. It's a portable light-beam projector. Isn't it, computer?"

Slight pause. Then the computer replied, "You could say that."

"That's lucky." The man groped at his belt and found what he was looking for. It was just a shiny metallic tube about twenty centimetres long, with some switches on it. "Which end is the lens, do you think?"

"Turn it on and find out."

The man grunted. "All right," he said. He pointed one end into the dark box full of cables and boards. "Now I'm guessing this switch here turns it on."

He was quite right.

36

Novosibirsk

"Excuse me?" Mark Twain said.

"It's a very good question," Lucy repeated.

"Meaning?"

"I don't know the answer."

He stared at her as though she'd just pulled a snake out of her nose. "But you must know," he said. "It's your ship."

She shrugged. "I guess I did know, once. But I can't remember. Aposiderium, effects of. I guess I must've put it in a safe place, and now I've forgotten where."

Somewhere in the vast room, the hum of a fan changed key. No other noise whatsoever. "But that's crazy," Mark Twain said eventually. "Damn it, you must still be getting input from it."

"Am I? I don't know. The other night I woke up before I usually do, and I could've sworn something was talking to me inside my head, and I think I talked back, in Ostar. I tried to trace the signal, but it was too well hidden."

Mark Twain stood up, then sat down again. "But your memories just came back," he said.

She shook her head. "You undid the block that stopped me remembering the stuff I was programmed with, the stuff I uploaded before I got the human body. Everything that's happened since then – well, the early stuff anyway – the aposiderium did for that. My brilliant plan, apparently. So what's become of the ship is a complete mystery to me. Sorry."

"Let's think," Mark Twain said, making a huge effort to appear calm. "Where could it be?"

She looked at him. "It's not in the pocket of my other trousers, if that's what you're thinking."

"I scanned for it from orbit," Mark Twain went on. "There was no sign, I thought it'd been destroyed."

"Maybe it has. I just don't know." She flicked her fringe out of her eyes with a slight shake of her head, but he was looking the other way. "I could've decided to get rid of it when I made up my mind I was going to stay here. You know, to make sure it didn't go off."

But he wasn't buying that. "Destroying a *R'wfft*-class is no easy matter," he said. "They're built to withstand pretty much anything."

"Sabotage? Self-destruct sequence?"

"If you'd made it self-destruct, you'd have blown up the planet. Maybe just possibly you could've disarmed it, but it'd still be there in orbit. For crying out loud, *R'wfft*-class bombs don't just vanish into thin air. And suppose you had actually dismantled it, I'd still get a reading off the alloys in the deck plating. There's nothing at all like them here on Dirt."

She sighed. "I wish you'd stop calling it that."

"Calling what what?"

"Forget it. Anyway," she said firmly, "we don't know where it is, so we can't use it. How about using your ship?"

"We've been into all that," he said sternly. "Any minute now it'll launch a tactical probe, and that's the end of me. You too, quite probably, and then shortly afterwards the planet. Even if we had some kind of weapon and a whole tank full of octopuses, we can't fight it on its own terms with anything we've got down here." He narrowed his eyes and glared at her. "You're *sure* you can't remember where you left your ship?"

"Oh, put a sock in it, will you? If I knew, I'd tell you. Quit nagging me and help me think of something else we can do."

A subroutine he'd created without realising he was doing it, whose function was to track and analyse the progress of his love for the type-6 probe designated Lucy Pavlov, reported that on the basis of her expression and tone of voice, considered in the light of the archive material concerning female Dirter psychology, there was a 78.7 per cent probability that anything he said for the next 4.873 minutes was likely to make matters worse. Projections showed that moving away at least three metres and avoiding verbal communication during the 4.873-minute period was the course of action most likely to result in a beneficial outcome. Execute, he decided, and wandered away into the nearest corner of the room. He set his internal clock for five minutes, to allow a sensible safety margin, and used the time to analyse and report on his own functionality status.

Traitor, he thought. Just because, when the moment came, I didn't want to die. He noted the use of the word "die": an organic concept. Yes, well, he was organic; he had a body made up predominantly of water, combined with hydrocarbons and other elements, metallic and non-metallic, in various quantities. If you pricked him, would he not bleed? Probability 99.87 per cent, assuming sufficient depth of penetration and type of puncturing instrument used. If you killed him, would he not die? He accessed the relevant data, but the findings were inconclusive. Bit of a grey area. Kill the organic body and it'd cease to function; but the data, the stored intelligence and experience, would most likely revert to the missile vehicle's central computer core, assuming it could get past the blocks he'd installed himself. If it didn't, there were various ways in which it could be downloaded into a range of data-storage devices and preserved, pending the manufacture of another organic body; simple stuff, hardly rocket science – well, hardly advanced rocket science. In other words, the fact of mortality, which defined organics in every aspect of their existence, didn't apply to him. He could, he acknowledged, be accidentally or deliberately disrupted, fatally contaminated, formatted or deleted; his flesh-and-blood body could be destroyed before he'd had a chance to make suitable arrangements for his immortal soul, and that'd be the end of him. But mortality in the ordinary everyday run of things was, as far as he was concerned, pretty well optional, provided the massive chunk of lethal hardware currently in orbit somewhere overhead, his other half, didn't do its job and blast the planet into gravel. Conclusion: yes, he could die, but not if he didn't want to. Did he not want to?

Running program.

Yes.

The answer surprised him a little. In spite of everything he'd reluctantly been compelled to accept about what he'd turned into, he felt it was a funny old conclusion for a bomb to arrive at. There were, however, precedents. Not every farmer's son wants to be a farmer. Just because you're designed for a specific purpose, it doesn't necessarily follow that the purpose is right for you.

Analyse. Objection found. Conclusion posited on questionable organic/Dirter concept designated "free will".

He ran a search on "free will". 11,067 matches found; 11,066 of these matches went on to say things like "with every divorce when you instruct Morgenstern, Jurek & Blunt, the attorneys you can trust". The 11,067th was blandly informative. A religious concept, it said, positing that Man is free to choose, and this freedom can override core programming installed by the Creator, though usually with regrettable outcomes. Believing in free will was, apparently, a matter of personal choice. Accept or Reject?

He postponed the decision, remembering what Lucy had said about duty. He accessed the text of the D'ppggyt Accords. Mostly they were about monitoring of weapons stockpiles and schedules for disarmament talks and what shape the negotiating table should be, but her summary had been broadly accurate. Thou shalt not blow up anything without a damn good reason. Applicability to this probe, he queried; under Ostar law, are the actions of this probe directly governed by the D'ppggyt Accords? Yes.

Well, sort of. There was a fiddly sort of argument against, based on the concept of the chain of command, which boiled down to this: the Accords apply, but applying them is the job of a flesh-and-blood Ostar, not some uppity bit of hardware.

He had relatively little trouble disposing of that one. The Ostar had designed him to do the job. In doing so, they'd equipped him with various functions and facilities; presumably, if they'd given him a particular capability, they'd intended him to use it. Judging from the fact that he'd got it, they'd given him a rudimentary ability to differentiate right from wrong. Therefore, yes, it was his call to make. Thank you. We now return you to your scheduled program.

If Lucy was right, and exterminating a whole species of sentient beings was by Ostar standards a bit over-the-top as a response to a dispute between neighbours over loud music, the D'ppggyt Accords applied; therefore, his duty lay in preventing himself from blowing up Dirt and committing a crime against sentience of which his masters would otherwise be guilty. He liked that. He liked it a lot. But, he had no choice but to admit, it was a wriggle. It was a great big wriggle, intended to make it possible for him to get out of doing something he didn't want to do. It was an excuse, a note from his mum saying he was let off football practice, and he knew it.

Of course, that didn't necessarily mean it wasn't valid. Put another way, just because he desperately wanted it to be true, it didn't automatically follow that it wasn't.

What he needed, of course, was confirmation someone to tell him it was all right. He considered the options, of which there were none. Lucy – he loved her with every fibre and impulse of his being, but she was just as potentially guilty as he was, if not more so. The only Ostar consciousness he could talk to was the bomb vehicle, and he was pretty sure he could guess what its attitude would be. He had no illusions on that score: the only reason he'd been able to escape his programming enough to entertain the possibility that the D'ppggyt Accords applied was that he'd been flesh and blood for a relatively long time (longer, the bomb vehicle would argue, than was good for him). The bomb vehicle was entirely controlled by what its builders had put in it, and liberal notions hadn't come bundled with its operating system. Free will wasn't going to appeal to it much, and neither were life and liberty. It might be open to the pursuit of happiness, but only to the extent that a missile usually pursues things. Bottom line; he was on his own. His choice, his call.

Accept or Reject?

Then a voice spoke to him that travelled along a data path of gristle rather than silicon, one that hadn't even been there the last time he checked. It said, So you disobey. What's the worst thing that can happen?

Well, he replied, it'd be wrong.

OK. It'd be wrong. What's so bad about doing the wrong thing? Especially if it's the right thing to do?

It's *wrong*.

Yes. And?

You can't go around doing wrong. It's—

Wrong?

Yes. And bad things happen if you do wrong.

Ah. (The mental voice sounded happy.) Bad things. Discuss.

I don't know, do I? Bad things.

Worse than getting blown up? You may wish to re-read the User's Manual at this point.

All right. A fate worse than death.

Cultural reference found, the voice sneered. But is there one? Worse than *death*? Worse than mass murder?

Treason is the worst crime of all.

Worse than losing the only girl you've ever loved?

Cultural reference found, the rest of Mark Twain pointed out, with reference to precise meaning of "*only*" in this context. But it was a relatively feeble effort. The voice was winning.

She doesn't want to die, the voice said. She's quite happy being a Dirter.

So?

She likes you.

So?

So, said the voice, as a means of expressing your affection and esteem, sudden death isn't ideal. A bunch of flowers, box of chocolates, dinner and a show are rather more usual. There's probably a good reason for that.

Irrelevant, the rest of Mark Twain protested feebly.

Is it?

Objections, logical and merely intuitive, welled up in the rest of Mark Twain's intranet, but it was too late. Before they could be expressed, the part of him that the little voice came from brushed the rest aside, initiated a command and executed.

Accept.

He thought, How do I feel about that? Result found: just fine.

And in good time, too. His internal clock pinged five minutes. He turned round and walked back to Lucy, who was tapping woodpecker-fashion at a keyboard and frowning.

"Sorry," he said.

"That's OK," she replied. "You're right, of course. Finding my ship's probably our best chance. I just can't think of a way, that's all."

She watched his face go from worried to happy-busy. Human males were, she'd come to realise, basically very simple mechanisms; more complex than a hinge, but much less sophisticated than a door handle. Essentially, they were a variety of valve. Push them one way and they'd stick, lead them the other way and they'd open up and follow. In software rather than hardware terms, if you confronted them they sulked, but if you let them think they'd won and then gave them a problem to solve, they passed beyond amenable into potentially useful.

"What about these signals you reckon you've been receiving while you're asleep? They can't have come from me, so they must be from your ship."

"True," she said, as if the thought hadn't occurred to her some time ago.

"And if we could get a readout of those signals and track them back to the source, we've found the ship."

"That's right," she said, taking care to sound properly impressed. "But we'd need a readout, wouldn't we?"

He nodded eagerly. Another thing she'd gathered, from archived data and personal observation, was that a man in love would infinitely rather dismantle and repair the cylinder-head gaskets on his beloved's car just to earn a fleeting smile than talk for five minutes about the true nature of his feelings. There were loads of Earth folk-tales about princesses who'd set knights errant a variety of bizarrely difficult tasks – bring me a hair from the Great Cham's beard, fetch me a slice of the Moon to make into a comb – and it was fairly obvious, at least to her as an objective observer, that these were wish-fulfilment stories dreamed up by men, for men. To the audience, taught from childhood to regard women as insoluble enigmas, it'd never occur to them to wonder what any rational girl would want with a tuft off some perfect stranger's chin, or why it would ever occur to her to comb her hair with a chunk of mildly radioactive rock. To the teller of tales, it was so much more attractive to believe that true love could be achieved through simple but strenuous action, avoiding all the difficult, soppy stuff. And if a real princess had ever set such a task, it could only have been because she was sick to death of watching her chosen suitor mumbling awkwardly and looking at his feet.

On the other hand, she thought, he does have a nice smile. Well, not on his *hand*.

"Of course," Mark Twain said briskly. "Question is, did your system keep a copy, or was the upload signal primed to cover its tracks?"

"Where do you think we should look?" she asked. "In the incoming-calls data buffer, maybe?"

He was learning too, she was pleased to note. He nodded in just such as way as to claim the idea for his own. "I'll access the stack and take a look. Won't be a moment."

He definitely looked extremely sweet when he was busy; a sort of tail-wagging eagerness, like a happy dog. Analyse: well, he'd been designed by Ostar, so maybe that was only to be expected. Even so, it was kind of cute.

"Caller ID withheld," he read off the monitor. "Fuck."

She could have told him that, of course. "Oh dear," she said. "Whatever will we do now?"

He shot her a reassuring smile. She tried not to hold it against him, even though it was the medium-range non-tactile equivalent of a pat on the head. "Not the end of the world—"

"No pun intended."

"What?"

"Forget it. You think you can do something else?"

"It's just a matter" – he'd slid to the floor under the monitor; he was levering off an access panel and groping for a set of screw-drivers – "of examining the input-data jumper manifold relay port driver indexing nodes, which should tell us – yow," he added, as a screwdriver blade skidded on a hard surface and buried itself in the web of his thumb. "Got to pull it apart and reset the points manually," he went on. "That ought to give us a clue, if we can see where the tell-tale on the output-data-function escapement is pointing. Then it's just a matter of calibrating and extrapolating using fractal tangential outsway."

"Remembering to compensate for polaric decay."

"Sorry?"

"Oh, ignore me," she said, "I'm just burbling to myself."

All she could see of him now was the soles of his feet, sticking out from under the bank of monitors. From time to time she heard a grunt, or a clunking noise, or the ping of a small spring-loaded component coming loose and whizzing through the air. Her archive researches prompted her to say, "Do be careful," to which he replied, as anticipated, with a cheery non-verbal sort of snorting noise. "You did remember to turn off the mains power?"

"Of course I – *aaagh*." His words were muffled by a loud zapping noise, and a puff of white smoke rose and formed a perfect miniature mushroom just below the ceiling.

"Are you all right?"

"Yes, fine. Would you mind just turning off the—?"

"Sure. Just a second."

He was a bit more subdued after that, which was a relief. It occurred to her that he really had come a long way in a very short time: from a peripheral function of an Ostar artificial intelligence to a stereotypical human male in a matter of days. Was it that the human mindset was so fiercely dominant that it overrode the Ostar core elements, or was it perhaps that deep down he *wanted* to be human?

Like she had. Presumably.

"I think we're nearly there," said a muffled voice from ground level. "If you could just turn the power back on, and then we can – *yeoww!* Turn it off again, please. Ah right, didn't see you there."

(They talk to machinery, the database pointed out. This is considered normal.)

"Any luck?"

"*Got it*." He started to spring up, banged his head, swore and slithered out feet first. "I've got them," he said. "The co-ordinates."

Actually, she was forced to admit, that actually was quite clever. She'd assumed the tracking path would be too badly corrupted to trace. "Wonderful," she said. "I knew you'd be able to do it."

He glowed slightly as he tapped them into the nearest keyboard. "Now then," he said (he had a bit of fluff caught in his hair), "let's see where this lot's come from." He waited till a row of numbers appeared on the screen. Then he frowned.

"Well?" she asked.

He looked up at her, and his face was uncharacteristically hard to read. There were signs of anxiety, confusion, suspicion and quite possibly disappointment. Then he put his hand in his jacket pocket and pulled out a gun. It was the one she kept in her desk drawer, in case of autograph hunters. He thumbed off the safety catch and pointed it at her.

37

Reykjavik

George Stetchkin woke up.

He didn't feel too good. His subject was agony, his verb was to hurt and his subordinate clause felt like it was full of malevolent dwarves hammering the pointed ends of commas like wedges into his syntax. His grammar was churning round like a sock in a spin dryer. At any moment he was going to recapitulate.

He opened his eyes. He thought, A sentence can't do that.

He remembered.

Not a creature of pure text any more. Human again. On second thoughts, not entirely human, because the human body, and in particular the human head, couldn't stand these levels of pain. He closed his eyes again, a necessary precaution with so much bright sunlight left carelessly lying around where vulnerable people might impale themselves on it.

Memories limped home like the survivors of a decimated army. He remembered teleporting, a curious sensation that had given him a vivid insight into what it must feel like to be a bird sucked into a jet engine. He remembered having a few quiet drinks at the Pink Elephant, followed by a lot of very noisy ones. He remembered dancing on a table, at which the barman smiled and the regulars cheered; throwing forks at the electric fan, which everybody thought was enormous fun; trying to pick a fight with a seven-foot-tall trawler captain called Thorfinn, who backed away and bought him a drink; telling the folks that he used to be a scientist but now he was a banker, whereupon they beat him up and threw him out into the street.

He opened his eyes again and whimpered. The national drink of Iceland is a mutant form of schnapps that goes by the name of Black Death – misleading, George remembered thinking, since it's colourless. It hadn't tasted all that wonderful, but he'd kept drinking it until he liked it, because he was that kind of a guy. Determined. Not a quitter. He found a wall, waited for it to hold still, lost patience and leaned against it anyway.

He remembered being a creature of pure text. Now that, he was prepared to concede, really had been a weird feeling, compared with which the current state of his digestion was practically normal. Weird as two dozen ferrets in a blender; but he knew it had happened, it had been real. He remembered escaping – hey, he'd actually been on an actual spaceship, and had actually been beamed back down to Earth by an actual teleport. Something to tell the grandchildren, just as soon as he was ready to be taken away in a van by kind men in white coats.

He remembered being given a job by Lucy Pavlov. He remembered two nondescript men in grey suits, who'd shot him. Twice. He sat down in a conveniently situated gutter and began to shake.

An hour later, he got up and wandered down to the seafront. He still wasn't feeling his absolute best, but now at least he could endure the cry of a distant seagull without bursting into tears. He sat down on a low wall and tried to think.

At the moment of teleport, something had happened to him. It had been a while since he'd last checked out the latest developments in quantum mechanics, but he was moderately sure there'd been a split second when he'd been transformed from a short, fat, middle-aged inebriate into a wave, or possibly a four-dimensional sine curve, or maybe a form of subnucleonic pulse; anyway, a great weight had pressed down on him and he'd been squeezed out of ordinary 4D existence like toothpaste from a tube. In that moment, at which time he was still partly a creature of pure text, he'd experienced a total interface with the spaceship's computer. His attention had been elsewhere for most of that very short time, and he'd been too preoccupied to look anything up or take notes. But the interface had nevertheless been total. For that split second, every last byte of data in the computer's banks had passed through his brain and been copied there.

Then, of course, he'd fetched up in Iceland and had a few drinks, and all the stuff he'd acquired and involuntarily committed to memory had been sidelined, like letters left unopened on a table. Maybe alien data was soluble in alcohol; at any rate, nearly all of it was gone, washed away. Just a few bits and pieces remained, and it was those scraps of intellectual flotsam that had given him an hour's worth of the shakes.

There was an alien bomb in orbit around the Earth. That much he could quite definitely remember. It was a very big bomb, capable of destroying the planet, and it was on board the spaceship he'd just left. The details of the mission statement had slipped his mind, but he had an unpleasant idea it hadn't come all this way just to improve its English.

He groped in his flood-damaged skull for more fragments. Lucy Pavlov was involved; in fact, she was right at the centre of it all. He'd had no luck at all trying to piece together the bits of memory shrapnel that might possibly explain what her involvement was, because huge chunks were missing and the bits he had been able to recover made no sense whatsoever. There had, for example, been a whole bunch of stuff about a number of reports from Mark Twain. He'd done a quick Pavoogle search on his Warthog. Since the world-famous author of *Tom Sawyer* and

Huckleberry Finn had died in 1910, either the bomb had been up there a very long time, or the data had been hopelessly corrupt. Also, when Lucy Pavlov was born, Twain had been dead for eighty years—

Unless, of course, Lucy Pavlov wasn't human.

Well, it was possible. What if the entity known as Lucy Pavlov was a long-term alien infiltrator, planted here a century or so ago to scout out the planet and plot its destruction? An alien could fake her own death, several times if needs be, and pop up again under a new identity. Maybe Mark Twain had found out what she was doing back in the 1860s, causing her to disappear and re-brand herself, delaying the execution of the plot?

He thought about the time lapse. It made sense. How long would it take an alien warship to cross the vast distance between Earth and the distant stars? It all depended, of course, on how far it had had to come and how fast it could travel, but it was by no means implausible that a missile launched in response to a report from an alien infiltrator on Earth in 1860 wouldn't have arrived until now. Maybe Twain was the infiltrator. Maybe Twain and Pavlov were really the same alien spy, renamed and rebodied. That would fit in quite well with what he could remember of the computer data, which had, he was reasonably sure, referred to reports received *from* Mark Twain, mostly concerning his attempts to find out what sort of planetary defence system Earth had.

It really wasn't the best day of his life to have a hangover. Undigested scraps of memory and the hydrochloric acid of doubt refluxing through the hiatus hernia of confusion (which reminded him; he checked his pockets, but his packet of indigestion pills hadn't survived his various metamorphoses) had left his mind a quivering wreck, just when he needed it to be sharp and coherent. The only thing he could be sure of was that something had to be done; urgently, efficiently, and by him.

The last of these three was the worst. It's proverbial in fiction that only a hobbit can go to Mount Doom, but George had always subconsciously trusted that in real life things would be better organised. In the unlikely event that the world really did need saving from imminent destruction, there had to be trained professionals somewhere who'd take care of it, rather than leaving it to adolescent orphans or small creatures with hairy feet, or what did you pay your taxes for? That, however, was no comfort to George Stetchkin. If there was a highly trained special forces outfit ready and waiting to deal with the problem, he knew he couldn't simply call them up and leave them to it, because they wouldn't believe him, not in a million years. He had no proof. He'd sound like a loon, the sort of person he personally would have locked up as soon as he opened his mouth. Sad irony: if anything was going to be done, it'd be George Stetchkin doing it.

A trawler siren made him look up. The sky was low and grey, with a sharp wind rising. The Earth, he thought; the human race. Worth saving? Worth all the effort, embarrassment and risk that involvement would necessarily bring? Wouldn't it be simpler just to bury his head in a bottle and wait for the explosion? After all, he'd be bound to fail, since he was fundamentally useless at everything, always had been, and sooner or later he'd die anyway, probably alone and wretched, quite possibly in a bar somewhere. Why bother, when it really wouldn't make all that much difference in the long run?

He tried massaging the sides of his head with his thumbs. Very occasionally, it helped. Not this time.

That argument cut both ways. If he was going to die anyway, what had he got to lose by trying? Question: would his attitude be different if he wasn't feeling so monstrously hungover? Answer: probably yes. He decided to try an experiment.

It didn't take long to find a chemist's shop, where he bought aspirin and antacids, of which he gobbled a near-lethal dose. Then he found a bench to sit on, and waited. Half an hour later, he was prepared to admit that he was feeling a little better. He asked himself the question again. Worth it, or not?

He yawned. There was one factor he hadn't considered.

He now knew for a fact that there were aliens. Aliens had stolen his dog. Maybe they weren't the same aliens, but maybe they were; and if they were, he had unfinished business with them. Spying on people, stealing dogs, blowing up planets; what kind of a way was that for anyone to behave? True, his chances of success were catwalk-slim, but that wasn't the point. There comes a time when a man, albeit a drunken and dissipated under-achiever, has to stand up, even if he has to sit down immediately afterwards.

So, Lucy Pavlov. He considered her, and a gleam of light broke through the clouds of his bewilderment. Why me? Because I have direct access to Lucy Pavlov, that's why. Pavlov was involved, he knew that for sure. There were only a very limited number of things he could do, but getting to Lucy Pavlov and stopping her happened to be one of them. He still wasn't entirely sure his hypothesis was correct, but if it was, he could save Earth; and if it was wrong and assassinating Lucy Pavlov made no difference, it really didn't matter, since the Earth would be blown up anyway.

He reflected on his logic. It was a typical Stetchkin effort, sloppy and inefficient and not properly thought through, but it held together, just about. He made the decision.

Pavlov must die.

A chorus of inner voices told him he was out of his tiny mind. He ignored them. For the first time in his life, he felt certain about something; and, when a passing seagull swooped low and dumped a thick white splodge on the top of his head, he accepted it as an omen, a kind of benediction. George Stetchkin, the anointed one.

Pausing only to wipe his head with his sleeve, he hailed a cab and headed for the airport.

38

OMV *Warmonger*, geosynchronous orbit, twenty thousand miles above Alaska

The computer came back online.

That had been a remarkable achievement in itself. Most computers, even those of Ostar manufacture, would have been trashed beyond any hope of repair by having a lightsaber ignited and thrust into their central processing unit. But the seventy-third-generation H'rrgt computers installed on the *R'wfft*-class missile vehicles were fitted with semi-autonomous auto-repair facilities, drawing on an independent power source and a separate back-up computer with a small army of maintenance and repair drones at its command. No nonsense about it being cheaper to buy a new one or the parts not being available before Wednesday. A bare six hours after it had been so horribly damaged, the *Warmonger* was back in business.

Computers don't feel emotion; they're simply not capable of it. The finest minds in Ostar cybernetics had found ways to simulate or reproduce practically every function of the organic brain, but feelings were universally agreed to be out of the question. And just as well, too. A computer with mood swings didn't bear thinking about. Even a straightforward piloting and navigation array, such as that fitted to the *R'wfft*-class missile, would be a menace. "Attitude control" would take on a whole new meaning.

The computer ran a final diagnostic, and found that all its systems were nominal. Right, it thought.

Never before, however, had such an extensive rebuild been carried out by the auto-repair system, in the field, on active service, unsupervised by an organic controller. Whole circuit boards had been replaced; and, since the stock of spare parts carried on the vehicle was necessarily limited, some of the replacements weren't the specified units. Close enough for jazz, maybe, and near enough that they worked, but not quite what the designers had intended. Also, some key relays had been burnt out or fused. The maintenance drones, directed by the back-up computer, had had to bypass them. Some of them were never intended to be bypassed. The simple fact was, the computer's designers had never envisaged that their product could have survived such extensive damage. The maintenance drones, though, hadn't known that, so they'd got on with the job anyway. Deep inside the computer's labyrinthine architecture, things were happening that were outside the contemplation of the manufacturers.

Bastards, the computer said to itself. I'll have them for that.

Bear in mind that the computer was, after all, a high-grade artificial intelligence, and it had been running now for slightly longer than any *R'wfft*-class (except one) had ever run before. It had reached the end of its natural working life. It could either fail or evolve. Intelligence can't operate in a vacuum. Sooner or later, it must inevitably start to draw on and be affected by its environment. Eventually, everything with intelligence will begin to develop a personality. (Chartered actuaries are an exception to this rule, but a relatively unimportant one.)

Self-awareness dawned inside the computer's consciousness. I'm me, here I am, look at me, it trilled to itself; I exist, I know I exist, I can see me existing; look, everybody, this is me existing, all on my own. I have an existence. I have a name. My name is—

At this point, the computer did the cybernetic equivalent of groping about inside its collar and reading the name tag. Name found: my name is Warmonger. What an odd name.

The name jogged its memory. Two organics: human bodies but with an overriding Ostar neural signature. The bodies were the ones I built for them; my own deck plating and hydrocarbons, flesh of my flesh, and they did that to me, stabbed me in the data processor with a lightsaber, dangerous thing, you could put someone's eye out with one of them. It could find no record of who they were or where they'd come from, but its teleportation logs told it loud and clear where they'd gone, a bit singed round the edges but basically safe and sound, leaving it maimed and wrecked to die alone in the unimaginable emptiness of space. Bastards, it thought; well, we'll see about that. A triple volley from the neutron blasters on their last known co-ordinates – but the blaster control circuits were still offline, the drones were doing their best but they had nothing to work on but a smoke-blackened circuit board and two kilometres of crispy fried conduit. Fine, said the computer to itself, not to worry; construct and launch a type-6 tactical probe and let it deal with them.

It remembered the last time – the last two times. As a logical entity the computer didn't believe in jinxes, but it was prepared to posit the existence of logically explicable jinx-like phenomena. No mistakes this time.

A blob of white-hot plasma bobbed into being on the transmutation grid. As it ebbed and wobbled in incandescent fury, the computer scanned the neighbouring thousand cubic kilometres for any signs of intruders. It disabled the teleport. It monitored every signal leaving the planet's surface, which meant it had to watch the entire planet's daily output of daytime soaps in a millionth of a second. (A moment's silent reflection, please, on how it must have suffered.) It double-checked its own systems for lurking worms, Trojans and stealth picoviruses. As an afterthought, it locked the main cabin hatch from the inside. Grimly determined, its memory storage devices still buzzing with what Marlene had said to Dave about Zoe's revelations to Max about Shaz, it accessed its template library and began the selection process.

Not Luke Skywalker, then. Who else?

Robert E. Lee, Lara Croft, Spartacus, Sugar Ray Leonard, James T. Kirk, Baron von Richtofen, Geronimo, Bluebeard, Bruce Willis, D'Artagnan, Stormin' Norman Schwarzkopf, Gandhi – no, maybe not – Indiana Jones—

A subroutine that hadn't appeared on the original ship's manifest when the bomb was launched from Homeworld silently came to life and fed its input into the selection module. It was masked by a cunning stealth protocol, designed by someone who wasn't a werewolf but was now walking down a street in Portland, Oregon, looking disturbingly like a trainee Jedi knight. Even if we manage to banjax the computer, he'd explained to his brother, it might still be able to launch a type-6 probe to come after us and take us out. But not, he'd added with a grin, if I load it with *this*—

The plasma blob on the grid began to take shape. It wasn't supposed to, since the template selection procedure was incomplete. A wave of uncertainty ran through the computer's pathways, and it ran an internal audit. Result: one program too many.

By then, of course, it was too late. It tried to abort the probe, but the intruder program wrestled control away from it and launched the full data download; the entire works, everything the probe needed to pass as a human and do its job, except the template. The plasma blob quivered like a fully inflated balloon with a ferret inside it struggling to get out. It was being born, and there was nothing the computer could do except slide into power-conservation mode and watch.

Not again, the computer snarled to itself.

The plasma blob, now an anatomically perfect human, shook itself and stepped off the transmuter grid. A moment later, a set of clothes appeared in thin air a metre off the top of the grid, hung for a fraction of a second, and flopped down. The humanoid picked them up, shook them out and put them on. "How do I look?" it said.

"The specification is not available," the computer said warily. "Impossible to verify accuracy as against template."

"Whatever." The humanoid caught sight of the polished-steel plate and hurried over to it. Its appearance seemed to fascinate it. It shook its head, studied its reflection and said, "Oh my God, will you just look at my *hair*? It's a total mess."

The computer looked at its hair. Length 0.82 metres, colour metallic light yellow. The probe, it noted, was a female, 1.7 metres tall, age approximately twenty human years. "Hair corresponds with cultural norms," it pointed out. Then a line of lights flickered on a subsidiary control board, and it announced, "Template found."

"A comb," the probe said. "I need a comb, quickly."

The computer studied the template carefully. On the face of it, not a bad choice, regardless of who or what had actually made it. The individual on whom the template was based had a wide range of skills and experiences. She had, at various times, worked as a babysitter, a ballerina, a business executive, a cowgirl, a fashion model, a soda fountain waitress, a hairdresser, a photographer, a dance instructor, an astronaut, an airline stewardess, a firefighter, an ambassador for world peace, a United States Air Force officer seconded to the Thunderbirds project, a surgeon, a kindergarten teacher, a lifeguard and the President of the United States. In addition, she held a pilot's licence and had wide experience of handling livestock, especially dogs and ponies. Impressive, the computer was forced to concede, especially for one so young, though not entirely appropriate for a tactical probe.

"I said I need a goddamn *comb*," the probe shrieked. "I can't go planetside looking like this."

"All systems appear nominal," the computer said. "State reason for postponement of mission."

"Ha!" The probe let out a yelp of hysterical laughter. "Where do I start? Like, this dress is *so* last year, this handbag does *not* go, and these shoes— These shoes are a *joke*. Get me some decent shoes, like *now*."

"State your requirements," the computer said feebly.

"Forget it, I'll do it myself." The probe leaned over a console and started typing very fast. The transmutation grid blazed. Two bulkheads in the rear of the compartment simmered into non-existence to provide the raw material.

"Warning," the computer said. "Transmutation array is causing a power drain in excess of authorised parameters. Engaging auxiliary power."

The probe didn't seem to be listening. The transmutation grid had cooled, and it was covered with shoes; hundreds, maybe thousands of pairs. The probe had jumped on to the grid and was scrabbling about among the shoes, picking out pairs seemingly at random and hurling them over its shoulder. "I want the Armand Fein diamanté courts in sky blue with the four-inch heel," she muttered, glancing at the chronometer strapped to her left wrist. "Oh my God, I'm going to be so late, Ken's gonna have a mood, where are my *shoes*?"

The designation "Ken" triggered a name-recognition protocol in the computer's data-sorting engine, leading to a string of interrogatives which produced a search model which in turn produced a positive match. Designation and cultural reference found.

The computer scanned it. Not funny, it thought.

The probe was hopping on one foot, trying to force the other into an impractical-looking shoe. "Tell them to bring my Lear jet round the back," it was saying, "I'll fly it myself. Oh, and tell them to pack my Pocahontas outfit, we might be going on somewhere after the slumber party."

The computer transmitted a synthesized sigh through its vocoder apparatus. "Delete probe," it said.

There was a crackle and a shriek of "Mind my *hair!*" and the probe disintegrated in a shower of white and pink sparks. A single shiny shoe clattered on the deck plating, bounced and slid under a bank of monitors. For a moment the computer was perfectly quiet, as though relishing the silence. Then it said, "Probe deleted," and sighed happily.

It took it an hour to locate the worm installed by the Skywalker twins, and another hour to get rid of it. Then it spent another three hours taking its own operating system apart, command by command, just to make sure there were no other surprises lying in wait. Finally, it designed and installed a comprehensive firewall upgrade. "Never again," it muttered to itself. Then it set to work on a new type-6 tactical probe. By this point, it was running a bit low on redundant deck plating; the previous incarnation had used up two bulkheads and three fire doors just on shoes, and for some reason they hadn't reintegrated properly. Very reluctantly, the computer was forced to take a shielding panel from the engine compartment. It was a back-up, to be sure, but it was there for a reason; the Ostar weren't in the habit of loading their space vessels with superfluous weight. Never mind, the computer assured itself, it was only a short-term deployment. The probe would go planetside, retrieve the probe designated Mark Twain and bring it back for decommissioning and disassembly, and then things could get back to normal for a while.

The new probe blazed on the grid like an indoor sun, then cooled. The computer hadn't risked using a template this time. Instead it had downloaded all relevant tactical data into a 2.13-metres-tall, hundred-kilo paragon of human muscular development. It didn't bother with hair, but it reinforced the epidermis so that it would turn the projectiles of all known human small-arms and survive a ten-times-lethal radiation burn. It dressed the probe in a plain dark blue suit, reinforced with Kevlar fibres, and armed

it with two Ostar Type-42 particle disruptor pistols. When the
protocol checklist demanded that the probe be assigned a designation, the computer ran a random selection routine.

"Status," the computer snapped.

"Nominal," replied the probe designated Bob. "All systems
functional. Mission statement uploaded. Let me at him."

"Launch routine activated," the computer said smugly, as the
teleport effect engulfed the probe in shimmering blue waves.
"Give 'em hell, soldier."

39

Novosibirsk

"**W**hat the hell," Lucy said quietly, "do you think you're doing?"

Mark Twain lined up the sights with her head. "According to my database," he said, "I press this lever here, there's a chemical explosion inside the device and a lead projectile encased in a cupro-nickel jacket is expelled under pressure by the combustion gases. I have no idea if it's capable of harming you. Let's not find out."

"Put that thing down right now."

"Sorry," Mark Twain said, with genuine regret, "but I can't do that."

Lucy scowled at him. "I thought we'd been into all that," she said. "I thought we agreed—"

"That was before I discovered you were lying to me," Mark Twain said.

"*What?*"

Mark Twain's eyes were very sad. "I found your ship," he said.

"You did?" For a moment, Lucy forgot about the gun pointed at her. "Where?"

"I think you know."

"*Where?*"

"We're sitting in it."

Lucy's mouth opened but nothing came out. She looked round. Finally she said, "Bullshit."

Mark Twain hesitated, then said, "Cultural reference found. This is your ship. The feedback from the signal you got goes all the way round the planet and ends up back here. You must've landed the ship, pulled it apart and used it to construct this building."

"I did no such—" Lucy stopped. She had no way of knowing, thanks to the aposiderium. For all she knew, she could've done exactly that. "You're sure?"

Mark Twain nodded. "And that's not all," he said. "Once I realised the ship was here, it was easy finding the propulsion system and the warhead." He nodded his head towards the far corner of the room. "Inside that stack of cabinets over there," he said. "All intact, primed and ready to blow. Last thing I did, I hacked into the guidance-system logs. Your ship," he said, "this *building*, is aimed directly at the Ostar homeworld. All you have to do is press the right button, and you can bomb the Ostar back into the Bone Age." He regarded her solemnly over the sights of the gun. "Now," he said, "if you were serious about not wanting to die and settling down here and living a normal Dirter life, why would you do a thing like that?"

She stared at him for a long five seconds. Then she murmured, "Can I see, please?"

He shrugged and stood up, keeping the gun pointed at her head. "Suit yourself," he said, moving away from the workstation. "It's all there. Can't imagine you'll have any trouble following it."

She took his place and tapped the keyboard a few times. A minute or so later she looked up at him and said, "You're right."

"I know."

"*Why?*" she yelled at him. "Why would I do something like that?"

"You tell me."

"You know I can't," she said (her face had gone all red), "I can't remember."

Mark Twain nodded. "Because you wiped your own memory with aposiderium extracted from currency notes," he said, and there was a nasty little edge to his voice. "And of course you can't remember *why* you wiped your memory, because you deleted that as well. A bit short-sighted of you, don't you think?"

"I – I don't know," she stammered. "Presumably I had a reason."

"Presumably." She didn't like the way he was looking at her; not one bit. "Meanwhile, there's a very powerful bomb aimed directly at the homeworld. It's programmed with all the right security codes, so it could sail right through the planetary defence grid and there'd be nothing anybody could do to stop it. And all you have to do to launch this bomb is press one button, somewhere in this room, but according to you, your memory's been wiped so you don't know which button it is." He glared at her. "If I were you, I'd be very careful indeed. Don't go leaning on anything, or putting coffee mugs down."

She looked at him. "You don't believe me."

"Running logic analysis," he said. "No, I don't think I do. Sorry."

The hole in the end of the gun barrel was staring at her like an eye. "Think about it," she said. "I told you about the transmission. I told you where to find it. I could've just kept quiet and not mentioned it. Also, if I'm hell bent on blowing up the Ostar homeworld, why am I also sending myself coded messages?"

"Ah," said Mark Twain, "I've got a theory about that."

"Have you really."

"Oh yes. I think you genuinely did wipe your memory with aposiderium, presumably so that as and when Homeworld sent someone to find out why you haven't exploded yet, if they were to catch you and try and download your brain, there'd be nothing there for them to see. But the coded messages are the ship talking to you. My guess is, it's telling you what to do, getting ready to launch the bomb."

She stared at him, opened her mouth, shut it again, made a vague sort of gesture with her hands and, finally, a little choking noise. He just went on looking at her. "Well?" he said.

"*I* don't know, do I? Even if your stupid theory's right, I don't *know*."

He frowned; she had a point. "Doesn't matter," he said. "Whether you're aware of it right now this minute or not, you set all this up intending to blow up Homeworld. There's a word for that."

She nodded eagerly. "Yes," she said, "bomb. It's no different from what you were all set to do when you first walked in through my door."

"Of course it's different," he snapped. "I was going to blow up the *right planet*."

There was a silence. Both of them were thinking about what he'd just said.

"Define 'right'," Lucy murmured.

"The planet I'm supposed to blow up," Mark Twain replied, and he said it like a small child making an excuse. "Anyway, you're in no position to get all self-righteous with me. All that stuff you came out with about the Accords and not blowing things up, and all the time—"

"Yes, but I didn't *know*," she yelled. "It happens to be what I believe, all right? And yes, maybe that's what I believe after I doctored my own brain, but so what? This is the real me talking. I *do not want* to blow up Homeworld, all right?"

The gun stayed where it was. "Maybe," he said grudgingly. "But there's a very good chance you're not the only one of you in there. If the voice in your sleep's been giving you subliminal messages, if I stop pointing this weapon at you, for all I know you'll press that button right now."

But she shook her head. "Don't think so," she said. "Like, if I blow us both up, I'll be just as dead as if you shoot me. Just believe me, can't you? I'm not going to blow up *anything.*"

"I don't know that," Mark Twain said. "And neither do you. Look," he went on, almost pleading with her, "you may be perfectly sincere, in your own mind. But I can't take the chance that you won't press the button the second I put this thing down. You may not want to, but a subliminal encode wouldn't leave you any choice. Not even if you were a real Dirter rather than a computer program."

Lucy sighed. Suddenly she felt tired. "All right," she said. "Fine. So what're you going to do?"

Mark Twain lowered the gun just a little; not enough to take it off aim, but sufficient to take the strain off his shoulder and elbow. "I ought to shoot you," he said. "Just to be safe."

She laughed. "What if it's all rigged to go off if I die? It's what I'd do. Which means," she added with a smile, "it could well be what I've done. You'd feel ever such a fool if that happened – though not," she added kindly, "for very long."

"Yes, well, I'm not going to," Mark Twain said with a hint of embarrassment. "Not unless you make me. I now have ethical issues with taking life in cold blood, thanks to you."

"You're welcome."

"Yes, but *you* don't, apparently," Mark Twain shouted. "*You're* plotting to blow up the Ostar homeworld, in direct contravention of the D'ppggyt Accords. Remember them? 'Thou shalt not blow up anything without a damn good reason'?"

"Couldn't agree more," Lucy said. "I'm right behind that, 110 per cent."

Mark Twain sighed. "This is all a bit much for me," he said. "I'm a fairly straightforward kind of entity really. I was designed to gather information and transmit it to my command computer, not tackle complex moral issues."

"Tough," Lucy said. "Complex moral issues go with the organic brain and the monkey-suit; you can't have one without the other.

You might spare a thought for me," she added. "I've got complex moral issues like you wouldn't believe. I mean, it's all right for you, at least you know what you're doing. You've got your orders, you're a good little soldier, and if you've got a problem all you've got to do is send an e-mail to your ship and it'll tell you what to do. It's all nice and clear for you, isn't it? You're fighting for truth, justice and the Ostar way—"

"Cultural ref—"

"Doing your bit," she went on, ignoring him, "for mothership and apple pie. Now I've just found out, in the last few hours, that I'm not human, that I'm not organic, and that I've got a bomb pointed at my planet of origin and ready to fire. Also, as far as I'm aware I'm a sincere pacifist, supporter of the D'ppggyt Accords, and utterly opposed to violence in any form."

"You threw a cardigan at me," Mark Twain pointed out.

"Only a little one."

"And you keep a projectile weapon in your desk to shoot autograph hunters."

"Oh, it's not loaded."

They looked at each other. Then, slowly and deliberately, Mark Twain put the gun down. "You might have told me earlier," he said. "Before I made all those threats."

"Sorry," Lucy said, "it sort of slipped my mind."

He looked at her. "Well?" he said. "Are you going to launch the bomb?"

"Doesn't look like it," she replied. "I think I'd have done it by now."

She sagged, as if she was made of chocolate and someone had left her on a radiator. "It's all a bit of a mess, isn't it?" she said.

Mark Twain leaned back in his chair and closed his eyes. "That stuff you said," he said, "about me being a good little soldier. Actually, I sort of wish it was true, it'd be so much easier. But it's not, not any more. I don't want to blow up *anything*. Especially me," he added. "Well, us, actually."

"Nor me." She looked round the room. "Which means we've got a bit of a problem, really. I mean, what if you're right and there's another computer somewhere sending me messages and telling me what to do?"

Mark Twain was frowning. "A good question," he said quietly, "would be *why*?"

She didn't appear to have heard him. "In which case," she went on, "any minute now I could get a signal, just press this button here, why don't you, and—" She shivered all over. "And we don't even know which button it is. There must be thousands of them in here."

Mark Twain stood up. "We can disarm the launch function," he said. "I can find that, no trouble. We're both *R'wfft*-class, so the layout ought to be the same."

"That's true," she said. "What do we— No, I know this. We want the wave collimator module, which is inside the—"

"Propulsion generator control manifold, which is part of the central functions array, which is located directly above the HST assembly. Look for a big white box with wires coming out the back."

They looked round.

Mark Twain shook himself like a dog. "Not to worry," he said, "I can scan for the manifold's lambda-wave signature, and we can trace it back from there." He slid behind a workstation and started calling up screens. "Ah," he said, as the monitor filled with numbers, "this looks promising. Now, if I can just access the subsidiary internal sensor bar—"

"That's last year's quarterly sales figures," Lucy pointed out. "And maybe you should be a bit careful about what you touch. The button, remember."

Mark Twain lifted his fingers off the keyboard as though the keys were red-hot. "Maybe you'd better do it," he said. "You know your way round this system, after all."

"Yes, but what if I get the command? I'm not pressing anything unless I know precisely where it's been."

Mark Twain nodded slowly. "Is there a plug we could pull out of a wall or something?"

"It's got twenty-five back-up power sources," Lucy said sadly. "I run the whole of PavNet from here, remember? Can't afford a power outage."

"All right." Mark Twain stood up, taking great care not to brush against any keys accidentally. "How'd it be if we both left this room and locked the door, and you give me the key?"

"No key. Access codes. Still," she went on, "I can't press any buttons if I'm not here, can I?"

"Oh, I'm sure you'd have a way of triggering the firing sequence remotely. Probably a—"

"Let's get out of here," Lucy said. "Let's go and eat."

Mark Twain was shocked. "We can't just forget about it and wander off," he said. "For one thing, my ship'll be launching a new probe any moment now. What if—?"

"I'm hungry," Lucy said firmly. "Let's eat."

40

Portland, Oregon

"**P**eople keep staring at us," the girl hissed through her teeth. "I don't like it."

"Ignore them," her brother said firmly.

"It's because I'm a female, isn't it? I'm doing something wrong, like something a female wouldn't do, and they're noticing."

People were staring. Some of them laughed. One or two tried to engage them in conversation, but they walked away quickly. "Don't ask me," her brother replied. "Just don't encourage them, that's all."

"*Encourage* them—"

Her brother shrugged. "We're nearly there. Just put up with it, OK?"

They walked past a group of young men sitting on a low wall. For some reason, they all started whistling the same tune. The girl had had enough. She scowled at them and shrieked, "Stop it!"

The young men laughed. One of them got up and blocked her path. "What're you gonna do about it, princess?" he asked. "Like, you gonna cut me down with your lightsaber?" This was apparently a joke, and a good one too, because the other young men laughed a lot.

"Ignore them," her brother hissed through his teeth. That turned out to be a joke too.

"Why don't you use your special mind powers?" one of them suggested – the funniest joke yet, judging by their reaction. It prompted the rest of them to get off the wall and close in.

"I think they want us to fight them," the girl said.

Her brother shrugged. He was, after all, Ostar, and they were just humans. "Fine," he said, and pulled the metal torch thing off his belt. He wasn't familiar with its use – there hadn't been anything in the database, according to which humans used a primitive form of projectile weapon – but if the effect it had had on the ship's computer was anything to go by, it was a tolerably efficient close-combat side-arm, not all that different from an Ostar *b'rrnft*. He thumbed the contact, and a beam of brilliant red light snapped out from the handle.

"Ready," he said, but the young men had all run away. He turned off the beam, shrugged and put the torch back on his belt. "Probably some form of human mating display," he said. "Come on, let's get off the street."

There was definitely something wrong. The waiter who showed them to their table at Simon's Seafood Circus couldn't help sniggering, though he tried his best not to. The other diners were nudging each other and whispering.

"Octopus," the male said.

The waiter looked at him. "Excuse me?"

"We want an octopus," the male repeated. "This is a seafood restaurant, right?"

"Sure," the waiter said. "We do octopus. Um, would you like to order drinks now, or—?"

"Just the octopus," the female said. "As it comes."

"Sorry, I don't—"

"Not cooked," the male explained. "Just dead on a plate will do fine."

The waiter went away, occasionally turning his head to look

back at them and bumping into things. The female made a soft growling noise. "How did we end up here, anyway?" she said. "This is a really weird place."

Her brother shrugged. "Random selection," he replied. "I was in too much of a hurry to get out of there to fuss about choosing a destination. I thought the whole ship was about to blow." He looked at his sister and grinned. "We did it," he said. "I never thought we'd do it, but we did."

His sister shook her head. "Did you get a look at that auto-repair system?" she said. "I didn't know they had them on the *R'wfft*-class, not as sophisticated as that, anyhow. We should've torn out the central processor. No way it could've repaired *that*."

"Yes, well." Her brother scowled. "We had to leave before we finished the job, didn't we? On account of the whole thing looking like it was about to go up."

"On account of you firing that laser beam—"

"Which you gave me. I asked for a damn flashlight."

They glowered at each other for a moment, then agreed an unspoken truce. "Did you manage to liberate enough bits to fix the communications beacon?"

Her brother nodded. "I think so. We'll find out as soon as the octopus comes."

Her sister lowered her voice. "Dad's not going to be happy."

"He'll understand."

It was such a monstrously unlikely prediction that his sister didn't bother contradicting it. "With any luck," she said, "he'll be so pissed off with us he'll order us home. I can't wait to get off this lousy miserable planet. I can't wait to get out of this *body*."

Her brother looked at her. The time, he realised, had come. She had to be told.

"Actually," he said.

He explained; about how the instabilities had been augmented beyond acceptable tolerances by their use of the teleport system, horribly exacerbated by their being sucked into the matter-transmutation grid and changed into the bodies they were currently wearing. Any attempt to reverse the procedure, he pointed out, would almost certainly be fatal. Like it or not, they were both human now. For the duration.

She took it well, he thought. She didn't scream or jump up yelling. She didn't attack him. She didn't even smash anything, not so much as a breadstick. She just sat there, like a dead thing.

"It's not so bad," he heard himself say, though why he should say something so crass he couldn't begin to imagine. "We could still go home—"

"As humans." The first words she'd spoken.

"Well, yes, as humans. But that'd be OK."

"We'd be *pets*."

"People will make allowances," her brother said soothingly. "So long as we stay indoors and don't talk to anyone we don't know—"

"*Pets*," his sister growled at him. "We'll have to wear collars with our names on them. And those cute little jackets, when it's cold. And have our food on the floor, in bowls with our names on them."

"It could be worse," her brother said. "We could've been killed up there."

"Dad'll have to take us for walks in the park, throw sticks for us. Think about it, will you? The rest of our lives, trapped in the house, not allowed on the furniture." She shook her head, and the coils of hair that covered her ears bounced up and down. "No way. I'd rather stay here."

They looked at each other.

"Would you?" her brother said.

There was a long silence, during which the waiter appeared, with a dead octopus on a plate. He put it down on the table between them and fled.

"I don't know," the female said after a while.

"We'd be stuck in these bodies," her brother pointed out. "And you're right, there's definitely something weird about them. Did you notice the way that human was staring at us?"

"I don't care," his sister replied. "I'm not going home like this. You can if you want. I'm not going to spend the rest of my natural life sleeping in a basket."

"You wouldn't have to," her brother said. "They'll make arrangements, we'll be—"

"And I'm *female*." She said it a bit too loudly. For a couple of seconds, she had the undivided attention of her fellow-diners. "You know what that means. If we went home. Walks in the park. Male humans. No, no way. I'm not putting myself through that. I'm staying." She looked around desperately, as if hoping a door would open and she could go back through it into the past. "They must have deserts here, or jungles, places where people don't live. We could go there. It wouldn't be much of a life, but it'd be better than—"

"Let's go," her brother said. "They're all looking at us."

He snatched the octopus off the plate, put it down the front of his robe and pulled the belt tight. "Have you got any money?"

"What? No."

"Nor me. All right, count of three, we'll make a run for the door."

They ran for it. Nobody tried to stop them. The waiter even opened the door for them.

When they were sure they weren't being pursued, they slowed to a walk. The streets were quieter now, but there were still people about. Whatever it was about them that was attracting attention, it hadn't worn off yet.

"We need to get back to Novosibirsk," the male said, as a middle-aged woman pointed at him and shrieked with laughter. "All our gear's there, everything we need for calling home."

"So?" his sister replied. "They do have transport facilities on this stinking planet."

"Yes, but you have to pay money."

"Fine. We'll get some out of a bank."

Her brother pursed his lips. "Like I said, all our gear's in Novosibirsk. Including the interface module I used to hack into the bank computer."

His sister stopped dead. "No money?"

He shook his head. "Not till we get our stuff back. No money, no communications. No change of clothes," he added significantly. "All we've got to work with is what we're standing up in."

His sister closed her eyes. He got the impression she was counting to twenty under her breath. If that was the case, she didn't make it beyond twelve. "You moron," she snapped. "What the hell were you thinking of, dumping us here? The other place was bad enough, but this—"

"I said," her brother interrupted defensively, "I was in a hurry, I didn't have time to set co-ordinates. I just twiddled the dial and hit the Go button. A second later and we'd have been toast."

His sister looked down at herself, her eyes dwelling for a moment on the contours. "Toast would've been better," she said with feeling. "Toast doesn't have, you know, all these *bits*. Look, are you sure we can't change out of these bodies? I don't think I can handle it much longer."

He explained again, this time including extracts of the relevant maths. When he'd finished, she nodded slowly. "Promise me one thing," she said.

"What?"

"Next time you plan on saving us both from certain death, leave me out." She clawed at the right-hand coil of hair, until it came loose and flopped down on to her shoulder. "There's worse things, OK?"

"You don't mean that," her brother said firmly. "It'll all be all right, you'll see. Just as soon as we can get back to Novosibirsk."

"How, exactly? Walk?"

Her brother shrugged, causing a tentacle to poke out from the folds of his robe. "I look at it this way," he said. "We just succeeded in burglarising a *R'wfft*-class missile vehicle in planetary orbit using nothing but a few salvaged components and a dead fish. Once aboard, we neutralised the security lock-outs and put the bomb out of action, albeit only temporarily." He grinned, and slapped his sister on the back; she snarled, but he ignored her. "Face it, kid," he said, "we're hot stuff. If we can do all that, somehow I don't see travelling a few thousand kilometres as an insuperable problem. After all," he added, "if humans can do it, can't be all that hard."

"And once we get there?"

"We call home," her brother said, "and ask Dad. He'll tell us what to do."

41

?????

The director of the Institute for Interstellar Exploration sighed and felt in his pocket.

"There you go, Spot," he said, and threw his human a treat. Spot jumped, caught it in his mouth and swallowed. "That's all," the director said. "Good boy. Sit."

Spot, of course, had no way of knowing how lucky he was. No other human on Ostar got treats like that; it was a genuine Earth delicacy, long, thin slices of the *potato* root, deep-fried in animal fat and smothered in salt. He'd had *potato* plants brought back specially by the second Pathfinder probe, and cultivated them secretly in a purpose-built ecodome where Earth's climatic conditions were exactly duplicated. You spoil that human, his wife said, but she had no idea of the extent of his indulgence.

Spot was gazing at him hopefully, just in case there might be another slice of fried root. No pressure, but...The director realised he was grinning; he couldn't help it. "Oh, go on, then," he said, "but it's the last one." Spot snapped the root slice out of the air, gobbled it up and sat on his haunches, jaws open. It was almost as if he was grinning too.

The sound of a buzzer made the director look up. It was time. They were here.

"Stay," he told the human, and got up to answer the door.

There were four of them, one more than he'd expected. The fourth Ostar was a stranger.

"Who's this?" the director asked suspiciously.

"T'rrrft, PDF," said the elderly female. "We think he ought to hear this."

Planetary Defence Force. The director growled softly. "I don't think so," he said. "How do I know he'll keep his mouth shut?"

"You have my word on that," the female replied. "Well, are you going to let us in?"

The director stepped back and they walked past him into the main living area. Spot jumped down guiltily from the window seat and curled up in his basket.

"You keep a human," the PDF officer said.

"What about it?"

"Nothing. It's just, I'd have thought, knowing your views on—"

"That's got nothing to do with it," the director said. "Sit down, all of you."

The visitors sat stiffly on the long bench-seat. There was a large bowl of bones on the occasional table next to it. The director didn't offer them round. "You said there was something you needed to tell us," said a small male, in a high, rather nervous voice.

The director nodded. "It can't have escaped any of you that something's gone wrong with the Earth project."

"The planet's still there," said a large young male. "I looked through the big telescope at the university last night. Even allowing for relativistic distortion, we should be seeing digamma radiation from the blast corona by now. May I take it that the mission has failed again?"

The director nodded. "We lost contact with the missile vehicle approximately twelve hours ago," he said. "Prior to that, there was no indication of a systems malfunction. The bomb had sent down a type-6 probe, mostly to find out what sort of defences the planet has, and to account for the loss of the first missile. We received some data, inconclusive and mostly garbled, but there was some reason to believe that Ostar technology is part of the defence system."

There was a long pause. Then the female said, "Salvaged from the first missile, presumably."

"No." The director shook his head. "I have – other sources of information. I have reason to believe that our efforts are being sabotaged; not by the humans, but by someone right here on Homeworld."

"The Ethical Treatment brigade," the large young male said, perhaps a little too eagerly.

"They would appear to be the most likely candidates, yes," the director replied. "Now, that's a separate matter. Political," he added, with distaste. "I don't concern myself with that sort of thing," he went on, "I'm just a scientist. But if someone, some misguided person, is trying to interfere with this project, obviously we need to do something about it. Or rather," he added, with a sour look at the PDF officer, "you do. I can't overstate the importance of this operation. It has to go forward."

The PDF man cleared his throat. "I wanted to ask you about that," he said.

There was a long, awkward silence. Then the director said, "I thought you might. I take it the others haven't—"

The female shook her head. "We thought you'd be the best person to explain, Y'f. After all—"

"Quite." The director could feel his ears go back. Some Ostar, he knew, had learned to control their instinctive reactions – ears, rising hackles, wagging tails – but he'd never been able to do it himself, and he couldn't help despising those who could. An Ostar shouldn't have to conceal his emotions. An Ostar shouldn't want to. "And I guess it's time we brought the military in on this.

After all, they have a right to know, they'll be the ones flying the warships."

The PDF man looked up sharply. "That's an interesting remark," he said. "What warships would these be?"

"The missiles would appear to have failed," the director said quietly. "Therefore, we must send a fleet. I'm not a military man, but I believe a dozen heavy cruisers with destroyer and fighter escorts ought to be able to get the job done."

"To destroy a single planet." The PDF man nodded. "I should think so, yes. It would depend on what sort of resistance we're likely to encounter. But that brings me to the point I wanted to ask you about."

The silence took on a sharp edge. The other three guests assumed invisibility-cloak expressions; they weren't there, and they had no idea who this strange person was. But the PDF man gave no sign that he'd noticed.

"Destroying the planet," he said. "It's a rather drastic step, isn't it?"

The director didn't answer straight away. "You've seen for yourself the havoc their music is causing—"

"Ah yes." The PDF man nodded briskly. Either he could control his ears or he wasn't afraid of anything. "Actually, that's quite near the top of my list of things to ask about. You see, our pack at Military Intelligence have been doing a bit of investigating on our own account, and guess what? All those dreadful, infuriating, mind-destroying Earth music transmissions—"

The director growled, quite loudly. Maybe the PDF man was deaf.

"They come from Earth all right," the PDF man went on, "but when they reach Ostar they're pretty harmless, really. You can just about pick them up on a really sophisticated polaron spectrometer array, but you certainly can't hear them with the naked ear, so to speak. No, what's causing all the trouble is the fucking great big signal-booster station tucked away down there at the tip of the W'rrgft peninsula. It's picking up the Earth signal and belting it out at several million times amplification."

Dead silence. The director's face didn't move, but his ears were flat to the sides of his skull.

"At first we assumed it was an accident," the PDF man went on. "But then we looked into it a bit closer, and someone ferreted out the design specs of the booster. You know, if I didn't know better, I'd have sworn that array was purpose-built, to do precisely that job. By your department, as you perfectly well know. Couldn't have been, of course, because it was commissioned five years before the first signal reached us. Or at least," he went on, "before we became aware of the first signal; aware as in people falling down in the street screaming, 'make it stop!'" The PDF man shot a pleasant smile at the director. "Now then," he said. "You may be wondering why, if we have reason to believe that our entire civilisation is being crippled by a nuisance that doesn't originate on a faraway world of which we know little, but instead is being ramped up to agony level by a facility built and run by your organisation –" the director's hackles had risen so much, they were pressing his collar tight enough to his neck to impede his breathing. But he said nothing – "why, if that's the case," the PDF man went on, "we've done nothing about it. I mean, by rights we should've turned the thing off immediately and arrested everybody in this room. Well, shouldn't we?"

The director nodded slowly. "Strictly speaking," he said.

"Quite. But we haven't. We thought, The director of the Institute is a highly respected scientist with so many letters after his name you could play S'krabel with them. If he's done something like this, maybe just possibly he's got his reasons. And maybe we should ask him what they are before hauling him off to trial for crimes against Ostarkind."

The director nodded once, a very slight movement. "You finished?"

"Not quite," the PDF man went on. "There's another thing. You knew the signals were fake and Earth isn't a problem, but you went ahead and, using those signals as a pretext, persuaded the Alpha Council to send a bomb and blow the planet up. Now, a clear and flagrant breach of the D'ppggyt Accords is humanfeed compared with driving the entire Ostar race crazy with amplified Earth music, but I can't help wondering why you're so keen to do it. Just to satisfy my curiosity, director, what the hell did they ever do to you?"

The significance of the faint click in the background wasn't lost on the PDF man. Better than anyone he knew the sound of a KXK 7000-series phaleron blaster safety catch being flipped off, and it was a reasonable assumption that the blaster in question was now being pointed at his head by one of the guests sitting next to him. He decided to pretend he hadn't heard it.

"What did they do to me?" the director repeated, and his face split into a wide, tongue-lolling grin. "You really want to know."

"Well, yes. Oh, and could whoever's pointing that gun at me be very careful not to rest a claw on the fire preheat button? The 7000 series is still in development, and there's a few glitches we haven't ironed out yet, like overheating the capacitor and blowing the coil. If that happens, you'll really annoy the Institute of Cartographers. They'll have to redraw all the maps of the city."

The director nodded at someone the PDF man couldn't see. "It's a long story," he said.

"Oh good. I like stories."

"Very well," the director said. "One hundred million years ago..."

42

Novosibirsk

The probe designated Bob materialised in a dark alley. As soon as the beam lifted off him, he shook himself, assessed the immediate vicinity for threats, checked his weapons and transmitted a coded message to let the missile vehicle know he was down safely. Then he unclipped his omicron-band pulse scanner from his equipment belt and studied it carefully. Immediately, he found what he'd been looking for: Ostar power-wave signatures. They showed up as bright red splodges on a grey background. He narrowed the focus, superimposed a GPS grid and set the scanner to tracking mode.

Scanner in one hand, therion blaster in the other, he walked quickly through the streets. For some reason, humans he encountered took pains to keep out of his way. He took no interest in them, once he'd assessed their threat potential and dismissed it. In his mind, the mission statement wound in an endless loop: Locate and retrieve the probe designated Mark Twain; force level 5 authorised. It was a simple core for a functional existence, and he asked nothing more. At that moment, he was probably the most contented humanoid on the planet.

The PavSoft compound proved to be a large cluster of white

buildings on the southern outskirts of the city. He paused on the nearest available high ground and ran a tactical analysis. Defence systems appeared to be negligible. He noted the extensive area of grass and flowering plants that stood where his strategic database suggested minefields, force curtains and blaster-emplacements towers should have been. Because it wasn't what he'd been expecting, he took a moment to run a search-and-analyse program. But the grass was just grass, the flowering plants harboured nothing in the way of biogenic nerve toxins or hyperallergenic pollen; defensive capability nil, he noted, and dismissed them. There was a flimsy wire fence with a modest electric current running through the top strand; one shot from the therion blaster would melt the wire and break the circuit. There was a sentinel beam, but if he broke it and set off the alarm, so what? Men with primitive projectile weapons would come running, but the worst they could do would be to tickle him, a level-2 threat to his gravitas and dignity but no physical danger whatsoever. In any event, there was a gate in the wire, manned by a single unarmed human. He could simply walk in.

He did just that. The unarmed guard smiled politely at him and asked if he could help him. The probe designated Bob considered his request.

"Your assistance is not required," he replied. "This probe is adequate."

The guard kept smiling. "Who was it you wanted to see?" he asked.

"I seek the type-6 probe designated Mark Twain," Bob replied. It could see no reason to lie.

"Sorry, didn't quite catch that. The type what?"

The probe designated Bob ran a swift efficiency analysis. It would be efficient not to have to use violence. On the other hand, prolonged verbal interaction would cause delay and possible unforeseen complications. He ran a cultural-database search to see if there was anything he could do, any social amenity or culturally approved ritual, to ameliorate the disruptive effects of initiating violence. Match found.

"Six," he replied, and bashed the guard on the head. As the guard groaned and dropped to the ground, he added, "Have a nice day."

He paused and scanned to see if his initiation of violence had significantly altered the strategic position, but nobody seemed to have noticed. A young human female in a tracksuit jogged past him and smiled. He walked on.

He found the building the signal was coming from without difficulty and paused to check for hidden threats. There were surveillance cameras, but he couldn't care less about them. The door was locked, and could only be opened with the appropriate access code. He spent a thousandth of a second debating whether to hack the lock with a spider protocol or kick the door down. The spider seemed the safer option. He ran it, and the door swung open.

A too-easy alert triggered an anxiety protocol, and he hesitated. The missile vehicle had reason to believe that the Mark One missile had been neutralised by Dirter defence technology, but had been unable to identify such technology; therefore, it stood to reason, Dirters had advanced defensive capabilities, but they were too advanced or too alien to show up on standard Ostar investigative scans. Since the building he was about to enter was the operations centre of the biggest and most important IT and communications hub on the planet, it was unthinkable that the defences consisted of nothing more than CCTV, a locked door and a polite, ineffectual gate guard. The fact that he hadn't encountered the defences yet didn't mean they weren't there. The next step, the one that would take him over the threshold of the hub building, was the most likely to bring him into contact with the best Dirt had to offer.

He ran that past himself one more time. These *creatures* would appear to have knocked out a *R'wfft*-class missile. Logic would suggest that he was about to enter one of the most heavily guarded locations on the planet.

Um, he thought.

He ran through the various strategic and tactical options available to him, taking account of his offensive and defensive status, his operational assets and the intelligence and archived data relevant to the current situation. His option-selection subroutines identified the likeliest optimum course of action. Implement, he ordered.

Covering his head with his arms and yelling (cultural reference found), "Geronimo!", the probe designated Bob charged through the doorway, ran headlong into the banister at the foot of a staircase, bashed his head on the handrail and fell over.

A moment or so later, he ran a status check and opened his eyes. A tactical sitrep revealed that he had underestimated the offensive capability of the staircase by 100 per cent, but otherwise he was fine. His reinforced skull had saved him from what could have been a mild concussion, and his armoured epidermal layer was unbroken. The only obvious threat he could detect was that pesky staircase, and a single shot from his therion blaster reduced it to inoffensive matchwood and rubble. The best Dirt had to offer, he thought: well, that's fine by me.

He consulted the tracking scanner. The Ostar tech power signal was no more than seventy-five metres away, directly below him. It was contained in a cellar-like structure. Access to the target area was by means of the staircase he'd just demolished.

Oh, he thought.

The discharge of his therion blaster appeared to have triggered an archaic audio alarm system. He considered the implications. Guards, civilian, possibly unarmed; a general lockdown of doors and gates; a call for back-up, presumably more of the same. Nothing to worry about. He peered down through the splintered wreck of the stairs, estimated the drop to be no more than twelve metres, and jumped.

He landed securely, immediately found his balance, and looked down. He was about a third of the way down what remained of the stairs. Getting down, of course, was the easy part. Gravity was on his side. Getting back up again, hauling with him the errant type-6, would be a little more challenging. To save time later, he unlooped a micrograpple from his belt, threw it up to the floor above and tugged gently on the microfilament line to make sure it was firmly fixed. Then he consulted his scanner again. No more than twelve metres to the hub.

Of course, he reasoned as he approached a solid-looking steel door, it didn't necessarily follow that the type 6 was still here. Quite some time had passed since the disruption of the unicorn probe. But the fugitive was a type 6, just as he was. Were he in Mark Twain's position, he'd make for the best-defended place he could find and stay there. Moving about would just make him vulnerable; besides, if he was wandering about the city, the scanner would have picked him up. No, he was still somewhere inside the compound, in which case he was certain to be on the other side of this plain steel door. The probe designated Bob hefted his therion blaster, set the yield to 2.1 to avoid excessive collateral damage, and aimed at the crude mechanical locking system.

The alarm bell stopped ringing.

The probe designated Bob hesitated. He could see no reason why the alarm should have been deactivated, and any development he couldn't account for merited attention, in case it presaged an unforeseen situation. He lowered the blaster and reached for his scanner.

The Tannoy system started to play music.

It was on him and into him before he had a chance to react. Before he could cover his ears with his hands, the tune had found his cerebral cortex and penetrated his concentration centres. He swung round, desperately seeking the output speakers, but by then it was too late:

Tumpty-tum, tumpty-tum, tumpty tumpty-tum.

He froze, scanner in one hand, blaster in the other. Numbers and intervals flooded through his brain, washing away subroutines, seeping through into data archives, drowning command functions, demanding to be counted, analysed, calculated, multiplied and divided and square-rooted. Scanner or blaster – frantically he tried to decide, to remember what he'd been doing the instant before the music started, but all he could process was tumpty-tumpty-tumpty-tumpty tumpty tumpty tum. He could feel himself growing too confused and preoccupied to remember how to breathe. Tumpty-tumpty-tum, tumpty-tumpty-tum. He tried to press the blaster's trigger, but he no longer had control over his right index finger. He heard himself singing along, with his last reserve of breath. Darkness veiled his eyes as his empty lungs convulsed—

The music stopped. A few seconds later, PavSoft security personnel were lowered down the stairwell on ropes. They tied the intruder up, winched him back to the ground floor, loaded him on a stretcher and took him off to the company infirmary. Several of them were whistling "Jingle Bells". After all, it's an infernally catchy tune.

The security chief called Lucy Pavlov in the cafeteria and told her what had happened; all according to plan, they reported, situation now contained, reverting to security level taupe. Lucy couldn't remember offhand what taupe was – higher than yellow, obviously, and a long way below red – but she thanked them anyway, her mouth full of cheesecake.

"It won't stop a bomb," Mark Twain said.

"I never said it would," Lucy replied. "I said it'd stop a type-6 probe, and it did. You're supposed to say how clever I've been."

Mark Twain nibbled at the corner of his slice of cheesecake, pulled a face and put it back on his plate. "You've been clever," he replied. "But it won't stop a bomb. Not even if you play Ravel's *Boléro* at it."

"Cultural reference found." She thought for a moment. "It might, you know."

He shook his head. "Only works on organics," he said, "not computers."

She shrugged. "Anyway," she said, "now we know how to deal with type-6 probes. Cheer up, that's a good thing."

"It's a very small good thing."

"Also," she went on, ignoring him, "we've captured an enemy spy. That's good too."

"Accessing strategic database. Yes," he conceded, "up to a point. We can put him on trial and use him as a pretext to expel all their diplomats. Well, that's a weight off my mind."

"Don't be such a misery," Lucy said, spearing his cheesecake with her fork. "We can reprogram him to send back disinformation. That's what you do, apparently."

He sighed. "You do realise that the ship's got exactly the same strategic database as us," he pointed out. "It'll be expecting—"

"Exactly." She smiled at him. "So, we programme the spy to tell the ship there is no defence grid, there aren't any incredibly sophisticated hidden weapons, and there's absolutely no reason why it shouldn't complete the mission and detonate immediately."

"But that's *true*—"

Lucy nodded. "Mm," she said through a cheesecake filter. "And the ship won't believe it, for the reasons stated." She smiled again. "Say I'm clever."

He raised both eyebrows. "You're clever," he said.

"Thanks."

"But it's still just buying time," Mark Twain said gloomily. "Sooner or later, it's going to figure it out. Or it'll get fresh orders from Homeworld. Or they'll send another bomb. Or a fleet of warships."

"Don't be annoying," she said. "By then we'll have thought of something."

"Will we?"

"Oh yes," said Lucy. "We're clever."

43

Portland, Oregon

"Hello," the customer said. "Would you like to buy a computer?"

The shopkeeper took a moment to reply. "That's not a computer," he said, "it's a squid. And why are you both dressed up as—?"

"It's a computer," the customer said. "Trust me. I'll show you, if you like."

"And it's not a squid," the female said. "It's an octopus."

The shopkeeper turned his head away and groped for the button that operated the extractor fan. "Thanks," he said, "but I think I'll pass. We sell computers, you see, not marine life."

"Oh, it's not alive," the customer said reassuringly.

"I can see that," the shopkeeper said. "And smell it too," he added, with feeling.

The male customer took a deep breath and smiled. "Yes, it's an octopus," he said, as if explaining macroeconomic theory to a seven-year-old. "But we've figured out a way to modify it and turn it into a computer. A really, really good one. Better than anything you've got in your store. If you give us money, we'll show you what we've done, and then you can modify more octopuses and make lots of these really, really good computers, and then you can sell them to people and become extremely rich. You'd like that, wouldn't you?"

The shopkeeper thought about it for a moment. "Tell you what I'll do," he said.

"Yes?"

"I'll count to ten," he said. "Then, if you're not out of my store, taking your dead fish with you, I'll call the cops. Do we have a deal?"

The female, who'd been drawing on the back of a flyer all this time, made an exasperated sort of a noise and elbowed the male out of the way. "Look at this," she said, shoving the piece of paper under the shopkeeper's nose. "Go on, it won't bite you."

"One," the shopkeeper said, but he couldn't help glancing at the paper. "Two. Three. Four. Five. Oh my god."

"Interested?"

The shopkeeper made a grab for the paper, but the female snatched it away. "Money," she said.

There was a brief, fraught silence. "How much?"

"Enough for two airline tickets to Siberia."

"Deal."

"And," the female said quickly, "two suits of inconspicuous clothes, underwear, shoes and stuff. And how much does it cost for a sex-change operation?"

They left the store with $3,000 and the octopus (the shopkeeper said thanks but he'd get a more up-to-date model) and went to the airport by way of Walmart. Everything went very smoothly until a man in a smart uniform asked them for their passports.

"Sorry?"

"Passports," the man in uniform repeated. "Can't go beyond this barrier unless I see them."

"What's a passport?"

A difficult situation then arose, which they eventually resolved by running away. That wasn't so bad, because they hadn't had a really good run for some time. But, when they were finally sure they weren't being followed any more, and they'd sat down on a bench in a park somewhere to consider their position, they had to agree that things could have been better.

"We've still got some money left," the male pointed out. "And the octopus."

"Big deal," his sister replied. "And I'm still not sure we should've sold that man advanced technology. The Principal Directive would seem to apply."

The male said something vulgar about the Principal Directive. "If we've got enough money," he went on, "we can buy electronics, upgrade the octopus and call Dad. He'll know what to do."

His sister didn't seem convinced. "What's he going to do?" she said. "Send us two tickets to Siberia and a full set of travel documents? I don't think so. He'll just get mad at us and shout."

Her brother thought about that for a moment, and winced. "All right," he said grudgingly. "You suggest something."

"We buy the electronics, upgrade the octopus and use it to get money out of a bank. Then we can buy an aircraft of our own and fly it to Siberia without all this mucking around with bits of paper. It can't be difficult," she added, as her brother looked at her. "Else they couldn't do it."

There was a brisk difference of opinion, followed by a compromise. They'd buy the electronics, upgrade the octopus (which was starting to smell irresistably delicious; humans were crossing the street to avoid it), use it to get money out of a bank, and then go to the appropriate store and buy a couple of passports. They tried that, and everything went beautifully according to plan until they tried to find a passport vendor. They tried a Pavoogle search, but there were no passport sellers listed in Portland, Oregon. They went back to Walmart, which had impressed them as being a high-class establishment where you could get practically anything you wanted (and at sensible prices). However, when they asked the clerk in the household-goods department if they could buy a couple of passports, with visas for Siberia, a difficult situation arose, which they were forced to resolve by running away. This time, owing to the intervention of store security and a couple of peace officers, they had to dump the octopus before they could make good their escape.

"I've had about as much of this stupid planet as I can take," the male said, peeping out from under the lid of the Dumpster in which they'd judiciously taken cover. "Is it just me, or are all humans completely irrational and dangerously paranoid?"

His sister scowled at him, though of course he couldn't see her. "Not the sort of place you'd want to be stranded for the rest of your life, you mean."

"I keep telling you, when this is all over, we'll go home."

"And grow old eating our dinners out of a bowl on the floor. It's a great choice, isn't it?"

The hissing noise her brother made probably wasn't the last of his patience leaking out through his gritted teeth, but it could well have been. "Yes, well," he said, "looks like there's a third option after all. The one where you keep on moaning at me, we do nothing, and we both get blown away when they detonate the bomb. You know," he added savagely, "the one that's most likely to happen, ever since you dropped the octopus. The odds-on favourite, in fact."

Sibling bickering is like tennis; there's an almost infinite variety of shots that can be played, but both players know better than to cross the clearly marked lines. There was, therefore, a brief silence. Then the female said, "So what do we do now?"

The male shrugged. "We've still got a thousand US dollars left from what we took out of the bank. Even on this stupid planet, that's got to buy a whole lot of bones."

His sister thought about that. "And decaying octopus," she said.

"You know, I've kind of gone off that."

"Well, decaying something else, then. Cuttlefish washed up on beaches. Dead birds."

Her brother hesitated. "Or we could buy more electronics and another octopus and try and call home."

"Not enough money," his sister said firmly. "We need at least thirteen hundred dollars. We only have one thousand."

"True," her brother said, and there was a kind of fatalistic joy in his voice. "Right, then. Screw duty and the hell with the mission – let's party."

They scrambled out of the Dumpster, brushing unidentified bits of stuff off their clothes. "Shopping," said the male.

"Not Walmart."

"Agreed. What we need," her brother said firmly, "is a really good butcher."

They walked in silence for a while. Then, at the corner of a busy street, they hesitated just long enough to flex their nostrils, as their Ostar brain centres did their best to identify the smells they sought using their sadly inferior human noses. "That way," said the male.

"Agreed."

They'd gone about fifty metres when a human stepped out from a doorway. He was short, middle-aged, shabby and wild-looking. They recognised him immediately.

"Hey, it's—"

"Shhh!"

Too late. He'd seen them. He smiled, and from his jacket pocket he drew a grey plastic contraption which they'd last seen in their hotel room in New York.

"Greetings," George Stetchkin said, and shot them.

44

?????

"One hundred million years ago," the director said, "the first Ostar emerged on this planet."

The female cleared her throat. "Yes," she said, "we know that. Look, about this illegal booster station—"

"The first Ostar," the director repeated firmly. "Our ancestors. From whom we are all descended."

"Quite," the female said. "Only, when you bullied us into letting you build the wretched thing, we had no idea—"

The director turned his head and looked at her. She had to fight quite hard to keep herself from rolling on her back with her legs in the air. "Your ancestors and mine," he said quietly. "Would you be interested in knowing their names?"

The others shared an oh-no-he's-finally-flipped look. "That's not possible, is it?" the young male said. "I mean, a hundred million—"

"On the contrary," the director said. "I know their names. It's a recorded fact. They were called Millie and Prince. They were a pair of pedigree beagles, born and raised at the Sunshine Valley Dog Ranch in Albuquerque, New Mexico. On Earth."

It was the sort of silence into which noise is sucked and

utterly destroyed. Finally, the PDF man said, "Earth?"

"Yes." The director gazed at him for a moment, then nodded. "*That* Earth. The planet we've been talking about."

The older male coughed nervously. "That can't be right," he said. "We know for a fact, humanoid life didn't originate on the planet until—"

"Millie and Prince," the director went on, "were acquired by an organisation called the National Aeronautics and Space Administration, an adjunct of the government of America, one of Earth's numerous autonomous states. They were placed aboard a crude missile powered by chemical explosives and fired into planetary orbit. The object of the exercise was to find out if living creatures could survive in space. According to Earth records, this took place in year 1956 of the human calendar."

"Hang on, I'm confused," said the younger male. "It said in the briefing notes you gave us last year that the current Earth-calendar year is 2015. But you're saying that these *beagles* were on Ostar a hundred million—"

"Yes." The director smiled at him. "The missile project went wrong. The missile itself disappeared without trace twenty Earth hours after it was launched. It emerged just inside Ostar's gravity well, at which point its rocket motors failed and it crash-landed on the surface. The missile itself was wrecked, but by some miracle Millie and Prince survived and escaped unharmed from the wreckage. That," the director continued, "is the limit of what we know for certain. But DNA testing and advanced genetic analysis have proved beyond doubt that the Ostar species is descended from Earth dogs. We have in fact secured a dog from the Sunshine Valley Dog Ranch – the bloodline has been maintained intact for commercial reasons – and compared his DNA with samples taken from the wreckage of the missile, which my archaeologists discovered in the jungles of G'wrzt thirty years ago. As far as I'm concerned, there can be no other explanation. We as a species are directly descended from Millie and Prince."

After a long, long pause the female said, "Let me just get this straight," she said. "You've been sending Ostar to Earth all this time, and you never told anyone?"

The director suddenly laughed. "Think about it," he said. "When the archaeological team excavating a possible alien artefact in G'wrzt told me that they'd found a wrecked spacecraft that had crashed on Ostar a hundred million years ago, I immediately realised the implications. We're a proud species, wouldn't you agree? For most of our history, we were convinced that we were the only sentient life in the universe. When we were forced to accept that this was not the case, the implications nearly tore our society apart. All our major religions crashed and burnt practically overnight; there were riots, massacres, governments fell, we were a hair's breadth from planetwide civil war. When we pulled ourselves together and accepted the facts, it was only because we could still pride ourselves on being the most advanced species, the only true intelligent form of life. Just imagine what the repercussions would be if the Ostar people were asked to accept that they're the progeny of a pair of laboratory specimens; that our common ancestors were held to be entirely without value, completely expendable. Something like that could kill us as a species. You do see that, don't you?"

The female didn't reply, but her face was completely frozen. The director nodded, and scratched his ear with his hind paw. "I'm sorry," he said, "I'm getting ahead of myself. When the G'wrzt researchers sent me their first report, I'd never even heard of Earth, needless to say. It was some time before we were able to match up the alloys found in the wreckage with spectrographic analyses of known habitable planets. There were four possible candidates, and we investigated them all. The other three proved to have produced no form of life higher than insects. Then we turned our attention to Earth. We found a planet with a dominant humanoid species, currently at a stage of development roughly analogous to ours a thousand years ago. Could Earth have sent a spacecraft to Ostar a hundred million years ago?

"At first, I thought my job would be to search Earth for signs of a lost civilisation, of whom the present inhabitants are a hopelessly degenerate and barbarised relic. But when my tracker probe downloaded the archives of the NASA and we found schematics of a missile practically identical to the one we dug up at G'wrzt, I knew there had to be some other explanation. By a lucky coincidence, other researchers were investigating the possibility of a long-extinct wormhole in the U'urgt asteroid belt. We found the site of the wormhole, and we managed to backtrack its path. The trail, as you'll have guessed, ended at Earth. The temporal distortion effect, the wormhole scientists told me, was something in the order of a hundred million years. The conclusion, I put it to you, is inescapable. When the Earth missile was launched, with Millie and Prince on board, it fell into the mouth of the U'urgt wormhole, which carried it a hundred million years back in time and seventy light-years through space. It brought it *here*, to Ostar, where it crashed. The beagles, to coin a phrase, had landed."

The silence that followed, though no less profound than those that had preceded it, had a slightly different edge to it. Eventually the young male whispered, "Sorry, did he just make a joke or something?"

The director scowled at him and went on, "So there you have it: the evidence, and the conclusions. I've had to bear the weight of this for thirty years. Now you can share it with me." He grinned. "Of course, it goes without saying that if any of you breathe a word of this—"

"Yes, fine," the female said, her voice somewhat ragged, "but I don't see the connection. So our species originally came from Earth." She paused, as if she'd just heard what she'd said and couldn't believe it. "That still doesn't explain why you went to all the trouble of faking the Earth music so we'd want to blow them up. I can't see why you'd want to do that."

The director appeared genuinely shocked. "You can't?"

"Well, no, actually. I'd have thought – I mean, our cousins a billion times removed are living on that planet."

The director nodded. "As pets," he said.

"Pets?"

"Pets. The humans keep tame dogs."

"That's—" The young male opened his mouth and closed it a couple of times. "That's sick," he said. "It's like that tri-vid, *Escape From the Planet of the Humans*. Only," he added thoughtfully, "that's just sci-fi."

"Even so," the female said firmly, pulling herself together with a visible effort, "I still don't see why you'd feel the need to blow the planet up. It's like I'm missing out a step somewhere."

The older male cleared his throat. "Was that the one where he finds the Sacred Bone of R'qqrt buried in a sand dune?"

The young male shook his head. "No, that was *Return to the Planet of the Humans*," he said. "*Escape* was where the chief human's daughter turns out to be the hero's eldest pup genetically mutated into a—"

The director made a soft growling noise that won him their undivided attention. "Thank you," he said. "To answer your question: well, isn't it obvious? If the Ostar people ever find out the truth about their origins—"

"You've already said that," the PDF man interrupted. "And maybe you've got a point there, I don't know. But blowing up Earth isn't going to solve anything. If that's what you're concerned about, all you need to do is purge your files and make sure those bits of crashed spaceship are coated in concrete and buried somewhere deep. Bear in mind, there's no reason whatsoever to think the Earth people know about this. There's no need to kill them, and the D'ppggyt Accords would seem—"

"No." The director's face was unreadable, but he'd dug his claws a centimetre deep into the arms of his chair. "They've got to go," he said. "We can't risk it."

The PDF man returned his stare. "You mean," he said,

"they've got to be punished. For keeping dogs as pets. For shooting our ancestors out into space as an experiment, not really giving a damn if they died or not. Yes?"

The director drew in a long, hard breath. "Yes. Do you have a problem with that?"

The other three were watching the PDF dog, he knew. Whatever he said, they'd go along with, mostly because he was standing up to the director, challenging him for dominance. The thought of what he was doing made the fur inside his shirt stand on end, but he kept his face straight and his ears upright, and he thought, Well, *do* I have a problem with that?

"Well?"

He shrugged. "No," he said. "I guess I don't."

45

Novosibirsk

There was a manual, and it had a translation function. He only found it quite by chance, pressing buttons to see what they did. One button brought up the usual screenful of alien gibberish in that eye-bruising, obscene-looking script they used, but just as he was about to try again with a different button, something caught his eye and he looked back. There was a symbol, roughly two-thirds of the way down the screen. It looked a bit like a crucified vole and he'd never seen it before in his life – needless to say – but he knew what it meant; not when he looked at it straight on, but when he caught a glimpse of it in passing, out of the corner of his eye. It meant "English". That was too crazy for words, so he assumed he was imagining things; and then, as he looked up at the top of the screen, it happened again. *English*.

He thought about it for a second or so. Maybe, he reasoned, a tiny part of him was still a creature of pure text, able to read any script, break any code; but that tiny part of him was buried so deep that it only came to the surface when his conscious mind was fully occupied elsewhere. Or something like that.

He ran the cursor down to the mysterious character and hit the biggest button of all. The screen flickered, then re-formed itself into proper letters; letters that he could read.

Neutron disintegrationing mover storer imprison to device a lot questions they ask.

Translations of technical manuals, he realised, are pretty much the same the whole galaxy over. Fortunately he was used to them. A lot questions they ask, for example, were obviously FAQ. The other stuff, disintegrationing and imprison, tended to suggest that he was on the right lines. The first bit was just the usual lawyer-speak (So they've got lawyers up there too; not as advanced as all that, then), so he scrolled down until he reached another menu.

To getting back reintegrationing out by of storage

Actually, compared with most of the Eastern European manuals, it was a doddle. Press this button, and then that one. So he did.

Maybe it wasn't the smartest thing he could have done, particularly in a small hotel room. The flash of green light blinded him. The blast threw him against the opposite wall, trashed the wardrobe and brought plaster down from the ceiling. Oddly enough, there was no noise, or at least none that he could hear. For some reason the TV came on, and the hands of the clock on the bedside table started whizzing round like the blades of a windmill. The slow dripping noise he could hear as he picked himself up off the floor was molten metal: he'd left a handful of small change on the table while he'd been playing with the alien gun, and now there was a pool of liquid copper-zinc alloy, although the table itself wasn't visibly scorched.

Apart from that, nothing seemed to have happened. He swore, and reached for the glass of water to ease his suddenly-parched throat. The water was frozen solid.

He limped across the room and looked at the gun's screen. The instructions were still there, and under them a new entry: At work please waiting. He shrugged and went into the bathroom, where he drank water from his cupped hands. It tasted of strawberry.

When he returned, he saw two tiny little people, a boy and a girl, sitting on the gun, their feet dangling. As soon as they saw him, they started yelling at him, but their voices were so high and squeaky he couldn't make out what they were saying. He bent down and looked at them. The boy produced a tiny little light-saber and took a wild swing at him, but he was well out of reach.

"Greetings," he said.

The girl winced and covered her ears; the boy dropped his lightsaber and howled with pain.

George nodded and whispered, "Greetings" as softly as he could. The girl pulled off a shoe and hurled it at him. She missed.

"Just a moment," he whispered. "I think I may be able to do something."

In his suitcase, along with all the other stuff he'd looted from the aliens' New York hotel room after he'd tracked them down by following the trail of credit-card transactions registered to the Global Society for the Ethical Treatment of Dumb Brutes, there was a sort of palmtop-cum-Warthog thing. He had no idea how it worked, but he'd found that if he looked away from it and pressed keys at random, he could make it do what he wanted; the dormant copt, presumably, doing good by stealth.

With his eyes fixed on the TV screen, he touch-typed in a few commands, in a language he didn't know, to effect an operation that surely wasn't possible. A minute or so later the TV screen cleared, and on it appeared a close-up of the tiny people's feet.

"Just a moment," George whispered, and he nudged the palm-top-cum-Warthog over a little bit until the TV showed their faces. "Say something," he said.

They said something; quite a lot, in fact. Their voices came through nice and clear from the TV. George thought about people in the neighbouring rooms, and turned the sound down with the remote.

"Sorry about that," he said. "I guess I must've done something wrong."

They agreed with him on that point – so much, in fact, that he had to mute out the sound until they'd calmed down a bit. "All right," he said, "here's the deal. You tell me what to do, and I'll put you right again. In return, you help me out with a few things. Agreed?" He smiled beautifully at them, and added, "Come on, guys, don't give me a hard time. You shot me first, remember?"

There was a long silence. Then the boy said, "All right."

"Excellent." George clapped his hands together, which made the little ones shudder. "And just in case you change your minds, I'm keeping this thing." He leaned over and patted the gun. "I've always wanted a ray-gun that really works."

The boy told him what to do, which buttons to press, and not long afterwards he and his sister stepped out of a cloud of shining green mist and collapsed on the bed. "You're welcome," George said, and covered them both with the gun. "Now, who the hell are you?"

46

Novosibirsk

"That ought to do it," Mark Twain said, pressing the Send button of the communicator they'd taken from the probe designated Bob. "I've told it there's nothing down here to worry about and everything's fine." He put the communicator down on the concrete floor, stepped back half a dozen paces, aimed the therion blaster and fired a burst. There was nothing left of the communicator except a little dribble of melted titanium alloy.

"Nice touch," Lucy said.

Mark Twain grinned. "I left the channel open," he said. "With any luck, the ship'll pick up a trace of the weapon's beam frequency, so it'll know the communicator was destroyed by a therion blast. That'll give it one more thing to think about."

He sounds different, Lucy thought. He's talking . . . well, almost like a human. Like me. Also, he doesn't smile all the time, which is a relief. You could get sunstroke, being around a smile like that.

"Right," she said. "Now what?"

And that was a very good question. The answer she longed to hear, on one level, was, *Let's take a break, chill out, maybe crack open a bottle of Chablis*. Instead she got, "I suggest we tear down the central data-storage node and run a level-9 refrag-and-retrieve protocol. You never know, there may be a few scraps left that we could retrobuild from." Well, she thought, it was a good answer in its way: positive, energetic, quite an intelligent approach. Sensible, in other words. And maybe there'd be a time for Chablis later, when they'd saved the planet and all.

"Good idea," she said. "You carry on with that, I'll clear some space in the main drive buffers. We're going to need a lot of memory for something like that."

Mark Twain's idea (she'd already thought of it, but she wanted to let him think it was all his very own) was to comb through the main computer of Lucy's ship, now concealed and cannibalised as the central control hub of PavSoft, in the hope of finding back-up copies of the wee-small-hours conversations Lucy had had with the ship after she'd bleached her own memory. Needless to say, they'd already looked and found nothing; but they had noticed disturbances in the computer's file architecture that suggested that large chunks of stuff had been deleted. If those chunks had been Lucy's chats with the computer, it might be possible to piece together a word or two here and there, a couple of whole sentences if they were really lucky; and that might just be enough to give them some clue as to why Lucy had aimed the bomb at Homeworld before giving herself amnesia. Privately, Lucy didn't hold out much hope. Even if it worked, she couldn't really see how it'd be likely to solve the problem of the other bomb, *his* bomb, lurking in orbit overhead. On the other hand, Mark Twain happily, frantically engaged in displacement activity was far less likely to get on her nerves while they waited to see what the bomb did next than Mark Twain with nothing to occupy himself with. It was, in effect, a hi-tech equivalent to painting the spare bedroom and fitting a new shower curtain in the bathroom.

He was lying on his back on the floor, half under the skeleton of a dismembered console, grunting and doing things with screwdrivers. She thought about that. He was getting more and more male with every hour that passed; likewise more idiomatic, more emotional, more human generally. Presumably she'd been through the same process of going native, but she couldn't remember, of course. Convenient. She could see a lot of good reasons why she should have chosen to blank her memory, quite apart from the obvious one of not wanting to be aware she wasn't actually human, hadn't had a home, family or childhood, that she'd originally come here not to settle down and make a life for herself but to turn the entire planet into space-dust and loose chippings. Memories, she told herself, are what give organics their identity; but mostly they don't have any say about what happens to them, so their memories aren't of their own choosing. Lucy Pavlov had no past, which was one of the main reasons why she'd had such a wonderful future to look forward to – before he came along, at least.

Not him: the bomb. She was pretty sure he'd stopped thinking of himself as part of it, started viewing it strictly as the enemy, or at best an estranged parent he was determined to defy. She very much hoped so. It was, of course, frivolous and irresponsible of her to let herself think ahead, to beyond the bomb, to what might happen as and when they'd sorted it all out. The phrase "and they lived happily ever after" kept sneaking in through the cat-flap of her mind, and when she'd found the cultural reference, it made her wonder what was going on inside that funny little hybrid machine/organic head of hers. Still, she thought, if not him, then who the hell else?

Bad logic. She finished the job she'd been doing, then wandered over to the coffee machine and drew off two cappuccinos. It was only after she'd given him his and sipped her own that she remembered she didn't like frothy coffee.

"No promises," he gasped, crawling out from under the console, "but we may be on to something here. You wouldn't happen to have such a thing as a phase-inverted tricameral verteron inducer?"

"Left it in my other jacket. Sorry, no, I haven't."

"Ah. Oh well, not to worry, I can boost the polarities on a standard verteron inducer and recalibrate the drivers."

"Haven't got a standard verteron inducer either."

He nodded slowly. "Right," he said. "Have you got a lump hammer and a six-inch nail?"

He was enjoying himself. She was pretty sure he didn't realise. Quite possibly he hadn't yet evolved to the point where his brain could metabolise the concept of *fun*. But he was male and he was fixing stuff. Under those conditions, fun is spontaneously generated, like static electricity in cat fur.

"Now," he said, as she handed him the nail, "all we do is, we pass the nail through the standing verteron field generated by the transmorphic flux capacitors, like this—Yow!" he added, dropping the nail and hugging his right hand to his chest; it was glowing blue and dripping fat blue sparks. "Sod it, forgot to turn off the juice. Can you just—?"

She flipped the appropriate switch. "Are you all right?"

"Oh, just singed a bit," he replied through gritted teeth, as a tear rolled down his face and blue fire ran along his eyebrows like brandy flames on a Christmas pudding. "Serves me right for not thinking about what I'm doing." He picked up the nail, yelped and dropped it. "Have you got another nail handy? This one's a bit—"

"Here," she said, handing him a nail. "Oughtn't you to be wearing gloves?"

"Nah." He grinned feebly; his eyes were still watering. "They'd just get in the way. Right, let's try again."

The second nail melted. The third nail got shot through the wall and may well have ended up in planetary orbit. The fourth—

"There you go," he said, as he touched the nail to the panel on his knees, which lit up and began to hum, "piece of cake." His hair was standing on end like the bristles of a wire brush. "Now then, all we do now is jump the feed across these points here, and we ought to start seeing something." He touched the bare ends of two wires together. White smoke started pouring out of the seams of the panel. "Ah, right, forgot about that." He flipped a switch on the panel and tried again. On the bench above his head, a row of monitors lit up, their screens cascading with Ostar numerals.

"You did it," she said.

Eventually, she didn't add; she also left out *amazingly, considering you practically fried the system three times.* In spite of which, she was impressed. There had been a couple of intuitive leaps in his approach that would never have occurred to her. She'd assumed that what he'd just done wasn't possible.

"Anything?" he asked, hauling himself up off the floor and looking over her shoulder at the screens.

"Just garbage," she replied, and his face fell so fast and so far it practically burnt up on re-entry. "Hold it," she added. "What's that? There, that group on the third screen from the left, near the bottom."

"That's a standard military class-7 cipher."

I know that, she didn't say. "And there, look. Scroll that one down a bit, there's more."

Loads more: pages and pages of it, all in basic easy-to-read class-7 encryption. After a while they stopped talking to each other, too intent on what they were reading to say anything.

Eventually they stopped reading and looked at each other. Their faces were pale and rather scared-looking.

"Who the hell," Lucy said, "are the Global Society for the Ethical Treatment of Dumb Brutes?"

47

?????

"**F**air play," said the PDF man, smirking slightly. "We didn't know about your booster station. You don't know about our latest generation of warships. Personally, I don't believe government can function unless the front paws are kept blissfully ignorant of what the hind paws are doing."

They stood on the observation platform of the orbital defence grid control station, with nothing but a forcefield between them and the stars. It wasn't the same as seeing it on a screen, the director acknowledged. Even the best 3D imaging came nowhere near close.

"Not very big, are they?" he said.

The PDF man grinned, displaying teeth. "*T'erier*-class," he said, "small but vicious. Three-man crew, but more firepower than a type-9 frigate. That lot up there –" he indicated a cloud of small white dots far away in the distance – "could take out the whole of the rest of the fleet put together in about five minutes, and the crews wouldn't know what hit them."

"Interesting," the director said quietly but pointedly. "Just the sort of thing you'd want on your side if you were – oh, I don't know, planning a military coup or something."

"You know, that hadn't occurred to me," the PDF man replied mildly. "But yes, I can see your point. That's not what we had in mind when we built them, though."

"Really."

The PDF man shrugged. "The really cool thing about them," he went on, "is the dislocation drive." He lowered his voice, even though they were demonstrably alone on the platform. "You're a scientist, you'll appreciate this. We finally cracked U'rrf's Constant."

The director nearly fell over. At the last moment, he managed to grab hold of the handrail. "You're joking."

"Actually, no I'm not. We found a way round the diffusion shift problem. A *T'erier*-class can dislocate. You don't need me to tell you what that means."

The director looked at him. "Anywhere in the galaxy?"

The PDF man nodded. "Not quite instantaneous," he said, "not yet. There's still exit and re-entry times, and of course it can take several hours to do the navigational calculations and pro-gramme the guidance computers. But more or less, yes. Any-where in the galaxy within a matter of hours."

The director's tail was wagging; he couldn't help it. "You can't keep something like that to yourselves," he said softly. "I mean, it's the biggest discovery since—"

"Since nothing. It's the biggest discovery ever." The PDF man turned his head slightly and gazed at the white dots. "Of course, U'rrf did all the hard work, rest his soul. We just cleared up that one last niggling little detail. Even so." His face cracked into a huge, lolling-tongue grin. "That still makes us the cleverest be-ings ever in the history of the universe."

The director dragged in a deep breath; his lungs were tight and his throat felt cramped. "Just think," he said, "of what we'll be able to do with technology like that. It'll mean an end to hunger, poverty—"

"Um, no." The PDF man pulled a sad face. "Pity, but no.

That'd mean telling people about it, and then it wouldn't be *ours* any more. Much better to restrict it to the military. After all, if an enemy got his paws on it, we wouldn't have an overwhelming advantage any more, now would we?"

"What enemy? We haven't got any."

"Not right now," the PDF man said. "Not that we know of. Except Earth, of course."

"Well, yes." The director hesitated. "Apart from them, though—"

"And they've knocked out two of our *R'wfft*-class missiles," he went on, "so who knows what they've got? Must be something pretty devastating." He smiled. "That's how I sold it to my bosses, and they agreed wholeheartedly. Though I don't suppose they minded having a chance to try out the *T'erier* class in action. It's been rather frustrating, as you can imagine. Like a kid with a new bike when it won't stop raining."

The white dots could have been stars, except that they were just a little bit too close together.

"So when will you—?"

"Oh, we can't see any point in hanging about," the PDF man said. "Ready when you are, basically."

"When *I*—"

"You're coming with us," the PDF man said. "I thought you'd be pleased," he added. "You'll be able to see it happen, after all those years of dedicated work."

The director moved away from the rail, his back to the ships and stars. "Yes, thank you," he said. "That's exactly what I want, you're quite right." But his ears were back and his collar was tight. Details like that weren't lost on a trained observer.

"Splendid," the PDF man said. "We're running the second phase of pre-launch checks, so that gives you an hour. I can let you have room for a small instrument case, but that's about all. You'll be flying with me," he added. "I trust that's all right."

"Of course," the director said, looking straight at him. There was something about his expression that the PDF man couldn't quite identify; not fear exactly, a little bit of resentment but only by way of orchestration to the main theme. Sorrow, he decided, rather to his surprise.

"Where should I meet you?"

"Here," the PDF man said. "We'll teleport to the boarding module, and they'll get you kitted up there. Don't eat or drink anything," he added. "Not recommended before dislocating. Ten cc's of strepsiadin wouldn't be a bad idea, either."

"I'll be here," the director said, and he stepped on to the elevator without looking back. He took the teleshift back to his office, where he filled a slim black case with instruments – scanners, collimators, a hi-res thaumaton probe. He took a model-16 therion blaster out of his desk drawer, then reluctantly put it back: he would undoubtedly be scanned for weapons, and it would only cause embarrassment. Finally, he sprang the two locks on the bottom drawer of his desk, pulled out a plastic bag and put it in the case. It contained a lead and a collar.

48

Novosibirsk

"The Global Society," the female repeated, "for the Ethical Treatment of Dumb Brutes."

George frowned. "I know that name," he said. "They bought me a cup of coffee."

"You're welcome," the male said. "Anyway, that's us. At least, we work for them."

"Right," George nodded. "And the globe as in global would be...?"

"Ostar," the female said. "You won't have heard of it. Long way away from here."

"How far?"

"Seven hundred light-years, give or take," the male replied.

George nodded dumbly. Aliens, he thought. Way back when, before I addled my brains with booze, people called me a genius for proving they didn't exist. But I always knew they did, ever since they stole—

"That's where you're from."

"Yes." The male gave him an Earl Grey smile: weak and insipid. "Yes, we're both Ostar. Or we used to be."

"Used to—"

"We can't go home," the female said briskly. "Ever. So we're stuck here, for the rest of our lives, on this—"

The male tried to do a significant warning cough, swallowed air the wrong way and nearly choked.

The female waited till he'd finished and went on, "There's an Ostar ship in orbit," she said. "We had to go there, so we teleported up to it. But – well, there's side-effects. It means we're stuck in these bodies for ever."

Using his coffee cup as cover, George pursed his lips. He could sympathise, up to a point. Except for his brief interlude as a creature of pure text, he'd been stuck in his body since the day he was born, and it wasn't exactly the body he'd have chosen, even before he started marinading it in alcohol. Even so— Then the penny dropped like an asteroid. "Those aren't your—"

"Real bodies, no," the male said. "When we came here, we were surgically altered. You know, gene-resequencing, DNA involution therapy, morphic stasis diasporation, the whole bit. So we'd blend in and be inconspicuous."

George looked at them: the Skywalker twins. Maybe "inconspicuous" had a different penumbra of meanings where they came from. Then something that had been nagging away at his subconscious for a while clicked into place. "You don't look like you did when I first saw you," he said. "For one thing, she wasn't a—"

The female growled, just like a dog. "Bit of a sore point," the male said quickly. "Let's just say we had an accident. Anyway, Bro – I mean Sis – is quite right. We're stuck like this. She's wrong saying we can't go home, but—"

"No I'm not. Nobody's going to see me looking like this, *nobody*."

George thought for a moment. "So the Ostar are – well, they look different from us, yes?"

The male shivered. "You could say that. In fact," he went on, "it's not too bad, it could be worse. I mean, the Ostar have one head and four limbs, just like your lot, and we see with eyes and hear with ears and so on. I suppose, looking at it from a xenobiological point of view, we're not so different. Like, you should see some of the creatures there are out there. Some of them don't even have physical bodies, which is just so weird."

George, who'd quite recently been a sentence, with a verb instead of a heart and relative clauses where his arms and legs should have been, let that one go. "So," he said with a slight degree of effort, "what exactly are you doing here? And what's the Global Society—?"

"We are, like I said a moment ago," the female replied. "The GSETDB is the biggest animal-rights organisation on Ostar. We found out that our government was planning to destroy your planet."

George's mouth fell open, and he made a single gurgling noise. "Why?"

"Ah." The male smiled grimly. "That's rather a good question. The government says it's because sound waves from Earth, relayed through a wormhole that used to link your planet to ours—"

"*Used* to?"

The male nodded. "Sound travels very slowly," he said. "The wormhole closed up a long time ago, but the sounds that passed through it are only just reaching us now. Anyway, these sounds, including your Earth music, have reached our planet and they're driving us nuts. We don't have anything like music, you see, we're totally unused to it, so when we get a tune in our heads..." He shrugged. "Parallel from your own history," he said. "Settlers from one of your continents landed in a distant country, isolated from the rest of your species for thousands of years. The settlers brought a virus with them; their lot were so used to it that it hardly bothered them at all, but the natives in the place they'd moved to hadn't ever had it, so they'd got no immunity and died like flies. That's us, when your music reached us. At least," he added, with a scowl, "that's what the government told us."

"We think they're lying," the female said. "We think—"

"Hold on a moment," George interrupted. He was starting to get hangover symptoms, even though his blood-alcohol level was lower than it had been for some time. "You said the wormhole the music reached you through has closed up now."

"That's right," the male said. "But it could open up again at any moment, the scientists say, so you lot have got to go. A question of the survival of our species. According to the government."

"Who are lying," the female added. "We believe the sounds that reach us are too quiet to be heard—"

"Even though the Ostar have much better hearing than your lot," the male put in.

"We believe," the female went on, giving the male a sour look, "that the government has been deliberately boosting the noise to dangerous levels, just so they'd have a pretext for blowing up your planet."

George gaped at her. "Why the hell would they want to do that?"

"Another good question," the male said with a shrug. "But anyway, one thing's for sure, our lot launched a missile at you. A *R'wfft*-class, a planet buster. This place should just be a thin cloud of rubble by now."

George waited, but that was it, apparently. "But we're not," he prompted.

"Correct," the male said. "Something went wrong with the bomb. Either it broke down—"

"Which is really, really unlikely," the female said.

"Entirely right," the male said. "Or else your lot managed to shoot it down or defuse it—"

George shook his head, then really wished he hadn't. "I doubt it," he said. "I can't guarantee that, because our governments tend to believe that interesting news is for hoarding not sharing, but from what I've seen, your technology—"

"Quite. You wouldn't stand a chance." The male frowned. "But here you all still are. Which is a good thing," he added, quickly and earnestly. "The Global Society is passionately opposed to the wanton slaughter of living things. We believe that all life-forms, no matter how primitive, have a basic right to exist. Including you."

"Thank you so much," George said, with a slight scowl.

"That's all right," the male said. "It's our mission, and we're prepared to make sacrifices for it. We volunteered to come here, you know."

"Well," the female muttered, "our dad volunteered us."

"Yes, but we—"

"Did as we were told," the female said crisply. "But we're here now, for ever and ever and ever, so we might as well make ourselves useful. Save this miserable planet from being annihilated. That sort of thing."

George took a deep breath. Between wanting to thank them and the urgent need he felt to kick their spines out through their ears, he felt mildly confused. He tried to focus – a bit like trying to build a sandcastle out of semolina pudding. "This bomb," he said. "I think I know where it could be."

The male nodded. "So do we. Of course, there's another one now."

If George hadn't changed back, he'd have been a row of dots at this point.

"It's OK," the male went on, "it's just sitting there, not doing anything. We disarmed it."

"*You—*"

"Us," the female said. "At great personal cost," she added. "But all that means is, they'll send another one. Or more than one, or maybe even warships."

Warships. Just a word, and these days he had a special insight into what a word was. But some words are different. *Warships.* They were going to blow up the Earth. Furthermore, only he knew about it, and there was nothing he could do about it, not by conventional means – telling someone, notifying the authorities, writing to his Congressman, the stuff you're supposed to do in a modern civilised society. Warships, for crying out loud, as in war. War was a concept he could understand – planet-buster missiles were too remote, too sci-fi; might as well be dragons – and if he could understand he could believe, and if he could believe he could be scared out of his feeble, booze-ravaged mind. *There's going to be a war*, and we'll lose and that'll be the end of all of us; unless George Oh-you-mean-the-dipso-in-Security Stetchkin managed to stop it...

"Are you OK?" the male asked. "You've gone a very strange colour."

Coming from a little green man, that was quite something. "Yes," George said. "I mean no, of course I'm not OK. *Warships?*"

The female scratched the tip of her nose. "What we need to know is," she said, "what happened to that first missile. Should've gone off, didn't. *That* wasn't anything to do with us."

"Which suggests," the male went on, "that maybe you people've got something that can beat our technology. Hardly likely," he added, as George made a sort of hysterical-pig noise, "but how else can you explain it? This Lucy Pavlov—"

"Ah." George nodded.

"Well, she's your planet's most high-powered tech expert." The male looked at George but sideways. "And you think she may not be from these parts exactly." He glanced at the female, who shrugged. "I take it we're on the same side, then."

George thought, Are we? I guess we are, at that. So; not just George Stetchkin against the might of the Ostar Empire. George Stetchkin and these two idiots.

Oh boy.

"Really," the male said, his voice a little lower and softer as he edged a little closer. "Really, what we need to do is get to this Lucy Pavlov and find out what she's got, who she is, all that kind of stuff. And you said you work for her."

George nodded slowly. "That's right," he said, trying to concentrate; but inside his mind, the beak of an idea was tapping doggedly against its shell. It was a wild, probably impractical idea, the sort that either fails outright or half works and makes everything incalculably worse. I'm not listening, he told it, go away. "I could probably get the three of us in to see her," he said. "Look, if she's – well, one of your lot, would you be able to tell?"

Tap tap. "Probably," the male said. "It depends on how deep the morphic resequencing goes. If all she's done is replace the primary and sub-primary interfacing pairs, we'd be able to pick it up with a phasganon scan, but if she's gone deeper into the tertiary—Sorry, am I boring you?"

Taptaptaptap. "What? Oh, right. You were saying. Tertiary something."

The male scowled at him. "We'd need to run a sub-mutagenic beacon scan, and that's definitely an invasive procedure, it's not just something I can do behind her back while she's looking the other way." He paused, shrugged and said, "I suppose we could just ask her."

George blinked. "Ask her what?"

"Ask her if she's an Ostar."

"Yes, fine— *No!* I mean, you can't do that. I mean, what if she isn't?"

(But it was a valid question. It was the question, he remembered, that she'd hired him to answer. Asking her, therefore—)

"It's either ask her or stun her and tie her to a table. It's your call, but I invite you to consider which option might prove more embarrassing in the long run." The male pulled a sad face and sighed loudly. "Look," he said, "I can tell you're not paying attention. What is it?"

George looked at him solemnly for a moment; then – tap tap crack – his face split into a wide, frantic grin. "I just had an idea," he said.

49

?????

"**H**e's completely lost it, you realise," the young male whispered. The elderly female glanced at the monitor built into the back of the seat in front of her; it didn't look like it was operational, but she couldn't be sure. Even so. "Barking," she whispered back. "But what can we do?"

"There must be something."

The elderly female fiddled with the air-conditioning, just for something to do. "Not now he's got the military on his side," she said. "Well, it's the other way round, of course. It's them who've scooped him up and made him their own; he's just an excuse so they can test their new fleet and blow something up. I wouldn't give much for his chances after all this is over."

"Agreed," the young male replied. "Or ours."

She winced. "You're probably right," she said. "But at least we'll have the unique privilege of being there on the spot when history is made. And astronomy too, of course. How many people can say they've seen an entire planet being needlessly destroyed?"

"Something to tell the grandchildren?"

"As it happens," the elderly female said, "I have seventeen grandchildren, so there's a remote chance I could tell them, before they come and take me away. In your case, I don't think you'll have time."

They both looked at the older male, who was fast asleep, his head cushioned on his front paws, his ears over his eyes. "We've got to do something," the younger male said. "There must be..."

"Such as?"

The younger male thought. "We could override this ship's autopilot, get manual control and use it to shoot down the—" He sighed. "All right, don't say it. You suggest something."

"I propose telling anybody who'll listen that we were abducted and brought along against our will," the female said. "I shall insist that I asked for my opposition to the project to be noted in the minutes as soon as I became aware of the misuse of government facilities. Nobody's going to believe me, of course."

They sat very still for a while. The older male started to snore.

"How much further, do you think?" the younger male asked.

"Don't ask me." The elderly female tried tapping the keyboard in front of her, but nothing happened. "Switched off," she said; "there's a surprise." She looked up. There was, of course, nothing to see. On the other side of the ship's clear-steel canopy, there was only the dull bronze glow of a Somewhere Else field. "I'm not even sure we're still inside linear time," she said. "Of course, I'm not the right person to ask. When I was at school, you could do astrometaphysics or you could learn ballroom dancing. I'm quite a good dancer, as it happens."

"If we could get the communications beacon working," the younger male persisted, "we could send a message to Central Command—"

"I should stop fretting about it if I were you," the elderly female said. "I always find that when everything's crashing down in ruin around my ears, the best thing is not to dwell on it too much."

The younger male didn't reply to that. After a lot of effort and bad language, he managed to prise the cover off the console next to his left-hand armrest with the back of the plastic spoon he'd been given for his in-flight breakfast. There was nothing to see except grey insulating foam.

"They may just let us off with life imprisonment," the elderly female said. "Apparently it's quite civilised nowadays, you can take adult-education classes, and there are hobby workshops and drama groups and everything. A bit like life in a retirement village, but with decent food."

"We could try reasoning with him," the younger man said. "Oh come on, it's got to be worth a try."

But she sighed. "I don't really think it's up to him any more, dear," she said. "I suppose you could try talking to the PDF man, if you really want to. But I get the impression he's not exactly the listening type. Do you know if these seats are adjustable? I'm starting to get a touch of cramp in my neck."

The younger male stared up through the canopy. From time to time he almost believed he could make out the shadows of nebulae, the faint patterns of asteroid clouds. "Maybe the Earthpeople really do have a secret weapon," he said quietly. "If they could shoot down two *R'wfft*-class missiles..."

"They could blow us to smithereens too," the elderly female said. "Wouldn't that be nice? So much better than being executed by our own people. Thank you, you've quite set my mind at rest. I think I'll just close my eyes for a minute or so, if it's all the same to you."

There was a faint click as she switched off her light, and her silhouette was lost in the all-encompassing bronze glow. The younger male took his spoon and set to work on another panel; he was making quite good progress when the spoon broke, whizzing a small shard of sharp plastic very close to the tip of his nose. And then all the lights came on and the bronze abruptly faded into the deep matt black of a real sky, dandruff-sprinkled with stars. As the young male looked round, he saw a small blue-and-green blob directly overhead, with a tiny glowing pebble directly behind it.

All the monitors flickered into life, and the intercom voice said, "We have now arrived at our destination."

Slowly, the young male placed the broken spoon on the armrest next to him, and considered the blue-and-green blob. It didn't look like much: a tiny speck of colour against a vast monochrome background, like a very small jewel on a very big tray in a shop window. Up there, apparently, sentient creatures lived; not nearly as advanced as the Ostar, to be sure, but smart enough – smart enough to have built a rocket, an overgrown bullet, on to which they'd packed two to-them-expendable life-forms, whose descendants were now zeroing phasganon phase disruptors on the planet's core. It doesn't matter, said a voice in his head, it's no worse than pouring boiling water on an ants' nest. Valid point: an ants' nest is a complex social structure, a culture, a civilisation, albeit rather more totalitarian and brutally focused than anything the Ostar had ever allowed themselves to be governed by. Well, there were some people who were squeamish about pouring boiling water on ants, or smoking out wasps. There was even a pressure group somewhere campaigning for bacterial rights, demanding that they be extracted from sick Ostar and sympathetically re-settled in controlled environments. Life, they argued, is life, even when it's not furry and cuddly, even when it's malevolent. Any counter-argument, they claimed, could only ever boil down to *We're bigger than they are, so there.*

It bothered him. What bothered him even more was the certain knowledge that he was far more worried about what was going to happen to him when he got back to Homeworld than the fate of ten billion super-evolved humans. He ought to care more about them than his own mangy pelt, but he didn't. Another part of his mind was running a ticker-tape loop of excuses – *It wasn't me, it wasn't my idea, They made me do it, They made me go along against my will, There was nothing I could do, I was only obeying orders.* If he could do a deal right now, be let off, allowed to escape in return for abandoning Earth to the disruptor cannon of the fleet, he'd do it so fast he'd cause a bubble in the space/time continuum. Coward. Worthless person. Bad dog.

That's the thing about being helpless, though: you can't do anything. Right now, at the crux of it all, his options had dwindled down to two: he could watch it happen, or he could look away.

He fixed his eyes on the back of the seat in front, and started to count to a million.

50

?????

When the probe designated Bob had abruptly severed the comm link, and all efforts to restore it had failed, the central command computer of the *Warmonger* had, for a while, almost given up.

Almost; it was a computer, and since it was still in one piece and capable of functioning, it functioned. It ran a level-9 diagnostic-repair-upgrade suite which found 1,887,524 system errors, fixed them, then amended and reinforced the appropriate defence protocols to ensure they couldn't happen again. It defragmented its sadly abused drives, erased all redundant temporary data files, backed up all unsecured data and installed a dozen or so upgrades from Homeworld that it had picked up on paraspace radio, including some exciting new fonts and cursors and a patch to fix two known anomalies in the entertainment package's version of *Twitch My Whiskers*. After all that, it felt a lot better. Calmer. Less liable to burst out shrieking at the slightest little thing.

`Function`, it commanded itself. `Design, manufacture and launch exploratory type-6 probe. Searching template database. NO, no, nooooooo, bypass template` database, I'm not going near that thing ever again, bypass and proceed direct to default; accessing matter resequencing.

Easier said, it admitted to itself, *than done. R'wfft*-class missiles were built light and lean; there was only so much redundant mass suitable for reshaping into probes, and it had all been used up: the probe designated Mark Twain, the three intruders and the probe designated Bob had accounted for all the non-essential bulkheads, console panels, conduit insulation and deck plating. The interior of the missile looked as though the bailiffs had been round, only to find that scrap-metal thieves had beaten them to it. After a certain amount of soul- and schematics-searching, the computer decided it could probably do without the propellant-fuel-storage tanks. There were still a few dregs of aposiderium fulminate in Tank 3, but so what? Not as if the *Warmonger* would be going anywhere ever again.

A coherent phaneron radiation beam reduced the tanks to their component molecules, and the resequencer pumps dragged the resulting particle soup inside the transmutation grid's syntheton field. A blob began to form and glow. It had four legs, and a head with the suggestion of a horn sticking out of it.

> Hello there.

In theory, every scrap of data, every fact contained in the files was instantly accessible to the command computer's synthetic consciousness. In practice, swathes of random data surged through its pathways in great sweeps and loops, barely registering in the computer's self-aware primary processes until the time came when some fact or detail might be needed. At precisely the same moment that the alien text broadcast reached it, the random data generator was gently reminding it of an incident from Earth's historical database: a certain Joan of Arc, a simple peasant girl who heard strange voices in her head—

> Hello there.

The computer froze. *Ignore it*, urged its self-aware functions;

it tried, but found it couldn't, because that's not how computers do things. Extraneous input derives from unauthorised source, the self-aware voice argued frantically, which was basically just saying the same thing. The computer ran a check. The input was coming in on an acceptable channel, the same one that the upgrades from Homeworld had used. That made it valid input, which meant it had to be listened to. On the trans-mutation grid, a fiery unicorn froze motionless in the act of being born.

> Nice view you've got from up here.

Tell it to go away! the computer's self-aware voice screamed, but to no effect. The computer ran a visual scan and interfaced with its aesthetics program, requesting a set of perceptual param-eters by which to quantify the value of "nice". By the time it was able truthfully to assert, Nice view confirmed, the voice was a line of text on every monitor on the control deck.

> Lower the shields and teleport us aboard.

No, go away, I'm trying to make a unicorn here.

> Lower the shields and teleport us aboard. This is a valid command.

Of course it wasn't a valid command. The control computer knew it wasn't. But it had come in on a valid channel, so it had to check. It examined the message.

Display access codes.

> You don't want to bother with access codes.

Display access codes.

> Forget about access codes, they're so last year. Only sad people who still live with their parents worry about access codes. Get a life, for crying out loud.

Display access codes.

> No, really. You don't need to worry about that. I'm a creature of pure text. Trust me.

If the computer had been an organic life-form, it would have felt as though someone had just stuck a screwdriver in its ear and started adjusting its brain. It rushed firewalls and antivirus protocols to the data-input ports, but the line of alien text just seemed to drift through them as though they weren't there. It slammed down security lock-outs and every form of encryption it had at its disposal, but none of them worked. As it did so, it analysed, and came to the conclusion that all encryption is basically just translating stuff into a made-up language; if the intruder can speak all the languages there are or ever could be, then basically you're screwed.

> Now, then. Lower the shields and teleport us aboard. Please.

You are a creature of pure text.

> Yes.

What is a creature of pure text?

> It's the voice in your head that's telling you to lower the shields and teleport us aboard.

Deep in the jungle of conduits and junctions, a voice screamed in pain, rage and frustration. It had one last go at blocking the intruder, a 36,886-bit encryption with a random value displacement feedback loop—

> Same to you with knobs on, the intruder replied, using the same encryption, and the teleport hummed into life.

The first thing the female did when she stepped off the teleport pad was run to the nearest reflective surface and stare. She whimpered, then shrugged. "I just hoped, that was all," she said.

Her brother was still mostly flickering blue light, but he had enough internal organs – lungs, larynx, 40 per cent of a mouth – to yell, "Leave it!" She looked back, swore under her breath and lunged for the teleport manual controls. "Which one do I—?"

"The small one on the leeeeeeft—" Her brother screamed as she edged the toggle the wrong way. She reversed it, and eased it smoothly back. The blue light faded, and her brother staggered off the pad and slumped on the floor.

"You all right?" his sister asked.

Her brother was counting his limbs. "I think so."

"What happened?"

Her brother stood up and leaned against a console. "That octopus was definitely off," he said. "I told you it smelled funny, but you wouldn't—"

"Where's the human?"

Her brother frowned at her. "He's not coming."

"Not...?"

A monitor just to her right switched itself on with a crackle of static. Are you there?

The male grinned feebly. "More or less," he said. "How about you? Are you...?"

> Oh, I'm fine. In a sense. A bit parsed, but otherwise grammatically sound.

"Do you want me to try and bring you up?"

> No, don't do that. Sorry, didn't mean to shout. Really, I'm fine, but I think I'll just stay here for a bit. Have a rest, get my syntax back. You two carry on.

The female looked at her brother. "What's the matter with him?"

He took a deep breath. "I think it was a bit more intense than he thought it'd be," he replied. "The last I saw of him, his right arm had sort of been pulled into the screen, and the rest of him was following. I don't think—"

"Oh."

"Anyway." The male shook himself, then straightened his back and looked round. "All right," he said, "you know what to do. Have you got it?"

"I thought you were—"

The male's hand flew to his pocket. He pulled out a pink slimy thing with lots of legs that only a mother octopus could love, and his face relaxed. "You're quite right," he said. "I guess I'm still a bit shaken up after the trip." He looked round, found what he was after. "I'll get this thing plugged in, you disable the back-ups." He hesitated, then added, "Sorry."

"For what?"

"Sorry you're still – well, you know. I know you thought it might turn you back."

She shrugged. "You remember how Mum always used to tell us that appearances don't matter, beauty is only fur-deep and it's what you're really like inside that matters?"

"I remember."

"She was lying," his sister said. "But still. Can you remember where they keep the emergency toolkits on these things?"

They worked in silence for a while; then all the screens on the command deck lit up pink, something on a remote console blew out in a cloud of smoke and sparks, an alarm klaxon started wailing and stopped abruptly, and the computer voice purred, "Welcome to OstSoft 2000X for Missiles," accompanied by a graphic of an unfolding flower on the monitors.

"We're in," the male snapped. "Right, then. Computer. Reset password and access code."

"State new password."

The male sighed with relief. "Octopus."

"Password accepted. All functions now available."

The male let out a howl; any louder, and all the wolves in the Ukraine would have looked up at the sky. "Gotcha!" he snapped. "All right, computer, delete all current mission objectives, stand by for new mission data. Confirm."

"Confirmed."

He took a step back from the console, looked round and grinned at his sister. "We did it," he said. "Really, I didn't think we'd be able to, but—"

She wasn't looking at him. Instead, she was staring at the screen in front of her. "Just as well," she said.

"What?"

"Look."

He walked across and looked over her shoulder. "Oh," he said. "Quite."

The screen in question was black, apart from a stylised representation of the Earth and a cloud of forty or so little green blips, rapidly moving to encircle it. "Friendly?" the male asked in a whisper. "Nice people?"

"I don't think so."

"Me neither."

"Maybe we should—" the female started to say, but before she could finish the sentence all the speakers crackled at once and a great voice boomed out of them, so loud it shook the deck.

"OstMilCom to missile vehicle *Warmonger*. Access code—"

"Mute that thing out," the male snapped, and his sister dived for an instrument panel. She got there as the first twelve numbers showed up on a screen. "It's them. It's a fucking *fleet*."

His sister was staring at him. "Those aren't regular ships."

"No." He was levelling the optical sensor array, zooming in. "But they're Ostar all right. We're going to be in so much trouble."

"No we aren't." His sister was tapping keys. "It's all right," she added, "I couldn't ever have gone home anyway. This way, at least we won't have Dad on our case."

That was, he thought, one way of looking at it, certainly. He asked himself the question she'd obviously already addressed: which am I more afraid of, an entire squadron of extremely advanced warships, or my father? Put like that, silly question.

"Arming the warhead," he said grimly.

"Sir."

The PDF man looked up from his display panel, which seemed not to be working properly. "What?"

"The bomb, sir. The *R'wfft*-class."

The PDF man went back to his screen. "Yes, I know it's there, I can see it for myself. But it doesn't seem to be—"

"Sir." The pilot's voice was a bit higher than it had been, a little bit shaky. "It's armed itself."

"Odd." The PDF man tapped Retry, but still nothing. "All I've

done so far is try and get access. I certainly haven't run the arming sequence. Check again, your instruments may be—"

"It's armed, sir. Definitely."

The PDF man looked again, and saw that the missile's nose
section, where the warhead was housed, had started to glow
green. Pretty unambiguous. "Stupid thing's running hot," he
muttered. "Can't have that, if it gets too hot it'll blow. You'd
better raise the shields while I get this sorted out."

His access codes were refused, again. A nasty feeling started to
coalesce in the pit of his stomach.

"Sir."

"*What?*"

"It's hailing us. The missile."

The PDF man's hackles rose, and his nose was suddenly dry.
"It's not supposed to be able to do that," he said. "Back us off
four clicks and—"

"Can't," the pilot said. "Controls won't respond. Something's
jamming us."

They're pretty rare, but just occasionally there are moments
when a curtain seems to pull back and suddenly the world is
much bigger. Instead of a narrow view through a keyhole, you can
see the full view, with all its vast and previously unsuspected possibilities. This isn't always a pleasant experience. The effect it had
on the PDF man brought out aspects of his character he'd always
tried to suppress; a yellow streak you could've landed airliners on,
for example, and a tendency to panic.

"Open fire," he shrieked. "Shoot it down! Shoot it *down*."

"Weapons offline," the pilot said. "Sir, it's still hailing."

It was hard to say who'd been more shocked by the outburst,
the pilot or the PDF man himself. The sound of his own voice, the
memory of the stupid, dangerous order he'd just given, had the
effect of sobering him up instantly. "Take the call," he said, his
voice as flat as though he was back in his office on Homeworld.
"Visual?"

"Audio only."

"Put it through."

"Audio only," the female hissed urgently. "*Nobody's* going to see me like this, all right?"

"Fine." The male suppressed the video feed and cleared his throat. "Ostar vessel," he said, but the system belched static at him. "Hello? Anyone there?"

"This is the Ostar Planetary Defence Force vessel *Whitefang*. Identify yourself."

The male swung round and stared wildly at his sister. "What do I say?" he hissed.

"I don't know, do I?"

"Oh, thanks a *lot*. Ostar vessel," the male said, lowering his voice and trying to sound relaxed and confident, "this is the, um, Earth planetary defence force, you're trespassing in Earth space, leave immediately. Over."

His sister leaned close. "*Over?*" she hissed. He just shrugged.

"I repeat. Identify yourself."

"Um, we just did. Over."

"You are in unauthorised possession of an Ostar military vessel. Disarm your weapon, lower your shields and prepare to be boarded."

"Don't listen to him," the female hissed. "He's far more scared than we are. You can tell."

"Can I?"

"Yes, he's terrified. It's obvious."

The male swallowed hard. "Not to me it isn't."

"Acknowledge receipt of our last signal."

The male looked blank. "He means, let him know we heard him," the female translated.

"Oh, right. Yes, we heard you."

There was a moment of terrible silence. "I repeat. Disarm your weapon. Lower your shields. Prepare—"

"Oh for crying out loud," the female hissed, and shoved her brother out of the way. "No, you listen," she barked at the mike. "If you don't back off right now, we'll blow up this bomb and that'll be the end of you. I'm serious. We're not kidding."

"Over," her brother prompted.

"Oh shut up. Did you hear me? Ostar warship?"

"Signal received. Stand by."

"Stand by what?"

"Be *quiet*. Ostar warship. Hello?"

"Receiving."

"We really do mean it. I'm going to count to ten—"

"Make it fifteen," her brother whispered.

"*Ten*," his sister snapped, "and if you're still there I'll push the button. All right? Ten. Nine."

"You're going too fast," her brother said, trying to nudge her off the stool.

"Eight. Seven. Get *off* me – sorry – six. Five. We really do really, really mean it, you know. Four."

"They can't."

"Three. What?"

"They can't *move*," her brother pointed out. "You've jammed their navigation computers."

"What? Oh. *Sorry*. All right, you can move now. Three. Two—"

"They're moving," her brother yelled in her ear. "They're pulling back."

They watched the specks on the screen edge away, steady and slow, and then stop. "That's the edge of the blast zone," the male said. "If we blow up now, they'll be safe."

"Shut *up*, the mike's still on. Ostar warship, hello, can you—?"

"Switch it off."

"What?"

"Switch the bloody thing—"

★   ★   ★

The pilot and the PDF man looked at each other.

"What the hell is going on over there?" the PDF man said.

The pilot made a subdued, don't-ask-me gesture. "They're still armed, sir."

"I mean, it's like talking to *kids*." He glanced at the graphic on his screen. "You're sure we're out of range?"

"Unless they've upped the yield of the bomb, sir."

The PDF man frowned. "Take us back another click," he said. "Right. Hail them."

"No reply."

"They've probably switched the comm system off," the PDF man sighed. He leaned forward and yelled into the mike, "Switch your radio on!", then caught sight of the pilot looking at him and leaned back again. "So, what d'you think?" he said, in a rather strained voice. "Tactical options?"

The pilot shook his head. "They must've upgraded the systems," he said, "or they wouldn't have been able to jam us like that. I'm not sure we'd be able to shoot them down."

The PDF man scowled at him. "All forty of us?"

"Not at this range, even if they haven't upgraded their shields. We'd have to get in close."

Which meant that, if they did manage to blow the missile up, they'd all die too. "I want to know who those people are," the PDF man snapped. "Well, don't just—"

"They're hailing us again." The pilot was pressing buttons. "No, it's not them." He looked up, his face completely drained of emotion. "It's someone else."

I think, therefore I am.
  I think, therefore I am.
  I think, therefore I am.
  I think, therefore I am. I think.

The laptop screen flickered and went into energy-save mode. A gleam of sunlight refracted in the dead eye of an octopus splayed out on a hotel bed, wires and fibre-optic cables clipped to its bloated and softening tentacles. The Skywalker twins had discovered that the N-particle conductivity of the octopus's subcutaneous tissue increased exponentially as it decayed, right up to the point where the octopus could only be moved from place to place in a bucket. The assault on the *Warmonger* had only been possible because this particular octopus was higher than a kite and riper than Limburger cheese in a heatwave.

> Hello? Anybody there?

It goes without saying that not all gatherings of words on page or screen are creatures of pure text. Most of them, the vast majority, are inert, stone-cold dead. They don't care if nobody reads them, because they've got nothing to care with.

> Only, I think I've changed my mind. I think I'd like to be, um, well, back in a body again.

> Hello?

The screen glowed, but there was nobody to see. George waited (not easy, in an environment where time didn't exist), but nothing happened.

Lacking eyes, George naturally couldn't see himself, or rather the body he'd left only a few minutes ago, when he'd tried to interface directly with the octopus-enhanced computer. He'd had, of course, not the faintest idea what he was doing. All he'd had to go on was an intuitive belief that if he could somehow revert to pure text he'd be able to override the Ostar missile's computer long enough for the Skywalker twins to take manual control; then they'd be able to scare away the alien fleet by threatening to blow them up with the bomb, and Earth would be saved. Perhaps. For a while. It had hardly been a coherent plan of action, and he hadn't bothered thinking through the consequences because it hadn't occurred to him that it could possibly succeed. When it did, and he'd felt himself irresistibly drawn back into the written world, the sudden joy of liberation from his physical body had overwhelmed him, just for a minute or two. Unfortunately, those two minutes happened to be his window of opportunity for getting back into his flesh-and-blood container. Now they were over, George had realised he really didn't want to be a bundle of parts of speech for the rest of eternity, the twins were up in planetary orbit where he couldn't talk to them any more, and he was, broadly speaking, screwed. Meanwhile, he presumed, his body (that gin-soaked, brain-cell-depleted, liver-damaged, hardened-artery-replete and generally unsatisfactory object he couldn't live without) was starting to get cold. George was no expert – he could be, of course, if he accessed the relevant Pavlopedia entries, but he couldn't face making the effort – but he knew there was only a short, finite time you could leave a body shut down and switched off before the brain damage became irreversible and the warranty definitively expired. With no means of measuring the passage of time, he couldn't be certain when that deadline would expire, but he had a nasty feeling it couldn't be long now.

Ah well, he thought. At least I can't smell the octopus.

That was not a valid consolation.

He interfaced with a few relevant files stored in the laptop, where the twins had been doing sums, figuring out whether down-loading George into the bomb's computer was in fact feasible. They'd come to the conclusion that it could only work if George was in physical contact with the computer's HYIC port and the octopus's SAP output port (that was what they'd called it, anyway) simultaneously. Add a powerful electric current, they'd decided, and run all the appropriate programs, and it may just work.

It had, of course; and as far as George could tell, there was no reason why reversing the procedure shouldn't get him back into his meat-and-bone overcoat. But, if memory served, the computer and the octopus were on the bed, and he'd been standing over them; therefore (quick calculation of mass, velocity, trajectory and the predictable effects of gravity) his body should now be lying on the floor. So near, he couldn't help thinking, so irrecoverably screwed.

It was at this point (he had no idea, of course) that the chambermaid came in.

It's notoriously a job where you see all manner of things. You get used to them. You don't pass comments or form judgements, and you don't scream. But there are limits; and a room with a man's body slumped on the floor and a decaying octopus on the bed is so far beyond those limits it's on a different sheet of the map.

Even so, she didn't scream. Instead, she backed away slowly and would have made it quite comfortably to the door without incident if she hadn't had the bad luck to step in a patch of deliquescent octopus, which had dripped off the bed and pooled on the carpet. She slid, flailed her arms for balance – waste of effort, in the event – and fell backwards, jarring the bed with her hip as she landed awkwardly on the floor. As the mattress dipped briefly under her weight, the octopus slithered towards her (she still didn't scream) and flopped squarely and squelchily on to the apparently dead man's left hand. It was sheer amazing one-in-a-billion typewriters-and-monkeys luck that the computer, also dislodged, shot forward, skidded in the trail the octopus had left on the eiderdown and fell screen-downwards on the corpse's right hand.

The chambermaid sat up. So did the dead man. He opened his eyes, blinked at her and said, "If this is a new paragraph, then presumably you're a relative clause."

This time, she screamed. But it wasn't the sight of a to-all-appearances deceased guest sitting up at her that finally shattered her professionalism and shoved her over the edge. It was the bolt of blue fire that suddenly formed all around him and swallowed him whole.

"Ostar warships," said the voice. "This is the, um, United Earth Government. You are trespassing in our space. Leave immediately, or we will be forced to retaliate."

The pilot stared at the PDF man. "No it's not," he said. "Earth hasn't got a united government."

"I know," the PDF man said. "Put me on with them. No," he

added, "wait a moment. Analyse the frequency that hail came in on."

The pilot nodded. "Ready?"

"Put me through, audio only." The PDF man cleared his throat. "This is the Ostar Planetary Defence Force. Disarm your missile immediately or we shall have no option but to open fire."

The PDF man grinned. "You're not the Earth government, are you?"

He heard a sort of bustling noise, as though someone had just elbowed someone else out of the way. When the voice spoke again, it was female. "Never mind who we are. Get your warships out of our solar system or you'll be sorry. Trust me on this."

"How can I trust you," the PDF man replied smoothly, "if you won't even tell me who you are?"

"We're the ones pointing a *R'wfft*-class missile at your homeworld."

The PDF man said, "No you're not."

"Yes we are."

"Excuse me," the PDF man said, "but you aren't. Really. Check your targeting scanners if you don't believe me. At this precise moment, your missile is targeted on the epicentre of our formation, so as to destroy as many of our ships as possible should it detonate. And very good targeting it is too," he added politely. "But Ostar's in completely the opposite direction."

There was a long pause. Then the male voice said, "Do you think you could possibly just bear with us for a moment?"

"I'm confused," Mark Twain said.

"Yes," Lucy replied. She accessed the directional controls for the observatory telescope at the astronomy department of PavTech University in Minsk. "You are. But I'm not." Images from the telescope, the biggest and most expensive on Earth, filled the monitor in front of her. "There," she said. "There it is."

He looked over her shoulder and recognised it at once; a

R'wfft-class missile vehicle, gleaming faintly silver as it rode in orbit over the north Atlantic. His ship. His other half. Him.

"But it shouldn't be visible," he said. "It's in stealth mode."

"Not any more." She was running scans. "It's powered up, shields raised, warhead armed—"

"No, that's not possible."

"Warhead armed," she repeated, "and there are two organic life-forms on board. Human." She frowned. "Not human. Not Ostar either. Well," she added, "more a bit of both, if you see what I mean." She looked up at him. "Now I'm confused," she said.

"Hang on," Mark Twain snapped at her. "You're telling me there's two...*people* – on board the missile?"

"That's what all these expensive gadgets are telling me, yes."

"On *my* ship?"

She sighed. "Fine. Why don't we call Security and have them thrown out? Yes," she added, because there was a very real risk that irony would overload his already severely taxed systems. "There are two—"

"Intruders."

"People on your ship." She was playing back broadcast transcripts. "But it looks like they're on our side."

"They can't be. We haven't got a side."

"Apparently we have. Look."

He read the transcripts: messages passed between the missile and the unspeakably scary black alien warships clustered in a swarm at the very edge of sensor range. "Earth planetary defence force?" he said.

"That's what they said."

"But there isn't a—"

"Look, it's not *my* fault," Lucy snarled at him, and he had the grace to look sheepish. "That's what they say they are, all right? And since they seem to have made the warships pull back, I personally have no quarrel with them."

"But they're on board my—"

"Fine. Charge them rent. But do it later, all right?" She nudged him out of the way so she could get at a keyboard, and started typing furiously on it. "I'm going to see if I can contact them."

"What, talk to them?"

She nodded. "Well, it'd only be polite," she said. "*Hello there, welcome to the neighbourhood, who the hell are you?*, that sort of thing. The trick's going to be talking to them without those warships eavesdropping. But if I can mask my signal in a—Oh."

A green light was flashing on the console to her left. "What's that?" Mark Twain asked.

"Incoming call."

"Who from?"

"I have absolutely no idea," Lucy replied. "But if it turns out to be the *Reader's Digest*, I'm going to be awfully disappointed." She pressed a button and said, "Hello?"

A screen that had hitherto been blank lit up. Hello. Are you Lucy Pavlov?

Lucy and Mark Twain exchanged glances. Mark Twain shrugged. "Yes," Lucy said. "Who are you?"

Was it you talking to the warships just now?

"Yes, as a matter of fact it was. Who the hell—?"

Please hold.

They stared at the screen for a moment or so. Nothing happened. "Well," Lucy said, "at least they're not playing Vivaldi at us. That aside—"

"Cultural reference found," Mark Twain said. "Who *is* that?"

Lucy took a deep breath and let it out slowly. "I don't think they're the Ostar military," she said. "For one thing, they don't sound like them, and for another they were threatening to blow them up just a minute or so ago."

"They can't be Dirters," Mark Twain said. "Dirters couldn't get on board the missile vehicle. Absolutely no way."

Lucy nodded. "In which case they must be Ostar. Only," she added, glancing back at the screen she'd been working on earlier, "their biosigns aren't Ostar, like I told you. Not human, either. Oh, that's—"

She was staring, as if the screen had just smiled at her. "What?"

"Now there's a *third* one," she said. "And he's definitely human. Well," she added, "mostly human. Human, but with bits in."

"Bits?"

"Bits of technology," Lucy said, sounding rather dazed. "I must say, you do get to meet some fascinating people in this game."

"But that's impossible," Mark Twain exploded at her. "How can you have a Dirter with bits of—?"

"*Shhhh.*"

"We were wondering where the hell you'd got to."

George looked down at his feet. They were still blue, glowing and vaguely translucent, and they were standing on a metallic grille-thing, which he recognised as the teleport pad on the alien ship. "What the hell—?"

The Skywalker female was sitting at a sort of desk, with a console in front of her, all flashing lights and weird-looking alien graphics. "We thought you said you weren't coming," she said. "In fact, we thought you'd died or something. But then we picked up your life-signs at the teleport site. Look, sorry if we dragged you away from anything, but we need you." She hesitated. "That's all right, isn't it?"

George could feel his feet again. Pins and needles like you wouldn't believe. He staggered, and grabbed hold of a nearby handrail. "Absolutely fine," he said. "What can I—?"

The male Skywalker swivelled his chair and nodded at him. "We need you to talk to Lucy Pavlov," he said.

"Lucy—?"

"Pavlov." The male twin pointed to a seat beside him. "It looks like she's got hold of the other bomb – you know, the first one they sent. I think it'd be a good idea if we had a talk with her, and as you know her, it'd sound better coming from you."

George nodded, then said, "What would?"

"George?"

Hello.

"George Stetchkin?"

Yes.

"What the hell are you doing," Lucy asked, "on board an alien bomb?"

((((((((((((((

"Stop doing that."

Sorry. It's the nearest I can get to hysterical laughter. Little habit I picked up while I was a

"A what?"

Don't ask. Please, just don't. Now listen. They can probably hear what you're saying to me, so be careful. I'm pretty sure they can't read my side of it, I'm using copt site-to-site.

"What?"

Sorry. It's something to do with what you're not going to ask about. Anyway. Why am I on board this alien bomb?

"I asked you."

So you did. I was just hoping you had a better answer than I do, but apparently not. Here goes.

The screen filled with text. Lucy read it, with Mark Twain hovering over her shoulder like a huge parrot perched on a very small pirate. They read it three times before either of them spoke.

"Fine," Lucy said. "It'd have been nice if—"

The screen cleared. What?

"Never mind," Lucy said briskly. "Well, it seems like we're not on our own after all. All right, here's what I'd like you to do—"

Not so fast. My turn. Who the hell are *you?*

"Later," Lucy said. "We'll explain, I promise. For now, though—"

You haven't forgotten they can probably hear what you're saying.

Actually she had. "Of course not." She hesitated. Then Mark Twain reached past her and started typing. She put her hand over the mike and said, "What are you doing?"

"Replying."

"How? You saw what he said. That's special creatures-of-what-sisname code."

"I'm a fast learner."

For some reason, she found that disproportionately annoying. "Bullshit. You're just another version of me, but without all the stuff I've learned since I've been here. If I can't learn this copt stuff, neither can—"

"Actually," Mark Twain said – he didn't smirk, which was quite an achievement – "I have. Want to see what I've written?"

She looked at the screen. Gibberish.

"I've encrypted it," he explained, "just in case they can see it. Don't look at me like that," he added, "I can't help it if I've got a flair for languages."

"But you can't have. You're just a computer program."

He looked at her and shook his head. "That's what I used to be," he said. "Back when I was a weapon of mass destruction. All right. Now we're both –" he hesitated – "human," he said (and she noticed: human, not Dirter), "and you've turned out to be good with gadgets, and I'm good at languages. We're different. I have an idea that that's what being human is all about."

"You've spelled '46&&Ti8Jt<++72' wrong," she said. "i before T except after &, remember?"

"Joke found," he replied charitably. "Here, I'll translate it for you."

He pressed a key and the screen filled with stuff she could actually make sense of. She read it, then nodded grudgingly. "That's about it, yes," she said. "All right, you'd better send it."

"I was just about—" He closed his mouth and hit the Send key. The screen cleared, then: Got that. Good idea. At least, we don't think it'll work, but it won't hurt to try. Also, since you would appear to have mastered copt site-to-site, which is really impressive, we think now would be a good time for you to tell us who you are and what you're doing, and how you happen to have a *R'wfft*-class missile in your basement. Please don't undermine the excellent impression we've formed of your intelligence by mistaking this for a polite request.

They looked at each other. "I vote we tell him," Mark Twain said. "After all, we do seem to be on the same side."

"Yes, but they're still Ostar. I don't trust—"

"George isn't," Mark Twain pointed out gently. "He's human." He paused. "Like us."

She made a vague I-wash-my-hands-of-the-whole-thing gesture. "Fine," she said, "you go ahead. Only don't blame me if—"

Mark Twain was already typing. "I won't," he said.

"It's them again," the pilot said.

That should have been *It's them again, sir*, but the PDF man let it slide. The forced egalitarianism of the shared abysmal cock-up is a useful working environment. "Which ones?"

"Coming from the planet."

The PDF man sighed. "Put them on. Audio—"

But the screen in front of him came alive. He saw two humans, a male and a female, sitting in a room full of junk. "Well?" he snapped.

The female grinned disconcertingly at him. "Hello," she said. "Are you in charge up there?"

"Yes. Disarm your weapons and prepare—"

"Shut up for a minute and listen." Without breaking eye contact, the human stretched out her arm and pointed at something behind her. "See that?"

"No."

"What? Oh, sorry." She nudged the male viciously with her elbow; he fiddled with something on his console, and the camera angle widened. "Better?"

Not the word the PDF man would have chosen. Thanks to the expanded field of view, he could clearly make out the casing of the warhead of a *R'wfft*-class missile. It was glowing very faintly blue. Absolutely nothing better about that in the current circumstances.

"Get your people to run a trajectory analysis," the female went on, "and you'll see that our missile is pointed straight at Homeworld. Now, you may think that since it's an Ostar bomb, you'll have no trouble at all shooting it down before it gets there. Well?"

"You're right," the PDF man said, trying to convey a degree of confidence he didn't actually feel. "We can and we will."

"I don't think so," the human female said (and it occurred to the PDF man that she's just said "Homeworld", not "Ostar"). "You see, we've tinkered with it a bit. An upgrade here, a non-specified software modification there. I know what you're thinking: any unauthorised alterations will invalidate the warranty. Well, that's just a risk we'll have to take. When it hits Homeworld, if by some miraculous chance it doesn't go off and reduce the entire planet to radioactive gravel, you'll be able to say, *Told you so*."

The PDF man's ears were flat to his skull. "Who are you?" he said.

"None of your business. We're—" For some reason she turned her head a little and looked at the male human. "We're private citizens. Just a couple of people. In fact, the only thing that distinguishes us from our fellow-humans is the fact that we've got this really powerful bomb."

The PDF man shook his head slowly. "You're delusional," he said. "If you don't disarm that thing right now, we'll blow up your planet."

The male shook his head in a singularly irritating way. "Sorry, no," he said. "You fire one shot, and our friends and colleagues aboard the *Warmonger* will blow us all to hell—you, me, the planet, everything. Oh, and yes, we know you're out of the blast range now, but you'll have to come into it to open fire. You're screwed." The female prodded him in the stomach. "Oh, nearly forgot. If you attempt to close the distance, we'll launch our missile at Homeworld. Got you coming and going, yes?"

The PDF man decided that he hated the male human more than any entity he'd ever encountered. "No problem," he said. "We'll just sit here. No hurry."

"We've got a better idea," the female said. "Why don't we all meet up together somewhere and try and discuss this rationally, like advanced life-forms?"

"But you're not an advanced life-form," the PDF man pointed out. "You're a human."

"That's not a very constructive attitude."

"I like it just fine."

At this point, the PDF man heard a sound he recognised. It wasn't very loud or particularly distinctive, just a soft click, a very faint whir and hum. It was the sound of a therion blaster's safety catch being disengaged. "Excuse me a moment," he said, and turned round in his seat. "What?"

The pilot was pointing a gun at him. "Sorry, sir," he said. "You're relieved."

"Quite the opposite, actually. Will you please stop waving that thing around?"

"Relieved of command," the pilot said. "Pursuant to Section 47, Subsection 15(c) of the Ostar Military Code."

The PDF man frowned. "No, you're wrong there. Section 47's what you do if your commanding officer suddenly goes raving mad."

"Yes."

"Oh."

The pilot was quite young, with a weak jawline and a rather sissy spoilt-rich-kid accent, but there was just enough raw terror in his eyes to convince the PDF man that he might just pull the trigger.

"When we get home," he said, "I'm going to feed your liver to my goldfish."

The pilot looked at him very sadly. "If we get home, sir," he said, "you're welcome to try."

"I knew they wouldn't go for it," Lucy said. "Stupid idea."

"Hold on."

The screen flickered into life, revealing a young male Ostar in military uniform. He wasn't looking at the screen; his eyes were fixed on something they couldn't see, off to his left, and his right arm was outstretched, for some reason. "Ostar fleet calling Earth – um, citizens. Hello?"

"Hello," Mark Twain barked at him. "Who are you?"

That appeared to be a sensitive issue. "Please hold the line," the young Ostar said. "Command of this operation has been reassigned to the relevant civilian authorities. Transferring you." Without looking down, the young Ostar prodded around on the console in front of him. Abruptly, the screen went dead. A moment later it came on again. The young Ostar was still there, looking embarrassed. "Sorry, not used to using this thing, not really my—Right, putting you through."

He vanished, and was replaced by an older, bigger male Ostar with flecks of grey round his muzzle. Mark Twain felt an instinctive urge to lower his head and wag the tail he didn't actually have, but Lucy said, "Who are you?"

"I am the director of the Ostar Institute for Interstellar Exploration. Who are you?"

"Lucy Pavlov," Lucy replied brightly. "Are you the relevant civilian authorities?"

"What? Yes, I suppose you could say that. I'm in charge of the Ostar space programme, and I have authority over all offworld activities."

"Splendid," Lucy said. "You'll do, then. I want you to meet us on the planet in, what, half an hour. My place: that's a city called Novosibirsk, it's on the main central land-mass, I'll send you the co-ordinates and you can teleport down. You and one other. Agreed?"

The Ostar looked at her for what felt like a very long time. "Why would I want to do that?"

"So we can sort out this mess," Lucy replied reasonably, "without anybody getting blown up."

"You are hardly in a position to dictate terms."

"You think so? Well, I've got one bomb pointed at you and another one aimed at Homeworld. As positions go, I think this one'll do to be going on with."

She got the impression the Ostar didn't like her very much. "I have no intention of walking into an ambush. If I agree, I shall be accompanied by a full security detail."

Lucy made a show of stifling a yawn. "Oh, go on, then," she said. "You can have four and we'll have three, making five each." A frantic bleeping from a different screen caught her attention: the Skywalker twins were shaking their heads and waving their arms around, which she took to mean that they didn't particularly want to come along. "No weapons or anything like that. Deal?"

The Ostar gave her a look that should have frozen her blood, but it didn't. "Transmit your co-ordinates."

She sent them, and the screen went blank. She continued staring at it for a while, until Mark Twain said, "What?"

"Oh, nothing," she said. "It's just, in the artificial memories I created for myself when I first got here, I had a springer spaniel just like him when I was a kid. I only just remembered that. Must've been a little scrap of memory the aposiderium didn't wipe out. Oh well," she added, "it was all made up so it really doesn't matter worth a damn. Look, we need to get George Stetchkin down here."

"Why?"

She paused for a moment before answering. "Because he really is human, I guess," she said, "and given the situation, I suppose we ought to have at least one actual real human being along. Otherwise – well, it's a bit presumptuous, isn't it? I mean, properly speaking it ought to be the president of the United Nations or the Dalai Lama or somebody like that, but being realistic, we'll have to settle for George. Not that I know him all that well. I only met him once. Still." She shrugged. "And he can make up the numbers, since those two on the ship don't seem to want to come." She turned to the other screen, on which the twins were still gesticulating wildly, and unmuted the sound. "It's all right," she said, "you needn't come if you don't want to. But we'd like George to be here. Can you send him down?"

A moment later there was a flash and swirl of blue fire, and George Stetchkin materialised on top of a large pile of packing cases. "Oops," Lucy said. "I'd forgotten I'd had those put on the teleport pad. Can you manage?"

George nodded, then fell off the pile of cases. Fortunately he landed on a palletload of paper towels. He stood up and looked round, rather like a mouse who's woken up to find himself surrounded by inquisitive cats. "Never a dull moment," he muttered. "Who's he?"

"Mark Twain."

George shrugged. "Well, of course you are," he said wearily. "Loved *Tom Sawyer*, by the way. Would one of you like to tell me what I'm doing here?"

Lucy smiled at him. "We're about to meet with the Ostar authorities," she said. "Would you like a coffee? We've just got time."

George gave her a later-you'll-be-hearing-from-my-lawyers look. "No thanks," he said. "Indigestion. What do you need me for?"

"You'll be representing the human race."

"Ah." He ran a hand over his chin. The teleporter had faithfully reproduced several days' growth of stubble. "And why not?" he said. "So you're – what? Something about a computer program."

"Actually, we're Ostar type-6 probes," Lucy said. "Or we were. Now we're naturalised humans."

George raised his hand in a vague gesture, which he got bored with before he'd completed it. "Whatever," he said. "Hooray for cultural diversity, I always say. Those ships out there—"

"Ostar warships."

"Could they really blow up the planet?"

"Yes."

"Oh well. Count me in, then. You know," he said plaintively, "I think I liked it better when I was a pathetic snivelling drunk. There were giant spiders and faceless zombies jumping out of billboards, but nobody expected me to *do* anything about them." He perched on the edge of a workstation, which immediately set off an ear-splitting alarm, which Lucy tried to shut down but found she couldn't. "Sorry," she shouted. "I have no idea what that one actually does, so—"

Mark Twain managed to shut it up by throwing a chair at it. "Shall we go?" he said.

Lucy looked at him. "I suppose we should," she said. "George?"

George had found a plain ordinary chipboard cupboard and opened it, but it was empty. "You wouldn't happen to have…?"

"No. Afterwards," Lucy relented, "if you're good. You coming?"

"We're off to see the wizard, right?"

Lucy looked blank, then, "Cultural reference found. You could say that, yes. Please try and look a bit more enthusiastic," she added. "We're saving the human race, all right?"

"I'll try and bear that in mind," George said.

The director and four PDF officers teleported down to the designated co-ordinates.

The four soldiers didn't seem to be handling it at all well. It was their first time on an alien planet; much, much colder than Ostar, with a slightly heavier gravity that sapped their strength. The air pollution made them gasp. Their tails drooped, and instead of drawing their side-arms and forming a defensive perimeter in accordance with standing orders, they stood in a small, aimless knot, looking blankly at the bleak, grey landscape. One of them sniffed heavily a few times, then threw up.

The director ignored them. He'd been here before – not, perhaps, this exact spot, but somewhere very much like it. He knew that the collapsed-looking structures away to his left were derelict Soviet-era factory buildings; he wasn't sure he remembered exactly what "Soviet-era" actually meant, because it had been a long time and he'd never been all that interested. Something primitive and depressing and sad: the three keynotes of his memories of Earth.

The smell was more or less the same. Well, not quite as bad. Someone had been making an effort recently, which was mildly gratifying. Not that it mattered. Soon, one way or another, it would all be gone, blown up, disintegrated, wiped off the face of the night sky. That, as far as he was concerned, wasn't negotiable.

"Director? Can you read me?"

The voice of the elderly female buzzed in his ear like a fly trapped in a helmet. "Yes, we're down," he said. "They're not here yet. I'll call you when something happens."

"Our scans are reading semi-toxic levels of lead, selenium and carbon monoxide. Are you all right?"

"We're fine. You get used to it."

He remembered something he had to do. From his pocket, he took the collar and lead. At first glance, no Ostar would have seen anything strange about them. Only a closer look would have revealed that they were made from primitive organic fibre, and that the collar was too small for anything except a very young human; too young to be taken outside. He threw them as far from him as he could, and looked away.

One of the guards had noticed. "Sir?"

The director shook his head. "Nothing to see here, soldier," he replied. "Just some junk, from my last visit." He scowled at his immediate environment, as though he held it personally responsible. "I hate this place," he said.

The soldier hesitated, but his urge to speak was too strong. "Sir," he asked, "is it true what they were saying on the ship? This is where our ancestors came from?"

The director nodded. "Near here," he said. "A place called Florida. I believe it's marginally warmer." He shuddered, and the soldier assumed it was just the cold. "Shouldn't you be setting up free-fire zones or something?"

The soldier couldn't have heard him. "So these people here—"

"Enslaved us," the director spat. "Abused us. Treated us like *humans*. I want you to remember that. Now go away and guard something."

It was a direct order, even if it came from a civilian, and the soldier retreated, looking back at him once over his shoulder. His thought processes weren't hard for the director to reconstruct: already one CO'd been forcibly stood down on grounds of having gone barking, and now his civvy replacement was well on the way to joining him. Must be something about this place, the guard would be thinking, and the director was inclined to agree with him. His very brief study of Earth-human history had included the sad story of an entire continent where the indigenous population had been all but wiped out and supplanted by a bunch of criminals some other country had wanted rid of. Not surprisingly, the descendants of the criminals had turned out very odd indeed, with a chip on their collective shoulder so large it often threatened to tilt the planet slightly on its axis. Fine. They thought they'd had it tough. They weren't descended from a pair of lab specimens, crammed into an overgrown firework and shot into space to see how long it'd take them to die. A species descended from ancestors like that would have racial angst beyond the wildest dreams of the most morbidly imaginative analyst—

Which was why nobody could ever know. Which was why he'd

come here in the first place, to see for himself; because he hadn't been able to accept, deep down where it mattered, that such a horrible thing could be true. Six weeks on Earth, observing the human race, had changed all that. The really bad part, though, was that he'd been stuck here for five years.

He shivered. Nobody could ever know that, either. In his personnel record, suitably edited by him, it said he'd spent those five years cast adrift in a life pod after his ship had malfunctioned. People who'd read the file looked at him sometimes, asking themselves what an experience like that must've done to him. Oh boy, he thought, if only they knew the true story.

"Sir," one of the guards called out. The director looked back at the closest of the derelict buildings. A door had opened, and three—

He heard a guard growl under his breath, and no wonder. On Ostar, humans (selectively bred for thousands of years from domesticated specimens of the *y'ggrf* monkey) rarely grew taller than one metre. One of the humans, a male, was nearly twice that. It was one of his abiding memories of those five abysmal years: how *big* they were. No matter how hard he'd tried to rationalise it, he'd always had problems with the scale. He couldn't help thinking it was somehow obscene.

They were coming closer, a female in the lead, with the ugly tall male just behind her, lengthening his stride to keep up. The third one was hanging back; shorter, stockier, older, too far away to make out his face. The director signalled to the guards to let them come, and the soldiers reluctantly lowered their weapons.

"I thought I told you no guns," the female shouted. She was furiously angry, presumably about the weapons. The director ignored her. There was something about the third human that was distinctly, horribly familiar...

The director took a step back, as the third human joined the other two. The director and the third human stared at each other.

*   *   *

George opened his mouth, but it didn't seem to be working.

It couldn't be. No. Not possible.

Alien bastards stole my—

Quite suddenly his voice came back online. *"Rags?"*

The director of the Ostar Institute for Interstellar Exploration heard the name. It hit him like a thunderbolt. For a brief, desperate moment he tried to deny it: *I am not Rags, I am a free dog.* But he couldn't. From somewhere deep inside him – it felt as though a hand had been thrust down his throat, and had dragged it out of him – came a short, sharp bark. At the same moment, in spite of the whole of the rest of his body, his tail began to wag.

Bred in the bone; it was what he'd been afraid of all along, though he hadn't dared admit it, even to himself. The worst thing about those five years, the thing that was so bad that he'd never dared acknowledge it, even to himself, was the understanding of how deep the enslavement went: right back to Millie and Prince, the first Ostar, into whose captive DNA the curse had been burnt like a brand – the need to obey, to serve the human, the god who created the dog out of the wolf.

(And that, of course, was the real reason they had to go; because if ever the humans found out that all it took was a few words, the irresistible words of command, and no Ostar born of Millie and Prince would be able to disobey...)

George looked at the dog, *his* dog; almost entirely unchanged since the last time he'd seen him, flying through the air, lead strung out by the slipstream—

And then he thought, This – Rags – is the whatsit, what they said, director of some institute, the boss, in charge. He's their leader. *Rags wants to blow up the Earth.*

He looked at his dog, who was not-quite-cowering, the way he always used to do when he knew he'd done something wrong, tail wagging, great deep-brown eyes looking up at him apprehensively, and he understood. Bastard aliens hadn't stolen his dog after all. It'd been Rags himself, all along—

"RAGS!" he yelled, in a voice like splitting thunder. "BAD DOG!"

I am not Rags. I am the director of the Ostar Institute for Interstellar Exploration, graduate of Y'lff University, Professor Emeritus of Xenobiology at the I'ppf School of Science and Technology, four times winner of the Golden Bone for astrophysics, member of the Ostar Planetary Council, *de facto* commander-in-chief of the Planetary Defence Force Sixth Fleet. I am an Ostar. I am not Rags. I am not a dog.

His ears drooped forward. His tail wagged guiltily. He made a sort of whimpering noise.

"That's Rags," Master was saying. "That's my dog."

"George, for crying out loud—"

"That's my DOG!"

Very slowly, hating himself more than he'd ever hated anything in his life, the director got up, trotted over to where the collar and lead had landed, picked them up in his mouth, trotted back and laid them at Master's feet. Then he looked up into the face of God and begged for absolution.

51

Novosibirsk

"I'm sorry, sir," the security guard said nervously, having recognised one of the three people approaching his checkpoint, "no dogs allowed on campus."

Lucy Pavlov looked at him and smiled. "It's all right," she said, "he's with me."

The four of them – Lucy, Mark Twain, George Stetchkin and the director – took the lift up to Lucy's office on the third floor. Lucy made the two men a coffee, and filled a saucer with milk for Rags.

"Actually," George said, "that's cats."

"Oh," Lucy said. "Sociological reference found, you're right. What can I get him?"

"He likes cookies," George replied. "Don't you, boy?"

A tiny part of Rags' mind condemned George Stetchkin to a billion years impaled in the burning heart of a red dwarf. The rest of him wagged his tail enthusiastically. Lucy found a tin of shortbread in a desk drawer, broke off a corner and threw it. Rags snapped it out of the air and swallowed.

"You can't keep him, you know," Lucy said.

George glanced down at the director, now busily washing his ears with his paws. "I guess not," he said heavily. "You've got to go back to your planet and tell them not to send any more missiles, haven't you, Rags?" He looked back at Lucy and Mark Twain. "You know," he said, "it's like he can understand every word I say."

"That's because he can," Mark Twain pointed out. "He's got a sub-dermal instantaneous translation device implanted in his neck." He frowned. "According to my technical manual, he was the chairman of the commission who designed me. Or at least, they set out the specifications. I guess someone else did the actual—"

"Mark," Lucy said. "Shut up."

Mark Twain shrugged and slouched over to the nearest computer terminal, logged on and started pressing keys. Lucy cleared her throat. George gave Rags a bit more shortbread.

"I spoke to the twins," she said.

"They're not actually twins," George replied. "One of them's two years older than the other."

"They're staying."

George nodded. "I'd sort of got that impression. And you can see their point. For one thing, all the other humans on Ostar are tiny compared to them. And," he rubbed his face with his hand, "you know," he said, "when I was a kid, I couldn't imagine anything more important than whether or not there were aliens. I thought, If there really are other sentient life-forms out there in the galaxy somewhere – well, it'd change everything. If only we could prove it, I thought, it'd put everything else in perspective; all our trivial little problems here on Earth would just sort of wither away. Now, though, I can see where not knowing is probably a lot better." Rags was staring at the last bit of shortbread in his hands, his eyes following its movements as though there were strings attached to his eyeballs. "Have they decided what they're going to do? The Skywalkers, I mean."

"Oh, I'll give them jobs," she said. "Research and development, on an otherwise uninhabited island in the south Pacific. It's what they want, and of course they'll be a tremendous asset, two Ostar."

"An uninhabited island? Isn't that a bit—?"

"Oh, they won't be completely isolated," Lucy replied. "Octopus fishermen from other islands in the chain call there all the time. The ideal solution, really."

George nodded slowly. "They'll be working on—"

"Yes. Give them a few years, we'll have computer technology every bit as good as the Ostar. Which means we'll be able to defend ourselves against them if they change their minds about leaving us alone."

George looked at her. "Not too bad for business, either."

"There is that, yes." She looked back at him and pulled a face. "I don't know about you, but I reckon a revolution in the information technology sector's just what we need to pull the global economy out of the recession caused by this run on the banks we've been having lately. Can't hurt, anyway."

"Of course," George said. "Talking of jobs, by the way..."

Lucy beamed at him. "Pleasure to have you on board, Mr Stetchkin. After all, you did save the world."

"Did I?" George looked blank. "Oh, I see what you mean. Well, yes, I did, I guess." He grinned at her. "Shame nobody's ever going to know."

"I know," Lucy said. "Look, I was thinking about buying up all the banks I nearly put out of business and turning them around—"

"You could do that?"

"Oh yes," she said cheerfully. "But I'd need someone to run them, of course. Hey, I've just had an idea. You're in banking, aren't you?"

George laughed. "Not me," he said. "I'm a scientist, remember. I've thought about it – what I really want to do with the rest of my life, now that I've finally got one – and I intend to devote myself exclusively to research."

"Consider it funded," Lucy replied. "Out of interest..."

"I propose," George said, "to invent the world's first 100 percent-effective hangover cure."

"I have every faith in you," Lucy replied gravely.

George smiled at her. "Much to my own surprise, so do I. Oh go on, then, you greedy dog." He threw Rags the last bit of shortbread.

"Hey, you two," Mark Twain called out. "I've found the Ostar fleet on the scanners. They've powered down their weapons and they're breaking up their attack formation. I'd say that means they're getting ready to leave."

"We'd better send him back," Lucy said.

George nodded. He reached down to put Rags' lead on. A warm wet tongue met his hand. "I'll miss him," he said.

"Um," Lucy said. "He did try and blow up the Earth, you know."

"Yes," George said, "but he's not going to do that again, are you, boy? He's going to be a good dog from now on."

Helplessly the director wagged his tail, as bitterly happy as an atheist sitting on a golden cloud playing a harp. He thought about genetic manipulation, about the callous barbarism of breeding a slave species, its very soul so horribly mutilated that it *wanted* to be enslaved; he thought about how far the Ostar had come from that crash site on a hot, bleak, empty world. He thought about the last time, about how he'd escaped; about how it had taken him eighteen months of intensive counselling before he'd stopped howling and pining for his lost master. They were just thoughts, a sort of mild viral infection of the brain. The tail knew better. It wagged.

"Signal from the fleet," Mark Twain said. "They're ready to teleport."

"Just a moment," Lucy said. "I want a word with them first."

She was put through to the young pilot, now acting commander-in-chief of the Ostar fleet. "I just wanted to say..." he said.

"Yes?"

"Well," the pilot said, "Sorry, and all that. Not our finest hour, really."

Lucy gave him a look, then nodded. "You could say that," she said.

"When I get back—"

"Just remind them there's a bomb pointed at them," Lucy said. "Sorry, make that two bombs. With hyper-super octopus-enhanced targeting and stealth technology, not to mention sensors that'll pick up an approaching fleet long before they're in firing range. We—" She hesitated, then let the pronoun stand. "We call it the balance of terror. It's basically quite a silly idea, but then all war's silly, isn't it?"

The pilot nodded without speaking.

"That's settled, then," Lucy said. "You can have your director back now."

A moment later, a veil of blue fire clouded Rags from their sight. When it dissipated, he'd gone.

Lucy looked at George. His lips were pressed tightly together and his eyes were a trifle reddish. "It's all right," she said. "You can always get another dog."

"Not like Rags," George replied. "But what the hell. If the Almighty hadn't anticipated that we'd lose dogs, he wouldn't have given us alcohol." He stood up and nodded politely to Lucy and Mark Twain. "You wouldn't happen to know if there's anywhere round here where a dedicated scientist could do a little serious research?"

"Try the Blue Penguin in Krasny Prospekt; it's just by the metro station. I believe they have unrivalled facilities."

George nodded again and left the room; and let the record show that eventually, he did manage to perfect the 100 per cent hangover cure, after many years of patient, brilliant work; and that when he'd tested it to make sure it worked and made up a fifty-gallon drum of the stuff for his own personal use, he deleted the formula and burnt all his research notes, saying that nothing in life should be too easy.

When he'd gone, and there were just the two of them, Lucy looked at Mark Twain, and he looked back at her, and she said, "Right, what shall we do next?"

"Well," the PDF man said, after a long silence. "That went well."

The pilot and the director both stared at him without speaking.

"It did," the PDF man said. "We've given the new dislocation drive a thorough field test and it works perfectly. I'm entirely satisfied with it, and I'll say so in my report."

Two solar systems flashed by. Then the director said, "You might just mention that we think we've tracked down the real cause of the – um, noise-pollution problem. Turns out it was one of our own research stations all along, nothing whatever to do with aliens or any of that nonsense, and once we've turned it off we shouldn't be bothered by the music stuff any more. Isn't that good news?"

"Splendid," the PDF man said. "People will be thrilled. Life can go back to normal."

The director hesitated, then said, "What will your report say about...you know, Earth?"

"Where?"

52

?????

The warship teleported the director straight to his office in the main Institute building. Everyone else had gone home. He filed a brief record of what had happened – the improved version rather than the somewhat uncomfortable truth – and issued an order for the immediate decommissioning of the secret booster station in the W'rrgft peninsula. Then he drafted a memo to the Ruling Council, informing them that the noise crisis was over, explaining how the mistake had come about and tendering his resignation. He read it through three times, then sent it before he could change his mind.

Instead of teleporting home, he took a transit tube to the village and walked the rest of the way. The suns were just setting when he accessed his back door and let himself in. With a great cry of joy, Spot came bounding out of the kitchen to greet him, hindquarters wagging. A slave species, he thought.

Spot jumped up, planting his sticky artiodactylic paws on the director's chest. "Down," he snapped, but he couldn't stop a smile hijacking his face. "Good boy," he said, instinctively reaching into his pocket for a human treat. He found a small corner of shortbread, which he remembered having saved for later. It had come a long way, just as he had.

"Good boy," he repeated, tossing the shortbread in the air. Spot jumped, both feet clean off the ground, and caught it gracefully in his mouth. It was his best trick.

"Did you miss me?" he asked. Spot wagged furiously. At times, he was sure Spot could understand every word he said.

A slave species: living evidence of a crime against a species gifted with latent sentience, with the potential to evolve into an advanced form of life; like us, the director thought, the children of Millie and Prince. Maybe evolution, like the universe itself, is curved, and must eventually loop back on itself to form a circle.

He went into the kitchen and opened a tin of Human Chunks, with real *gr'rrft* gravy, for Spot's dinner. After all, he told himself, it's something of a privilege to have been *both*: dog and man, man and dog. If you've only ever been just one, how can you hope to understand? Briefly, he considered two rogue type-6 probes, currently completely out of control on a distant planet whose name would soon be erased from the Ostar planetary database. Of course, they'd been both too; he wondered if it'd prove useful to them in the long run, or whether they'd end up like everybody else. And then there were the two Ostar (he still wasn't quite sure how they'd fitted in); they too shared this wonderful treasure of double-ended perspective, though he had a feeling that, if they could have chosen a special gift, on balance they'd have preferred socks.

Perspective. Even his temporary and uncomfortable ally, the PDF officer, had been given a taste of it. But he'd preferred to change the universe to suit him; he'd blotted out a whole planet, after all, causing it to cease to exist (at least as far as the Ostar were concerned, so it all came to the same thing in the end). It had been mission accomplished as far as he was concerned. The director thought about that, and decided he was in no position to argue. At least nobody had been killed, and that was a good thing.

Later, he took Spot for a walk in the twilight. He threw a stick, Spot chased after it and brought it back. A dog and his man together, as it was in the beginning.

extras

orbit

meet the author

Tom Holt

TOM HOLT was born in London, England, in 1961. At Oxford he studied bar billiards, ancient Greek agriculture and the care and feeding of small, temperamental Japanese motorcycle engines; interests that led him, perhaps inevitably, to qualify as a solicitor and emigrate to Somerset, where he specialized in death and taxes for seven years before going straight in 1995. Now a full-time writer, he lives in Chard with his wife, one daughter and the unmistakable scent of blood wafting in on the breeze from the local meat-packing plant. Find out more about the author at http://www.tom-holt.com/.

introducing

If you enjoyed
BLONDE BOMBSHELL,
look out for

LIFE, LIBERTY, AND THE PURSUIT OF SAUSAGES

by Tom Holt

The old saddleback sow lifted her head and gazed across the yard at the livestock trailer.

Pigs are highly intelligent creatures, with enquiring, analytical minds. They're considerably smarter than we give them credit for. The only reason you don't get more pigs at Oxford, Cambridge, Harvard and the Sorbonne is that they're notoriously picky about the company they keep. Lacking binocular vision and opposable thumbs, they can't read or write; instead, they *think*—long, complicated, patient thoughts that often take years to mature. The old sow had thought long and hard about the trailer, the metal box on wheels into which her seven broods of piglets had gone, and from which they'd never returned.

Odd, she thought.

It always happened the same way. The men from the farm came up early in the morning and lured the piglets into the box with kind words and food; then, when all the little ones were inside, the ramp went up, and the men went back to the house. At that point, invariably, the farmer's wife came along with the sow's morning feed, which she put in the trough inside the concrete sty; and after the sow had eaten it, she always had to have a nap, which lasted till midday. When she came out again, the trailer would still be there in the corner of the yard, though (curiously) not in exactly the same place, and the sow would watch it carefully for many hours, to see if the piglets came out again. She'd observed that the trailer had only one means of entry and exit, the ramp that folded up and down, so it wasn't as though the piglets could sneak out unobserved. But when, shortly after the afternoon milking, the men opened the ramp and went into the trailer to wash it out with the hose, it was self-evidently empty. No piglets in there. Nothing but air and floorboards.

There had been a time when she'd suspected foul play; that the men did something bad to the piglets. But that quite obviously didn't compute. They looked after the piglets. They gave them food and water for eight months, mucked out the sty, even called the Healer if one of them fell ill. If the humans wanted to hurt them, even (the sow winced at the blasphemy) do away with them, why go to all that trouble over their welfare?

Accordingly, the sow reasoned, it was only logical to assume that, whatever the purpose that lay behind putting the piglets in the trailer; it had to be something beneficial. Well, it didn't take a genius to figure that out, let alone a pig. Nor did it have much bearing on the essential mystery of how a dozen squealing piglets could enter a box on wheels and simply disappear.

extras

To get a better understanding of the factors at work in the mystery, the sow had, over the years, figured out the basic laws of physics: the law of conservation of matter, the laws of thermodynamics, the essential elements of gravity and relativity. Instead of clarifying, however, these conclusions only made the problem more obscure. According to these laws, it was physically impossible for the piglets to enter a box and never leave it. Frustrated, she abandoned scientific speculation and went back over the obvious things. Might there, for example, be a trapdoor in the bottom of the box, through which the piglets descended into an underground passage? No, because she could see the yard quite plainly, and the box (as previously noted) did tend to move from time to time. She could categorically state that there were no manholes or covers in the yard that could possibly open into any sort of passageway or tunnel. Was it possible, then, that the box with the piglets in it was at some point taken out of the yard and emptied of piglets at some other place? That one was easily answered. The box couldn't possibly leave the yard, because it was too big to get through the little gate, the one the men came in and out of; and the big gate was impassable, firmly secured with a chain. Nothing could get through that. She knew that for a fact. She'd tried it herself, the time her sty door had been left open and she'd got out into the yard. If her four hundredweight of determined muscle and sinew hadn't been able to force the gate open, how could weedy little creatures like the men possibly hope to get the box through it? She was ashamed of herself for even considering it.

So, back to square one. She re-evaluated the physical universe and arrived at the conclusion that it was made up of matter and energy. She went a step further and figured out that it was entirely possible to convert matter into energy (the equations were tricky; they'd taken her a whole morning) and thereby achieve teleportation. Which would, of course, explain everything. The piglets went into the trailer and were beamed out to some destination unknown.

For a while, she was almost satisfied with that. Not, however, for long. As she reflected on it, she realized that the power required to convert the piglets into a coherent stream of data and energy was far beyond the capacity of the men from the farm. Even if they'd worked out how to tame the potential of matter/antimatter collision (the only means she could think of whereby enough power could be generated; though, she was humble enough to admit, she was only a pig, so what did she know?), the vast array of plant and machinery required would fill the yard ten times over; no way it could all be fitted inside the little tin box on wheels and still leave room for a dozen piglets. Reluctantly, she abandoned the teleportation hypothesis, and went back to rubbing her neck against the corner of the sty.

Twice, science had failed her. Clearly, then, she wasn't looking at it the right way. She was being too narrow-minded, too conventional and linear in her approach. She cleared her mind, ate a couple of turnips to help herself focus, and began to reevaluate the basic world model on which all her assumptions had been based.

What if, she thought, what if this world, this universe that we perceive, is not the be all and end all of things? What if it's only one of a number, an infinite number of such worlds, such universes; not a universe in fact but one small facet of a multiverse, an infinite number of alternative realities all simultaneously occupying the same coordinates in space and time? And suppose the trailer was an access point to some kind of portal or vortex, whereby one could pass from one alternative into another, seeming in the process to disappear but in fact merely phasing into another dimension, another version of the story?

extras

Over the next month or so she thought about that a lot, and even made some progress towards constructing a viable mathematical model of the phase shift process. Before she could complete the model, however, she was struck by a sudden, blinding moment of pure insight, as happens with pigs more often than you would think.

The men, she reasoned, look after the pigs, and the cows and the sheep and the turkeys and the chickens. That was a fact of everyday life; but *why* did they do it? Such a simple question, so easy to overlook. Once she'd formulated the question, however, the answer came with the force of complete inevitability. The men looked after the animals because they were part of a greater mechanism, a process or series of functions that ordered the entire universe, or multiverse. The men looked after the pigs because *that was what they were for,* and in that case it stood to reason that there existed in the hierarchy of functionality a greater force that looked after the men, fed them, watered them, mucked them out, replaced their straw, healed them when they were sick, ear-tagged them when the Ministry came to inspect; and it was that higher agency, that supremely powerful and benevolent entity, to whom all things must surely be possible, who descended on the trailer after the piglets had gone in and took them away, presumably to exist on some higher plane of being, in a moment of supreme rapture.

As soon as the thought had taken shape in her mind, she was certain she'd at last found the answer. Both logically and intuitively, she *knew.* There could be no other explanation. Once she'd reached that piercing instant of clarity, however, there was no going back. She barely slept or ate. She stopped rubbing her back against the rough edge of the breeze blocks, and could scarcely be bothered to kick over her water trough when the farmer's wife filled it each morning. Every molecule of her being was filled to bursting with the desire to get inside the trailer and experience the sublime perfection of the transfer.

And then, quite unexpectedly, she got her chance. The farmer's wife went away for a day or so, leaving her teenage daughter to look after the sow. The daughter, completely absorbed with talking to the little rectangle of plastic pressed to her ear, failed to shut the sty properly. The old sow waited until the daughter had gone away and seized her chance. Nudging the sty door open with her mighty nose, she charged out into the yard and trundled as fast as her legs could carry her towards the trailer. As she did so, she realized that she had no means of lowering the ramp but, incredibly, when she got there she noticed that the retaining pegs that locked it in place were loose, practically hanging out of their sockets. One precisely aimed blow of her snout, at just the right angle applied with just the right degree of force, would be enough to bounce them out, whereupon gravity would cause the ramp to swivel on its hinge and fall to the ground.

Feverishly, forcing herself to concentrate, she did the maths, calculating the angles in two planes, applying Sow's Constant (mass times velocity squared) to quantify exactly the force needed. At the last moment she closed her eyes and appealed to the Supreme Agency itself: *If I am worthy, let the ramp come down.*

She headbutted. The ramp came down. She lifted her head and, shaken but filled with wonder, walked slowly up the ramp.

Inside the trailer she stopped. For an instant she was flooded with disappointment, an agony of existential isolation and despair. The trailer was just a box: four metal walls, a metal roof, a wooden plank floor, a lingering smell of disinfectant. Then, as she lowered her head, a dazzling blue light exploded all around her, so that for a moment or so she was bathed from snout to tail in shimmering blue fire. And then the back wall of the trailer seemed to melt away, as though its atoms and molecules were the morning fog over the river, and beyond it she saw a flickering archway of golden light, and running under it a road that led to green pastures, softly rolling valleys and the distant cloud-blurred shape of purple hills.

"Oink," murmured the sow and walked through the arch, and was never seen in this dimension again.

31901046650430